Hidden Depths

By

Ally Rose

Fahrenheit Press

A Hanne Drais Novel

PART ONE

1. 31st December 2004

The prospect of working on New Year's Eve when others are free to go out and celebrate or simply welcome the incoming year at home isn't the most appealing of options. At St Engel's hospital in Berlin, the night shift on the coma ward on the last night of the year turned out to be quite a lively affair.

Twelve years in a coma in intensive care, attached to a monitor, meant that Lotte Holler was the longest patient in residence. Home was a small room where a few family photos adorned a bedside dresser and fresh flowers gave a bit of colour to a white, clinical space overlooking a school playground that often echoed to the sound of energetic children. Except for the grey flecks that peppered her dark hair, Lotte, now aged 41, showed few signs of the laughter lines or wrinkles that would normally be found on someone her age.

Lotte had arrived in a blaze of publicity, the victim of a violent attack on a bleak winter's night who had been left to die of hypothermia on the banks of an icy lake. A passing dog walker had found her, barely alive. The crime remained unsolved and the culprit was apparently still at large due to lack of evidence. The victim, although she had survived, could not be questioned and the investigation was eventually filed as a cold case entitled the 'Lady of the Lake'. Lotte remained in a coma, although MRI scans showed brain activity that the doctors attributed to the presence of her devoted younger sister, Julia, who was convinced Lotte could hear her but was unable to respond.

Julia visited regularly and did everything she could to stimulate her sister's mind.

She read to her daily, chatted about trivia and recalled their shared childhood memories. She had always looked up to the elder sister who had played a protective role after their mother ran off with her lover and severed all contact. Their father had had a stroke soon after, forcing Lotte to leave school, find a job and look after the family financially, becoming a substitute mother for the young Julia. He never fully recovered from his stroke and died a few years later, leaving his daughters only a rented apartment and each another for comfort. It seemed for the next few years that life was looking up - but then Lotte was attacked.

Julia was in the ward corridor getting a coffee from the dispenser when she recognised the man in a white coat passing by.

'Dr Roth, could I have a word?'

Dr Jonas Roth, a tall, middle-aged man with a bulbous nose and rugged face, stopped and turned around. He was often waylaid by the slender woman now standing in front of him. Although he was usually busy he always stopped to talk to Julia, reminding himself it wasn't only the coma patients who suffered: their family members experienced a waking trauma. Also, he had an unspoken attraction to Julia and thought she was pretty and feminine with her intense, chocolate-brown eyes.

'Frau Kessler… How can I help?'

'You'll never guess… I saw on the news today that a man in America has just woken up after 19 years in a coma, just like that, and he's completely normal. He'd been listening to his wife all the time.' Hope and excitement was evident in her voice.

'I see,' Dr Roth said, wondering if it was true.

'My sister can hear me… she'll wake up someday as if nothing has happened,' insisted Julia.

'Anything is possible,' he replied, unconvincingly.

'I don't suppose you've had any news yet about any funding for an operation?'

'Brain implants are still in the pioneering stages of surgery,' the doctor began. He noticed Julia frowning with disappointment and softened his voice. 'No, I haven't any updates for you but I'm sure your presence here really does help your sister.' He put his arm briefly on her shoulder. 'I must go… Happy New Year.'

'And to you, doctor,' said Julia, and returned to her sister's room.

Dr Roth continued along the corridor to the ward office. He popped his head round the door. 'I'm off now. See you next year,' he said to his colleagues.

Martin and Lena were the two nurses on duty on the ward.

'All right for some,' Martin joked.

'Bye, Jonas,' Lena replied warmly, watching him go.

Recently single, the thought of going out to her local bar and bumping into her ex boyfriend wasn't appealing, which is why she'd volunteered for the New Year's Eve shift. Martin on the other hand, liked to party. Sulking at first when his name appeared on the duty rota, he perked up when he discovered he'd be working with Lena.

'Just going to turn Lotte Holler,' Lena told him. 'I won't be long.'

Julia knew Lena and Martin - in fact she knew all the doctors and nurses on Lotte's ward by name. Over the years she had grown to trust the staff and enjoyed her daily chats with them.

Lena knocked and entered. 'I need to turn Lotte, her last one for today. Are you staying to see the New Year in with

Lotte?' she asked.

Julia shook her head. 'I'm taking my sons to midnight mass.'

'Oh, that's nice.' Lena knew Julia lit a daily candle for her sister but didn't want to be drawn into a theological discussion and diverted the conversation away.

'Well, we'll see you soon.'

'Tomorrow,' Julia replied, looking at her watch. 'I'd better go, got to collect my boys- their father doesn't like driving in Berlin during the winter.'

'Hasn't he heard of the U-Bahn?'

'My ex husband doesn't go out of his way to help me,' Julia confided. 'Thank you, Lena. Happy New Year... you'll call me if there's any change.'

Lena smiled and nodded. 'Happy New Year.'

Julia repeated her good wishes to Martin as she passed him in the corridor. Martin went into Lotte's room to find Lena.

'You done?' Martin asked.

'Just about. You know, Julia's been saying for 12 years, 'Call me if there's any change' and we never call her. She just refuses to give up hope.'

Martin nodded in agreement. 'Hopelessly devoted. They must have been close.'

'Shame the police never caught the psycho who put Lotte in here,' Lena mused.

'It had to be a man,' Martin said. 'And unless he was a madman and it was some kind of random attack; he must have known her. The thing that interests me is the motive. What were the circumstances to provoke such an attack?'

'You've been watching too many episodes of Tatort.'

'I know... Hey, it's time we saw in the New Year,' Martin announced, cheerily.

Towards midnight with just minimal patient surveillance duties to carry out throughout the night, Martin and Lena felt free to relax. They put some tinsel around their starched white uniforms to add a little festive colour and switched on the television in their office.

The news was, unsurprisingly, still dominated by the tragic scenes coming from Banda Aceh and the carnage and aftermath of the tsunami in Asia less than a week ago.

'Bitte! I can't think about all those kids lost in the tsunami, not tonight.'

Martin groaned. 'Ok. How about we listen to the radio?'

Lena nodded and Martin switched on the stereo and fiddled with the channels. A broadcast of Bizet's opera Carmen and the aria 'Toreador' came on.

Martin clapped his hands. 'I love this! It's from Carmen, and I was in kindergarten when I first heard it. I had hair then. All those years; where did they go?'

'Let's ask Lotte Holler,' Lena said in a deadpan voice, fully aware that irony had its place on a coma ward.

Martin turned up the volume, put his hands above his head and made mock bull charges at Lena, singing loudly and encouraging Lena to join in and dance with him out in the corridors. The song resonated along the corridors and throughout the ward.

'Allons! En garde! Allons! Allons! Ah! Toreador, en garde! Toreador, Toreador! Et songe bien, oui songe bien encombattent, qu'un oeil noir te regarde, et que l'amour t'attend. Toreador, l'amour, l'amour t'attend.'

Lotte Holler heard the song and opened her eyes.

2. Awakenings

Lotte Holler looked around her small room. Her vision was a bit blurry but it soon cleared enough for her to see white clinical walls, the bunch of fresh flowers by her bedside and a photo of herself and Julia. A rhythmic beat from a heart monitor was audible despite the volume of the music coming from the corridor. Looking down, tubes were attached from her chest to the monitor. What was going on, what was she doing here?

Panic set in as she started to remember. The last time she heard this music was when a masked man had taken her at gunpoint to a lake outside Berlin, made her strip to her underwear in the cold night air and dance to this song. Where was this man now? Was he keeping her captive in this room and coming back any second?

She tried to get out of bed but her muscles felt heavy and slow. Lotte began to shiver, recalling the icy night. She had the feeling she knew the man behind the balaclava mask, whose cold eyes had gazed down on her. Was her memory playing tricks, hadn't she asked for his mercy and forgiveness? He knew her and he was taking revenge... The fog in her mind began to clear.

The music grew louder.

'Toreador en garde! Toreador, Toreador!'

Her attacker had ordered her to dance to this exact song,

stripping her of her dignity, so she had danced. Biting her lip, she had tried not to cry as the dancing warmed the chill in her bones. The last thing she recalled before being hit on the head and falling unconscious to the freezing ground was worrying for the safety of the unborn baby she was carrying.

The music transported Lotte back to that horrific night.

'Toreador, l'amour, l'amour t'attend.'

'NEIN! Turn off that SCHEISSE! Lotte screamed. 'Help! Julia, help me,' she yelled, her voice surprisingly strong after such a long period without use.

Martin and Lena stopped dancing in the corridor and raced to Lotte's room.

'She's awake!' Martin gasped.

'Lotte! It's OK, you're safe, you're in hospital,' Lena told her. 'Martin. Call the night doctor, Jonas, anyone… and turn off that bloody music.'

Martin quickly disappeared down the corridor.

'Turn it off!' Lotte cried, repeatedly.

Instinctively she began caressing her lower abdomen.

'My baby… my baby,' she cried.

In another part of Berlin, Julia and her sons were just arriving home around midnight to a backdrop of fireworks ushering in the New Year. A plethora of colours lit up the night sky as her mobile phone vibrated in her pocket. It was Lena calling with the amazing news that Lotte had woken up and was asking for her. Julia burst into tears, throwing her arms into the air in the middle of the snow- covered street and sinking to her knees.

'Mutti!' Frank and Tomas helped their mother to her feet and she hugged them tightly.

'It's a miracle!' she proclaimed. 'Tante Lotte has come out of her coma. We need to go to her right away.'

'Mutti… Tante Lotte doesn't know about us- it might freak her out if she meets us now.' Frank spoke with a wisdom and thoughtfulness beyond his 11 years. 'We'll go back to papa's, eh Tomas?'

Julia smiled at Frank. She could discuss most things with her eldest son even though he was at an awkward age with his hormones showing signs of puberty and a few spots appearing on his forehead. In contrast, Tomas was a young nine-year-old and still her baby. Frank nudged his brother to respond to his question but Tomas just shrugged his shoulders and played with the snow.

The miracle Julia had hoped for for so long had finally happened and she was bursting to see her sister. She wanted to drive like a tornado but thought of her sons and stayed impatiently within the speed limit, detouring back to their father and Jurgen's flat, where less than an hour ago she'd collected the boys. Jurgen and Julia had divorced a few years ago after growing apart during 10 years of marriage. He had felt the burden of Lotte's coma hanging over the family like the sword of Damocles; tonight he was truly glad for Julia, who looked visibly lighter than she had in a long time. Lotte's subsequent recovery would be pivotal in lifting the weight of responsibility from her shoulders.

At the hospital, an exuberant Jonas Roth had returned as soon as he got the news. Martin spoke excitedly, explaining the sequence of events that had precipitated Lotte's arousal. 'Lena's with Lotte- she hasn't stopped talking, it's incredible!' Martin informed him. 'Her sister's on her way.'

'I'll see the patient before Frau Kessler arrives and do some tests before unplugging her monitor. It seems Frau Kesslers' faith was justified!' said Dr Roth, smiling.

'Julia will be over the moon,' Martin replied.

The doctor patted Martin on the back. 'Thanks to the opera Carmen, we all are.'

It seemed an eternity waiting for her to arrive. Dr Roth was overjoyed when Julia appeared and rushed along the corridor to greet him. Smiling warmly he quite forgot himself and took her hands in his, then reprimanded himself for dropping his usual professional standards. Julia did not recoil. It was comforting to have his large hands envelop hers in a brief, shared and very poignant moment.

'Frau Kessler, I know you've waited so long for this moment but please, just a few minutes longer.'

Julia was so ecstatic she wanted to run along the corridor and take her sister in her arms but contained herself a little longer and complied. Dr Roth could see she was in a conflicting state of euphoria and anxiety, and overwhelmed by it all. He was careful to speak in a soft and sensitive manner in the way he delivered any information.

'Just to tell you a few things,' he began. 'We'll need to do more tests but for now, her heartbeat is normal and she's breathing well and independently. The good news is she's no longer in a comatose state- Lotte's awake and very obviously cognisant.'

Julia was pleased but still anxious. 'She won't fall back into a coma, will she?'

'I don't have all the answers to such a phenomenon as has been witnessed here tonight. We'll do our best to see she gets the finest treatment possible regarding physiotherapy, diet, psychotherapy or whatever she needs to make a good recovery,' Dr Roth told her.

'What can I do to help?'

'You said she was listening to you all this time and you were probably right! May I suggest that at the moment you answer any of her inevitable questions on a need to know basis. Don't volunteer information that might shock her, and remember, don't lie to her.

You know, the police will have to be informed because her case will be re-opened, but I won't let the police interview Lotte until she's ready.'

Julia frowned. 'Must the police be told? I don't want Lotte to be some freak in the news. They didn't find her attacker back then and they won't find him now.'

'I'd be breaking the law if I didn't inform the police. I'll do my best to keep the media circus away and make enquiries into compensation for your sister.'

'Thank you, doctor. Sorry to rush you, but is that all for now?'

Dr Roth smiled, understanding her impatience. 'Doch!'

Julia galloped down the corridor and burst into her sister's room. 'Lotte,' she cried.

'Julia! Lotte responded, attempting to raise her arms, weak from the years of inactivity, into the shape of a hug.

Tentatively, Julia held her sister in her arms. Lena wiped her own tears and made a discreet exit from the room, leaving the sisters to their poignant and long-awaited reunion. Lotte was now unattached to a monitor and although vocal, she was speaking as if she'd just awoken up from a deep sleep. Julia helped her take frequent sips of water to lubricate her dry throat because Lotte simply didn't want to stop talking and was highly animated.

'There was a man, he attacked me.' Lotte's voice resonated with a palpable fear.

'You're safe now,' Julia said, softly. 'You're in hospital and I'm here.'

'And my baby? You know I'm seven weeks pregnant. Is the baby OK?'

Julia remembered Dr Roth's words of wisdom: don't lie. 'Lotte... I'm sorry, you lost the baby.'

Lotte let out an anguished howl and began to sob. Julia held her sister close until her breathing returned to normal.

'I've been here every day, talking to you,' said Julia. 'Did you hear me, could you understand anything I was saying?'

Lotte nodded. 'I heard your voice rambling on.'

Julia laughed. 'Oh, poor you; listening to my ramblings! You were a captive audience.'

Lotte smiled, which brought a mixture of tears and pleasure to Julia's eyes as she remembered mannerisms she'd long forgotten.

'Why are you crying? I'm the one in hospital.'

Julia smiled and wiped her eyes thinking that Lotte didn't

realise she had just woken up from a coma.

Lotte stared at her. Julia looked different from the last time she'd seen her. At first she couldn't fathom what exactly it was but then she realised that Julia looked older. Quite a lot older.

'What's happened to you?' she asked, bluntly. 'Being married to Jurgen has aged you.'

'Jurgen and I are divorced.'

'What? You never told me. But you only married last year; I don't understand.'

Julia hesitated. 'I told you while you were sleeping.'

'I never liked Jurgen anyway, and he was far too old for you. He was just a substitute father.' Then it dawned on her. 'What do you mean, you told me while I was sleeping?'

'Lotte, I don't think you realise… you've been in a coma.'

'A coma?'

Julia nodded. 'You suffered blows to the head followed by severe hypothermia.'

Lotte still didn't ask how long she'd been in a coma. Instead the colour rushed to her cheeks as rage against her attacker took hold.

'That bastard! My attacker knew me, I know he did.'

Julia was dumbfounded. 'Wirklich?'

'When I worked at that place for unruly kids, he was one of the kids. He said he'd got rid of other wardens the same way, in the lake, and now it was my turn.'

'You've got to tell the police,' Julia insisted.

'I'm not telling the police I worked at Torgau! I told you that when the Berlin Wall came down and Germany reunited; it was a social stigma to admit working there. Julia, you haven't told anyone, have you?'

'Of course not. But the police will ask because they'll have to re-open your case.'

Lotte was curious. 'Have I been in the news then?'

'Not for a while.'

She noticed her sister's reticence. 'There's something you're not telling me? What are keeping from me? You and me, we don't have secrets. Come on, out with it.'

'You've been in a coma.'

Lotte frowned. 'Yes, you said. Julia, how long have I been in a coma?'

It was all happening too quickly for Julia. She wasn't ready to tell the truth, yet it was impossible to lie. Terrified how her sister would take it, Julia took Lotte in her arms again.

'I'm so sorry, my darling. Lotte, you've been in a coma for 12 years.

'NEIN!' howled Lotte, repeatedly.

Her cries could be heard throughout the ward.

3. 1989. The Boy

The moon over the lake at Motzen in East Germany on a clear and crisp November night was a few days short of being full, yet still offered sweet temptation to be outside under the stars.

Fourteen-year-old Felix was restless. It was 6.30pm and moonlight was shining through the window of his hideaway, brightening up his dimly lit, microcosmic world: a storage room high in the rafters of an old, aircraft hangar. He had adjusted well to nocturnal habits since his arrival at the lake in the spring. Felix felt the night belonged to him. No one noticed him in the still of night when he went out for a run, and afterwards, he'd take a rowing boat out onto the lake, whatever the weather. He enjoyed the rocking movement of the boat whilst listening to the sounds of the rippling water and the owls hooting under the stars.

Motzen Lake was roughly an hour south of Berlin, in a verdant, agricultural area. It was one of the many lakes in the area with a large expanse of water, an ideal oasis for aquatic sports and outdoor activities, with dense woodlands surrounding the picturesque lake interspersed with bicycle and rambling nature trails.

If he did go out in the day, Felix avoided the areas near the campsites during the summer because they were risky for someone who didn't want to be noticed. As instructed, he wore a dark wig and a baseball hat to hide his fair hair and his real age, 14. He limited his time outside to just a few hours in the middle of the day when the sun was at its hottest and most visitors would be in the shade.

But now summer had turned to autumn and tranquillity had returned to the lake, in stark contrast to the political unrest taking place in the Eastern Bloc countries during the summer of 1989. Under President Gorbachev's glasnost policies, demonstrations for political reform had grown and its domino effect was the gradual toppling of what the West called the Iron Curtain. In Hungary, Czechoslavakia and Poland the borders were opening and East Germany was cracking under the pressure. In East Berlin in October, over 100,000 demonstrators walked in peaceful protest and as a result, the East German President, Erich Honeker resigned supposedly due to ill health, and was swiftly replaced by another Kremlin puppet; Egon Krenz.

Felix kept up to date with these events as they unfolded by listening to a small radio in his room. The antenna on the roof of the hangar could pick up West German radio, and Western news gave a clearer, uncensored picture of unfolding events in the East. As his optimism grew, life would soon be changing.

Felix's onkel and tante, Klaus and Ingrid Felker, were careful to keep him safe and live a life of subterfuge, knowing only too well the pitfalls and the punitive consequences should their deception be uncovered. Ordinary folk in East Germany regularly informed on their families, friends and neighbours for the 'good' of the Communist party and eavesdropping was worse in small towns than cities as people were more exposed and couldn't disappear into the crowd. Conversations could be twisted and personal circumstances discovered by watching and listening. No one knew who was a Stasi informant, but you instinctively knew whispering voices led to betrayal.

Klaus and Ingrid, a childless couple in their late 30s, after 20, happy years together failed to produce an offspring. Tests had shown there was no medical reason why they couldn't conceive: it was simply a case of unexplained infertility. After much disappointment they had accepted their family would consist of just the two of them and made the most of their life together.

Klaus, a tall man with a thick head of hair and a protruding chest, was a little more rotund these days though he was strong and active. He liked to pat his belly and say to his wife, 'Look what your fine cooking has done to me!'

Ingrid, a tall and slender woman of subtle beauty, would throw back her hair and point to the flecks of grey in her long, fair locks. 'And look what you've done to me!'

Klaus preceded his brother Bernd by two years and a sister, Maria, had come along five years later. Klaus had always worked in the boatyard for his father Werner, and when he died 15 years ago Klaus had taken over the reigns of the family business. Gisela, Klaus's widowed mother, then moved with Maria to the island of Rugen on the Baltic Sea.

The land around the cottage had a small garden leading to a tiny beach and boatyard where Klaus, who was often dressed in blue overalls, worked fixing up fishing and rowing boats and hiring out pleasure boats during the tourist season. There was an old aircraft hangar set back from the waterside and everyone called it 'Das Kino'. It was used as a cinema at weekends for the townsfolk and tourists. Ingrid ran a café next to Das Kino, which she combined with selling flowers at local markets. Life was busy.

Younger brother Bernd was on the committee of a town council just outside East Berlin. His political job of functionaire in the Communist party came with privileges such as 'vouchers' to spend in special, Western-style shops. He dressed in a suit and a tie and his wife Ute, dressed in Western clothes. They both enjoyed the perks of the job, especially driving in the comfort of a Western car rather than the ubiquitous, under-performing, East German car, the Trabant. Their teenage daughters, Anna and Heidi, also disliked wearing

outdated clothing predominant in a country known for its

anti-consumerism.

It would have been easy for petty jealousies to spoil things between the brothers but Bernd didn't resent Klaus for owning the land at Motzen and Klaus didn't resent Bernd for his perks. The brothers were close despite their different lifestyles.

When Felix turned up at the lake in the spring of 1989, Klaus and Ingrid thought long and hard about their actions and anticipated that Bernd would be at risk of repercussions if a family member was found to be hiding a runaway. They came to the conclusion it was best not to compromise anyone but themselves and to safeguard Felix at all costs. Thus Bernd was not told and he never suspected Felix was in hiding in Das Kino - a safe place away from spying eyes.

Pacing in his room and mumbling in the silence of his mind, Felix counted three paces to the sink and three paces back to his bed. He muttered, constantly berating himself. He began rubbing his hands, quickening the speed as he did so, and before long his palms started to tingle with pain from the friction. The last part of this ritual was to scrub his hands with carbolic soap, which he always carried with him, but no matter how much he scrubbed away he never ever felt clean.

Once his panic had abated, Felix could no longer contain his feelings of cabin fever. He grabbed his rucksack and climbed down the spiral staircase and out into the moonlight. He ran along the pathway at the side of the lake with a torch to guide him. He was unafraid. Tonight, as he often did, he detoured into the village and climbed over a familiar gate, happy to be back in his oma Gertrude's garden. He would sit and look at the dark and empty house where once there was light and laughter, imagining the aromas coming from her kitchen. Gertrude had been a good cook, and used vegetables from her garden to create a variety of delicious dishes. Felix and his twin sister Susanne had loved coming to stay at Motzen on extended visits. But as he remembered his grandmother, an unpleasant memory filtered through. The final time he had stayed in Motzen was when Gertrude died. After the funeral, his mother, Sofie, had had a bitter argument with her sister Ingrid and then dragged Felix and Susanne away. They had never returned to Motzen after that, and Klaus and Ingrid never visited them again in Berlin.

Felix used to ask his mother why they couldn't go back to the lake but she just said, 'One day. Not now.' Without really understanding why, he accepted her explanation and after a while stopped asking.

Things went from bad to worse for his family after that. His parents separated and his father, Jakob, continued in a drunken, downward spiral until luck abandoned him not only at the bottom of a glass, but in the depths of a river whilst attempting to escape to the West. A few years later, Sofie was knocked down by a speeding cyclist on a busy East Berlin street, sustaining serious head injuries. She never recovered consciousness.

The twins were 12 when their mother died. East German authorities tended to view those who attempted to escape to the West as traitors to the Socialist State. Jakob Waltz was a traitor and also a drunk, therefore his children were tarnished by his genes and guilty by association and were punished in their father's place. Without consulting the two bereft young twins, or bothering to contact any of their relatives and thereby reflecting the cruelty of the quelling system, the social services declared Felix and Susanne orphans and therefore wards of the state.

In East Germany at this time, orphans and disruptive youths were often sent to institutions where abuse was rife and punishments were inflicted by staff without mercy or moral conscience. So it was that in 1987 Felix and Susanne ended up in an institution called Torgau, approximately two hours south of Berlin on the outskirts of Dresden. Its reputation meant it was only ever mentioned in undertones and the only way out for anyone to escape was to risk their lives by jumping into the swirling River Elbe, far below.

For two years Felix and Susanne suffered mental, physical

and sexual abuse in this notorious institution, a place totally lacking in humanity and empathy. The perpetrators of these crimes went unchallenged by the authorities or their colleagues because abuse was conspiratorial and hidden. They grew to believe they were invincible and there would be no retribution for their heinous crimes, no price to pay. Children who were unfortunate enough to be put in Torgau were out of sight and out of mind to the rest of the world and were later given the name the Weggesperrt, which meant the forgotten children.

Felix left Gertrude's garden and made his way slowly out of the village. As he walked along the main street it seemed every house in the village was in a party mood. It was late but many lights were on with music playing amidst the sound of laughter. It wasn't normally like this so he felt bemused and wondered what was going on.

Felix headed back to the lake and at the water's edge stripped to his swimming trunks, wading out to waist high with a bar of carbolic soap in his hand. The coldness of the water was bearable. At Torgau, punishments were handed out indiscriminately for trivial and minor offences. He'd sometimes been made to stand knee-deep in a darkened cellar for hours on end, or hosed with icy water in a slippery, cobbled courtyard whilst the wardens looked on in amusement. The cold water held no fears for him as the urge to feel clean now overwhelmed him.

Felix found it difficult to stop washing himself repeatedly, even though his excessive daily scrubbing had left him with dry skin that resembled eczema, especially on his hands. Despite the pain it caused, his obsessive washing was a comforting ritual.

'Felix!' shouted a bemused Klaus, appearing out of the darkness and making him jump. 'What are you doing? You'll catch your death.'

Felix hadn't heard his onkel approaching or noticed the light from his torch in the moonlight. 'Onkel, I'm OK, just cooling down,' he replied, hiding the soap in his trunks, trying to keep his obsession with cleanliness a secret.

But how could anyone really keep Torgau a secret? The damage and effects were there for all to see. The first time Klaus and Ingrid had set eyes on Felix after he'd escaped from Torgau they noticed the cigar burns on his ears, his dry, red skin and pale, thin body. They also logged the torment in his eyes. The night he arrived, Felix answered all their questions as best he could. Klaus and Ingrid listened patiently and compassionately and on hearing about the abuse he'd suffered they reassured Felix he shouldn't feel guilty for escaping and leaving Susanne behind, promising him he would be safe with them.

Love might not be enough to heal Felix but that was all Klaus and Ingrid could offer him, and they just hoped it would be enough after everything he had suffered.

'Come to the house, it's important,' Klaus pleaded, his usually stoical voice faltering and close to tears.

Felix felt a lump in his throat and a wave of sympathy towards his uncle. 'Are you crying? Onkel, you never cry.'

'Yes, I'm crying, even me. Promise me, boy, you'll never be too proud or afraid to cry. It doesn't make you less of a man.'

It was the first time Klaus had spoken to Felix with such paternal warmth. Until now, he'd shown kindness and generosity through his actions but often stumbled to say what he felt with words. Klaus and Ingrid were inexperienced in parenthood and were growing into this role but had agreed their relationship with Felix needed to develop over time and for trust to be built with the boy. Ingrid soon discovered how Sofie had died, crushed on her bicycle on the streets of Berlin with no one to comfort her as she slipped away. Ingrid dealt with her own pain and regrets, crying herself to sleep for many nights, but knew her pain was nothing compared to Felix's sufferings at Torgau.

As Felix came out of the water there seemed no more barriers between them. They were not just uncle and nephew, there was at last the hope and possibility they could become like father and son. Klaus picked up the towel and wrapped it around his nephew and rubbed his back to warm him.

'You'll never guess what's happened... I thought I'd never see the day.'

'Onkel, what's going on? Celebrations are going on all over the village.'

'Come and see for yourself,' Klaus exclaimed. 'The Berlin Wall is down.'

4. The Wall

On 9th November 1989, the Berlin Wall came down. The sequence of events leading up to this was clearly influenced by the fall of Communism throughout Eastern Europe throughout the year. However, there was one East German who gained much notoriety for precipitating the fall of the Wall on this night rather than any other night. His name was Gunther Schabowski.

A Politburo minister, Schabowski announced on television that East Germans were free to travel outside the country immediately. In his second, revised and corrected version later the same day he announced citizens could apply for a visa on 10th November, valid for travel the following day. Confusion and chaos reigned as crowds, full of expectation, gathered at checkpoints throughout East Berlin.

The Stasi uniformed officers and border guards at the checkpoints who previously would not hesitate to open fire with their shoot to kill policy of anyone trying to escape from the East to the West, started to have doubts. The guards noe questioned their role, their job as supposedly, keepers of the peace, their power to enforce it and ultimatcly their purpose. The gentle push of the crowd met feeble resistance; the guards opened the borders and looked on passively in amazement, stunned and powerless.

Klaus, Ingrid and Felix ate their dinner on trays in front of an open fire and watched, in awe, the live coverage on East

German television. Ingrid had cooked fricasee with bread, one of her mother's recipes, and their bellies were warm and full. Life couldn't get any better watching the events in Berlin unfold on this historic night.

'I've been keeping a bottle of Schnapps just for a special occasion,' Ingrid cheerily announced, opening the drinks cabinet.

The telephone rang. It was Gisela, Klaus's mother.

'Mutti. Yes, it's great news... We're watching the television coverage right now... Yes, Ingrid's fine... Can I call you back a bit later? Thank you. Tschuss.'

'You always get your mother off the phone as quick as possible. Poor Gisela.'

'Ingrid, don't nag!'

The telephone rang again. This time it was Bernd.

Klaus listened a few minutes and suddenly burst out laughing.

'Poor Ute... she'll get over it.' Klaus told his brother. 'Tschuss.'

Klaus returned to the fireside.

'Bernd said he thinks he'll soon be made redundant from the Communist party.'

'Don't be silly Klaus. And what's that about Ute, is she ill?'

Felix was quick on the uptake. 'I think you mean tante Ute will miss the privileges of being a functionaires' wife. Isn't that right, Onkel?'

Klaus winked at his nephew. 'Glad to see you've got your brains from Ingrid's side of the family, my boy.'

Ingrid gave Klaus a nudge for his cheek. 'Well, I'd take advantage too, given the option of shopping in Western stores. Maybe soon we'll all have that privilege.'

Felix had often been afraid to speak for fear of the consequences at Torgau, realising his politeness, silence and obedience usually kept him out of trouble - except when trouble had knocked on his bedpost at night. Whatever he did or said made no difference then. Now, he was hearing rare praise for his opinions and his confidence grew.

'Tante, don't jump the gun,' Felix warned. 'They'll close up the borders again just as quickly as they've opened them.'

Ingrid took Felix's hand. 'Don't you worry, as life only goes forward and tonight is a big step forward. Whatever happens, you're safe with us.'

Felix was adamant. 'I won't leave Motzen again.'

'You won't have to. You can live in my mother's house.'

Klaus rolled his eyes. 'Ingrid! Not now.'

It seemed inappropriate to bring up the subject now. Ingrid had never mentioned Gertrude's house in front of Felix before.

'Oma Gertrude's house? It's in the village, near the pond. Susi and I used to visit her there. We loved staying in that house.'

'Yes, that's right,' said Ingrid, looking at Klaus, knowing she'd now have to explain things to her nephew, if only to appease her disapproving husband.

'Sometimes, when I'm out running at night, I go and sit in oma's garden,' he confessed.

'You do? Good job you haven't been seen, my boy,' said Klaus. 'Well, we keep an eye on it, opening the windows a few days a week to freshen it up and tend the garden.'

'Gertrude's house belongs to you and Susanne,' Ingrid declared.

Felix shook his head. 'I don't understand.'

Ingrid couldn't face telling Felix how she'd alienated Sofie, breaking their close sisterly bond. To give Sofie's children the house was a small gesture in reconciliation and would give the twins some security. Ingrid and Klaus had agreed on this act of atonement and giving up Gertrude's house was a small sacrifice they were happy to make. Ingrid lived with her guilt about Sofie on a daily basis. Felix reminded her of her sister in the way he moved, his looks, his mannerisms, and his smile. One day she'd be brave enough to tell him, probably when he was a man, to ensure he had no false illusions about her. She hoped when he heard the truth he'd be able to forgive her even if she couldn't forgive herself. Tonight a half-truth would suffice.

'Well, it's like this. Klaus and I have our home and a little plot of land here and Gertrude wanted Sofie to have a home here too. When you and Susanne are adults, the two of you can decide.'

Ingrid had spoken from the heart. Klaus gave her a look of approval. Suddenly, Felix felt overwhelmed and vulnerable. 'We've got to get Susi out of Torgau and bring her here,' he urged them, beginning to sob.

Ingrid reached out to him and held him in her arms.

Felix blurted out, 'She's all alone in that scheisse place!'

'We'll get her out when the time's right, I promise,' Klaus told him.

After a few deep breaths he became calmer, feeling he could melt into the safety of tante Ingrid's arms. It had been a long time since anybody had touched him in a comforting, non-threatening way, let alone hugged him.

'Now the Wall is down, must I stay hidden?'

Klaus reassured him. 'Let's wait a little longer, just to be sure. Events are unfolding very quickly. But I'll tell Bernd about you. I'm sure his last assignment in the Communist party will be to help us reintroduce you to society and get Susanne out of that place. Can we all agree on that?'

'Agreed,' echoed Ingrid and Felix.

'Now, how about a Schnapps?'

5. Fated Coincidences

A few days after the fall of the Wall, the full moon went almost unnoticed amongst the blaze of lights from the worldwide television networks encamped in Berlin near the Brandenburg Gate. The celebrations had continued non-stop, day and night, with crowds gathering at this symbolic place; an obvious focal point of a once divided city.

It was here in June 1963, two years after the wall had been erected, that President John F. Kennedy visited the city to show moral support and stood by the Wall with the incumbent West German Chancellor, Willy Brandt. Later that day, at the Schoneberger Rathaus, JFK gave a rousing after-dinner speech, proclaiming 'Ich bin ein Berliner'. Berliners who witnessed the enigmatic and influential American's speech that day knew the speech could be literally distorted into a joke, as a berliner is also a doughnut pastry. But taken in its intended form, 'I am a Berliner', or rather 'I'm one of you and on your side', the President was given a warm and rapturous applause.

The Wall was slowly being dismantled. Chunks were now missing where 'woodpeckers' had chiselled away with their hammers until the holes were wide enough to walk through. Pieces of the wall would later be sought-after souvenirs and sold as memorabilia. For now, though, the crowds were not thinking about future money-making ventures. They were ecstatic, climbing the wall to wave German flags without the risk of being shot. The atmosphere was jovial and euphoric; the German nation was in union at last.

These images were broadcast around the globe. Against this backdrop, dignitaries up to be interviewed and the biggest cheers were saved for the German Chancellor, Helmut Kohl. He made a daily appearance and mingled amongst the crowd making daily, televised speeches to the crowds and his popularity soared.

Klaus and Ingrid wanted to experience the atmosphere in Berlin first hand. With them on the train to Berlin was Felix, wearing his usual disguise of a dark wig and hat. At Ost Bahnof they walked amongst the crowds along the Wall by the River Spree to the Oberbaum Bridge. Here, those from the East who attempted to climb over the Wall had to swim across the river to freedom in the West. Felix had been desperate to come here to see where his inebriated father Jakob had perished in a futile attempt to escape to the west. But despite the dismantling of the Berlin Wall, the bridge remained closed and impenetrable. Felix found a small hole in the wall and peered through.

'This is where my father ended up,' he told them. 'The fool somehow got as far as the middle of the bridge before the guards opened fire.'

Klaus understood. 'That's why you wanted us to come here.'

'Yes, Onkel. Mutti hid the report but I found it. Jakob didn't die from being shot. The bullet hit his cigarette case in his breast pocket. How lucky was that? No, he was stupid enough to jump into the water, and drowned because the drunken fool couldn't swim.'

Ingrid put her arm around Felix.

'I'm ok,' Felix shrugged. 'Come on, let's get over to Checkpoint Charlie.'

They walked along the U-Bahn to Friedrichstrasse and waited patiently in line to pass through. It felt surreal. At Checkpoint Charlie the guards were relaxed and friendly but even so, no one in the crowd dared to ask the guards why they were still there. It was in stark contrast to the recent shoot to kill policy for escapees, because if it was deemed the guards had missed on purpose, they were court-martialled. But they rarely missed their targets. The Stasi held great fear for East Germans and this wouldn't disappear overnight. No one could predict this really was the end after 44 years of the Socialist era in East Germany. Political idealism seemed split: those who fully believed in the Communist system versus those who were celebrating a glimpse of freedom from suppression and a new vision of the future. However, fear had long bought silence and obedience and it was hard to trust the miracle unfolding before their very eyes.

The three of them walked hand in hand to the western side of Berlin. Cheers and the popping sounds of champagne corks greeted them. A tall young woman, with closely cropped hair, carrying her baby in a pouch, passed by, shoving a banana into Felix's hand then disappearing into the crowd with her baby and bag of bananas. Felix, knowing how rare and sought after bananas were in the East at that time, offered to share it.

'You eat your little pot of gold,' Klaus told him with Ingrid nodding. They enjoyed watching Felix wolfing down the banana with gusto.

They continued to the wide avenue of Unter Den Linden, with its long alley of Linden- Lime trees, beautiful in summer and now bare of leaves on this autumnal evening. Ahead were the lights and sounds of the celebrations in Pariser Platz by the Brandenburg Gate.

A catering truck offered free warm drinks to the East Germans - known in the West as Ossis - who showed their identity cards. Ossis were easily spotted with their antiquated and unfashionable clothing in contrast to the West Germans -Wessis, with their access to Western consumerism. The Wessis were affluent in comparison and had to buy their drinks, thus the catering truck made money in spite of its spirit of altruism.

Klaus queued for coffees whilst Ingrid and Felix waited

nearby. A loud cheer rang out as another chunk of the wall crumbled under the pressure of the constant chiselling. A gaping hole opened, like a gate to a secret garden, an opening to the possibility of an unknown enchantment on the other side.

Bravely, Felix announced, 'I'm going through the hole in the wall. Tante, don't worry, I know where you are and I won't be long.'

Ingrid watched Felix disappearing into the crowd. She was anxious about losing him in the crowd but watching Felix taste the air of freedom in the last few days, she could not let her fears stand in the way of his excitement and pleasure.

Felix reached the gap in the wall. A 10-year-old boy was running in and out of the hole. A girl, about three or four years older, grabbed the boy's hand and pulled him away.

'Nein!' The boy screamed as he tussled for control with his sister.

The girl stubbornly insisted. 'Papa said not to!'

Felix could tell they were Ossis by their clothes as he was dressed in a similar fashion. For some reason, which was making him feel uncomfortable, he couldn't take his eyes off the pretty girl.

'Martha, Friedrich! Stop that,' boomed a familiar voice.

Felix froze as a small, athletic man of about 50 arrived to chastise his children. Surreptitiously pulling up his collar and wrapping his scarf around his face so only his eyes were visible, Felix shrank into the shadows. Luckily, the children's father didn't notice him but Felix knew the man standing less than five metres away from him; Dr Jens Wissemann, an employee at Torgau - the man who had helped Felix escape.

'Come on, you two,' he told his children, pulling them apart and returning them to their mother who was standing with her back to Felix. In the midst of this activity something fell unnoticed from the doctors' coat pocket - his identity card. He'd shown it to get his family the free hot drinks on offer at the catering truck and shoved it carelessly into his pocket. Felix swooped to retrieve it. Before he had time to return it, Dr Jens and his family had disappeared into the crowd.

In his haste to find the doctor, Felix almost collided with the banana lady with the baby he'd seen earlier that evening.

'Like a banana?' she asked.

'You already gave me one, near Checkpoint Charlie,' he reminded her.

'Did I? Then have my last one.'

'Thank you.' Felix couldn't refuse another delicious banana. He offered to shake her hand, intending to make a quick getaway.

'I wanted to do something tonight,' she began. 'To be a part of history and offer a symbol of sorts. One day, my daughter will ask where I was and what did I do when Wall came down? And I'll say, bananas!' she laughed.

'Thank you, it's very kind of you,' Felix told her.

The baby was wrapped up snugly and was quite content amongst the noise and excitement of the crowd. A young woman with spiky, punk-style hair appeared and the baby smiled, recognising her mother's companion.

'Here you are!' said the other woman, kissing the baby.

'I'm all out of bananas. This young man was my last recipient,' she said, pointing at Felix. 'What's your name?'

Felix gave the first name to come to mind. 'Jens.'

'Hi Jens, pleased to meet you. I'm Hanne, this is my friend Claudia and my daughter Audrey. Where are you from?'

Felix felt uncomfortable about giving away too much information. 'Berlin.'

'Whereabouts?'

'I live in Treptow, near the Oberbaum Bridge.' It wasn't such a big lie, he used to live there, near to the place where his father drowned.

'Oh, we live the other side of the bridge, in Kreuzberg,' Hanne told him.

Cheerily, Claudia said, 'We're all Berliners and there's no

more Wall to divide us,'

'Jens, do you mind if we all have a photo together? Hold up your banana for banana posterity?' Hanne said, laughing at herself.

Hanne quickly asked a passer-by to take the photo and Felix reluctantly agreed. What harm could it do? He couldn't foresee that it would be kept on Hanne's kitchen wall as a souvenir of this historic night for the next 15 years.

As their brief encounter was about to end, Audrey reached out her tiny hand and tugged at his hat, which fell, with the wig, to the floor. Hanne glimpsed the scars on the boy's earlobes and felt a wave of sympathy for him, although she was puzzled as to why he disguised his fair hair under a dark wig.

'I'm sorry,' Hanne said, empathising and embarrassed for him.

Felix quickly picked up his wig and hat and ran off, back through the hole in the wall to find Ingrid and Klaus.

'There you are! Onkel Klaus has gone looking for you. You were gone ages and your coffee's gone cold.'

'Sorry,' he muttered, having readjusted his wig and hat just moments before.

Klaus breathed a sigh of relief when he returned and saw Ingrid and Felix together. 'We were worried about you.'

'Onkel, I didn't go far. Sorry.'

'Well, you're here now. And can you believe it? Tonight, us three, we're a part of history. It's a miracle!'

In the crowd, people were shaking hands and hugging one another. The euphoria and party atmosphere would last for days. Klaus felt a little guilty, being in Berlin and not telling his brother, but Felix had to be protected a while longer and hoped Bernd was somewhere in the crowd with his family, enjoying the celebrations.

Felix patted his pocket regularly to check if Dr Wissemann's identity card was safe inside. It meant he had the means to contact the man who had smuggled him out of Torgau, if necessary.

'Oh, I forgot. I was given another banana. Here, I'd like you two to share it.'

Klaus smiled cheekily at Ingrid, peeled back the banana skin and put the fruit in his mouth while Ingrid took the opposite end in her mouth. They nibbled the banana until their mouths met in the middle for a sticky kiss as with a sudden loud bang, fireworks were set off from the Brandenburg Gate and an explosion of colours lit up the night sky.

6. The Brothers

Felix knew that the repercussions from the fall of the Wall would dictate when he could re-emerge back into society, out of the darkness and into the light. Klaus and Ingrid were confident that Torgau would face closure in the new, united Germany, and with this in mind, Klaus rang Bernd and asked him to come alone to Motzen, without delay.

Meanwhile, Felix stayed hidden in Das Kino as a precautionary measure. Fear was a crippling companion after years of state security exercising blanket surveillance and the East Germans knew that severe consequences always followed if the regime was compromised or challenged. Consequently, most ordinary citizens were reluctant to step out of line.

When Bernd arrived, he and Klaus wrapped up warm and took a rowing boat out onto the lake to be sure no one could overhear their conversation. Ingrid had made them a flask of coffee and sandwiches, which they tucked into. The lake was calm and winter seemed milder here than in the snowbound streets of Berlin. Klaus dropped anchor in the middle of the lake.

'The party's moribund. I'm not sure what to do next, job-wise that is,' Bernd confessed.

'You can always work here with me.'

'Thanks, no shame in that. I may just do that,' Bernd replied.

'So, what's all this talk of giving us in the East one Deutschmark for one Ostmark?'

'It's true. It'll be announced on television on 3rd December. And afterwards the Politburo will resign and the central committee will assist Helmut Kohl with the integration of one Germany, moving the capital back to Berlin from Bonn.'

Klaus gasped, '3rd December? That's tomorrow! It's all happening so fast.'

'Aren't you glad?'

'More than you know, little brother.'

'Hey, we could really build this place up for the tourist trade and make a lot of money in the process,' Bernd enthused.

'I think so too. There's a bit of land around here, and the Russian Army recently left their military base about 10 kilometres from here that's ripe for development. I'd be interested in opening up a golf course.'

Bernd laughed. 'Golf? My dear Klaus, you know nothing about golf!'

'But you do. Ask about the possible sites and use your connections. I think there's a lot of money to be made in golf,' stated Klaus.

Bernd nodded. 'We sound like capitalists already.'

Klaus spoke in a sombre tone. 'Now, is there anything you've done that'll bring repercussions? You're my brother and we stick together no matter what, but I need to know, just to be prepared.'

Bernd knew what his brother meant. 'No. I've not shamed you, my family or myself. Nor have I been a part of any decisions made within the party that have compromised the safety and security of any individual. My conscience is clear, you have my word.'

'Good lad,' said Klaus, patting his brother on the back.

'But you didn't ask me here to talk about golf.'

Klaus smiled. 'No. You see, I've a confession of my own… I've been hiding a runaway in Das Kino.'

Bernd was flabbergasted. 'Scheisse!'

'I know how dangerous a situation it was, so Ingrid and I told no one because we had no choice. We had to protect the boy at all costs. Luckily, events have gone in our favour and now is the time the boy can come out of hiding.'

'Klaus! Are you mad? Who is this boy you risked your life for?'

'Felix.'

'Sofie's boy?'

Klaus nodded. 'Yes. You remember when Ingrid and Sofie fell out at Gertrude's funeral and they lost contact? A few years later, that stupid drunk of a father, Jakob, drowned, and then Sofie died in an accident. Nobody told us so we never knew, and the twins ended up in Torgau.'

'Nein! Fic! Fic!' Bernd screamed, banging his fists on the hull of the boat.

'Sofie was knocked off her bicycle, and never regained consciousness.'

Bernd sighed. 'That's tragic. Poor Ingrid.'

'She's not forgiven herself. She's been very brave, hiding her grief from Felix. He was in a state when he turned up here in the spring, with bouts of shaking and nightmares, the poor kid. He needed us to be strong. He's on the mend now, thanks to Ingrid's love.'

Bernd admired his brother's modesty. 'Sorry to hear that. How can I help?'

'We need to know what's happened to Susanne,' Klaus told him.

'Ok. We'll go there today.'

'Before we go, I want you to meet Felix.

'Hopefully, he'll remember me,' he ventured.

Klaus spoke with an air of pride. 'He's got a fine eye for detail and he's incredibly bright. We don't want Felix to be just a Torgau boy.'

Felix was in Das Kino, reading in his room. He heard footsteps down below and Klaus calling his name. Appearing on the balcony, he looked down to find his Onkel was not alone. There was another man with him, similar in looks to Klaus but a better dressed and slimmer version.

'Felix, don't be alarmed. Guess who's here to see you?'

'Hello, Felix,' Bernd said warmly. 'Do you remember me?'

'Onkel Bernd?'

While they all had lunch together in the cottage, Felix was pleased to hear Klaus and Bernd were going to Torgau that very afternoon.

'I want to come with you,' he told them.

Klaus was adamant. 'No, I'm sorry lad.'

Frowning, he cried, 'Bitte! I'm not afraid. Please let me come with you.'

Bernd concurred with his brother. 'Sorry, best not.'

'Susi needs me! Onkel, she might not even recognise you,' Felix insisted, growing more and more frustrated. 'She'll think you're just another bastard wanting to take advantage of her!'

'Felix!' Ingrid cried. 'Mind your language.'

Angry, tearful and frustrated, Felix ran out of the room.

'He's got a mind of his own,' observed Bernd.

'Feisty, like his mother and tante,' said Klaus, glancing at Ingrid. 'When he's calmed down, we'll be able to reason with him.'

'What if he's right and Susanne doesn't recognise you?'

'Susanne will know her onkel Klaus,' he replied, assuredly.

Bernd telephoned a colleague in the Dresden Politburo and was given the information he needed about Torgau. Arriving a few hours later, Klaus and Bernd were taken aback at the size of the imposing, fortress-styled building on the River Elbe as it came into view. The main prison was not their destination; the annexed fortress was where the children had been housed. The gates were open so they drove through a cobbled courtyard and parked. It was getting dark and they noticed that the only lights were coming from a reception area in the entrance hall. The place seemed empty. As they went inside, a middle-aged man with a bird-like face and glasses greeted them.

'Gentlemen, how may I help you?'

Bernd spoke for his brother. 'I'm from the Politburo,' he said, showing his official identity badge. 'We're looking for a girl… our niece.'

'You'll need to fill out a form and it'll be dealt with in about ten days.'

Klaus was instantly livid. 'Ten days! We want news today!'

'As you can see, we're working with a skeleton staff here,' the man explained.

Bernd intervened. 'That's convenient. Everyone does a disappearing act so there's no one left to answer any questions.'

'You're from the Politburo, you should know,' the man said, accusingly. Everyone knows Egon Krenz is yesterday's man and so you'll excuse me for asking, but what jurisdiction do you have in the party?

It was the first time Bernd had experienced his authority being challenged.

'Krenz was an arschloch!' spat Bernd. 'I believe orders came through last month from my colleague- our newly-elected minster from Dresden, Hans Modrow. Torgau's penal colony for children closed with immediate effect. All detainees should have been sent home to their families, fostered or released.'

'Correct… and I'm here with a few colleagues to deal with enquiries.'

'And all the bastards who worked here, disappeared to?' Klaus shouted.

The man defended himself. 'Sir, I am not here to be abused.'

'No. Only the kids were abused,' was Klaus's riposte.

'I'm only doing my job,' the man replied.

Klaus banged his fist on the desk. 'You don't have to deal

with the aftermath of these screwed-up kids!'

Bernd intervened. 'Klaus! Calm down. Let me deal with this. Do you have a list of where these kids have gone?' Bernd asked, in as civil a voice as his mood allowed.

The man nodded. 'I do. Child's name?'

'Susanne Waltz. She's 14.'

'I'll get you a form.'

Bernd read the man's name on his identity badge. 'Herr Stokowski, you have files in your office. I want details of our niece, today. Is that clear?'

Bernd and Stokowski faced one another and stared. After a brief pause, Stokowski nodded, conceding defeat and disappeared to a back office.

Bernd shook his head and wiped a trickle of sweat from his brow. 'Believe me when I tell you, this is the best day of my political life.'

Klaus winked. 'It's great to have perks if you use them wisely. Welcome to the real world, little brother.'

Stokowski returned. 'Susanne Waltz. Date of birth 30th January 1975.'

'Genau!'

Stokowski looked uneasy. 'She left sometime in September.'

'September!' Klaus exclaimed.

'Where'd she go?' demanded Bernd.

'To a nursing home down in the town,' Stokowski informed them.

Klaus was worried. 'A nursing home? Was she ill?'

'I'll give you the address of the nursing home. They'll fill you in on the details.'

There was no one to take out his anger out on and no one to blame. A frustrated Klaus went outside into the courtyard and punched the cold air.

Bernd was a calming influence. 'Klaus, she's alive! This isn't the time for revenge, just get in the car and let me do the talking when we get there.'

Convinced another spanner would be put in the works once they got to the nursing home, Klaus was amazed when he was told Susanne had been there over a month and with Torgau's closure the doctors were wondering what to do next for her, believing she didn't have any relatives.

'Susanne can go home with you, just as long as you can prove you are related to her,' said the nurse.'

Bernd handed over the necessary proof of kinship: Gertrude Baum's will, stating her grandchildren Felix and Susanne Waltz will inherit her house in Motzen. With Klaus's marriage certificate to Ingrid, whose maiden name was Baum, it was adequate proof.

'Is she all right? Can we see her?' Klaus asked.

The nurse said she would arrange for them to see her. 'Susanne is fine and much improved, but still a little weak. She's recovering slowly from the complications she experienced giving birth,' she announced.

Gasping, Klaus looked at Bernd, both were stupefied.

The nurse added, 'Susanne had a baby eight weeks ago; a healthy boy, called Axel.'

7. The Girl

Susanne recognised Klaus even though it had been five long years since she'd last seen him. He hadn't changed much - but she had. Gone was the carefree girl, with flowing, sunshine locks and happy, hazel eyes. She had been replaced by a young woman with shorter, mousey, lank hair that fell on slightly hunched shoulders, and a smile that no longer sparkled. She showed little emotion when the nurse told her that her onkel Klaus had come to take her home. She'd said nothing to anyone about having relatives and had long stopped believing that people were fair and kind. In fact, she was sceptical that anything positive was ever going to happen in her life. At 14, the birth of her son had taken its toll on her young body. She was exhausted, emotionally and physically, from the abuse she'd lived through at Torgau, although at the nursing home they just viewed her as a troubled teenager from Torgau with a baby in tow. No one knew or even thought to question whether she was also suffering from post-natal depression.

The tiny baby slept untroubled in his cot. Susanne glanced at Axel. She was supposed to bond with him; love him, yet she felt numb. She breastfed him and looked after him in a perfunctory way and that was all she could manage for now.

Bernd met with the superintendent at the home and dealt with the legal formalities while Klaus went alone to see his niece. He didn't know what to expect as he knocked and opened the door to a small, clean room but he was taken aback when he saw Susanne, thinking she looked in a worse state than Felix had when he'd turned up at Motzen. Klaus attributed her lifelessness to the trauma of giving birth and motherhood.

'Susanne, it's me. Onkel Klaus,' he said softly, wanting to put his arms around her but holding himself back.

'Onkel, is that really you?' she said, managing a half smile and holding out her hand.

'Yes. Onkel Klaus has come to take you home,' he told her, taking her small hands in his and holding them.

'This is Axel, my son,' Susanne said, pointing at her sleeping baby.

Klaus peered into the cot. 'He's a handsome devil.'

'Did Dr Jens tell you I was here?' she asked.

Klaus shook his head. 'Who is this doctor?'

She sighed. 'It doesn't matter now. Besides, I haven't seen Dr Jens since Axel was born. I thought you'd all forgotten me.'

Klaus was emphatic. 'Never! We just didn't know and weren't able to help you until now. I'm so sorry.'

'Will you take me and Axel home with you?'

'Doch! Ingrid and Felix are waiting at Motzen for us all.'

Susanne's face crumbled with confusion. 'Felix? He's alive? But I thought he'd drowned, jumping into the river.'

'Is that what they told you? No, it's not true. Wait a minute, Dr Jens! That's the man who helped Felix escape.

Her eyes had the look of betrayal. 'Then he had more luck than our father then. Felix never told me he was planning to escape. Neither did Dr Jens.'

'Maybe they couldn't,' Klaus began. But Felix is alive and well and so are you. You know the Berlin Wall came down and Germany is reunited?'

'Yes, I heard. And I really don't have to go back to Torgau?'

Klaus shook his head. 'No. You won't ever have to go back.'

Susanne looked afraid. 'Promise?'

'I promise,' Klaus said, reassuringly. 'We're a family again. Come on, get your things packed, bring your baby and let's go home.'

Klaus called Ingrid from the office of the nursing home to say they were on their way and update her on all the necessary news. He asked her to break the news to Felix that his sister was coming home.

Ingrid got a bedroom ready, hastily ironing some clean sheets, and prepared a dish she remembered was one of Susanne's favourites, a green bean stew; grune-bohneneintopf.

She heard the latch of the door click open. It was Felix who had just returned from a long run as he tried to work off the frustration of his earlier outburst. The aroma of the stew filtered through from the kitchen.

'Tante, I'm sorry I behaved badly earlier.'

'Oh, it's forgotten. If it means you feel safe enough to speak your mind with Klaus and me, well, that's a good thing - from time to time,' she said, with a wry smile.

Felix nodded in agreement but he understood that poor behaviour wouldn't be tolerated on a regular basis.

'Mmm, something smells nice.'

'I've good news,' cried Ingrid. 'Susanne is on her way home with Klaus and Bernd.'

He was ecstatic, and hugged Ingrid. 'Is she all right?'

'She's as well as to be expected but there is something else. She's had a baby.' Ingrid told him, and waited for his reaction but realised Felix was not in the least bit surprised.

Felix frowned. 'A boy or a girl?'

'A boy. Felix, did you know Susanne was pregnant when you last saw her?'

'Yes.'

Ingrid's disappointment was tangible. 'Why didn't you tell us?'

'It was Susi's secret. I couldn't tell anyone.'

'You can't keep a baby a secret!'

'I hoped she'd lose it, or get rid of it.'

Ingrid was shocked at her nephew's attitude. 'Nein! Felix!'

He was adamant. 'Who wants a Torgau baby? Not my sister, that's for sure. He'll be a constant reminder of… I didn't want Susi to become a mother at 14. Who would?'

'No, but it's happened and she is a mother. We'll all have to help her and just get on with it as best we can.'

Susanne was quiet on the drive home and Klaus and Bernd didn't tax her with questions or force conversations. Mostly, she stared wistfully out of the window at scenery she'd long forgotten whilst Axel slept peacefully in the carrycot beside her.

Felix heard the sound of a car engine and tyres crunching on the snowy terrain as they drew up outside and began to panic. He had betrayed his sister by leaving her behind in Torgau. Would she, could she ever forgive him? Nervously, he waited in inside the cottage with Ingrid. It felt like an eternity waiting for the door to open and Susanne to walk in carrying Axel in his carrycot. She smiled at Ingrid and Felix but they could tell by the look in her eyes she was vague, disorientated and fragile. Klaus and Bernd followed her inside.

'Susanne, it's so lovely to see you,' Ingrid said, embracing her niece.

'For me too,' Susanne replied and looked her brother in the eye. 'Hello, Felix.'

Felix smiled. 'Susi… You're here at last.'

Brother and sister held one another briefly and each could feel the other trembling as they hugged.

Klaus broke their awkward moment. 'Well, we're all hungry, let's eat.' And turning to his brother he asked, 'You'll eat with us before you go?'

'I wouldn't turn down Ingrid's cooking,' Bernd said, winking at his sister-in-law.

Klaus patted his belly. 'Nor me.'

Felix turned his attention to the baby. He bent down and held the boy's little fingers in his. 'What's your name, little man?'

'Axel. I named him Axel. Do you like his name?'

Felix smiled at his sister and nodded approvingly, which seemed to please her.

After supper, Bernd had the option to stay overnight and enjoy a few glasses of schnapps but it was only an hour back to the Berlin suburbs and Ute and the girls would be excited to hear all the news. It had been a memorable day. Klaus walked Bernd to his car to see him off.

Klaus patted his brother's back. 'Thank you for all you've done today.'

Bernd smiled and shook Klaus's hand. 'Brothers in arms. We did it together.'

'Susanne's got a long, tough road ahead,' Klaus mused.

'I'll bring my girls down next week. A bit of girlie company, that'll cheer her up.'

'Great! Now, don't forget what we said.'

Bernd raised his brow, 'We've said a lot today.'

'Golf!' Klaus reminded him. 'Let's find out about our options for a golf course.'

The brothers said a fond farewell and Klaus returned to his newly expanded family and the warmth of the fireside.

'How about a game of cards? Skip-bo?' he suggested.

Klaus was glad to see Susanne's mood from earlier in the day had improved a little. He thought it was possibly a mixture of being with the family, Ingrid's home cooking and the realisation dawning on her that she was finally free. However, his optimism was flawed: it would turn out to be the brief sunrise of a false dawn.

Playing cards, they relaxed together without the pressure to talk about the traumatic events of the past. Personality traits are often revealed through play and their game of Skip-bo quickly took an interesting turn.

Klaus nudged his wife. 'Come on, Ingrid, it's your go.'

Ingrid eventually put down a card.

'No! You'll help Felix that way,' Klaus objected.

Ingrid scoffed, 'I'm not ruthless when I play cards, unlike some.'

Felix put down a few cards and then hesitated, perusing the other cards on the table.

'Thinking about your next move?' Susanne asked her brother.

Susanne's words were cryptic, meant as a double entendre, but Felix didn't respond and she continued to dig at him. 'You must have a joker, to get you out of trouble.'

Ingrid didn't know whether the tension between Felix and Susanne was sibling rivalry but sensed an unspoken edginess between them.

Felix felt under scrutiny. 'When a door closes and a window of opportunity opens it's best to climb through it,' he said, finishing the game with a flourish. 'I'm out.'

'The winner takes it all,' muttered Susanne, stony-faced.

Ingrid observed the twins closely, deciding it was simply sibling competitiveness. 'Good job we weren't playing for money,' she remarked.

'You know what they say? Lucky at cards; unlucky in love.'

'Well, my dear husband, you always win at cards. What does that say then?'

'Exceptions to every rule, my dear,' said Klaus, blowing a kiss at Ingrid.

Axel began to cry.

'Oh, he's hungry again. I'll go and feed him.' Susanne picked up her son and left the room.

'I'm ready for my bed, it's been a long day,' Klaus confessed.

'Onkel, can I use your carpentry tools tomorrow?' whispered Felix.

Klaus was curious. 'What for?'

'With the spare wood in the boathouse I thought I'd make a crib for Axel.'

'Ok. Good idea. I'm off to bed, gut nacht,' Klaus said, yawning and went to his room.

Felix,' Ingrid began. 'I was thinking about going to see the principal at the village school, to ask when you can re-start your school life.'

'Can't I just start working in the boatyard?'

Ingrid shook her head. 'You haven't had a proper education for the last few years. It'll be good for you, to mix with young people again. Onkel Klaus can wait for his apprentice.

Susanne returned to the room with Axel, who was crying incessantly. 'He won't feed! I think my milk is drying up,' she said, anxiously.

Ingrid called Klaus out from their bedroom. 'Quick, go into the café… Under the counter there are baby bottles and some powdered baby milk that I keep for my customers, in case of an emergency. Don't worry Susanne, it's quite common, and lots of babies take bottled milk.'

Klaus hurried out to the café and Ingrid disappeared to the kitchen. Felix and Susanne were left alone with Axel.

'Susi, you're exhausted. Let me have him.'

Susanne handed Axel to her brother who rocked him in an attempt to calm him.

Once the bottle was ready, Susanne asked Ingrid to feed Axel as she was afraid he would be frustrated in suddenly coming off the breast. But Axel took to the bottle easily and Ingrid was surprisingly natural at feeding him.

'Babies are fickle. All he needs is feeding, changing and a few cuddles and he'll take it from any source,' Susanne observed.

'He's a nice healthy size, you've done a good job,' Ingrid told her niece. 'We'll go out tomorrow and get a sterilising set, some new bottles, nappies and clothes for him.'

'I wanted to keep him,' Susanne began. 'They asked me if I wanted him adopted but I refused. If the Berlin Wall hadn't fallen and changed things I wouldn't have been allowed to keep him and bring him home to my family,' she said, bursting into tears.

Ingrid handed the baby to Klaus to finish feeding and swept Susanne into her arms.

'Come on, young lady. Let's get you into bed. I'll check on Axel during the night. You need a good night's sleep, and then you'll feel so much better in the morning.'

Susanne didn't argue and went with Ingrid to the bedroom. Klaus propped Axel on the sofa, between some cushions and finished feeding him.

'You haven't winded him,' Felix noted. 'I'll do it.'

Klaus watched Felix carefully handling the baby and gently rubbing his back. Axel soon let out a loud, healthy burp.

'Onkel Felix, when did you become an expert on babies?' Klaus joked.

'It's common knowledge. First you feed them, then wind them and then change them. Look, he's straining, I bet he's trying to poop.'

Klaus smiled. 'I'll get a fresh nappy and you can change him.'

'Sshush.'

At first Klaus thought Felix was making soothing baby sounds but he was actually doing was asking for quiet.

'Onkel. Listen… Tante is singing Susi to sleep.'

Ingrid's dulcet voice could be heard, singing a lullaby.

'She's a good woman,' Klaus said, proudly. 'Felix, why don't you sleep here tonight?'

'I'm fine in Das Kino, and the straw insulates the room really well.'

'My boy, you don't have to stay hidden any more,' Klaus reassured him.

Felix nodded. 'I know. But for now, I'd rather stay in my own little space.'

Ingrid tiptoed out of the bedroom, closing the door quietly behind her. 'She's asleep. Poor girl, she's so very tired. Even if she sleeps all day, let her. We can all muck in and look after the baby. What's that smell?'

Klaus joked, 'Not me! Axel needs changing.'

'Well, what are you waiting for, Great Onkel Klaus?'

Ingrid did the night feeds and Susanne had an unbroken sleep until late the following morning. When she awoke she didn't recognize her surroundings but catching sight of an old photo of her oma Gertrude on a bedside dresser she remembered where she was. But where was Axel? She dressed and went to find him sitting quite happily in his carrycot, Ingrid talking baby-talk to him while she was ironing.

'Morning,' Ingrid said, putting down her iron. 'Sleep well?'

'Yes. Did Axel wake you in the night?'

'Only once. It's fine; I'll do the night feeds until you're feeling better.'

'Thank you,' she said, stroking her son's head. 'You've got so many people to love you. What a lucky boy you are!'

'Hungry?' Ingrid enquired. 'I'll make you some breakfast, anything you like.'

Susanne nodded. 'I'll help myself, if that's ok.'

'This is your home now, yours and Axel's.'

Susanne suddenly doubled over in pain.

Ingrid grew concerned. 'What's wrong?'

Susanne sat down and eventually the pain eased. 'It was a difficult birth. They had to cut me. I get the cramps sometimes.'

'You take it easy,' Ingrid advised.

Susanne went to the bathroom and checked herself. She'd been menstruating for a month now and although it was a light flow of blood and the doctors at the nursing home had told her it might last for six weeks, it was draining her. After showering she dressed again and went to the kitchen to eat some porridge and a strong cup of coffee. Observing how kind Ingrid was being to her, she decided to say something lasting to show her gratitude.

'Thank you for singing me to sleep last night. Mutti used

to sing to us.'

Ingrid looked wistful. 'I heard her sometimes. Sofie had a sweet voice.'

Susanne thought about asking Ingrid about what happened between the two sisters but decided it would only bring back painful memories. Sofie was long gone and everyone had their regrets for one reason of another. There had been a lot of water under the bridge since then. She barely recognised herself these days. What was important for her was to try and focus on the present, and today she needed to tie up some loose ends.

'Where's Felix?'

'He's in Das Kino.'

'I want to talk to him.'

'No, don't go, I mean… It's a secret,' Ingrid blurted out.

'A secret? Tante, I don't like secrets, please tell me.'

'He's making something for the baby. Sorry, it was meant to be a surprise.'

'I've kept secrets just to stay alive. Tante, I can't do it any more.'

There was nothing Ingrid could say. Implicitly, she understood.

Sussanne announced, 'There will be no more secrets between Felix and me,' putting her coat on. 'Please look after Axel for me,' she said, kissing her son and embracing Ingrid warmly before going outside.

Felix was working in Das Kino, making the baby crib. He was good at woodwork, good with any task where he could use his hands. Under Klaus's tutorage, given a piece of wood, he was rapidly developing the skills to turn it into something interesting and useful. One day he hoped to build a small boat but for now, he made chairs, tables, anything practical.

Initially when his sister came in he was irritated.

'Susi! What I'm making was meant to be a surprise,' he said, with disappointment.

'You know I don't like surprises… It's a lovely crib.

Thank you… Felix, please. We need to talk.'

It was approaching lunchtime. Ingrid had made eisbein - pickled ham - with sauerkraut. A hungry Klaus came in and was promptly kissed by his wife.

'Klaus, look after Axel for me. I'm going to call the twins for lunch. Won't be long.'

'What's that lovely kiss for?'

Ingrid kissed her husband again. 'For bringing the family back together.'

Klaus smiled. 'You like having a baby in the house, eh?'

'It's lovely,' Ingrid said, smiling broadly.

The snow crunched beneath her feet walking along the path to the Das Kino. The doors were wide open and she witnessed Felix come out of the hangar briefly only to disappear inside again. Then she heard the twins' raised voices, followed by a wild, falling scream, a heavy thud and the crack of bones on concrete. It was a moment that would change all of their lives forever.

Ingrid ran to the entrance of Das Kino, her heartbeat racing so hard it was audible. Inside the hangar, she saw Susanne's broken body lying lifeless on the floor. She had landed not far from where Felix was standing, frozen in horror.

'NEIN!' Ingrid cried. 'Scheisse!'

Screaming wildly, Felix suddenly bolted into action, rushing to cradle his sister's bloody head in his arms.

'NO!' he screamed, over and over. 'NO!'

8. The Doctor

Felix carried his sister from Das Kino to the cottage, her blood dripping a trail of red on the pristine white snow. The warmth of her body was ebbing away, yet as Felix laid her on a bed she looked as if she was sleeping, peaceful at last. Axel was asleep in his cot, blissfully unaware that when he awoke crying for the comfort and sustenance of suckling his mother's breasts, his cries would forever go unheard.

Klaus and Ingrid stood watching at the bedroom door, stunned and quiet.

Felix broke the silence. 'It's my fault. Susi and I argued… then she jumped.'

Ingrid was adamant. 'No! It's not your fault. You couldn't know she'd do that!'

'But I left her in that fucking place! She wouldn't forgive me,' Felix yelled.

'Stop that!' Ingrid insisted. 'Whatever you were arguing about, she'd made up her mind to jump. Now, what we are going to do?'

Felix reluctantly left Susanne's side and carried Axel in his cot out of the room.

'We need a doctor,' Klaus said, picking up a telephone directory.

'I know a doctor,' Felix began. 'Dr Jens. He helped me escape.'

Klaus nodded. 'I remember. And Susanne spoke about him too.'

Felix was distraught. 'You must call him,' he cried, handing over the identity card with Dr Jens's details.

'Where did you get this?'

'Onkel, no questions, bitte, not now. Dr Jens will help us. Just call him.'

Klaus decided to trust Felix's instinct and rang the number. A man answered.

'Dr Wissemann?'

'Yes. Who is this?'

'Please, don't hang up. I'm Felix and Susanne Waltz's onkel. There's been an accident.'

Dr Wissemann was shocked by Klaus's tragic news and knew he had to help. He thought back to his days at Torgau where he'd sat on his hands for too long, telling himself it was not his business what the wardens got up to. In the hospital wing he'd seen the effects of abuse that some wardens inflicted on the children on a regular basis, and his job was somewhat perfunctory: to tend to their wounds, get on with his tasks and say nothing.

In East Germany at that time, as a man of 50, he felt he was unlikely to find another job, and he had his family to think of. A steady income paid the bills and gave them a reasonable lifestyle. He'd convinced himself that challenging the system would be futile and feared the consequences of such a challenge. But his growing sense of guilt at his collaboration of silence had gnawed away at his conscience and by tolerating it, his apathy made the evil possible. When news of the fall of Communism spread throughout Eastern Europe during 1989, Jens decided to take a few risks.

Dr Wissemann had been one of a dozen or so doctors and nurses who worked shifts in the Torgau hospital wing, tending the wounds of children who'd been subjected to a long list of injuries: cuts, bruises, horrific weals from beatings with belts, broken fingers and toes. All were commonplace. But those he found most pitiful were the children sent to the hospital wing suffering from constipation and anal sores from the effects of the buggery they endured.

The most infamous paedophiles at Torgau were three men known by their pseudonym of 'The Three Musketeers'. Their real names were Horst Gwisdek, Gunther Schukrafft and Harald Plaumann and their reputation at Torgau was legendary. Children spoke about them in whispers, hearing about them from friends and fellow victims. Resting uneasily in their beds at night, they would pray it wasn't their turn and feel guiltily relieved when another kid received a knock on their bedpost, to be taken from their bed and led to the evil trio. For those unfortunate enough to be chosen, a long night of terrifying, painful, drunken debauchery lay ahead, ensuring the Musketeers lived up to their motto of 'all for one, and one for all'.

The Musketeers used a go-between to take the children from their beds at night, a young, female warden who obeyed orders and never questioned her superiors. Her name was Lotte Holler.

When Dr Wisscmann was on duty at Torgau he listened surreptitiously to the BBC World Service on his small radio. His English was good enough to understand what was being said and the historic news that the Soviet control of the Eastern bloc countries was loosening enraptured him. One crisp, spring night, he heard the sound of footsteps approaching his office and turned off the radio and returned it to its hidden place- his private medical bag. There was a knock on the door. It was Lotte Holler.

A young, fair-haired boy cowered behind her, crying in the corner. He recognised the boy immediately as one he was particularly sorry for, a little chap called Felix. He and his twin sister Susanne were regular victims of the Musketeers who, before they sexually abused the twins, made them dance to music. Dr Wissemann treated Felix and Susanne when they were brought to him afterwards, sad and sore. He used to offer them a brief respite, letting them stay overnight on the ward together.

Lotte explained, 'Herr Doktor. One of the inmates has been playing silly fools with a cigar, and he's burned his ears.'

'How did he get hold of a cigar?'

Lotte shrugged her shoulders. 'These kids get up to all sorts.'

Jens knew she was lying, as she usually did, and guessed the cigar burns were inflicted by the Musketeers. Felix's ears had blistered and he was trying to be brave and not cry, but his legs gave way beneath him and he sank to the floor in agony, muffling his cries by biting on his shirt collar.

'Stand up!' barked Lotte, in a fierce and merciless voice.

Felix stood up. He didn't know if this was the start of another game where the wardens repeated 'stand up, sit down' ad infinitum, simply for their amusement.

'I'll keep him here overnight. Burn wounds need to be dressed every few hours or so and he can sleep in the hospital ward tonight.'

'Yes, Herr Doktor,' Lotte replied and marched off.

Felix yelped when Jens applied an antiseptic gel to his ears and gave him some strong painkillers. 'There, that'll soothe them, although I'm sorry to say you might have some lasting scars.'

Felix lay down in the dark of the small room that housed four single beds. The pain from his ears over-rode the pain from his body after his evening with the Musketeers. Sleep would only come when the pills began to work.

A short while later, Felix heard footsteps coming into the room but didn't dare open his eyes for fear it was that bitch warden, Lotte Holler, coming to take him away. He slyly opened one eye and saw Dr Wissemann opening a nearby window, tying a few bed sheets together and attaching them to the bed to hang out of the window. Felix was afraid. It was a long drop to the River Elbe, below. What was the doctor thinking?

The doctor whispered. Felix, wake up. The night nurse is on her break, we haven't got long. I'm going to get you out of this place.'

There was a flight of stairs next to the escalators used for deliveries to each of the floors of the children's wing at Torgau. In the hospital wing, Jens used this staircase to avoid entering the main gates, preferring to come in at the electronically controlled delivery gate, for which he had a coded pass. The store room where food and medical supplies were delivered was patrolled by armed guards during the working day while a small number of non-uniformed staff worked in the storehouse, to help log data and distribute the supplies. At night it was locked and unmanned.

Dr Wissemann wrapped a blanket around the bewildered boy and led him down a few flights of stairs, past the storeroom and empty reception desk and into a small courtyard to where his Trabant car was parked.

'Felix, lie down in the back, stay very still and try to sleep. I'll return before sunrise.'

'What about my sister?'

'Sorry. It's too dangerous to get both of you out tonight and you know Susanne is three months pregnant. I insisted she wasn't forced into a termination because she wanted to keep the baby and that means the wardens will leave her alone now. Things are changing outside these walls and when the time's right, I'll get her out of here, I promise.'

Dr Wissemann returned to the ward as the duty nurse was coming along the corridor.

He lied with ease. 'Nurse! A patient has escaped. Quick, call the wardens.'

Before long, an armed male warden called Jochens turned up with Lotte Holler.

Jochens looked through the open window where the sheets were hanging, blowing in the breeze. 'It's a long way down and difficult to survive a fall in the cold water,' said Dr Wissemann, giving a convincing performance. 'I saw him climbing out of the window and I shouted at him not to do it, but he jumped. The outside security lights helped me see him struggling in the water below, and then he went under.'

Lotte chuckled. 'I heard the boys' drunk of a father drowned trying to escape over the River Spree. Maybe the boy got hold of a bottle of schnapps. Stupid boy - like father, like son, eh?'

Jens ignored her cruel comments. 'I only went to the bathroom and when I returned, the boy was halfway out the window!'

'No one will miss him,' said Lotte. 'Felix Waltz has danced his last dance.'

'No one's to blame, Herr Doktor. But what if the boy did survive and got out of the water down river? Maybe we should send out a search party?' Jochens ventured.

Dr Wissemann thought it best to flatter the warden's authority. 'Whatever's best Jochens, you decide.'

Fortunately, Jochens decided to trust the doctor and began untying the sheets. 'No, you just write your report. I mean, it's not as if anyone will care about a Torgau boy.'

'We are, after all, only doing our job,' stated Lotte.

'And no one's to blame,' Jens echoed, trying not to look at Lotte with contempt, thinking some of the most despicable human behaviour has been conducted in the name of 'I'm only following the law' or 'I'm only doing my job'.

'Genau, Herr Doktor.' Lotte had felt the doctor's look of disapproval. 'We're all just doing our job under difficult circumstances. The boy didn't suffer. It's for the best, as the kids here don't have a future and nothing to offer society. That boy won't be missed by anyone, it'll be as if he never existed or he was left comatose. Kids here are the forgotten children. Who'd want a life like that?' Lotte believed she'd acquitted herself well in front of the eminent doctor.

Before sunrise and at the end of his shift, with no more questions asked and no suspicions raised, Dr Wissemann drove out of Torgau with Felix hidden under a blanket on the back seat of his car.

'Don't say a word, Felix,' he instructed.

Felix obeyed and was silent until the doctor began talking to him. 'You can talk now. But stay lying down for the time being. How are your ears?'

'I'm trying not to think about them.'

'I'll dress them when we get home.'

'Home?' Felix asked.

'Yes, where I live. I've thought it through and I'm sure my wife will be fine about it. You can stay hidden at my house for as long as it takes.'

'Please, I can't stay with you. I want to go home.'

Jens was surprised. 'Home? But, I thought you and Susanne were orphans?'

Felix trusted the doctor implicitly and without hesitation said: 'I've an onkel and tante. Because of a silly family row I'm sure they never knew my mother died, and Susi and I knew if we told the wardens we had relatives it wouldn't have made any difference.'

Jens felt a mixture of sadness and delight for the boy. His relatives could have saved him from Torgau, but perhaps they now could offer Felix new hope.

'Where do they live?'

'South of the Spreewald.'

A few hours later Jens, with Felix sitting in the front of the car, saw the aircraft hangar and Motzen Lake coming into view.

Felix grew animated. 'Look! Dr Jens. Das Kino!'

Jens was bemused. 'Das Kino?'

'The aircraft hangar, that's what we call it, Das Kino. We show films in there at the weekends.' Felix couldn't contain his excitement. 'And look, there's the cottage.'

Jens parked and looked out onto the peaceful lake. It was a beautiful spring morning with a gentle breeze and freshness to the air. Felix would do very well here, he thought, it was a perfect place to heal. 'You'd best go,' he told him.

Suddenly Felix felt afraid. 'What if they don't want me?'

'They'll want you,' Jens reassured him.

'Will you come in with me?' Felix pleaded.

'Best not. It would compromise your family and mine if we met face to face. I tell you what, I'll take a walk to stretch my legs and if you're not back here at my car in one hour, I'll know all is well.'

Jens gave Felix a few sterile dressings to take with him and shook his hand. 'I'll make sure Susanne's ok. Once she's had the baby, I'll do my very best to bring her home here but it has to be our secret, just for now.'

'Danke, Dr Jens. I'll not forget you.'

'You should. Because I'm a constant reminder of the hell you've come from.'

Felix threw his arms around the doctor, then took a deep breath, left the car and started his short walk towards the cottage. Jens watched him go and crossed his fingers for the boy.

An hour later, he got into his car and drove home to the outskirts of Dresden without Felix. Feeling good about himself for the first time in ages, Jens started to dream of different schemes to get more kids out of Torgau. The problem was, if he helped anyone else escape, where would they go? It wasn't viable to hide more than one kid at a time and they wouldn't all be lucky like Felix and have a family to return to. Escapees couldn't be left to fend for themselves in the outside world, leading a life on the run; the Stasi authorities would pick them up like stray dogs and return them to their kennels.

Under the pressure of torture, tongues would be loosened and that would compromise Jens and his own family. He'd have to be content that he'd acted responsibly with Felix and that would have to satisfy his moral conscience for the moment. But he'd safeguard Susanne during her pregnancy and try to keep his promise to return her to her family.

He attended Susanne at the nursing home just after Axel was born. Life was going to be hard for a 14-year-old teenage mother but he had believed there was a promise of something better to come.

Jens's wife had persuaded him to let events unfold and not have any further involvement with anyone from Torgau and to concentrate on their own children, just in case the authorities caught up them. Jens reluctantly agreed and tried to distance himself from his Torgau past and make a fresh start. He paid the owner of the nursing home out of his hard-earned savings to keep Susanne Waltz and her baby safe throughout the winter months of 1989. If the political climate allowed, Jens promised himself to return to the nursing home and help Susanne Waltz the following spring.

Motzen, in the midst of a bleak, snow-covered winter, looked vastly different from when Jens had last been there in the spring. Klaus and Ingrid welcomed him into their home; the mood was sombre. The ticking of a grandfather clock and its' chimes were the only sounds Jens could hear as he clasped Felix's hands in his, noticing in a distracted way that they were red and flaky.

'I'm so sorry for your loss,' he said, softly.

Klaus shook the doctor's hand. 'I'm sorry we had to meet under these circumstances.'

'Herr Doktor, would you like something to drink?' Ingrid asked.

'A coffee would be fine. Please, call me Jens.'

Felix handed Jens his identity card. 'You dropped it - it's how we knew how to find you. I tried to give it back when you were only five metres away from me in Berlin, but I lost you in the crowd.'

Jens was surprised. 'You were in Berlin too? How strange. Thank you. I felt quite a fool, losing my identity card.'

'Susanne's in the bedroom,' Klaus began. 'We haven't called for an ambulance or the police, we waited for you. I hope this was ok. Felix told us how much you helped him and Susanne and we are forever in your debt.'

'You owe me nothing. I'll see her now,' he told them.

The sight of her lying lifeless on the bed brought tears to his eyes. 'Dear girl,' he whispered to her angelic corpse. He stayed several minutes with the body before returning to the living room.

'Will you call an undertaker?' Ingrid asked.

Jens nodded. 'First, I'll check the baby, to make sure he's all right.'

'We want to keep him,' Ingrid announced. 'We don't want to lose Felix or Axel.'

'Well, you're Felix's next of kin and he wants to stay with you, so I can't see there being any problem. The courts could award you legal guardianship until he's 18. As for the baby, I don't know.'

Ingrid frowned and shook her head. 'I'm sure they won't let us keep either of them when they find out what's happened to Susanne.'

Jens could see the fear in her eyes. 'It's no one's fault. Would you like me to help you with Axel's adoption?'

Ingrid's eyes lit-up. 'Would you, Jens?'

He reassured her. 'Yes, of course I'll help, and with Felix's case.'

'When I'm old enough, I'm going to change my name to Baum. Felix Baum, my grandmother's family name,' Felix told them. 'Waltz has been an unlucky name for me, and I think Susi would want Axel to have the name of Felker. We'll both have a new name and a new start.'

Ingrid was full of angst. 'Klaus and I haven't any children of our own. Now we have two sons and I'm so afraid they'll be taken from us.'

'The new Germany can't possibly object to our family reunification,' Klaus remarked bitterly. 'Ingrid, don't worry, we've lost Susanne but we'll not lose our boys.'

'I'll sign a death certificate, deal with the police, etcetera,' Jens told them. 'You said she jumped from the balcony at the top of the hangar, so there's only one thing I can write for cause of death: suicide.'

'Couldn't you lie for us?' Felix implored. 'Axel will suffer one day when he learns the truth. Couldn't you say it was an accident?'

'Felix!' Klaus exclaimed. 'You can't ask the doctor to lie on a death certificate. He could get struck off!'

Ingrid concurred with her husband. 'Felix, we can't compromise the doctor. What difference does it make what Dr Jens writes on the death certificate? She's gone.'

'Tante! It'll make all the difference in the world to Axel. And maybe it'll affect your chances of adopting him,' declared Felix, turning his attention the doctor. 'Dr Jens, I'm just a kid, so what do I know? But I know about stigma from being a Torgau boy. I don't want Axel to have any labels forced on him and live his life under a cloud or grow up thinking his mother didn't love him or want him. How do you think he'll feel if he learns someday she jumped to her death because she thought it was the only way out?'

Klaus and Ingrid agreed. 'We'll never tell him the truth.'

'The truth's bound to come out someday,' Jens began. 'But by then, our lies won't look like anything compared to some in East Germany. I should've realised that Susanne was depressed- it was probably post-natal depression, and helped her when she was alive'

'Then help her son,' Felix said, crossing his fingers behind his back.

Jens nodded. 'Ok, I'll do it, if it means protecting Axel. Poor Susanne's death certificate will say 'death by misadventure' and the truth remains hidden. Agreed?'

They all nodded in a tacit acceptance that sealed their collaboration.

9. A New Dawn

Christmas was a sober affair. Susanne's funeral a few weeks earlier meant they weren't in the mood for festive merriment. Gisela was disappointed that Klaus would not be in Rugen for Weihnachten, but understood their family reunion would have to wait. Bernd and his family travelled to the Baltic for the festivities with his mother and sister Maria, whilst Klaus, Ingrid and Felix adjusted to life in Motzen without Susanne - yet with an intrinsic part of her: baby Axel.

The cottage was now filled with nappies and with a baby waking everyone up at night and when Felix found it all too much, he would run off into the woods. Alone, his thoughts usually turned to Susi. The lucid, nightmare visions of his last conversation with his sister and her flight through the air ending her short and tragic life at his feet, had not abated. He felt her blood on his hands and no amount of scrubbing would make him clean. He was now free to integrate back into society but he'd become self-conscious about many things, especially his raw hands, and was summoning all his inner strength to curb his obsessions.

In the world outside Motzen, retribution was in the air. In January 1990, thousands of protestors stormed the Stasi Secret Police headquarters in East Berlin and managed to get inside. The files full of secrets and lies, stealthily gathered and assembled, were thrown out of the windows, to the delight of the crowds below. There was snow on the ground and the floating paper gave the effect of a sudden snowstorm. Those who had used their position of power and authority unwisely were challenged and motions were set in place to bring them to justice.

A few months later, in March, elections were held and Lothar de Maziere became the only democratically elected Prime Minister of East Germany. As Premier, he signed the 'two plus four treaty' which ended the rights and responsibilities of the four wartime Allies - France, USA, Great Britain and Russia - in Berlin. For the two Germany's, East and West, it was vital for unification. Things were changing rapidly. East Germans had more money and access to Western consumerism. They threw away their outdated goods and bought into the modern world. No longer could Ossis be defined by their clothes.

In the spring of 1990, Felix started school again. He'd avoided it as long as possible by helping out Klaus in the boatyard. Felix only had to read a manual to give a project a go but at school he felt as if he'd learn more by being at home and experiencing life rather than sitting bored in a classroom. But he soon made friends and settled in, to his surprise discovering he was good at debating in class and could manipulate situations to his own advantage.

Math's master, Herr Janowicz, a tall, spindly man with a dowager's hump, was soon to retire. A teacher of the old school, he adhered to the motto 'Do as I say, not as I do' and his arrogance was well known. In class one morning he cleared his throat and began a long monologue. 'The implication of substituting one Ostmark for one Deutchmark is paramount for parity between the two Germanys. Of course it will affect the economy, the budget and the national debt for years to come,' pronounced Janowicz. 'Changing to a capitalist system will mean the days of full employment under the socialist era are over. Unemployment will grow steadily and so will crime.'

Janowicz stopped. He had noticed Felix yawning and

mistook it for a sign of boredom whereas in truth, Felix had been up early to help Ingrid take a delivery at the café. Determined to put the new boy in his place, he shouted, 'Waltz!'

His name bellowed across the room and Felix jerked upright. 'Yes, Sir.'

'Waltz, perhaps you could offer the class some insight,' Janowicz sneered.

Felix began to feel defensive. As he had grown stronger, a feeling that nobody would abuse, mistreat or belittle him ever again was developing. Perhaps this growing dislike of authority was hormonal and just his age, because at home he also wanted to please less and not always be a 'good' lad. Felix didn't have many problems with Klaus or Ingrid but now he wasn't so afraid; he was ready to debate and disagree with them.

Today, feeling confident, he thought, 'I'll see how far I can push the old fool.'

'If we didn't have 'one for one' monetary values, those of us in East Germany would continue to feel inferior to our fellow Germans in the West,' he said succinctly.

Janowicz was surprised. 'You're suggesting East Germany was inferior because we were Socialists?' he asked.

The class bolted upright, listening intently.

Felix was adamant. 'We were inferior. Look at the way they made us dress. We were controlled under the pretext of Socialism. Those in the higher echelons of the Communist party didn't have the same experience; they lived with privileges and perks. They got to wear decent clothes, drive a nice car and accumulate a bit of money.'

Janowicz was a staunch Socialist who wasn't going to be persuaded to think any different by an adolescent boy who'd grown brave enough to speak out since the fall of the Wall.

'Communism was a fairer system. The State looked after its people, now we'll all fending for ourselves. Greed will be the new motto,' Janowitz stated, sharply.

'I'd rather have a free society with everyone given an equal chance than an Orwellian state where 'some pigs sleep in beds with sheets on' - and eat bananas!'

The class laughed en masse, amused by this allegory and a reference to bananas.

'Quiet!' Janowicz barked. 'Waltz! I see you've read George Orwell's Animal Farm. But you've missed quite a lot of schooling and your knowledge is limited.'

Felix felt this remark was personal. 'Sir, with respect, East Germany was a Russian enclave run by the KGB or the Stasi, if you prefer. Yes, people had jobs, but there were food queues. It was always a case of double standards; those that had the power and those who had none. Not everyone in a position of authority used their power wisely. And some became Spitzel's to feel important, informing on their countrymen. And did they care about the rest of us? They didn't want to give up their power or privileges and if anyone dared complained they were dealt with, severely. And we all know what I'm talking about. We were controlled by fear.'

'You have no fear now,' Janowicz observed.

Felix agreed but was trying not to sound arrogant. 'Once people lost their fear and faith in the system, the Wall came down and Communism was dead and buried.'

Janowicz disagreed. 'The Socialists didn't lose faith. World events took us by surprise.'

Felix was really animated now. 'Yes, and it probably all started at the ship works in Poland with a union led by a brave man - Lech Walesa, who encouraged the people to fight back. He's the real unsung hero, but because Gorbachev was forward thinking, his policies took the praise. I think the Americans were influencing Gorbachev far more than he cared to let on.'

Janowicz's tone was incredulous and sarcastic. 'Wirklich? Please, do go on.'

Felix ignored the derision. He had the class captivated and in the palm of his hand. 'Well, what if the Americans were winning the race in the Star War policies and in an effort to keep up were bankrupting the Soviet Union? Gorbachev offers to introduce glasnost, or perestroika, whatever you call it, as a means of saving face and to avoid facing the costs of civil uprisings in the East. The Russians couldn't afford to keep control of all the countries mortgaged under their wing of communism in Eastern Europe as well as keep up with the Americans. They had to get a grip of their finances and not go bankrupt. Gorbachev may well have been progressive but he also got on the world's stage and was validated as the good guy from Russia, for a change.'

'Ludicrous!' Janowicz bellowed. 'Bankruptcy, my... We, in East Germany, loved being Russia's favourite son. Poland's Lech Walesa was just another trouble making Pole! We never wanted to cut the strings with the Russians. Events just spiralled out of control.'

Felix stifled a laugh. 'Well, I for one am glad the strings to the Kremlin have been cut. Now we are no longer puppets and like Pinocchio, we can be real boys.'

The class laughed and clapped simultaneously.

'Ruhr! Waltz! Look what you've done! You've disrupted the class. How arrogant you are with your ridiculous ideas. Who do you think you are? You're just a Torgau boy!'

Defeated, Janowicz was resorting to insults to try and regain power and control. Felix knew he'd won the debate and the moral argument. No one could hurt him now. At Torgau he'd learned all there was to know about humanity; who has it and who doesn't. He wasn't even angry with Janowicz, viewing him now as just a silly old man. The kids in the class knew the Torgau swipe was below the belt. They wouldn't judge Felix this way, nor constantly remind him of it in an attempt to belittle him. No, this was a game of one-upmanship that the old fool Janowicz had lost because he couldn't win the debate any other way. It was cowardly. Most of his contemporaries in the class had some understanding of this and realised Felix had been through a tough experience and survived. And some of them were now on his side, his allies and his future friends.

One of the boys stood up and shouted. 'Janowicz, leave him alone. No one's listening to you anymore! Don't you know there's a new order? And you're not part of it!'

Janowitz was outraged. 'Carsten Berger! How dare you? Shut up and sit down!'

Carsten refused to sit down or stay silent. The momentum was growing in the classroom.

Felix decided to leave and no one would persuade him otherwise. 'For the record, Herr Janowicz, I was sent to Torgau, but only because my parents died. That was not a crime, it was a tragedy! I'm going; I'll not stay another second in your classroom.'

'Waltz!' Janowicz screamed. 'Show some respect.'

'Respect has to be earned,' Felix told him. 'To be a teacher, you need to be someone the kids look up to, someone they respect. In Loco Parentis.'

The class cheered even if they didn't understand Latin.

Another classmate, Paul Scheer joined in Felix's defence. Shut up, Janowicz!'

'You old Commie!' Carsten yelled and began banging open and closed his desk.

The others in the class joined in with a loud cacophony of desk lids clashing in unison.

Felix smiled at his classmates as he left the room. The noise from the disruption travelled along the corridors as Felix left the school and the chaos in his wake.

Klaus was outraged when Felix told him about Janowicz but Ingrid was proud of her nephew, especially after hearing about the Torgau provocation. They both felt Felix had handled himself and the situation without losing his self-control and respect.

'Who does Janowitz think he is?' Ingrid said, indignantly.

'Herr Janowicz can't teach me anything. I know that sounds arrogant but I've learnt about life in the last few years from human nature and through all the books I read when I was a hidden away. I don't want to go back to school; I want to work for the family, in the boatyard, at the café, or help looking after Axel. Anything, I don't mind,' Felix said, imploringly.

Klaus was fuming. 'I'll complain to the education board, and get Janowicz fired. I'll bet he was a Stasi Spitzel. Then you can go back to school, with your head held high.'

'Onkel. You'll need extra workers if you and Bernd get the golf course.'

'But your education is important!'

Ingrid was concerned. 'Felix, please. Don't jeopardise all we've built up here. It's illegal not to attend school and I don't want the authorities turning up here, not with the ongoing adoption process with you and Axel.'

Felix understood immediately the ramifications of keeping a stubborn line of resistance.

'Ok, I'm 16 next year and legally allowed to work - I'll go to school till then.

Herr Janowicz didn't get away with his behaviour. Klaus vehemently complained to the school, who were embarrassed and apologetic and Janowicz was sidelined and retired slightly early. However, the staff were wary about Felix returning to school in case of further disruption but he settled down and completed the rest of the term without further disruption.

In summer of 1990, the Football World Cup in Italy captivated the Germans' imagination in their year of reunification like no other tournament ever had. All over Berlin, satellite dishes adorned the flats in anticipation that the West German footballers would do well in the tournament, but around Motzen, satellite dishes were uncommon. Bernd brought a satellite dish on his last visit, installing it on the roof of Das Kino in time for the opening ceremony, and it became a celebrated village affair.

The locals and visiting tourists were charged a small

entrance fee, just as they were when films were shown on the large screen at the weekends, to watch the matches live from Italy. Klaus and Bernd shared the profits and this enterprise made a good profit for the month of the tournament. Here, the seeds were being sown for their future working partnership, which would bring the hardworking brothers and their families a rich and rewarding harvest.

Felix worked in the café, helping Ingrid serve drinks and snacks during the matches at half-time when the surge of customers was at its' highest. Axel, now nine months old, sat in his playpen at the back of the café. Ingrid took him everywhere with her. He was a happy and contented baby and with his blond quiff of hair, he enchanted all who set eyes upon him.

The mood in the country was euphoric and football fans as well as abstainers were caught up in the buoyant, party mood. West Germany reached the semi-final, played in the heat of an Italian summer in the city of Turin. It was a tense, nail-biting and gripping spectacle against an old adversary; England, which after playing extra-time, the score was 1-1. The outcome was decided on penalties. The Germans scored four out of their five penalties whilst the English missed two out of their five. Final score, West Germany 4, England 3. Germany was in the final. Das Kino erupted with a giant roar.

'JA!'

Klaus turned to Bernd and hugged him. 'We won!' And when he'd calmed down a little added, 'We deserved to win. We were cheated by the England in the World Cup final in 1966. That was never a goal- the ball didn't cross the line!

Bernd was used to his brother's weird concepts. 'Who cares? We're in the final!'

Four days later, on 8th July, the final of the World Cup in Rome, West Germany beat Argentina. Das Kino was again packed to the rafters and the ecstatic crowd in the hangar, was audible at the far side of the lake. Everyone had lost any apparent reserve, embracing the moment and one another.

Felix hugged his family and laughter and tears filled the air, a sense of national pride welling in most Germans, both East and West. This camaraderie and unity wasn't just about West Germany winning the World Cup. It was about the German people becoming one nation, no longer divided by political ideology or enforced walled borders.

Directly after the match, the Three Tenors, Luciano Pavarotti, Placido Domingo and Jose Carreras, gave a memorable concert live in Rome. Many of the crowds at Das Kino dispersed but some remained to have picnics and barbeques on the beach, enjoying an open air concert from the open doors of the hangar. At the lake, the mood was euphoric and Felix drank a few beers with his friends Carsten and Paul while Klaus and Ingrid turned a blind eye. It was the first time Felix got drunk and he didn't need anyone to remind him about his father's alcohol addictions because he would forever be conscious of not falling into the same trap.

On 3rd October the German nation was reunited. The reunification party went on for days. It was like a simultaneous World Cup fever and New Year all over again with fireworks on top of the symbol of Berlin, the Brandenburg Gate, bringing the people of this once divided city and nation officially together again.

In Motzen, Bernd and his family escaped from the volumes of people that had descended upon Berlin and the relatives from Rugen made a surprise appearance. For the first time since he was very young, Felix met his oma Gisela, and his tante Maria- who was a younger version of Gisela. She was a stout and friendly woman in her early 30s, married to Olaf, a robust farmer. With them was their 12-year-old son, Lutz.

Gisela, although in her 60s, was used to young teenage boys as she'd lived with Lutz since he was a toddler. She had a relaxed manner with Felix that made his initial awkwardness subside and with tante Maria and onkel Olaf cracking jokes with Lutz, being in their jovial company felt easy to Felix.

The family gathered outside around an open fire, the smell of cooked meat from their barbeque mixing with the smoky wood. Knowing the practice was illegal they daringly lit some fireworks and afterwards stayed huddled around the crackling fire, watching the smoke parade upwards into the night sky.

Klaus looked at Ingrid holding Axel in her arms, and pulled Felix towards him, putting his arm around his nephew.

'Today is a very special day,' Klaus began. 'It's the day of Einheit, German unity. And today of all days, Ingrid and I received confirmation that we are Felix's legal guardians And Axel's adoption has been approved.'

Felix whispered in his nephew's ear. 'Axel, we belong to Klaus and Ingrid now.'

Everyone cheered and clapped and there wasn't a dry eye witnessing Klaus, Ingrid, baby Axel and Felix all huddled together in an embrace. The sad memories of Susanne's death the previous year were fading and it seemed the beginning of a new dawn. Felix felt he was starting to live up to the Latin meaning of his name, Felice: the fortunate one.

10. Encounters

There was an area about five kilometres from Motzen that was once a virtual no-man's land, interspersed with landmines that were controlled and used by the Russian army for target practice and military training. The ground was apparently polluted by ammunition and nearby there had been a waste depot and landfill site. The West Germans had paid the East Germans to deposit their waste and though it was fenced off, those in the East had risked searching through the waste for 'Western' dregs to re-use. After German reunification, environmentalists acted quickly to change these blots on the landscape, adding nutritious new soil to both areas, and within a year, verdant fields were the result. However, cases for remuneration and claims for compensation from those with ill health linked to the previously contaminated area were growing in vast numbers.

Those that had fled to the West before the Wall and its borders that divided Germany now claimed their share of the properties and any land they'd left behind. Disgruntled family members who had remained in the East looking after the family's inheritance and ageing relatives for years, with limited or no access to their family on the 'other side'.

When East Germany ceased to exist in 1990, families were reunited, only to be torn asunder once again when a claim for ownership under the inheritance laws was registered. When the Wall was up, those in the West had waited up to 10 years for the right to visit their families in East Germany. Now, the split was irreconcilable, engendered by a wall of greed and misunderstanding.

However, whilst some families throughout the early 1990s bickered, claimed and counter-claimed, Bernd and Klaus used their energies to purchase the Russian's no-man's land at a greatly reduced price. As owners of such a contentious site it was vitally important to ensure that impregnable terms and conditions were written into the contract so they would not be liable for any future claims made against them. Bernd didn't give up politics and was elected Burgermeister - Mayor - of nearby Zossen. The family rented out their flat in Berlin and moved to a large mansion provided in the town. Ute was in her element as the Mayor's wife in charge of the functions for the self-appointed dignitaries in town and their daughters settled well in a new, local school.

The golf club was built the following spring, a grand affair complete with an 18 and 9 hole courses, a licensed clubhouse, a driving range, putting green, a club shop selling the latest equipment, and a small restaurant. It was named 'The Motzen Mayor Golf Club' and was opened by the golfer Bernhard Langer. Klaus had secured a government grant to employ a multitude of staff and by the summer of 1992, the golf club was providing a comfortable income for the Felker brothers and their families.

At the lake, the boatyard continued to be Klaus's main source of work. Using some of the profits from the golf club, they hired instructors ready for the tourist season and opened a water activity centre offering waterskiing, scuba diving and hiring out boats. They also paid for lifeguards for the swimming area on the small, sandy beach near the boathouse.

Ingrid had hired help in the café to make sure she had ample time every day for Axel, now a beautiful and energetic toddler of nearly three who was running about all over the place. She had grown into the role of motherhood and didn't want to miss out on his development and precious moments. Klaus too, enjoyed fatherhood but his busy and industrious life meant he only had half the weekends and holidays free. He always tried to be present when Axel awoke, at mealtimes and for the last few hours before the boy went to sleep. With constant juggling they made time for Felix as well as each other, going cycling on mountain bike rides, hiking around the lake, with or without their boys. Klaus had also joined a gun club with Bernd, shooting at targets with small, rapid-fire pistols.

Felix, now a muscular, handsome lad of 17, was happy to work in the boathouse with Klaus and help run the waterside activities. He also helped out at the golf club, collecting and refilling the balls in the machines on the driving range or assisting the ground staff around the golf courses. He was the proud owner of a 50cc, light blue Schwalbe - 'The Swallow' - one of the most popular mopeds from the East German era with three speeds and a manual clutch. This was Klaus and Ingrid's present for his birthday in January. Ingrid didn't want Felix driving a more powerful and faster motorbike, and the Schwalbe was her compromise, plus paying for his driving lessons in Klaus's old car, a VW estate.

The girls in the village had begun to notice Felix. Tall, athletic, with shoulder length, fair hair which he usually let blow in the wind except at work, where he tied it in a ponytail; he had turned into quite an Adonis. He remained wary of intimacy, though. Happy to make friends with the opposite sex and hang out with the village girls or his girl-mad pals Carsten and Paul, he was slightly remote around them, which only added to his appeal.

A deep thinker, Felix believed life was about a series of moments. He'd managed to survive in Torgau by being in the moment, dealing with whatever life threw at him, good and bad. He'd learned to take whatever pleasure he could in small things, such as being with the family, enjoying nature, pushing his body to its physical limits of whatever he was doing at the time. He tried not to think too far forward or stay too much in the past. One of his greatest pleasures, much to everyone's surprise, was looking after Axel. He liked nothing more than playing on the beach with him, taking a bucket and spade to build snowmen in the winter months or sandcastles in the summer, and trying to teach him how to kick a ball or swim. By nurturing his nephew he felt close to Susi, who was often in his thoughts. Axel was surrounded by love, and he adored his onkel Felix.

The summer Olympics of 1992 were held in Spain, and the opening ceremony was in the last week of July. In Motzen, it was a bit cooler than the heat the athletes were enduring in Barcelona. Ingrid arranged for the café and the golf club to hold weekend Spanish nights of tapas, paellas and flamenco dancing for the duration of the Games. The screen in Das Kino beamed the various sporting events live throughout the day and they'd also installed a satellite dish at the golf club to cover sporting events for the patrons to watch in the bar lounge.

During the Olympics, Klaus and Ingrid invited Dr Jens and his family to the lake.

'Hola!' said the doctor, with Latin gusto, on arrival.

'Jens was happy to come to a Spanish night to practice his language skills,' Angele, his wife told them. 'Please humour him.'

Angele was an attractive, stylish lady in her early 40s and Jens was a decade older, but there was warmth and humour between them that was natural and the age gap didn't show or matter. Jens clearly adored his younger wife and children: Martha was a pretty, 17-year-old with long auburn hair, who took after her graceful and poised mother, and her brother Friedrich was a lively 13-year-old.

The last time Felix had set eyes on Martha was in Berlin, a few days after the Wall came down. When he saw her again, he had the same feeling of butterflies in his stomach.

'Can we go out on a boat?' asked Friedrich.

'When you've eaten,' his mother told him.

'I'll take you later, if you like,' Felix offered, unable to take his eyes off Martha.

'Thank you, Felix,' Jens said. 'Haven't seen you since I played golf with you and Klaus, back in the spring. How are you?'

Unusually tongue-tied, Felix muttered, 'Oh, I'm keeping busy.'

Ingrid noticed Felix's discomfort. 'Yes, we keep you busy, working hard for the family business, here at the lake and up at the golf club, she told the visitors, adding 'He even helps me with Axel.'

'Saint Felix,' quipped Klaus, poking his nephew playfully in the ribs.

Felix felt embarrassed. 'Onkel!'

'What do you think about the latest hand-sized mobile phones? Jens asked Felix, thinking the subject would take the heat off him.

They're handy!'

Jens smiled. 'You have to be German to get this joke. I think mobile phones will catch on but personally, I'll wait till the price comes down.'

'Where's Axel?' Angele asked.

'As it's Spanish night, my son's having a siesta,' Ingrid informed them. 'Tomorrow I'll call it a nickerchen again.'

Jens loved playing with words or language. 'I believe the English call it a nap.'

'We usually speak English with the tourists,' Felix said, turning to address Martha. 'I hear you don't have to learn Russian in school anymore, now the second language is English.

'That's right… and you don't have to go to school, lucky you!' Martha ventured.

So began their first, tentative conversation.

Felix kept his word, taking Martha and Friedrich in a small motorboat out onto the lake. Friedrich draped his hand in the water as they sped around whilst Martha sat on the bow, her hair blowing behind her, as Felix steered the boat and watched her surreptitiously out of the corner of his eye.

Before she went home, Felix got a chance to talk to

Martha alone. Would Jens approve if he asked to see his daughter again? He wondered what Martha knew about him and if her father had told her about his background. Rejection was a risk worth taking because he wanted to see her again, to get to know her and didn't want to wait until another get-together was arranged between the families, which could take six months or more.

'How long will it take you to get back to Kopenick?'

Martha raised an eyebrow. 'Less than an hour. Why?'

Felix began tentatively. 'Oh, well, I was wondering, there's a bus in Motzen, it goes to Berlin and stops in Kopenick.'

'Really?' Martha said, smiling inwardly.

'Well, you're welcome here any time.'

'Or maybe, Felix, you could come to Kopenick, to see us?' Martha suggested, adding 'I'd like a ride on the back of your Schwalbe.'

'It's a deal.'

For the following two months, Felix and Martha spent a lot of time to-ing and fro-ing between Motzen and Kopenick. The long summer days while Felix worked were more enjoyable when Martha visited- she was always ready to lend a hand and even babysit Axel until his shift had ended. After eating with the family they'd take a relaxing walk, staying outside on starry nights to share moonlit kisses. By this time, Felix had moved into Gertrude's house, and Martha would stay overnight in the cottage under Klaus and Ingrid's watchful eyes. They were so young that they were more than happy just to hold hands, hug and kiss. It was an innocent kind of love and their sceptical guardians decided not to interfere. After all, who could stop two young, headstrong people falling in love?

As summer drew to a close, the youngsters sat nestled in each other's arms under a blanket on the end of the jetty with their feet dangling in the water, listening to a chorus of night owls over the lake. The night sky seemed endless and full of promise.

Martha sighed. 'School starts next week.'

Felix joked, 'Never mind.'

Martha was curious. 'You don't regret leaving school at 16?'

'Not at all, I enjoy my work,' Felix told her.

'I don't want to think about work just yet. In two years I'll finish school and before I go to university, I'm going to take a year off and travel the world.'

Felix felt happy for her but equally, was afraid to lose her. 'What, on your own?'

Martha squeezed his hand. 'Are you fishing for a compliment?'

Felix was thinking she knew him well and was comfortable with this. He believed he could trust her and tell her most things about what he thought and felt, except the darkest secrets from his time at Torgau. He tried to block out those experiences and for the most part, he was successful. The love he had for Martha made him feel vulnerable and insecure but he tried to deal with his fear.

'Naturlich! I'm a fisherman, aren't I?'

Martha realised he needed reassuring. 'I'd like to go travelling with you.'

Felix's anxiety was assuaged. 'What, you'd travel the world with someone like me, even though I was sent to Torgau?'

'I know all about what happened to you. Papa told me.'

'Everything?'

Martha nodded, looking sad. 'You were abused by those sick bastards and no one helped you. Papa did, but by then the damage was done.'

Quickly, Felix let go of his embarrassment and was adamant. 'I don't blame your father, he was kind to me and my sister. But If I ever see any of those wardens again, I don't know what I'd be capable of.'

'Who would blame you? Felix, remember, it wasn't your fault.'

'I know.'

'Do you really know it, deep inside? Say it. It wasn't your fault.'

He faltered with his words. 'It wasn't my fault.'

'Again,' she insisted.

'It wasn't my fault.'

She squeezed him tight. 'Really believe it.'

'It wasn't my fault.'

And with this Felix broke down.

Martha held his shaking body until his tears stopped falling and he could speak.

'And it doesn't make any difference to you, knowing I was an abused, Torgau boy?'

'Not one bit.'

'I feel I could tell you anything.'

'You can, you must. Let it out- don't keep it all inside, festering and sabotaging your potential happiness.'

'I'll try not to. Martha... I love you.'

'Darling Felix... I love you, too.'

Kissing, they sealed their declaration of love.

In Gertrude's house that night, Felix and Martha became lovers. Their lovemaking was gentle, caressing and exploring each other's bodies, discovering the intimate details and preferences that only lovers can share. It wasn't the first time for either of them, but it was a life-changing moment for them both, as they slept in each other's arms.

Returning to the cottage to sleep simply for the sake of appeasing Klaus, Ingrid and her own parents felt unacceptable to Martha. They returned to the cottage for breakfast, hand in hand, and it was instantly obvious to a concerned Klaus and Ingrid what had occurred the night before. Axel, however, was delighted to see them.

'Fe-wix,' Axel squealed and ran into his onkel's arms.

'Hello, little man,' Felix cooed, covering the boy with kisses.

'Can we play?' asked Axel.

'Later, I promise,' Felix told his nephew.

Axel pouted his lip and wandered off to play with his toys in a corner of the room.

Ingrid shook her head. 'What will Jens and Angele say? They'll feel we've let them down, not looking after their daughter.'

Felix announced proudly, 'We're in love.'

'Ingrid, I'll deal with my parents, so don't worry,' Martha said confidently.

'Just because you kept our sleeping arrangements apart doesn't mean you could have stopped anything happening,' Felix stated.

'That's true, Klaus observed. 'I just hope it doesn't interfere with Martha's schooling.'

Martha reassured them. 'It won't. And before you ask, I'm on the Pill.'

Martha's parents weren't surprised at her news. They'd seen it coming and hoped she wouldn't get too hurt if it all went wrong, as was so often the case in teenage love affairs. Martha's first boyfriend had broken her heart last year when she was a much less self-assured girl of 16, and it took her a while to feel better, so if she did get hurt, they'd be there to pick up the pieces again. Jens and Angele genuinely liked Felix and felt he was a good lad at heart, but given his background they worried whether he could cope with the demands of a relationship at his young age - or with their daughter, for that matter. Only time would tell.

Summer and romantic trysts for Felix came to an abrupt end at the golf club. A few months after the German Masters golf tournament was played in Stuttgart, the golf clubs in the Berlin area were touting for the honour to hold next year's tournament. At the Motzen Mayor Golf club, their annual open tournament began and was one of their biggest events of the year. Various personalities in golf turned up, including the winner of the German Masters, 1992, England's Barry Lane.

The club hired extra staff for security purposes, not only

to protect the professional golf players but to keep the crowds off the greens and fairways, safely behind ropes. Bernd had arranged for the event to be televised, striking a lucrative deal with a satellite television company and opening the tournament in his official capacity of Mayor. Felix was keen not to be seen in front of the omnipresent television cameras. He was happier behind the scenes, working, repairing the divots with the ground staff.

But on the opening day of the tournament, the world he'd built for himself that had seemed safe and full of promise was irrevocably torn asunder. Felix recognised one of the hired security stewards at the staff briefing. It was Horst Gwisdek, one of the Musketeers at Torgau.

11. Horst

Horst Gwisdek was the eldest of three boys, brought up by an authoritarian mother in a Berlin suburb in East Germany. After she had caught Horst's father in bed with a 14-year-old boy she had divorced him, denying him any future access to his sons in exchange for her silence and not informing the authorities.

Frau Gwisdek worked all the hours under the sun to support her three children. Horst was the eldest and a surrogate father at the age of nine, helping look after the younger children. His overworked mother often came home tired and irritable, regularly taking her frustration out on her eldest son, belittling his efforts and beating him indiscriminately for a perceived or trivial mistake. The young Horst saw brief glimpses of her love but it made for a fractious relationship when he became an adult. By then all he felt for her was bitterness, whereas she had mellowed, but he couldn't forgive her. A strong man now, he towered over his mother and harbouring deep resentment, took a final, satisfactory retribution, hitting her so hard that he fractured her cheekbone causing her eyeball to

come out of its socket. Smiling smugly, he then left the house, never to see his mother or his brothers again.

The Russian Army was serving in Afghanistan in the 1980s and this appealed to Horst. Here, with the protective cloak of a uniform to hide his actions, he found he enjoyed torturing imprisoned men, especially the teenage militants who were captured and alongside a few of his fellow soldiers, crossed sexual boundaries. After five years, Horst left the army and ended up as head of security at Torgau's youth prison. Gradually, he made friends with the other Musketeers whom he soon discovered shared his proclivities for sexually abusing young boys. They formed a tight bond and if anyone working at Torgau outside their paedophile unit dared to oppose them, Horst used his considerable and formidable strength to deliver his message: 'cross me if you dare'.

When Torgau was closed down, the authorities began dealing with complaints from the survivors of abuse. As yet, none of the children Horst had abused spoke out against him or his fellow Musketeers and he remained at large in the community to continue his life as a paedophile. He kept in regular touch with a paedophile ring of comrades, especially the two Musketeers, but lived a solitary life in Leipzig in rented accommodation that he changed frequently, never developing personal relationships with other adults of either sex. He preferred a life of hiring boy prostitutes to share with the Musketeers during their opportune moments when they went out 'hunting' in Horst's motor home. On these trips they would kidnap a young, unsuspecting kid, often a young male aged between 12 and 15, off the streets of some distant city. After days and nights of abuse too vile to document, they would dump the abused child, barely alive, onto the streets and disappear into the night.

Horst was now a burly man in his 40s, working as a freelance security guard. He was happiest mingling with celebrities at prestigious events and jumped at the chance to work at the Motzen Mayor golf club tournament in September 1992.

After the first day's play, when all the crowds had dispersed, Horst was enjoying a drink in the clubhouse lounge, filled with the players, their wives and children. A blond Adonis caught his eye. It was Felix, dressed in staff overalls, chatting to the Mayor. He began thinking this lad was a little bit older than his usual hors d'oeuvres of teenage boys but gave him a second look and his curiosity grew.

Horst went to the bar. 'Who's that young, lad with the Mayor?'

The barman, Carsten Berger, looked across the crowded lounge. 'Oh, that's Felix.'

'He's very matey with the Mayor. Doesn't the Mayor own this club?

'Yeah, Mayor Felker and his brother Klaus. Felix is their nephew.'

Horst remarked. 'Nice to keep all that money in the family, the brothers have quite a lucrative business here. Lucky lad, that Felix Felker.'

'Felix's name is Waltz,' contradicted Carsten.

Horst's suspicions were confirmed. So, Felix had somehow escaped from Torgau and wasn't dead as they had all been told. How had they allowed him to slip past them? And Felix was now in a fortuitous position. How the fates of fortunes change, thought Horst, knowing there was no alternative but to take action.

It was twilight when Felix emerged from the party that was still underway in the clubhouse. Horst watched him unlock his Schwalbe and flashed his car headlights. Intrigued and sensing no danger, Felix crossed the car park and as he neared, Horst emerged from the car to stand in front of him.

Felix felt his pulse race. He'd almost thrown up when he saw Horst earlier but the hectic day's schedule had taken his mind off his anxiety. What was he to do now he'd been recognised? Felix knew the next few hours would be critical and mustered all his strength to show his Torgau abuser he was unafraid and no longer intimidated.

The two men faced one another with icy stares.

'Felix Waltz, we meet again. I thought you were last spotted drowning in the River Elbe,' Horst said, breaking the silence.

'I jumped a sinking ship.'

Horst smiled smugly. 'You got lucky and rode with the current, ending up here.'

Felix stared. 'I deserved my luck.'

Horst scratched his chin. 'I think we should talk.'

'I agree, but not here.'

'Well, you're on home territory young man; the balls are in your court.'

Felix had a plan. 'I know a place where we won't be disturbed, about half an hour from here. Do you know Muggelsee?'

Horst nodded. 'Sounds good to me.'

'Follow me and I'll park by the lake.'

Horst followed Felix to the banks of Muggelsee, avoiding the main jetty in Kopenick. Here, a large ferry on the River Spree linked residents and commuters directly to Berlin. There were four other jetties on the water, at the north, south, east and western sections of the lake where smaller ferries passed, and visitors and residents could hop on and off around the lake. Felix knew his way around this area now from visiting Martha and like the locals he also knew the murky depths of the water.

It was dark and quietly eerie on the lake, which was devoid of people when Felix parked his Schwalbe and joined Horst in his car at the south jetty. The car headlights stayed on lighting up the water. It felt strange to be in close proximity to someone whom he despised and was repulsed by, smelling Horst's still familiar pungent after shave which he had always scrubbed away ferociously once the Musketeer had finished with him. It made Felix feel nauseous to breathe the same air as Horst.

'Well, so you're the Mayor's nephew, no less.'

'I can see you're impressed.' Felix's tone was sarcastic. 'Don't be expecting an invite to the Burgermeister's for dinner.'

'Think you're better than me now, do you?'

'I'm from a good family. I should never have ended up at Torgau.'

'So I see. The Stasi made mistakes too,' Horst mused.

'And you?' Felix challenged him. #Are you from a good family?'

Horst's answer was composed. 'Families can lift you up or drag you down. I have no family, no dependents, I'm a loner and I like it that way. You've grown up since we last met, how long has it been? Two or three years, I think.'

Felix spat, stony-faced. 'How could I forget your ugly face?'

'Oh, Felix, don't be so cruel to a former lover.'

Shaking his head, Felix took umbrage. 'That's not what we were!'

They both felt their hackles rise. It was going to be a strategic game of chess with the outcome unknown and undecided.

'And your sister?' Horst enquired.

'She died,' Felix announced, not showing any emotion.

It was a form of weakness to show empathy, Horst reminded himself. 'Did she die in childbirth?' he enquired, with a certain vitriolic relish.

'Something like that,' Felix replied, the rage inside him beginning to swell.

'Well, you came back from the dead. So, what are we going to do now?'

'Let the police decide,' Felix declared.

Horst wasn't expecting this. 'No way! There'll be no Nuremberg trial for me. I'm not going to turn myself over to the police or face a life on the run.'

Felix was adamant. 'You're a paedophile. Talk yourself out of that.'

'It was only sex. We both enjoyed it.'

Felix wanted to hit him but held himself back. 'You're a sick bastard. You abused my sister and me and I'm not going to let you get away with it.'

Horst tried to remain calm but was getting hot, so he wound down the car window. He couldn't lose this battle- he wasn't going to be outwitted by this Torgau kid.

'I can see you're not afraid anymore.'

'No!' spat Felix, emphatically. 'Maybe it's you who's afraid?'

Horst scratched his chin. 'If you tell the police and it goes to trial, you do realise you'll be in the dock too, giving evidence. You'll have to say in front of everyone what I made you do, how you and your sister were shared by the Musketeers.'

'If it means stopping you abusing other kids, I'd do it.'

'Oh, Felix, don't be naïve,' Horst smirked. He opened the glove compartment and pulled out a red diary and waved it about. 'In here is a list of all my colleagues at Torgau and lots of other men with my, let's say, proclivities. The list is endless... It would only take one call from me and they'd very quickly be up your arse again... literally.'

Felix was so angry he was at bursting point. 'All for one and one for all. Wasn't that your sick motto?'

'Felix, you're a little too old for my liking but if you involve the police, your nephew - Axel, isn't it? I saw him at the golf club, such a sweet little boy - will be kidnapped by one of my pals in my little red book. And that's a promise.'

Their game of psychological chess had reached its climax. The next move for either side was checkmate.

Felix reached in his coat pocket and pulled out a gun. Horst was visibly taken aback.

'See this? It's a rapid fire pistol, similar to the one used by Ralf Schumann when he won the Olympic gold medal for Germany in Barcelona last month. When I recognised you at the club today, I had the feeling our paths would cross and went home for the gun.'

For the first time, Horst felt fear. 'Now, don't be silly, we both know you're not going to use it.'

'You don't know me, or what I'm capable of. You're right about the trial, though. I'd find it hard, telling my family and the court how you fucked with me, and I'll never forgive you for taking my sister from me.'

Horst lunged at Felix, trying to grab hold of the gun.

Taken by surprise, they struggled, hitting, punching, pulling and tugging as their veins pumped with adrenalin before Felix took control and hit Horst on the head with it, time after time, stunning him and giving Felix a few seconds to run to his Schwalbe. There was no one in sight and in his rucksack he collected his boat knife and some anchor rope and returned to the car.

Binding Horst's hands to the steering wheel, he then tied the Musketeers' legs together.

Horst stirred from his daze. 'Untie me, you bastard!'

'Fic dich!' Felix snarled.

Horst tried to wriggle free. 'Stupid Torgau boy. I'll fucking kill you!' he screamed.

Laughing a deranged kind of cackle; something powerful was driving Felix on. 'Don't you like being the underdog to the Torgau boy?'

He was in control now, it was his choice whether to call the police or take retribution of his own. He debated the pros and cons. Allowing justice to take its course would all be so complicated and the outcome wasn't a foregone conclusion - Horst would manipulate and lie through his teeth. The decision was made for him when he saw Horst's red diary on the passenger seat. There was only one thing he had to do; protect Axel.

'You'll regret this, Waltz.'

'Shut up!' Felix bellowed in Horst's face.

Horst struggled to free himself and began screaming. 'Help! Someone help me!'

'Shall I burn your ears? When I look at my ears in the mirror I'm reminded of you!' He spat, grabbing Horst's ears and making a few wild swipes, cutting indiscriminately with his boat knife.

Horst's lobes split at the bottom and blood spurted out as he screamed.

Felix smirked. 'Now we'll both have scarred ears. One for all and all for one!'

'Help! Someone help me!' Horst yelled.

'No one can hear you. You'll be a weggesperrt, forgotten... No one will care or miss a fucking paedophile!'

His beloved Susi flashed into his mind. He remembered what she'd said just before she jumped to her death, how she'd spoken about the shame of the identity of Axel's father and how it had destroyed her. Felix now had an opportunity to find out who the father was and in a moment of lucidity, hacked off a hefty chunk of Horst's short hair, wrapping the cuttings in a tissue and putting it in his rucksack, knowing DNA testing would confirm parentage.

'Let me go!' Horst pleaded.

Felix looked at the pathetic, bloodstained Musketeer and decided to give him one last chance to speak. 'Tell me you're sorry that you ruined my sister's life - and mine.'

'I'm sorry,' Horst said, quickly and unconvincingly.

'Liar!' Felix screamed and grabbing Horst's hair, he rammed his bloody head repeatedly against the steering wheel until he lost unconsciousness.

There was no turning back now. Felix sat on the grass next to the car to catch his breath. Noises from the surrounding woodlands amplified all around him and he imagined something was lurking in the shadows but it was only the natural sounds of the night carried by the breeze. He was alone and no one could hear or see him, and the deed was only half-done. He picked up Horst's diary, and searched Horst's floppy body for personal belongings, finding a mobile phone and a wallet. He put all these items into his rucksack by the Schwalbe.

Stripping to his boxer shorts, Felix started Horst's car and drove it slowly onto the jetty. He untied Horst's hands from the steering wheel and shoved his heavy, blood-soaked frame over to the passenger side, retying Horst's hands to the passenger door. Then he got in at the driver's side, accidentally switching on the car radio. The aria 'Toreador' from the Bizet's opera 'Carmen' blared out into the dark night.

'Toreador, en garde! Toreador, Toreador!'

Felix understood the paradox of this operatic song - a bullfighter in the ring with an enraged, black-eyed beast charging the matador - and himself, confronting a Musketeer. He turned up the volume, opened the car window on the driver's side and both window in the back to ensure the water would flood in but that he could escape. He revved the engine and drove as fast as he could along the long jetty until the car took flight, projecting into the air and out over the lake before landing flat on the water.

With difficulty, Felix scrambled out onto the roof of the car where he stood, feeling like a mountaineer reaching the summit after a long, arduous climb. The ascent had been breathtaking and now he could admire the view.

'Et songe bien, oui, songe bien en combattent, qu'un oeil noir te regarde…'

Feeling vindicated and invincible, Felix began a jumping jig of a dance on the rooftop, hoping the pressure of his bouncing weight would make the car sink quicker.

The music resonated in the night air.

'Toreador…'

The water was rising and flooding through the car windows. Felix felt strangely elated and began to sing the words of the song.

'Toreador, l'amour, t'attend! Toreador, Toreador, l'amour t'attend!'

The last thing Horst heard at his dying breath, hoped Felix, was that the boy from Torgau was singing and dancing, having got the better of him.

The music suddenly muted and the headlights dimmed. The

car was rolling in a lopsided fashion and sinking fast as the water had reached the roof. Felix dived away from the drag and pull of the car as it went under, swimming back to the safety of the jetty. Quickly, he dressed himself and fetched a torch from his rucksack, shining it on the water, anxious to see that Horst hadn't miraculously escaped. Ten minutes later, Felix felt satisfied the evil Musketeer had sunk without a trace.

12. The days that followed

Felix woke up the next morning alone in Gertrude's house. He hadn't slept well, tormented by the images of what had happened last night at Muggelsee. He was now a murderer. Unplanned, but that was the outcome and the sum total of all his actions the previous night. How was a murderer supposed to feel?

Horst had made him feel dirty again and his hands were sore from constantly washing them during the night. And what did he think about himself? Was he proud of the choice he had made to kill Horst? In addition to his Torgau secrets, was this going to be the hardest secret to keep? Could anyone understand if he shared this secret with them? Would he lose Klaus and Ingrid's love, and now, more importantly, Martha's love?

Felix knew he had to stay silent and live a lie, keeping his secrets, as he always did, locked in the dark recesses of his mind. He believed he had left no clues at the scene of the crime and surreptitiously returned to the cottage when nobody was around to return the gun, wiped clean of his fingerprints. Horst's mobile and wallet he secreted safely in his old hideaway in Das Kino. The hair clippings he placed in an envelope and wrote the letters 'HG' on it. A thought crossed his mind: what if Horst had telephoned one of his friends in the red diary and told them Felix Waltz was alive and where to find him? Felix switched on the mobile phone and looked at the last calls and texts Horst had made. No calls or text messages had been sent for two days - before the golf tournament had even begun. Felix was in the clear.

Looking through Horst's diary, some of the names inside seemed familiar and it began to dawn on Felix that he couldn't just get rid of one of the Musketeers. He needed the DNA from all three, to find out which one was Axel's father, and he couldn't take it from them if they were alive. No, all three Musketeers had to die.

But was taking the law into your own hands ever justified? The saying 'Two wrongs don't make a right' echoed in Felix's brain, yet he was a murderer and to convince himself he was a vigilante acting on his nephew's behalf was a paradox. Axel was not free of danger if the Musketeers stayed alive and Felix couldn't relax knowing that they or their paedophile associates might turn up unannounced in the future to harm Ingrid's precious little boy.

There was no turning back. Felix went over and over it in his head, wanting to be sure he was making such monumental decisions for the right reasons. There were three that he rationalised: to safeguard Axel, first and foremost, for his own revenge, and to uncover the truth about Axel's true parentage. To label his motives for murder seemed a bizarre ritual, but in Felix's complex mind it was clear and succinct.

Revenge was perfectly understandable given the circumstances at Torgau: an eye for an eye. He recalled the surprisingly powerful adrenaline rush and the thrill it had given him to be in control of Horst and ultimately, his destiny. Perhaps this made him no better than the depraved monsters he was seeking to punish? And yet who else would punish them for their heinous crimes if he himself didn't? He hadn't gone looking for trouble, trouble had found him. Felix had taken a gun to defend himself if necessary and certainly without a premeditated intention of using it. The gun was simply a bargaining tool.

But why hadn't he fired the gun? It was clear he'd wanted

Horst dead. One single bullet to the head would have done the deed without the added fuss and danger he put himself in. It would have been over too quickly and that wouldn't have caused the Musketeer enough suffering, he decided. He'd wanted Horst to feel weak, helpless and afraid; to feel like 'little Felix' and 'little Susi' had felt. The Musketeer had showed no sense of shame or remorse and instead had taunted Felix with threats, waving his red diary in front of him. By doing this, Horst had decided his own fate.

Felix convinced himself that he could live with the truth that he was as capable of murder as any man, given the circumstances and opportunity. There would be a limit to how many paedophiles needed to die to ensure Axel's future safety. His four targets were the Musketeers and their go-between. As for the rest of the paedophiles in the red diary, he had to be clever and plot a plausible subterfuge, informing the police by surreptitious means, thereby diverting attention away from himself. It needed a clear head to think and manage this; he would do his best not to get caught and hope no one ever found out.

At the golf club, the players arrived early to practice on the second day of the tournament whilst television crews took their positions alongside the stewards, and the public were let in. Felix arrived a little bleary-eyed, greeted by Bernd in the men's locker room.

You left the party early, so why do you look so tired? Bernd joked.

'Herr Burgermeister, it's far too early for your pathetic jokes! Felix snapped.

Bernd wasn't going to take such rudeness. 'Don't you dare talk to me like that!'

Felix realised he'd stepped out of line and made a mistake. His tone was sincere. 'Onkel, I'm sorry.'

Noticing the scratches and bruises on Felix's face, Bernd said sternly: 'Don't take your bad moods out on other people,' and looking at Felix's swollen face, he softened his tone. 'What's happened? Have you been in a fight?'

'No.' Felix said the first thing that came into his head. 'I fell off my Schwalbe.'

Bernd was concerned. 'Are you all right?'

'Just cross with myself. Sorry.'

'Best not tell Ingrid, she hates motorbikes and she worries about you. Now, one of the security guys hasn't turned up, so they're a man down. If they need help, can you give them a hand later on?' Bernd asked.

'Sure.'

Left alone in the locker room, Felix glanced at his face in the mirror. In a few days the marks from Muggelsee would fade. He needed to get stronger and fitter if he was going to overcome the other Musketeers. Horst had been no pushover and Felix's body ached from their pugnacious encounter.

Over the next two days, Felix wondered if Horst had been officially reported missing. It unsettled him every time the news came on and he felt mightily relieved every time when nothing about Horst or his car being discovered at Muggelsee was mentioned. Horst had clearly been telling the truth about not having a family or any close relationships because he had disappeared without a trace and no one seemed to miss him.

The golf tournament ended and everyone deemed it a great success. Bernd and Klaus threw a party for the family and staff at the club and Martha came for the celebrations. Felix was his usual gentle self with Martha; he couldn't behave any differently with her, although she noticed his bruises immediately.

You look as if you've been in a fight?'

'Yeah, I had a fight at Carsten's boxing club. You don't mind if I take up boxing do you? he lied.

Martha laughed. 'It'll ruin your good looks, but I'll love you anyway. And don't think I haven't noticed how red your hands are. What's up?'

'When I'm stressed, I wash them - excessively. It's

something I started at Torgau and it returns occasionally.'

She was concerned. 'What's happened to make you feel so stressed?'

Felix lied again. 'The tournament's been manic here all week, I've worked from the crack of dawn till midnight and I'm tired, that's all.'

'Relax and leave your hands alone,' she said, softly squeezing them. 'We'll have a lie-in at Gertrude's house tomorrow.'

He kissed her and smiled at the thought.

'Oh, and I've some news for you,' Martha began. 'I've just found out, there's a ten week, foreign exchange trip to England soon with my school. It'll really help my English and you can come and visit me for the last week, I've already asked.'

'When are you going?'

'Mid-October to mid-December.'

'I'll miss you.'

'Ich auch. But we can phone and write. Please say you'll come?' she implored.

Kissing her, he said, 'Of course I'll visit you. Whereabouts in England?

'Brighton. It's by the sea.'

After the weekend Martha returned home to Kopenick and Klaus and Ingrid asked Felix to stay with them at the cottage. He was more than happy to have the company because being alone with his tormented thoughts in Gertrude's house was proving too difficult. When he was busy or with other people it was easier.

'We made a lot of money out of the golf tournament,' Klaus began. 'We'd like you to have a car for your 18th birthday in the New Year.'

Felix was surprised at their generosity. 'Wirklich? Danke!'

'Well, you'll be a man, and it's time you had your own bank account too.'

'Onkel, thank you,' Felix enthused, hugging Klaus.

'You deserve it, lad. I imagine Martha will like to ride in a nice, new car. No one likes riding a Schwalbe in the middle of winter.'

Ingrid came out of Axel's room. 'Felix, Axel's asking for you.'

Felix put his arms around Ingrid and kissed her. 'Tante, thanks for the car.'

'I'm sure you'll still ride your bike in the warmer months but I'll worry less with you in a car,' she told him.

Felix went into the little boy's room. Axel's delight at seeing his Onkel was tangible and he jumped upright in his bed. 'Fewix. Read me a story?'

How could Felix resist?

Axel fell asleep during his bedtime story. Felix kissed his nephew softly on his cheek and tucked him in. Tears welled in his eyes. At this moment, as he looked at this beautiful, innocent child, he realised that killing Horst to protect his family was the only choice he could have made. Felix decided he would no longer harbour regrets about Horst and his premature demise. He believed it was the children that mattered most in the world and they had the right to be loved and protected.

Felix came back into the lounge. 'He's fast asleep.'

Ingrid gave Felix a discerning look. 'I haven't asked you yet where you got those bruises?'

Felix fobbed her off. 'Boxing… I went to the gym with Carsten and I'd like to take up boxing. Do you think I could have a punch bag and a few weights? I could set up a mini gym in Das Kino.

'I don't see why not, but it'll spoil your good looks,' Ingrid told him.

'That's what Martha said but I need to get fitter. Onkel, 'can I join your gun club.'

Klaus was surprised. 'Ok, but you'll need your own pistol.'

'I've been practicing with yours, at targets in the woods.'

Ingrid was unimpressed. 'Felix! You can't just take guns into the woods or you'll have the police on our doorstep;

you need a licence.'

'You should have asked me,' Klaus told him.

'Sorry. You're right, I should have asked.'

'Well, all right, I'll get another gun and you can have mine when we get you a licence. Did you hit your targets?'

'Yes, I hit my target,' Felix replied, thinking of Horst.

'Your hands are sore again,' Ingrid observed. 'Everything ok with you and Martha?'

'I've been a bit stressed lately, but Martha and I are fine. Do you know, she's going to England next month on a school exchange? She'll be gone eight weeks and I'm invited for the last week. I'm going to miss her.'

'So will we,' said Ingrid. 'It's nice having a girl about the place.'

'The weeks will go quickly. What will you do with all that free time?'

'Onkel, I thought that as it's the end of the tourist season at the lake I could have a little break from work and enrol in an English course, to be on a par with Martha and to be prepared for when I go to England.'

'Good idea, but I guess you'd have to go to a city for that; there's not any language schools near us.'

'Tante, I thought I would go to one in Berlin, travel up in the mornings, do an afternoon course and return here at night,' Felix suggested.

Klaus nodded his approval. 'Fine by me.'

When Felix went to bed that night, all his thoughts seemed crystal clear. He would put Martha's absence to good use and was free to plot his crimes and stalk his victims in their home environment. Flicking through Horst's infamous diary, Felix began working out a plan. The die was cast; his course was set.

13. Gunther

Gunther Schukrafft was a small man of 40. He had never married and lived next door to his disabled, 60-year-old mother, Marlene, on a council estate, a plattenbauten in the suburbs of Leipzig. At Torgau, he was the warden who had supervised the running of the library, distributing the books to the children as well as being a fully-fledged Musketeer. After Torgau's closure, his sexual proclivities regarding children went undiscovered and his crimes unpunished, and Gunther found work as senior librarian in his home town.

Neighbours thought well of Gunther. After his father died 10 years ago he looked after his mother, who had developed multiple sclerosis. She was gradually losing her ability to walk and Gunther was her dutiful and only son. The locals had no inkling of Gunther's past or private life because he had few friends. Apart from the Musketeers, he kept in touch with a few ex-Torgau colleagues and other paedophiles scattered around the country in a secret ring. His short trips away with the Musketeers raised few eyebrows as the explanation would be that he needed regular respite from looking after his wheelchair-bound mother, who was tended by professional carers during the day when he worked or when he went away. Gunther looked forward to his jaunts away: a few days of sexual abuse in a motor home with unsuspecting victims, shared with Horst and Harald.

Marlene had not met any of Gunther's friends and never

suspected her son was anything other than a man who was shy with women. Gunther spoke about his friends occasionally and told her when he was going 'fishing' and 'hunting' with his ex-colleagues. She was always happy to have Gunther at home; he was a good son and she missed him when he went away. Their conversations after a trip away, usually followed the same pattern.

'Did you have a good trip?'

'Yes, Mutti.'

'Where did you go this time?'

'Rostock.'

'Oh, lots of sea fishing then. What did you catch?'

'Small fish. We fried them for supper in the motor home. Mutti, did you have a nice time

while I was gone?'

'Yes. My carers are fine but it's nice to have you home.'

Gunther left home the same time every morning, driving to work on the other side of Leipzig, returning at lunchtime to take his disabled mother for a walk in the park. Felix, unseen, sporting a dark wig, was watching him, noting what time the library closed, which car he drove and plotting his optimum form of attack. Once he'd gathered enough information about Gunther's routine, Felix returned to Leipzig on the train, with his onkel's gun.

The crepuscular light on the fallen autumn leaves scattered in the streets turned them assorted shades of pink, orange and yellow. Children trampled on them and gathered them in colourful heaps to playfully throw into the air- or at one another. To catch falling leaves was an autumnal pleasure children could enjoy as the days in October grew shorter and colder.

Felix looked at his watch. Six pm. He wondered what Martha was doing in England and remembered how wonderful she smelt when he kissed her goodbye a few weeks ago. It would be over a month before he saw Martha again and he missed her. Inside the library in Leipzig the lights were being turned off. The library doors opened and a few members of staff trickled out and dispersed, bidding their colleagues goodnight before disappearing into the night. Gunther was the last one out, locking up the library before his walk across a dimly lit pathway to a car park. The streets were empty as Felix lay in wait. He put on his balaclava and gloves and primed his gun.

CLICK.

Felix heard footsteps and quickly crouched down behind the Musketeer's car. As Gunther approached, he delved in his pockets for the keys. Suddenly, he felt a gun pushed against his temple.

'Don't say a word, or I'll blow your brains out,' Felix barked his instructions. 'We're going for a ride. Give me the keys!'

Gunther wet himself. He had no choice other than to obey. He prayed someone would see what was going on with this masked man but there was no one in sight. Gunther fumbled with his car keys and passed them to the masked man.

'My mother's expecting me, she's disabled. Please, what do you want with me?'

'Schukrafft, your mother is of no concern to me.'

Gunther found this shocking. 'You know my name?'

Felix swung out with the gun and hit Gunther on the head. He slumped to the ground and Felix bundled him into the back of the car, tying the Musketeer's hands and feet with boat rope and covering his mouth with duct tape. Driving lessons had come in useful. Felix drove with ease to the banks of Muggelsee and this time parked near the north jetty. He hoped to repeat the same ending for Gunther as Horst, using similar methods.

Gunther was stirring in the back as Felix ripped off the tape and dragged him to the water's edge. 'Let's see how you like a darkened cellar, knee-deep in water,' Felix spat, menacingly.

It was quiet and dark. The lights illuminating their evening came from the car headlamps and Felix's torch.

'My mother will be worried,' Gunther pleaded.

'Poor little mummy's boy. Does your mother know the truth about you?'

'What do you mean?'

Felix's voice was cold and emphatic. 'That you're a sodomite.'

'I don't know what you're talking about.'

'Do you think your mother would still love you if she knew the truth about you?'

'You're mistaken. You've got the wrong man!' Gunther spluttered.

Felix took out his boat knife. 'I'm going to strip you. Stand still and don't try anything clever or I'll shove this knife up your arschloch!' he barked. 'And empty your pockets.'

Gunther handed over his wallet and mobile phone whilst Felix slashed away at Gunther's clothes until the Musketeer was left in just his underpants.

'I'm just a librarian. Believe me, my disabled mother will be very worried about me by now,' he implored.

'What's your mother's pet name for you?'

'Gunty… Why?'

'I'll text her, to tell her you'll be home late.'

Felix turned on the Musketeer's mobile and texted the following to Gunther's mother.

'Mutti, gone for a drink with colleagues, don't worry. 'Gunty.'

The night air gave Gunther's wiry frame goosebumps. 'Who are you? What do you want from me?'

'Scheisse! I don't want anything! Don't you get it? I'm taking something from you!'

Gunther was afraid to know the answer. 'What are you going to take from me?'

'You'll see!' Grabbing at a handful of hair, Felix began hacking chunks off.

Gunther screamed.

'Shut up!' Felix snapped and pushed Gunther into the cold water, where he fell on his knees.

'Please, don't hurt me,' he sobbed.

Felix wrapped the hair cuttings in a tissue and placed it in his rucksack. He took out his Walkman radio cassette and switched on his recording of 'Toreador' from Bizet's opera 'Carmen'. No one was around so he turned up the music.

'Allons! En garde! Allons ! Allons ! Ah!'

'Dance!' Felix barked.

Gunther started to jig about on his knees in the cold, muddy water, dancing awkwardly. He felt small, pathetic and afraid. Felix watched, smiling behind his balaclava as he picked up Gunther's shredded clothes and shoved them into the boot of the car. Laughing, he and made a mock charge, like a bull at the quivering Gunther.

'How's it feel, Gunther? To be stripped of your dignity?'

'Toreador, en garde! Toreador, Toreador.'

'I'm cold. Please stop!' he cried.

'Stand up!' Felix bellowed.

Gunther watched the man in the balaclava charge at him, back and forth like a raging bull, simultaneously waving his knife menacingly and somehow managed with his feet still bound to haul himself up before toppling down again.

'Bitte!' he pleaded.

'No one cares. You and your Musketeers didn't care about us kids at Torgau. Don't expect any sympathy from me.'

Gunther wet himself again. 'Torgau? Were you one of my boys?'

'Finally; a confession. I've got the scars on my ears to prove it, branded by you!'

Gunther gulped out his words. 'I'm sorry.'

'Sorry you got caught you mean…You're not much of a Musketeer now. Did you think you'd get away with it, you immoral coward?'

Felix ignored Gunther's pleas and slashed the knife at Gunther's ears. The Musketeer howled as his earlobes were ripped and the blood gushed.

'Et songe bien, oui, songe en combattent, qu'un oeil noir te regarde…'

'How's it feel to be branded?'

Gunther's ears burned with pain. Stripped of his dignity, on his knees in cold water at the mercy of a madman, feeling terrified. 'I know what I did was wrong and I'm sorry.'

'Et que l'amour, t'attend, Toreador, l'amour t'attend.'

'You've ruined lives,' Felix told him, while rinsing his knife in the water.

'You can have all my savings, anything! Please, let me go,' Gunther wailed.

'I don't want your blood money!' Felix snapped, and picked up his gun. 'Your sense of remorse is touching. Horst had none.'

Gunther's eyes were wild with fear. 'Horst? Horst Gwisdek?'

'That's right, one of your fellow sodomites. Horst is lying at the bottom of this lake and that's where you're going to end up. That's what I'm taking from you… your life! One less paedophile to destroy lives.'

'No!' Gunther screamed, attempting to escape his fate proved futile.

Felix quickly overpowered Gunther, and stood towering over Gunther. The hate inside him was so strong that he couldn't bear to look at him. Hitting him on the back of the head with the gun, he dragged Gunther's limp body to the car and threw him in the back. Before long Gunther's eyes flickered and the monster stirred.

'Mutti! Help. Someone, help me!' was Gunther's last, desperate cry.

'Fic dich!' Felix yelled in Gunther's ear, giving him another whack with the gun.

Felix turned off the music, tied Gunther's hands to the door handle, bound his feet to the handle on the opposite side and locked the doors. He put on a wet suit and aqua shoes and opened the windows in the front so the car would fill with water and he had a means of escape. Then he drove the car off the end of the jetty at breakneck speed, hitting the water hard. The car began to sink and Felix climbed out with ease to repeat his ritual of dancing on top of the car roof before diving off and swimming in the cold, cleansing water, back to the jetty.

Shining his torch over the water he double-checked that the deed was done. It had surprised him how easy it was to dispose of someone and how good he felt about it.

A euphoric feeling without any regrets. Felix didn't have any bruises this time, not even a scratch - but he knew the third Musketeer wouldn't be so easy.

Dressing himself at the side of the lake, he got ready to leave. The next part of his plan was to contact the relatives with news that would hopefully throw them off track. Felix texted the following message to Gunther's mother.

'Dear Mutti,

I have to get away. News is about to break, the police will come after me for what I did as a warden at Torgau. I sexually abused the kids. Tell no one. I have to lie low for now. I'm sorry.

Your loving son, Gunty.'

Felix sent the message and it registered a beep, successfully delivered. He quickly turned off the mobile, not wanting to receive any messages or calls from an anxious and frightened old lady in Leipzig. Triple-checking the crime scene for any clues he might have left, he departed the lake thinking it had all gone well and surprisingly to plan.

As he walked along the dark, wooded pathway at the side of the lake towards the street lights of Kopenick, Felix decided there was no time to lose and would start stalking his third Musketeer immediately. With growing impatience, he looked forward to returning to normality at Motzen and get on with the rest of his life. A life with Martha.

Two down, two to go, he told himself.

14. Harald

Harald Plaumann was a married man in his mid-30s with two children: a boy of eight and a girl of six. A devoted husband and father, his wife had no idea he was a paedophile and would have vehemently refuted any suggestion that he was.

As a young and impressionable warden at Torgau, Plaumann's latent proclivities for under-age sex, predominately with boys, were kindled and truly ignited under the influence of Horst Gwisdek.

After Torgau's closure, Harald got a job at Berlin's Schonefeld Airport as a security guard and within two years became a deputy manager of the security team. He was regarded as an upstanding pillar of the community and moved his family with him, settling in a nearby village on the edge of the Spreewald. To outsiders, Harald seemed like a 'normal' person - a regular guy, tall and strong, raising a family and going to work, where he strutted around the airport like a puffed-out peacock, anyone or anything suspicious feeling the full force of his wrath. But he also kept in touch with his fellow Musketeers and enjoyed their depraved mini breaks in Horst's motor home.

Horst's diary helped lead Felix to Harald's home. At the crack of dawn, he parked his Schwalbe in an alley and began stalking his prey. Hidden between the large recycling bins he felt safe and protected and also had a prime view. Harald came out of his house wearing his uniform, with 'Airport Security' emblazoned on the back of his jacket. Following on his Schwalbe, Felix couldn't keep up with Harald's fast car but it seemed logical that the Musketeer was heading for Schonefeld airport, about 15 kilometres away. Felix parked at the nearest U-Bahn station, put on a dark wig and took the train to the airport.

At Schonefeld, Felix found and observed his prey, pompously patrolling the arrivals hall. He decided it would be far too dangerous to try and abduct someone here, with masses of security measures and cameras clearly visible. Harald also carried a gun during his working day. This Musketeer was going to be tricky, he thought. Felix didn't fear him, because with all the boxing training he had bulked up his athletic frame and now felt he was Harald's equal in terms of strength. In Das Kino, he boxed to the music of the 'Toreador' song and every time he hit the punch bag he would shout out, 'The Torgau boy wins!' Hopefully, he'd prove more than a match for Harald, using his brain as well as his newly-developed brawn to achieve a successful outcome. And as with the other Musketeers, Felix believed luck was on his side.

He watched Harald's children play outside their semi-detached home in a cul-de-sac near open fields. For the first time Felix felt a surge of guilt, knowing it was his intention to deprive these children of their father; his plans for retribution impinged on their young lives and were in direct contradiction to his thoughts about protecting children. But then he thought, 'What if Harald abused his own children, or planned to in the future?' and his guilty feelings were soon assuaged.

After 10 days of surveillance, watching the house and following Harald's movements, Felix felt ready. A different strategy was necessary as the cul-de-sac was far too exposed. He decided the optimum choice would be to make his move at the gym. Harald finished his working day at 4 p.m. when he picked his children up from school and spent time at home with them. In the early evening he went alone to a local gym and afterwards, drive to a nearby bar for a beer with colleagues. Felix checked the gym car park for security cameras. There were none.

On a quiet October evening just after twilight, Felix waited behind a tree near to the Musketeers's parked car. Harald emerged from the gym and walked over to his car, pressing a remote control keypad to open the vehicle and put his bag in the boot. For a brief moment, anything or anyone in front of him was invisible and it was at this optimum moment of surprise that Felix sprang into action. Harald closed the boot of his car and found a man in a balaclava standing beside him pointing a gun at his head.

'What the fuck?'

'Hands up!'

Harald dropped his car keys and obeyed, putting his hands in the air. Felix body searched him for signs of a gun.

'I work with the police. You're making a big mistake.'

Felix snarled. 'You need policing! Keep your hands behind your back.'

Harald obeyed and his body was shoved spread eagled on the bonnet of the car. He also felt something he hadn't felt in years; fear.

Felix tied Harald's hands tightly together with some rope and duct taped the Musketeer's mouth, dragging him to the back seat of the car, pushing him inside, face down, and using more rope to bind his prey's feet together. Picking up the car keys from the ground, Felix started the car and drove steadily out of the car park.

He kept a close eye on Harald through the rear view mirror. The Musketeer was wriggling in the back but remained tightly bound. Before long, Felix reached the scene of his previous crimes, parking this time by the banks of the east jetty. The night was cold and dark and nobody was about.

Keeping the car headlamps on, Felix shone the lights on a nearby tree as he went into the bushes. Earlier in the day he'd camouflaged his Schwalbe under a bush before stealing a bicycle in Kopenick, taking it on the train to Schonefeld and cycling onwards to his destination; Harald's gym.

His Schwalbe was still there. He rummaged in his top box for his wet suit and aqua shoes and quickly changed. Returning to the car, Felix opened the back door, leaning the full weight of his body on Harald while holding him firmly in place. He proceeded to take off his abuser's shoes and socks, cutting away at his clothes with his knife from top to bottom and throwing the rags out of the car until Harald was left lying in his underpants. He then took Harald's wallet and mobile phone and ripped off the duct tape.

'What's your wife's name?

'You leave her alone!' Harald yelled.

Hacking at Harald's hair, Felix got his DNA cuttings.

Harald was incensed. 'You bastard!'

'Your wife's name? I'll text her, tell her you'll be late home.'

'Ina... my wife's name is Ina,' Harald blurted out.

Felix took the hair, wrapped it in tissue and placed it in his rucksack. He was feeling confident and prematurely sent Harald's wife the following mobile text.

Darling Ina,

I have to get away as news is about to break and the police will come after me for what I did as a warden at Torgau. I sexually abused the kids. Tell no one. I've got to lie low. I'm sorry. Kiss my children for me.

Your loving husband,
Harald

The message beeped a successful delivery. Felix switched off Harald's mobile phone and returned to the car with his knife in one hand and a gun tucked into the top of his wet suit. He dragged the Musketeer from the car into the cold night air and threw him onto the muddy banks, kicking at him, shoving him into the shallows of the cold water, rolling him like a log as he stood over his prey, watching him through the eye slits of his balaclava.

Harald managed to pull himself upright, balanced on his knees. 'Who the fuck do you think you are?' he screamed.

'Plaumann, I'm your worst nightmare.'

'You know my name?'

Felix spoke with venom. 'Every kid knew your name; at Torgau.'

Harald was shivering knee deep in the water and mustered all his strength and bravado in an attempt to save his life. 'I don't know what you're talking about.'

Felix fetched his Walkman and turned on the cassette.

'Toreador, en garde, Toreador, Toreador.'

'This is such a perfect song for all of you. Don't lie to me or treat me like an idiot! Now, dance for me, Musketeer, like I danced for you.'

Harald tried to stand up but his feet were bound and it was all he could do to stop himself toppling face first into the water.

'I can't stand up... Cut me loose and I'll dance for you.'

'Idiot! Dance on your knees!' Felix bellowed and made a mock bull charge at his prey.

'Et songe bien, oui, songe en combattant, qu'un oeil noir te regarde...'

Harald moved from side to side on his knees in rhythm to the music, trying to think of a way out of this nightmare. It was obvious his life depended on it. He asked himself, if this is a Torgau boy, why would dancing for him be important? Then he realised and stopped moving. There was only one boy at Torgau who had danced for him.

'Et que l'amour t'attend, Toreador, Toreador, l'maour t'attend!'

'I said dance!' Felix barked.

Harald was adamant in his defiance. 'No! Take off your mask… Felix Waltz.

Felix switched off the music. The game had taken a different direction to the one he had anticipated. He wasn't afraid to show his face and gladly pulled off his balaclava. 'My sister and I danced for you so it's the least you can do for me.'

'Well, well, Felix Waltz. You didn't drown after all. We should have got together, you and your sister and the Musketeers, just like the old days.'

Furious, and unable to contain his temper, Felix slashed the knife at Harald's ears, cutting his lobes. Blood splattered and gushed into the water.

'My sister's dead because of what you did to her!'

Harald screamed out in pain, but refused to cry or beg in front of the Torgau boy. 'You'll regret that, Waltz!'

You're branded now. How does it feel?'

Harald didn't reply. He blocked out the pain in his ears and moved his body to stay warm. He felt something sharp dig into his back - a rock, hidden under the surface. Placing his tied hands over the rock he began to rub the rope against it, up and down, in an attempt to cut it loose. He disguised his actions as best he could, trying not to give himself away.

'I've had enough of this scheisse! Your revenge stops here,' Harald snarled.

'Revenge? I've only just started. This is payback time. Of course, if you don't like my kind of justice, I'll hand you over to the police and you'll be thrown into prison with all the other sodomites. You'll think you've been fucked by a train when they get at you.'

'You've no guarantees I'd be prosecuted. I'll deny everything.' Harald said, stony-faced.

'That's what I thought,' Felix mused.

'Horst hasn't said, but I suppose you pulled the same stunt on him, bringing him here.

Felix smiled like a fox. 'Yes, I brought that paedophile here, and Gunther.'

Harald thought it was odd his fellow Musketeers hadn't warned him. 'I guess we'll swap stories about how a Torgau boy outsmarted the lot of us. Ok, you've made your point. What is it you want, money?'

'Screw your blood money! That's not what I'm taking.'

Harald had not understood the deeper meaning of Felix's words. He felt the rope around his hands loosening and stalled for time.

'My wife and children will be worried about me by now.'

Felix stared hard. 'And when you tuck your children in bed at night, are you tempted to, you know, touch them?'

'Nein! Nein!'

'Liar! Bet you've thought about it. Have you already abused them?'

By the shock in Harald's eyes, Felix could see he'd found Harald's Achilles heel.

'No!'

'People like you think children enjoy having sex. You're a sick bastard. They'll be better off without you.'

'I love my children,' Harald cried.

Felix was adamant. 'It's deeply rooted in you to abuse, over and over again.'

'I wouldn't touch my children … I couldn't…not them.'

'I don't believe you… I bet Horst and Gunther would.'

'They wouldn't dare! I'd kill them.'

Felix smirked. 'I've saved you that job.'

Harald was now in fear for his life. 'What did you do with Horst and Gunther?'

'I, Felix Waltz, was the judge and the jury. They're at the bottom of this lake and that's where you're going. The Torgau boy wins!' he yelled at the top of his voice and bashed Harald on the head with his gun.

He dragged a slippery, wet and stunned Harald out of the water and into the back of the car. The blood trickled from his forehead and ears and his body was blue from the cold. Felix collected Harald's clothes and put them in the boot of the car. There was no one around and no one in sight. He picked up his balaclava along with his gun and knife, placed them in his rucksack and switched on the headlights of his Schwalbe, ready to guide him back to the jetty.

Returning to the car, Felix could see Harald lying motionless in the back. He quickly unwound the car windows at the front, leaving the back windows closed and locking the back doors. With his adrenaline pumping and losing sight of any sense of order, Felix forgot to repeat the success of Gunther's demise and failed to re-tie Harald's hands to the door handle and his feet to the opposite side. As he drove the car at high speed off the end of the jetty, with the car in mid-flight, he felt a rope around his neck.

'Waltz! I'll fucking kill you!' Harald bellowed, having freed his hands.

The rope tightened around Felix's neck, choking him. He took his hands off the steering wheel and grappled with the rope to try and loosen Harald's lethal grip. His foot on the accelerator pressed down hard and generated more height and speed than expected, projecting the car close to a small island of trees. He could hardly breathe as the car landed on the water and quickly began filling up. Felix thought of Martha, Klaus and Ingrid; they would never know what happened to him. He saw a vision of Axel's smiling face; Susi's little boy would forget him and never remember he existed. The silver crucifix hanging on the driver's mirror caught a prism of moonlight and with his strength ebbing away, Felix grabbed it and stabbed at Harald's eyes.

He'd struck home. Yelling in pain, Harald loosened his grip on the rope and Felix managed to wriggle out of the window but Harald grabbed his foot and held on, tugging him backwards. Suddenly the car went under the water and with the rocking of their movements, nose-dived quickly towards the bottom. Branches from the roots of a tree invaded the car on the front passenger side, just missing Felix's head. Felix tried to swim upwards, kicking Harald full in the face. The Musketeer's grip on Felix's foot loosened and he was left holding only an aqua scuba diving shoe in his hands. As Felix escaped out of the only remaining open window the car rolled slightly and the branch speared through the entire width of the front window, blocking any exit. Harald's feet were still tied and he gave up struggling to undo them, diverting his efforts to pulling at the branch to find an escape hatch by the window. It was futile. The tree closed off any hope of life and Harald's lungs filled with water and delivered him to his watery grave.

Felix struggled to swim upwards; it proved the darkest and longest swim of his life.

Finally reaching the surface, he could barely breathe and felt as if he were swimming through treacle as he headed for the lights from his Schwalbe. On reaching the jetty, he hauled himself out of the water and collapsed.

15. Ingrid's secret

Felix managed to drag his exhausted body onto his Schwalbe and drive slowly away from Muggelsee, arriving back in Motzen in the middle of the night. He left the motorbike in Gertrude's garden and went into the darkened house, switched on all the lights and ran a bath. He looked at his neck in the bathroom mirror; it was sore and a deep rope burn was visible. Scheisse! Can't hide this, he thought, hoping it would have faded by the time he was due to go to England to visit Martha.

He took a bottle of beer from the fridge and once the water was ready, scrubbed and soaked away his aching body in the bath. But in bed, sleep would not come. He put on the television and watched an episode of Tatort and drank another beer. How easily the detectives solved the crimes in this programme.

He looked at the four small, white envelopes in front of him. The initials on the envelopes were HG, GS, HP and AF. Now that he had all three Musketeers' DNA he could send them off to be analysed. The envelope with AF written upon it contained hair clippings from Axel, collected surreptitiously when Felix had taken his nephew to the hairdressers to get a trim. Soon the mystery of Axel's parentage would be solved.

Felix began typing out a list of all the male names from Horst's diary to send to the police, some were those he remembered from Torgau. They were all potential suspected paedophiles as far as he was concerned and if they were innocent then they would have to prove it.

There were not many female names in the diary but there was one woman who Felix was going after: Lotte Holler. As she wasn't a Musketeer or a paedophile, it didn't matter if he omitted her or any other females from the list but Lotte, the go-between, would get her come-uppance and that would more than satisfy him. He went to bed feeling his family were safer now that he'd murdered all of his Torgau Musketeers.

In the morning, he overslept. Ingrid let herself in and finding a few empty bottles of beer near the sofa in the living room and Felix asleep in bed at 10 a.m, knew instinctively that something was wrong.

'Felix, wake up. Are you ill?'

Felix stirred and pulled the covers over his head. 'No. Tante, please, leave me be.'

'Axel's at the kindergarten till lunchtime, Klaus is working and you and I, young man, are going to have a talk. Now get up!' Ingrid snapped.

Felix peered over the duvet. 'I'm not a child!'

You've been behaving like one of late,' she remarked gruffly and left the room.

A little while later, an aroma of coffee filled the house. Felix, downstairs now, sat opposite Ingrid with a scarf around his neck.

'Are you cold?'

'No.' Felix didn't want to lie. If anything, he felt, Ingrid was the one person he could tell the truth to, but dare he?

Ingrid thought she would test her nephews' integrity. 'Look at the time. Aren't you supposed to be catching a train to Berlin for your English course?'

Felix was perceptive enough to counter Ingrid's ruse. 'Tante, you know I haven't been to going to Berlin or going to English lessons.'

'Thank you for not lying to me. Axel and I came to meet you at the train station a few weeks ago other and the ticket cashier said you'd caught the train to Leipzig. What the hell were you doing in Leipzig?'

'Not an English course, that's for sure.'

She frowned. 'Felix! It's no time for flippancy.'

He nodded. 'I'm sorry.'

'I'm really worried about you. You haven't been yourself these past few weeks- you've been moody and lost in your own world. What's going on?'

'I've needed to sort out a few problems.'

Ingrid was concerned. 'Problems? Please, talk to me, or if not to me, talk to Klaus. Are you in trouble?'

Felix took off his scarf and revealed the rope burn on his neck.

'What happened?' she gasped.

'I got into a fight… I met someone from Torgau, one of men who buggered me.'

Ingrid's heart sank and she was afraid for him.

'And this man, he did that to your neck?'

He nodded. 'I'm ok. I hurt him too.'

'What did you do to the man?' she asked, afraid of the answer.

'It's best kept a secret.'

'Secrets can become great burdens. Tell me, and if need be, we can go to the police.'

Felix was adamant. 'Too late, the police can't help me now.'

'You can trust me,' Ingrid implored.

'I trust you,' Felix said, his eyes filling with tears. 'Tante, I'm made of secrets… I've buried myself in them.'

'There's nothing you could do to stop me loving you,' she said to reassure him.

He smiled. 'I'll remind you of that someday. Tante, trust me, there are others who would expose me, and my secrets would wreak repercussions on the whole family. I couldn't allow that. I'd die to protect my family but hopefully now I won't have to.'

'Felix, you're talking in riddles. If it helps, I've done

things I'm not proud of… We could swap our worst secrets, I'll go first. It's something I've wanted to tell you but was afraid to. I lost Sofie's love and as a result, you and Susanne ended up in Torgau.'

'It was no one's fault we ended up in Torgau. Blame the Stasi and their regime, I do, but not yourself,' he declared. 'But you're talking about the argument you and Mutti had at Gertrude's funeral, aren't you?'

Ingrid was surprised. 'You remember it?'

'Sure, I was in the garden, and I heard your raised voices. I didn't know what you were arguing about, Mutti never told us, but I knew it was serious because we never came back to Motzen.'

Sighing, Ingrid remembered it was here in this very kitchen that she'd lost her sister. He's still so young, she thought, but she knew Felix had insight and understood things at such a deep level that she could tell him anything. The timing could never be right but she was ready to admit her failings and tell her nephew the truth.

'Your father messed up all your lives. Gertrude, Klaus and me, we watched the fall out - the bruises on Sofie's arms, her face and on both of you children. We begged her to leave Jakob and bring you and Susanne here to live with us in Motzen. It made Gertrude ill to witness it all. We told her Jakob was no longer welcome here to push her into making a choice, but Sofie thought it was her duty to try and help her husband.'

'Mutti was stubborn like that. A bit like you, she couldn't be told.'

He knows me well, Ingrid thought. 'Yes, but my darling sister thought love would be enough. It wasn't. When people are in denial they can't help themselves and Jakob's alcoholism had you all trapped in a cage.'

Felix looked at the empty beer bottles beside the kitchen sink. Ingrid must have brought them in from the living room. 'Before you say anything else, I had two beers last night, the first I've had in ages: I am not my father.'

She nodded. 'I know.'

'I remember… Jakob used to get angry over nothing, take off his belt, give us a whack and send us to bed without any supper. When he started on Mutti, I'd get out of bed and scream at him, not to hit Mutti, and I'd get another whack for my troubles. He never said sorry or showed any remorse. Later on, he'd come into the bedroom and wake us up just to sing us to sleep again as if nothing was wrong. We had to pretend it wasn't going on and it never happened, until the next explosion. I remember his smell, of stale cigarettes and alcohol. My father was an angry, controlling, and bitter drunk.'

'He made your lives a living hell.'

'Well, I guess we thought it was normal to live like that. When Jakob tried to escape over the river, he got his just rewards. Maybe, at some point or other we all get payback for our sins,' he mused.

'If you believe that, then I lost Sofie as a punishment. I was unkind to your mother- I blamed her for Gertrude's death.'

Felix finally knew the reason why his mother had refused to kiss and make up with her sister: the wound went too deep.

'That's why I believe I'm partly to blame for you and Susanne being sent to Torgau, and for Susanne dying. What you suffered could have been avoided. If Sofie and I had been on speaking terms, we all might be here now, together as a family. Felix, can you ever forgive me?' Ingrid begged, tears running down her cheeks.

'Tante, there's nothing to forgive. Mutti would agree with me.'

Ingrid wiped her cheeks. 'Now I've told you my secret, won't you tell me yours?'

Felix had murdered three people and was planning to kill a fourth. He could not condemn Ingrid for an argument with his mother, whatever happened afterwards. He would never dare be self-righteous and judge Ingrid for her actions. His beloved Tante had shared her darkest secret with him but he felt he could not burden her with his.

'Secrets and lies are a lethal combination. No, sorry. Tante, I'm not ready to tell you my darkest secrets.'

She understood and would bide her time. 'Ok. I'm here for you, whenever you feel like telling me.'

'I know. You and Klaus gave me a home and a life and I love you both.'

'We love you, too,' Ingrid cried, embracing her nephew. 'Now, what are we going to tell Klaus about the rope burns on your neck?'

Felix quickly came up with a plausible idea. 'I'll say I was swinging on a rope over the lake and it got tangled round my neck. If you want to tell onkel Klaus, I'll understand, but I'd rather you didn't. I just hope my neck looks better when I visit Martha.'

'I'll get some arnica, that'll do the trick,' she ventured.

'Tante, just so you know. I lie sometimes to stay out of trouble and to hide the truth.'

'So do I,' Ingrid told him, smiling. 'So do I.'

16. The Ring

When Gunther's mother Marianne received the text sent by Felix about her son she did not know whether to believe it or what to do. Hearing her beloved boy confess to paedophilia in a text message came as a great shock and when Gunther didn't return home she feared the worst. Two weeks later, having tried unsuccessfully many times to contact Gunther on his mobile, the police turned up at dawn. They had been sent a typed, anonymous letter with a Berlin postmark containing a suspected ring of paedophiles. Gunther's name was on this list and he was wanted for questioning.

Marianne was extremely anxious about Gunther's disappearance and had felt his absence deeply, because without him there was no one to love or even to care for her except those whom she paid. She had deleted Gunther's texted confession and when the police asked her about her son's alleged paedophilia she denied any knowledge and was adamant; it was all a big mistake. Not long after the police left, Marianne had a heart attack and slumped to the floor. She died shortly afterwards, believing her son was a good boy down to her very last breath.

Harald's wife Ina had also been in a state of panic since receiving Felix's text about her husband. She had two young children to think about and they missed their father as much as she missed her husband. When the police tur ned up at dawn wanting to question Harald about alleged paedophilia she told them he'd gone missing, which only added to their suspicions.

Perhaps Harald was not the person she thought he was? Ina wondered if what the police were suggesting could be true. As a worried mother, it crossed her mind that Harald might have abused his own children and because of this, Ina decided to show the police the text message she'd received and kept from Harald - sent, of course, by Felix.

The police were immediately sympathetic and offered Ina and her children psychological help to cope with the trauma. Police protection was available should anyone find out the truth about her husband and turn up unexpectedly at her home to cause trouble. The news that day was full of the paedophile dawn raids so they also advised her not to allow her children access to any media reports.

Felix was in the cottage looking after Axel when he saw the breaking news about the dawn raids on the television. He left Axel to his puzzle on the kitchen table and turned up the volume. The television presenter was saying that various male suspects had been arrested and taken in for questioning, and then switched to a live report from Berlin. On the steps of police H.Q against a backdrop of the Brandenburg gate, a female journalist was conducting an interview with a craggy-faced detective sporting a five o'clock shadow of facial stubble.

The journalist began enthusiastically. 'I'm here at police headquarters in Mitte, Berlin, with Kommissar Kruger, what can you tell us about the success of this operation?'

Kruger scratched his stubble. 'We received an anonymous tip-off which has proved to be reliable. As a consequence, we've made a number of arrests of potential sex offenders in an operation by our undercover team of police officers. It's been a great success.'

'Am I correct in assuming these potential sex offenders were in a paedophile ring and worked in childrens' institutions such as Torgau?'

Kruger nodded. 'That's correct. I'd like to make an appeal to any young person who was interned in places such as Torgau to come forward and give us vital information to help secure the imprisonment of those connected to this paedophile ring. I will personally guarantee anonymity to anyone giving evidence in court.'

The journalist probed further. 'Surely those who have been sexually abused might be reluctant to go over such sensitive and painful memories?'

Kruger nodded. 'I understand, but can assure anyone who comes forward can be assured that we have a team of dedicated individuals working in conjunction with the police who will offer psychological support. Anyone coming forward would ultimately not only help themselves, but other victims of abuse, in the past and in the future.'

Felix felt vindicated. By sending the police a list of names from Horst's diary he'd saved some of the next generation of children from suffering at the hands of the Musketeers and the rest of paedophile ring. Moreover, Axel was now safe.

In the last few weeks, Felix had turned his attention to his next and last victim: Lotte Holler. He had found her details in Horst's diary and wondered if the Musketeers had kept in touch with their go-between once they no longer worked together. He thought it unlikely - they would have had no use for her after her role in bringing to them their favourite kids became obsolete.

Lotte lived in the Berlin suburb of Kreuzberg, not far from the Oberbaum Brucke, where Felix's father Jakob had lost his life. Felix had been stalking Lotte on daily visits to Berlin for the past few weeks and he didn't have long before he left for England to see Martha. It was now or never.

Once Felix had planned his strategy he announced to Ingrid he was going to Berlin for a few days. 'I've some unfinished business to settle.'

Ingrid was afraid. 'I've heard on the news about the

police after this paedophile ring. I have the feeling…?'

'Tante. We promised. No questions.'

'You can't expect me to stay silent!' she cried.

Felix was adamant. 'I've no choice!'

She shook her head, frowning. 'Your quest might be the death of you.'

'Parents can rest easier in their beds knowing their children are a little bit safer. You're a mother now, you understand.'

'Stop it!' Ingrid was crying now. 'You're not some kind of vigilante who has to take the law into his own hands, and you don't have to do anything. You've come so far, you've got a good life now. Forget about those Torgau bastards!'

'Susi couldn't forget, and neither can I.'

'Felix, I'm scared. I don't want to lose you.'

'Tante, you won't lose me. I'm scared too, but it's something I have to do. Like you say, it is my quest.'

Ingrid cried, 'Stop talking like you are Don Quixote or something! He was delusional and was taken for a crazy fool.'

'Maybe Quixote was a Toreador in disguise,' Felix mused, thinking about the role he played and the music he used against the Musketeers. 'I may be crazy, but I'm no fool. Tante, let me ask you some questions. If anyone abused Axel, what would you do? Would you be satisfied if the police locked up the sicko, or would you want some revenge of your own? And onkel Klaus, what would he do?'

Ingrid concurred with a reluctant sigh of tacit approval, before asking, 'Won't you let me help you? I could be Quixote's mule.'

17. The Go-Between

Felix meticulously packed all the essentials for his task in a large rucksack. It was late

November and thick snow had arrived in Berlin. Undaunted by harsh winters and sometimes months of snow, it didn't stop people wrapping up warmly and going about their daily lives. The streets were gritted daily and the traffic continued to flow.

Felix arrived by train at Ost Bahnof, just as he'd done for the past few weeks in his surveillance of Lotte Holler. He took his usual route, walking along the long and wide avenue of Muhlenstrasse by the riverside where the city's infamous four metre high Wall was now a tourist spot called the East Side Gallery. Artists had the privilege of writing and drawing political messages and images on this section of the wall. The two murals Felix found the most striking were Erich Honecker and Leonid Brezhnev's mouth-to-mouth embrace and the Trabant bursting through the wall. Throughout the rest of the city the Wall had gradually been taken down, except for a few preserved areas that reminded modern Germany not to forget its past but to confront and acknowledge it.

Passing the imagery at the East Side Gallery Felix continued on, crossing the Oberbaum Bridge. The train rattled overhead, whilst the cars, cyclists and pedestrians passed through the bridge's ornate arches. Felix looked down into the icy water and thought, about the river going all the way to Muggelsee. With luck, he'd be taking the go-between to Muggelsee later that night; to her final destination.

Lotte Holler lived alone in a high-rise apartment building. She had a regular daily visit from a younger woman who came at lunchtimes when Lotte went home on her break. Felix worked out they were sisters from listening to Julia repeat her daily ritual as she rang on her sister's bell.

'Lotte, it's your one and only sister, Julia. I'll let myself in,' she often said.

Lotte drove an old car- a red VW Polo estate, that she used for shopping although she mainly walked or took the U-Bahn and the car remained parked outside her apartment in the street. She worked within walking distance of her apartment as a plain clothed security officer at Karstadt, one of a chain of large department stores found throughout Germany.

Felix had visited the store on his stalking visits to Berlin over the past few weeks, smartly dressed and disguised with a dark wig under a trilby hat. He'd eaten daily in the open-plan restaurant on the top floor, spending a few hours inside the store away from the icy winds outside, watching Lotte at work. There were security cameras all over the place and he'd been careful not to draw attention to himself. On one occasion Felix thought he'd been caught out.

'Excuse me, sir?' Lotte Holler said, in an accusatory tone. 'Come with me.'

Felix's pulse raced, turning slowly around to witness Lotte apprehending a young, male shoplifter, not much older than himself.

'Don't know what you're talking about!' the shoplifter yelled, lying through his teeth.

Lotte's voice grew hard and intimidating, speaking on her walkie-talkie. 'Hello, security, can I have some back up? I'm in the music department.'

'Be right there,' came the response.

'Empty your pockets,' she demanded to the shoplifter. 'You've got two unpaid items, namely CDs, in there.'

The shoplifter refused and turned to Felix. 'Did you see me take anything?'

Felix shook his head. He looked at Lotte, and was thankful she didn't recognise him, and swiftly moved along. The shoplifter made a dash for the exit and the security team was on him immediately, pinning him to the floor.

Felix put on his wet suit under his clothes in the male toilets in Karstadt. Luckily, it was lightweight and didn't restrict his movements. He'd already verified Lotte was at work having seen her in the toy department and stayed inside the store until it was about to close. He passed the store's post office on the way out and remembered it was here that he'd posted his typed letter to the police, detailing the paedophiles from Horst's diary. The memory made him smile. His quest was almost at completion.

Felix felt protected by the cold, snowy shadows of the night as he walked quickly to Lotte's apartment building, ice crunching beneath his feet and rubbing his gloves to warm his hands. He took off his wig and thermal hat, exchanging his headwear for a balaclava, and waited for half an hour in a darkened doorway for his victim to arrive.

Checking over his shoulder that the coast was clear, he primed his gun and crossed the road. Before Lotte knew it, a masked stranger was pointing a gun at her head and she was being dragged into a doorway. He applied duct tape roughly to her mouth and tied her hands behind her back.

He spoke in a menacing tone. 'Don't say a word. Give me your car keys.'

Lotte fumbled in her handbag. Felix checked the street to see it was clear and quickly dragged her the short distance to her car. She offered little resistance and he lifted her into the boot of the car, threw his rucksack and Lotte's handbag into the front passenger seat and drove out of Berlin, crossing the Oberbaum Bridge, heading for Kopenick. The journey took around 40 minutes and Lotte, after a few kicks and muted shouts remained eerily quiet throughout. She'd decided to save her energy until the car stopped at some unknown destination.

At Muggelsee, Felix remembered to park by the west jetty, and took a few minutes to gather his thoughts. The Musketeers and their cars were spread around the other jetties from North, South and East. Purposely, he'd chosen the West jetty for Lotte; a veritable wicked witch. There was light covering of snow on the ground and he needed to urinate. With the headlights on, he could see the snow change colour as he emptied his bladder. He felt a little strange, abducting a woman: it didn't seem right or natural but reminded himself that this was the heartless bitch who had time and again taken him and Susi to the Musketeers. He primed his gun and tentatively opened the boot of the car.

She had only just managed to free her hands and pull off her duct tape and her screams were loud enough to be heard on the opposite banks of the lake. Lotte kicked out at him and caught his hand with her foot, kicking his gun to the ground behind him. By the time she had wriggled out of the car, Felix had quickly retrieved the gun and was pointing it at her head.

'Not another step,' Felix barked.

Lotte screamed again. 'Help! Somebody help me!'

'Shut the fuck up! Or I'll hurt Julia.'

Lotte heard her sister's name and stopped screaming. How on earth did this man know her sister was called Julia? 'Nein. Bitte nicht! Don't hurt my Julia.'

'Fraulein Holler, now that I've got your attention…'

'What do you want with me?' Lotte asked, her voice trembling, alarmed to hear her name. Even more worrying was the fact that this crazed man knew Julia's name as well. 'You know me?'

He nodded. 'And you know me. So, let me tell you the rules. If you scream, try to run away or disobey, I'll not only go after Julia, I'll bash your skull in before I put a bullet between your eyes. So, listen to me and answer truthfully. Is that clear?'

Lotte nodded and bit back the tears. 'Where are we?'

'On the banks of Muggelsee.'

'Why have you brought me here?'

'I'm going to strip you!'

She gasped and began to cry. 'Are you going to rape me?'

'Don't flatter yourself. That's not what this is all about.'

'But it's so cold. I'll freeze to death.'

'Then you'll know how it felt when you hosed me regularly with icy cold water at Torgau,' he reminded her, cutting away at her clothing to leave her in just her underwear.

'You're a Torgau boy?'

'Yes. It's payback time,' he told her, in a spiteful tone.

Lotte stood in front of him in the freezing night air and began to shiver. She never thought a day like this would come and now it had. Someone wanted revenge. Her survival instinct kicked in and she told herself to outsmart this Torgau kid, knowing her life depended on it.

'What now?' she asked, standing tall and proud, not wanting to show any weakness.

Felix kept the gun pointed at her. 'A few questions,' he began. 'You knew what was going on and I want answers! Why did you take me to the Musketeers?'

'I was only obeying orders,' she replied.

'That's a Nazi kind of answer,'

'I'm not a Nazi,' she cried.

'You behaved like one. You were a go-between for the sodomites.'

Lotte was adamant, insisting, 'You were in Torgau as a punishment.'

Felix was outraged. 'I was an orphan, not a delinquent! Is rape your idea of punishment? Rape is a crime, and you assisted in systemised rape and buggery.'

Lotte was lost for words. She knew she had to be careful how she responded. He was a hurt and angry man but she felt no guilt for what she had done. All she could think about was how cold and afraid she was, and the mind blowing news she'd received earlier in the week. Lotte had discovered she was seven weeks pregnant with her married lover's child; she was going to keep the baby. She'd told Julia but no one else.

'I'm sorry,' she muttered feebly.

'You're not sorry. You enjoyed being in charge, dishing out punishments. You obeyed the Musketeers without question.'

'I was afraid of them too… I took you to the hospital ward, afterwards, didn't I?'

He scoffed at her reply. 'Luckily, there was one kind man at Torgau who didn't abuse us kids. He helped us and he saw you for what you are, a sadistic, heartless bully.'

Lotte was in denial. 'I'm not a bully. I'm a kind person, ask anyone.'

Felix wanted her to understand why she was in this predicament. 'You got control of us by taking away our dignity. You belittled us constantly and we didn't have a voice, we were beaten and sexually abused and no one listened to us. You turned us over to the Musketeers and persistently showed no empathy. It's what makes us human, our empathy and capacity for mercy.'

She didn't understand, and simply thought her assailant was mad. She was in denial about what he'd said. 'Who are you? Let's talk about this. Show me your face,' she demanded.

'No, I won't, and not because I'm afraid to. I don't want you looking at me the way you used to, when you thought you'd get away with it. Well, I'm the judge and jury now. Go into the water up to your knees and dance for me,' Felix said, turning on the music on his cassette and making a mock bull charge towards her.

'Allons, En garde! Allons! Allons! Ah! Toreador, engarde! Toreador, Toreador…'

Lotte obeyed. The temperature of water was zero degrees. She was feeling light- headed but jigged about to the music, hoping it would warm up her body.

'Please, stop this,' she begged.

He was adamant. 'Dance!

'Et songe bien, oui songe en combattent…'

'Please stop… I'm so cold.'

'Sit down!' Felix barked.

'What? In the water?' she asked in disbelief.

'Yes… Sit!'

'Qu'un oeil noir te regarde…'

Lotte obeyed and sat down in the water.

'Stand up!'

'Et que l'amour t'attend…'

She stood up.

'Sit down!'

Lotte sank back into the water.

'Toreador, Toreador, l'amour t'attend!'

'Stand up!'

She obeyed, stood up and cried, 'I'm sorry. I really am sorry.'

Felix turned off the music.

'I don't believe you! Sorry you got caught, more like. Anyway, the damage is done. Tell me, when did you last see Horst, Gunther and Harald?' he asked her. 'You do remember your friends - the Musketeers of Torgau?'

She nodded. 'A few years ago, we met up for a drink but I've nothing in common with them. I didn't want to keep in touch with them.'

'Oh, you think you're better than them?'

'I was only doing my job. I made mistakes at Torgau and I wasn't the only one… I'm a good person. Doesn't everyone deserve a second chance?'

'Second chance? Why? To abuse more kids?'

'I don't understand,' she wailed. 'Please, just let me go.'

Lotte Holler, I know who you are and so did the Musketeers. They knew you'd help them. Now you'll be joining them, your Torgau friends.'

'Where are they?' she queried.

'At the bottom of this lake.'

'No!' Lotte screamed, wetting herself with fear and warming the water around her.

'Did you think you were going to get away with it, like all the others who abused their positions of authority?' Felix spat, menacingly.

'You can't murder all of us! Who do you think you are?' she bellowed, with her last ounce of defiance.

'You've only got yourself to blame.'

Lotte fell to her knees. She couldn't swim and the icy waters beckoned. 'I don't want to die! Forgive me. Please, forgive me.'

'No one can hear you. Feeling sorry for yourself are you? Self-pity has a sell-by date and besides, you never felt sorry for me. Julia will miss you.'

'I'm pregnant! Please, think of my baby,' Lotte screamed in desperation.

This was unexpected. Maybe she's lying to save herself, Felix thought. He was not going to weaken now. Something he'd read jumped into his complex mind.

'In loco parentis,' he told her.

'What? I don't understand?'

'In Latin it means, 'In place of a parent'. You're not fit to be a mother!' Felix yelled and cracked the gun on the side of her head.

Lotte fell like a rag doll. He dragged her cold body to the

car and put her on the back seat. He took off his clothes to reveal the wet suit underneath and hurriedly stuffed all his belongings, including the gun, into his rucksack. In his haste, his knife jolted out and was left, unseen in the darkness, hidden behind a wheel of the car.

Felix switched on his torch, leaning it upright, illuminating a path to guide him when he would be swimming back towards the safety of the jetty. The thought of the icy water didn't deter him because with this final act, his quest was complete.

He turned the key in the ignition. It wouldn't start. 'Scheisse!' he cursed.

Felix looked at Lotte, lying comatose in the back and tried the ignition again. Flat battery. 'Stupid bloody car!' he shouted and pummelled the steering wheel.

He stopped to think about a solution. Luck had been with him previously, on the banks of Muggelsee with all three Musketeers. Had his luck deserted him? He could give Lotte a few more whacks on the head or hold her face down in the water to finish her off? But she was a female and it went against all he knew.

Felix had never hit any female before. The crack on the head he'd administered was simply to stun her and make it easier to get her into the car. He looked at Lotte. Blood from her head wound seeped onto the back seat and her body now had a strange blue hue. She looked pitiful and although Felix tried to suppress and dismiss it, he began to feel sorry for her.

What if she wasn't lying and she was pregnant? Then he'd knowingly be killing an unborn baby. He thought of Axel and how, despite the circumstances surrounding Susi's pregnancy and birth, he was glad he'd been born. Felix realised then that he could do no further damage to Lotte Holler. He'd inflicted enough pain and punishment and felt he'd got a satisfying revenge. Whether she lived or died didn't really matter anymore.

Felix put on his clothes again and collected what was left

of Lotte's garments from the jetty. He dressed her as best he could with the rags he'd shredded and put her thick coat over her body. The cold mist on the car windows predicted a long, hard night. He left her mobile phone beside her should she wake up, so she could phone for help.

He tried to start the car again, thinking about driving to a place where it would be quickly discovered, but there wasn't even a sputter from the engine. He found himself hoping she would survive the night and an early morning dog walker would discover her in the abandoned car. As he walked for about half an hour from the lake into the town of Kopenick, passing people, Felix worried that someone would remember him and give his description to the police once Lotte was discovered.

As a precaution, Felix decided not to travel south in the direction of Motzen but to go north. He caught the train back to Berlin and stayed the night at one of most expensive hotels in Berlin; Hotel Adlon by the Brandenburg gate. He signed in under a false name and paid for the luxurious accommodation in cash. It cost him 200 marks, money he felt was well spent. But as he unpacked his rucksack in the privacy of his room, he realised his boat knife was missing. The only time it could have fallen out was when he was changing at the lake, which meant it would be found near Lotte's car.

Felix berated himself for his carelessness. He'd left another clue at a crime scene- the first was his aqua shoe - but that couldn't be helped and was safely hidden in the depths of Harald's watery grave. Although he'd used gloves to handle his victims and their belongings, his boat knife had his fingerprints on it. He would have to ensure the police never got hold of his fingerprints to put in their data base files and tried to put this fear to the back of his mind.

The end of his successful quest was celebrated with a few beers in the alabaster marbled bathroom as he soaked away the chills and mental torments in a long, hot bath. He wished

Martha were with him and sharing the king size bed. It wasn't long before he would be with his beloved Martha, he thought, smiling, and now he could get on with the rest of his life. As for Lotte Holler, luck would decide her fate.

PART TWO

17 January 2005. Lotte Remembers

Lotte Holler looked in the mirror. The last time she looked at her face, a young reflection had smiled back. Now, a woman of 41 stared at her, a woman she only half recognised. She swore. Twelve years, she said to herself, twelve years of my life wasted lying in a bed, comatose.

She steadied herself on the Zimmer frame and took a deep breath. Her muscles were still weak even though the hospital physiotherapists had massaged her regularly over the past few weeks. They had helped improve her walking skills in the specially-equipped therapy studio where she had exercised in the warm waters of the hydrotherapy pool. Tentatively, she shuffled out of the bathroom in her room towards her armchair by the window, hearing the sounds outside of children's boisterous voices resonating in the school playground below. She looked out of the window and watched these children, apparently oblivious to the cold, running about in the snow, some of them making snowballs to throw at one another. They had their whole lives in front of them, she thought, as the painful memory of losing her own baby flooded back.

'You're not fit to be a mother!' Her assailant's words resonated in her head.

Was he right? Most children irritated her but maybe she'd have been different with her own. She'd never know now, because this option had been taken from her. How dare he, a Torgau boy, decide this for her? Lotte was full of hatred for what he'd done to her. If only she could work out his identity.

She needed time to think and the children outside disturbed her with their joviality. Play quietly, she grumbled inwardly, wishing these school children were as obedient as those at Torgau. They were quiet, sombre and hardly ever playful when they were outside in the prison's exercise yards.

Lotte's thoughts drifted to Julia's diluted yet diverse summary of 12 years of world events. Gerhard Schroeder was now the German leader, following Helmut Kohl who had stepped down in 1998. The Deutschmark had disappeared, replaced by a single European currency called the Euro. Germany was the figurehead in Europe now, having sufficient fiscal strength to dominate European politics. When Julia had told her Germany had bailed Greece out of debt a few years ago, Lotte found this amusing.

Lotte quipped, 'We didn't have to invade Greece this time. We just bought it!'

Julia had chuckled and continued with her news. Around the world there had been an aerial attack on the Twin Towers of the World Trade Centre in New York in September 2001 and the Towers collapsed with the world looking on. The new American President, George W. Bush, with the co-operation of British Prime Minister Tony Blair and the backing of the United Nations Security Council, then went to war in Iraq for the second time within a decade under the premise that weapons of mass destruction were being manufactured there. The access to oil may have played its part but Saddam Hussein was their main target and eventually he was toppled from power.

'Is oil any cheaper?' Lotte asked her sister, tongue in cheek.

'As expensive as ever,' Julia replied, with a wry smile.

'Do tell me something funny or unusual.'

Julia thought for a moment. 'Well… scientists cloned a sheep in 1997.'

Lotte shook her head in disbelief. 'Whatever next? I don't

think I've missed too much.'

Concluding her brief update, Julia told Lotte that Boris Yeltsin had been replaced by Vladimir Putin but the Germans had long left the Russians in their wake since the fall of the Berlin Wall. Modern technology had led the way forward, especially the advancement of mobile phones and computers, and communication had never been easier with the invention of a world wide web of instant information.

'Computers! I've got to learn how to use a computer?'

'Lotte, I'll help you. Frank and Tomas helped me. They use them all the time in schools and colleges and we've got a laptop at home.'

Frank and Tomas: Julia's children. This was the most important news she'd been given. Julia had become pregnant not long after Lotte had fallen into a coma. Lotte would have liked to see her sister's sons grow up but now they were eleven and nine and she'd missed so much. As yet, she'd only seen photos because Lotte didn't feel she should meet them until she felt stronger.

'Good looking boys,' Lotte commented, looking at a photograph of her nephews.

'I think so too. But then, I'm their Mutti,' Julia said, with pride.

'Thankfully they take after you and not Jurgen.'

'I think Tomas takes after Jurgen, Frank's more like our side of the family.'

'I'll be their Tante… Tante Lotte. I like it.'

'They'll love you like I do,' Julia assured her.

Lotte smiled at the memory of her conversation with her sister. If it wasn't for Julia, she thought, she wouldn't want to be alive.

The door opened. Half hidden behind a bunch of flowers was Julia. Lotte was now strong enough to put her arms around her sister. It touched her deeply, not only to have the strength to hold her but to be held in Julia's warm and safe embrace.

'Not more flowers, Lotte began. 'Don't waste your precious money on flowers.'

'The room needs a bit of colour,' ventured Julia.

Lotte smiled, 'You aside, I can't remember being shown such kindness. In here, I'm treated like royalty. I'm wondering if it's a case of mistaken identity and they think I'm Princess Diana in disguise!'

'Princess Diana died in a car crash about eight years ago.'

'Oh, How tragic,' exclaimed Lotte.

'London was full of flowers for her. It was very sad. I took the boys to London a few years ago.'

'You did?'

Julia nodded. 'When Jurgen and I separated, we needed to get away. The boys and I had our first holiday in years and we went on the train, through the Tunnel.'

'The Tunnel?'

'The Channel Tunnel- between England and France. It opened about ten years ago. You can take a train direct from Paris to London. We went from Berlin to Paris, had a few days there and went on to London. The boys loved it and so did I.'

Lotte took her sister's hand. 'I'm glad you had a holiday. I hope you had lots of holidays in the last 12 years because if you'd never had a break from visiting me, I'd feel you were trapped in this room just as much as I was.'

'I never left you for long, I couldn't. I know this sounds strange but I knew, I had no doubt at all, that you'd wake up one day.'

'Must be all those candles you lit for me.'

Julia frowned. 'Who told you that?'

'Never mind who told me! I'm just sorry you had to wait so long.'

'Can you remember any more details about what happened that night?' Julia asked.

'I get flashes,' she began. 'I get so angry when I think about it. A Torgau boy took my life away from me. All those precious, stolen years.'

Julia squeezed her sister's hand. 'I hate him too, but you know what goes through my mind? He wanted to kill you but at the last moment he changed his mind and dressed you to keep you warm until the dog walker found you the next morning.'

'Well, he obviously wasn't normal, attacking me in the first place. If he was here in the room with me, I'd know his voice and remember the athletic way he moved' Lotte stated, suddenly recalling, 'He insisted I dance for him and got quite a kick out of it. I remember he charged at me like a bull.'

'You've got to tell the police all this,' Julia urged. 'With all the modern forensics and psychology they can catch criminals for past crimes from all sorts of clues.'

'No! They'll bring up the past. What's done is done.'

'Oh, Lotte, don't be so silly. You're not on trial just because you worked at some youth prison in East Germany. It was attempted murder. He tried to kill you! And if he told you he'd killed before then he's a serial killer and has to be caught.'

'Ok, ok, don't nag. I'll talk to the police,' she conceded. 'I don't suppose I'll find peace of mind until he's brought to justice.'

'Good. I'll pop out and speak to Jonas - I mean Dr Roth,' said Julia, trying to conceal her feelings for her sister's doctor. 'I won't be long.'

Jonas Roth was in his office. The door was ajar and he sat up when Julia popped her head around the corner. 'Frau Kessler. Do come in and take a seat.'

She sat down. 'My sister is finally willing to talk to the police.'

Jonas smiled. 'Good. Well, then, I'll arrange things.'

'Thank you. I don't think this is going to be easy and I'm afraid the press will make life very difficult for me and my family. I've seen reporters sniffing around at the hospital entrance, asking if it's true about the Lady of the Lake waking up.'

'Frau Kessler, the staff are sworn to secrecy.'

'I trust you but when all this gets out, it'll be all over the news.'

'I understand your concerns but I think it's the right thing to do. All this can't stay a secret for too long. Lotte's a victim and the criminal must be caught, or at least the police given the information that will give them a chance to catch him.'

Julia nodded. 'You're right. My sister's a victim and she needs to tell her story.'

19. The Psychologist

Hanne Drais pushed her hand through her short, cropped fair hair. The style gave her a fresh, impish look for a woman of 36. She stretched out her long arms, releasing the tension in her back. She thought about getting out of her trouser suit - her usual choice of work clothes - and back into her preferred casual wear of jeans or jog pants, sweatshirt and T-shirt. She was looking forward to doing her back exercises once she got home, and it usually did the trick after a long day at work. She had just decided to call it a day and head home when there was a knock on her office door.

A whiff of cigar smoke blew into the room heralding the appearance of Kommissar Oskar Kruger. He popped his head around the door. 'You off?' he asked.

'Just about, Audrey will be home from school shortly, and she's cooking me dinner,' Hanne replied.

Kruger smiled. He had a rugged, lived-in face for a man approaching 50 and a greying stubble to hide the pockmarks of youth. The white shirt that his wife of 30 years had pressed for him that morning looked crumpled.

'Drais, give your daughter a call and tell her to have a meal waiting for you in the next hour or so. I need you for about half an hour, tops.'

Hanne looked at her daughter's photo on her desk. 'I feel like a bad mother. I hardly ever cook for Audrey.'

'She wants to be a chef like her father, doesn't she?'

Nodding, Hanne said, 'Her father lets her help out in the restaurant where he works, but she's 16 soon. You've got kids, you know they change their minds all the time.'

'Can't remember, my kids left home years ago,' Kruger said. 'Drais, you're not much of a cook anyway.'

'That's true. I'll text her, she hates me calling when she's with her friends,' Hanne said, picking up her mobile phone. 'So, what can't wait?'

'I've just been assigned a new case. You're going to love this one. You remember the 'Lady of the Lake' assault, back in 1992? I just got a call to reopen the case. She's woken up! Fucking miracle, eh, Drais?'

'Indeed!'

'The family are keen not to create a media circus but you know the press, they'll have a field day once we release an official statement. The 'Lady' in question, Lotte Holler, woke up on New Year's Eve. She's all there mentally and it's as if nothing has happened. She's been having intensive physiotherapy and psychotherapy at St Engel's hospital in Templehof to cope with her new life.'

'So you're opening the cold case file and opening a new investigation?'

'Damn right we are! The doctor we're liaising with said Lotte Holler heard loud music – some song the nurses were playing - and woke up, freaking out at the music.'

Hanne was curious. 'What was the song?'

Kruger looked at his notes and laughed as he read aloud. 'God, I hate opera. It was the Toreador song from the opera Carmen.'

Hanne ventured, 'This music must have great significance or trauma attachment deep in her psyche.'

'Well, you're the psycho-cop, you should know.'

'Has she got any family?'

'A sister. Apparently she's devoted to Lotte.'

Hanne's mobile chimed and she read her daughter's text. 'I'll need to talk to both sisters. Let me have the doctor's contact details and get me a copy of the cold case file and I'll do a preliminary profile of the assailant,' she said. 'Ok, I'm out of here… Audrey's cooking won't wait.'

Hanne took her bicycle from the police yard and set off through the snowy Berlin streets along the city's cycle paths adjacent to the gritted roads. She was into keeping fit. When she had turned 30, she'd decided the years of smoking, not enough exercise and fast food were taking their toll on her tall, lean frame. Her new fitness regime coincided with the break-up of her long-term relationship with her girlfriend, Claudia. In the past, Hanne had lacked energy and vitality but when she turned to yoga, walking, swimming and cycling it gave her a new lease of life. She fitted her new fitness regime around Audrey and juggled them both with her work as a criminal psychologist.

Neu Kolln was about half an hour cycle from police HQ. It was one of the most run-down areas in Berlin but rents were cheap and this made it fashionable for artists who had moved into the area. The gay community was at its largest here alongside neighbouring Kreuzberg as well as being home to Berlin's largest Turkish quarter and a wonderful array of Turkish food and delights.

Hanne had lived in this area since the fall of the Wall, when many buildings were empty and abandoned, squatting with groups of political females whilst attending Berlin's prestigious Humboldt University. As a young and socially conscious woman, similar to the rest of the group who married men without papers to assist their entry into Germany, Hanne wed a short, dark and handsome Chilean refugee called Rafael Solares but kept her own name.

At this point in her life Hanne was discovering her sexuality and when Rafael moved in with her at the squat they put up a united but false front as 'husband and wife' for the authorities. A brief fling produced Audrey, and by then Hanne met Claudia and fallen in love. Rafael continued to see his daughter on a regular basis and after three years and an amicable divorce, met his future wife, a German woman his own height. This time he married for love. Once Hanne received her psychology degree she began her police training and moved with Claudia, who worked as a nurse, and baby Audrey, into a three-bedroom flat overlooking the River Spree.

Three years ago, though, Claudia had moved out, ending their 11-year relationship. She quickly met a new girlfriend and moved in with her, keeping in touch with Hanne intermittently, more for Audrey's sake than her own. Hanne was devastated at the split and Audrey had mourned the loss of her second mother.

Hanne arrived home to the smell of ginger and spring onions wafting through the flat. Audrey was in the kitchen. A much shorter version of Hanne, she took her height from her father's side, although mother and daughter were similar facially. Both had fair hair but Audrey had exotic hazel eyes in contrast to Hanne's blue ones.

Audrey was a fashion-conscious, self-assured and independent teenager who knew her own mind. Sometimes she seemed more grown up than her mother, possibly because of Hanne's estranged relations with her own mother, Traudl. Though Hanne had a degree in criminal psychology, it was easier to work out other people and their motives than fathom her own relationships. Audrey understood her mother's complex personality and they got on reasonably well, both playing to each other's strengths and nurturing one another.

Hanne greeted her daughter with a kiss. 'Something smells good.'

'It's quorn, with spring onion and ginger sauce, with coconut rice.'

'Fab!' Hanne said with enthusiasm. 'Did you have a good day in school?'

'I've got a new maths teacher, Herr Lankwitz. He seems friendly enough.'

'Being friendly with the students isn't always a good thing. Is he a good teacher?'

Audrey shrugged her shoulders. 'Well, he's offering after-school maths classes.'

'Prima! Sounds as if he wants to make a good impression for his head teacher. I think you should go.'

'Mutti! Are you saying I'm rubbish at maths?'

'Audrey Solares Drais, your maths is about as good as my cooking!'

Later that evening mother and daughter sat on the sofa, nestled close to one another after watching Wallander, one of their favourite programmes, when Audrey brought up the touchy subject of Claudia.

'Claudia phoned today,' Audrey began, watching her mother's face showing signs of discomfort. 'She's got a spare ticket for the Banda Aceh relief concert at the Olympic stadium next week. Every German band or singer you can think of, past and present, will be there and Claudia wondered if I'd like to go.'

Hanne sat up. 'Then you must go.'

'Mutti, it's been three years. Claudia has moved on. Why can't you?'

Hanne sighed. 'Easier said than done. I wanted to be with Claudia for the rest of my life, then one day she woke up, took a look at me and didn't like what she saw. Said she didn't love me, said she'd made a mistake. How do you think that felt after 11 years? How can I ever trust anyone else again?'

Audrey delivered some tough love. 'You've got to! Stop feeling sorry for yourself. And remember; Claudia hurt me too by leaving.'

Hanne frowned. 'Well, you're obviously better at forgiving than me.'

'I'm not as stubborn as you or oma Traudl. You two won't forgive each other for past mistakes and usually, I have to tiptoe around the pair of you whenever we get together.'

Hanne laughed. 'My mother and I enjoy arguing!'

'I know it's easy for me to say, but there's plenty of people out there who've been hurt yet still go looking for love. Why can't you?'

'Hey! Who's the adult here?'

'I wonder that myself,' Audrey said, pouting her mouth in mock disapproval at her mother. 'Mutti, when was the last time you went on a date?'

'Cheeky! I had a few dates last year but it's all too much bother. I've got you, a few friends, work and besides, I'm busy keeping fit.'

'Mutti, I won't always be here, living with you. I don't want you to be lonely.'

Hanne put her arms around Audrey. 'Thank you, sweetheart, you've a wise head on young shoulders, but don't worry about me. If you must know, my friend Karin has arranged a blind date for me next weekend. A group of us are going to see 'Kill Bill 2' at the cinema, followed by a meal.'

Audrey's face lit up. 'Prima!'

'Her name is Brigitte, and I'm probably not her type.'

'Mutti, you're beautiful. Promise me you'll leave Claudia's ghost hidden before you meet Brigitte. Even if she's not your type, give her a chance - she could grow on you. Now, I'm off to bed. Don't sit and wallow too long.'

Audrey kissed and hugged her mother goodnight. Hanne thought how lucky she was to have such a lovely daughter: bright, sensitive, and full of insight. And feisty, just like all the women in the Drais family.

She went into the kitchen and started on the pile of washing up. Covering the walls were framed collages of photos from various stages of Hanne's and Audrey's lives. Perusing the photos and trying not to be over sentimental, her attention was drawn to the photo taken on the night the Berlin wall came down. Hanne called this her 'banana' photo. Four people in a time capsule: Audrey, her beautiful baby, a younger, punky version of Claudia, herself - and the boy in the photo, holding a banana, wasn't he called Jens?

He was a funny little thing, she remembered, with his wig and scarred ears. 'I wonder what happened to him?' she asked herself.

20. Birthday surprises

At the end of January, 2005, Felix Baum celebrated his 30th birthday with his friends and family at their golf club. He was no longer Felix Waltz: he'd changed his name to Baum when he was 21 after inheriting his oma's house in Motzen. Felix lived there with his wife Martha and their two-year-old daughter, Peonie. The past decade had been kind to the former Torgau boy. Felix had a happy marriage and enjoyed fatherhood, and the profits from the golf club and the lake had made him and his family comfortable beyond their dreams.

Now in their early 50s and semi-retired, Klaus and Ingrid remained fairly active. They were happy to oversee the management side of their business and enjoy the profits, along with Bernd, who was still the Mayor in nearby Zossen. Axel was now a bright young man of 15 with long fair hair, who outside school hours enjoyed helping wherever he could, working alongside his onkel Felix who was now the manager of the family enterprise.

These days Felix sported short, fair hair just long enough to cover the small but visible scars on his ears. Marrying Martha once she'd finished her law degree, they took a gap year and backpacked their way around Britain, Europe, the USA and Australasia. On their return, Martha got a job as a junior lawyer in a large, Berlin law practice and commuted daily from Motzen.

Felix, Axel, Klaus and Bernd shared a love of golf and as

well as playing together liked to take annual trips to prestigious golfing events: the British Open, the US Masters and Open and - the one they enjoyed the most - the bi-annual Ryder cup between Europe and the US. These trips served to strengthen their close bonds.

Peonie's impending birth in late September 2002, around the same time as the Ryder Cup Golf tournament was being played in England at The Belfry. This tournament had been cancelled in 2001 after the attacks on the World Trade Centre and the tournament had switched to even years. It had been a three-year wait for their anticipated trip and Martha insisted Felix went with Axel, Klaus and Bernd, as it wasn't far to travel home should she go into labour. They felt the break was worthwhile especially after seeing their fellow German, Bernard Langer, win his singles match, and Europe won the Ryder cup by three points. Felix returned home and luckily, his daughter was overdue and born a few weeks later on 11th October.

Peonie Angele Sofie Baum was the image of her mother, a beautiful, energetic and happy child. All the adults fussed over her and she was a source of great pride and joy to her family. Klaus and Ingrid were helpful, first-time grandparents and Ingrid caught glimpses of her beloved sister Sofie's smile when Peonie laughed.

Dr Jens had recently retired and Martha's mother, Angele, took the role of looking after her first grandchild when her daughter eventually returned to work. Angele drove down daily from Kopenick to look after Peonie, sometimes accompanied by Jens. Their son Friedrich had married a local girl, Heike, and lived close by Jens and Angele in Kopenick. They were expecting their first child in the summer and Jens and Angele would be in demand as babysitters.

Felix awoke on his 30th birthday morning to his wife bringing him breakfast in bed.

'Thank you, sweetheart,' he cooed, smiling broadly and

putting the breakfast tray aside to kiss Martha and pull her into his arms. Felix never wanted their kisses to stop and often it turned amorous but sometimes they were interrupted by the patter of tiny feet.

Papa! Peonie squealed, rushing in and jumping on the bed, separating the lovers.

Felix listened to his wife and daughter singing 'Happy Birthday' to him, and applauded them. 'Thank you, my darlings.'

Martha pulled a bag from under the bed filled with presents. 'I was thinking, what do you give the man who has everything? Hopefully, I've come up with a few surprises. Peonie helped me wrap them, didn't you sweetie?'

Felix kissed his daughter. 'What a lovely surprise. I wonder how many more surprises I'll have today?' he ventured, looking at his wife.

'Who knows?' Martha replied, and her eyes held a mischievous glint.

It was a change for Felix to lie in bed. He was usually up at the crack of dawn, but today was his birthday; a Sunday, and he was taking the day off. He had not forgotten about his twin sister in any of the many celebrations he'd experienced since her death and wondered how different life would have been if Susi were alive and sharing this birthday with him. He was in good health and had a good life. He loved his family and felt lucky to have a loving wife and daughter, and then there was Axel. He loved his nephew in a different way to Klaus and Ingrid, and luckily, the bond Felix shared with Axel had remained special.

His Torgau life now seemed foreign to him. He'd read somewhere in an opening line of a book, about the past being like a foreign country, where people do things differently. Felix was different back then but he had changed and grown up. Nevertheless, there was always something nagging away in the dark recesses of his mind to remind him of who he was and what he'd done. Over the years, Felix had hidden his secrets well.

Klaus, Ingrid and Axel came for lunch, bringing more presents. Felix felt boyishly happy to be spoilt by his family. After a jovial meal, they sat around the fire, together, with a freshly made pot of coffee and pastries. The lunchtime news came on. Dominating the headlines was the news about the Lady of the Lake. Felix almost choked on hearing the breaking bulletin and spat out the coffee, surprising everyone in the room. 'Sorry,' he apologized, 'I burnt my mouth.'

Ingrid wasn't so sure it was the coffee. She paid attention to how intently Felix watched the news and for the first time since he was 17 and had returned home with rope burns on his neck, she had an uneasy feeling in her stomach.

The newsreader made the following announcement.

'Earlier today, the Berlin police announced that the 'Lady of the Lake', Fraulein Lotte Holler, is now recovering in hospital in Berlin having awoken from a coma on New Year's Eve. Attacked by an unknown assailant in 1992, she was left to die in freezing temperatures in her car on the banks of Muggelsee, near Kopenick. At the time she was seven weeks pregnant but the baby did not survive. Fraulein Holler is responding well to treatment and is now helping police with their inquiries.'

The archive television footage showed Lotte's car on the banks of Muggelsee. The rest of the family was only half listening to the news but Felix was feeling sick and desperate for some fresh air.

'Who's up for a walk?' he asked. 'Or a boat ride?'

'It's snowing!' Martha replied. 'I know it's your birthday but you don't mind if I stay by the fire, do you sweetheart?'

Axel chirped up. 'Onkel, I'll go out on a boat with you.'

'You're on,' Felix told him, and hurried out to the entrance hall where he put on his coat and boots. He ran out of the door, managing to reach a nearby tree just in time to vomit behind it, hopefully unseen by his family.

Felix and Axel took turns steering a small, motorboat

with a cabin out onto the lake. They both enjoyed being out on the water. There wasn't a need for conversation: they could be quiet together, taking in nature and their environment. It was just what Felix needed to gather his thoughts and try to calm himself.

He was ruminating how the go-between had come back to haunt him, on his 30th birthday of all days. Was this more than just a coincidence? Lotte Holler had been telling the truth about her pregnancy. Would she remember any details that could lead to his door? Regurgitating it all in the whirling torments of his mind, Felix worried about the clues he'd left behind at the scenes of his crimes.

In Plaumann's car was his aqua shoe but more importantly, he had mislaid his boat knife when he was with Lotte Holler. It wasn't an ordinary knife; it was a Herbertz, a classic, top of the range, German knife made of stainless steel with rivets elaborated with a cocobolo wood handle. It had a lanyard hole, a rescue gut hook blade, a razor sharp, three-inch, serrated blade, a marlin spike and sturdy pliers attached to it. Felix kept this knife proudly in a black leather sheath with a Herbertz crest emblazoned on the handle as well as the blade - and his fingerprints were all over it. This boat knife, which the newspapers reported had been found by Lotte Holler's car, would have indicated to the police that the perpetrator of the crime had more than a keen interest in watersports and boats. He knew that clues that seemed innocuous in the beginning could magnify and profiles of perpetrators would be formed and trails followed.

Felix reminded himself that he'd never been in trouble with the police and they didn't have his fingerprints on file, yet he knew that if he was discovered he stood to lose all he had, and especially the love of his family and the life he had built with them. He tried to block out the many imponderables and 'what ifs' from his mind because his family would be disappointed if he wasn't enjoying himself on his birthday and instead, was looking troubled and unhappy.

When he returned home after his boat ride with Axel, all the family had disappeared. Felix knew Martha was plotting a surprise party for him and was glad to be alone for a while, so he steadied his nerves with a beer and a bath.

His thoughts raced around in circles as he regurgitated over the details of the murders and Lotte Holler's abduction. He believed he'd successfully diverted the police away from his doorstep by sending them the list of names in Horst's diary. The Musketeers' prolonged absence from their families as well as the police wanting to question them meant there was substance to the charges against them. Evidence pointed to the belief that the Musketeers had fled the country or were possibly hiding under a pseudonym. No one thought they had been murdered and were hidden in watery graves.

As Felix lay in the bath, he asked himself if a person deserves to die. Death, he reasoned, is, after all, everyone's final destination but what if a person does not respect the sanctity of life? Behaviour towards others is a measure of ourselves. If there is not any dignity, compassion and respect of personal boundaries for others, there is always a ransom to be paid - and a forfeit.

But who decides the forfeit? Felix had decided the price to be paid. He had played God, judge and jury. Who gave him this right? But then who gave the Musketeers the right to abuse him? This question could be asked of anyone in the annals of time who had participated in genocide, murder, crimes against humanity and rape, to name but a few. It came down to choices, personal preferences where it was the individual's free will that decided their actions. The Musketeers and the go-between had made their choices and Felix had made his. And he was resolute: he had no regrets about it. The forfeit he chose for them was to pay with the most precious thing anyone can ever have: life itself. With an obvious exception: Lotte.

When he heard Lotte Holler had woken up on the news

he was at odds with what he was feeling. He'd thought about her regularly over the years but without remorse, and the case remained unsolved as the years passed and Lotte remained in a coma. Felix found himself strangely glad that she would have a second chance at life. All the hate inside him had long since subsided and although he was anxious she'd give the police clues that might incriminate him he was fairly confident he'd got away with it.

The press had unkindly revealed Lotte Holler was pregnant at the time of her attack and Felix felt a certain vindication because he hadn't actively killed an unborn child. No, he felt the price she'd paid was justified. Her forfeit for her years as the go-between had been 12 years in a coma and the loss of her unborn child and possibly the rest of her childbearing years. As for himself, he hoped that losing Susi and all the abuse he'd suffered at Torgau balanced up what he'd done to Lotte. Maybe he'd be lucky and there would be no further price for him to pay.

Felix sank under the warm water. Retribution was morally wrong and unlawful, he told himself, but if Axel or Peonie were threatened he would do it all over again. No qualms about it. Not someone who prayed, he now prayed not to be caught. A crucifix had helped him survive when Harald was choking him to death and he had nearly drowned along with the Musketeer. Maybe, a little prayer might help him now.

Felix heard movement in the house and Martha came into the bathroom.

'Hi, sweetheart. You ok?' she asked. 'You've been miles away today.'

He lied. 'Sorry. I'm tired, that's all.'

'Why don't you have a siesta? We've a late night planned.'

'Oh, you have, have you? So, what's happening later?'

'Wait and see. All you have to do is put on a nice shirt for me, and smile!'

Felix smiled. 'Ok.'

Martha winked. 'Tante Ingrid's got Peonie for a while… and I'm joining you in bed.'

Later that day the family threw a party at the golf club. They waited patiently in the dark when they knew the VIP's arrival was imminent. Axel relayed a message to the guests that his Felix had just pulled into the car park. The lights were swiftly turned on when the guest of honour; Felix, with Martha and Peonie walked through the door.

'SURPRISE!'

Everyone who was important to Felix seemed to be present. Bernd, Ute, his cousins Anna and Heidi with their spouses, his parents-in-law, Jens and Angele, Martha's brother Friedrich and his pregnant wife Heike. The relatives from Rugen made a surprise visit: Gisela, Nadia, her husband Olaf and their son, Lutz, with his wife; and Felix's friends Carsten and Paul came with their girlfriends.

Ingrid pushed a trolley with a two-tiered chocolate cake out of the kitchen. Stevie Wonder's 'Happy Birthday' came over the loud speakers and everyone began to sing before an excited Peonie helped her papa blow out 30 candles.

The family had a good time together dancing to the music that Axel had mixed on a computer console in his role as the disc jockey for the night. Felix, with various members of the family watching him, opened a pile of presents. His face dropped for a second

unwrapping Bernd's present: a top-of-the-range Herbertz boat knife in a case.

'And look after this one!' Bernd told him. 'That's the third Herbertz knife I've bought you in a decade.'

'Thanks onkel Bernd. I'll try not to lose this one.'

Felix knew he'd lost the first one at the scene of the crime when he was with Lotte Holler and he'd replaced it himself, so not to cause suspicion at home, but this one had fallen overboard into the lake at Motzen. Felix felt it was an omen that he wasn't meant to own such a prestigious knife. Possibly, it brought him bad luck and he'd made do for several years with a marine knife of a lesser brand and quality.

Ingrid noticed Felix's discomfort at Bernd's gift. He couldn't hide things easily from her, she knew him too well. She noticed his nuances, his mood swings and tonight she knew something was troubling him. Her instincts were often right and began to feel worried about him. It was time they had a private talk. Not tonight though, she told herself; let him enjoy his birthday.

Jens was thinking along the same lines. He'd heard the news about 'The Lady of the Lake' awakening from her coma and that it was his ex Torgau colleague, that notorious witch, Lotte Holler. Jens and Felix had not spoken about Torgau since Susanne's funeral, although in the beginning of Felix's relationship with his daughter Martha he used to advise her how to handle a boy from Torgau. Jens didn't intend mentioning anything about their shared Torgau past with his son-in-law, and certainly not on his birthday, not unless Felix wanted to talk about it. It was a subject that was best left buried.

Instead, Jens patted his son-in-law on the back. 'So, young man, how's it feel to be 30?'

Felix quipped, 'No different to yesterday.'

'Angele and I hope you like your present from us. I thought now you have entered another decade, you might appreciate a night at the opera,' Jens ventured, passing Felix an envelope.

Felix opened the envelope and pulled out a pair of tickets. To his dismay, they were for Carmen. The last time Felix heard the Toreador song was on the banks of Muggelsee with Lotte Holler. He never wanted to be reminded of that night or hear the music again and he'd thrown away his recording of the aria.

'Thank you, Jens,' he said, trying to hide his feelings of discomfort.

'You're welcome. It's on at the Berlin Opera House so you'll have to wear a tuxedo. I rather like the Toreador song, and if my French is up to scratch, I believe the chorus translates as something like, 'Toreador be ready, dream even when you're fighting, that a black eye is watching you' - that's the black eye of the bull — 'and love awaits you, Toreador'. I hope you'll love it as much as I do,' Jens enthused.

'I'll go and find Angele to thank her,' said Felix, trying to make a quick escape.

Jens noticed Felix's discomfort and glancing down at his hands saw new signs of eczema.

'Felix, you know if there's anything troubling you, I'm here for you. You're like a son to me and if you want talk it'll be between us,' Jens told him.

'I'm ok, but it's good to know,' Felix replied and hugged Jens.

Approaching midnight, Martha led Felix onto the dance floor.

'Peonie's asleep in the back office. Gisela's watching over her.'

'It's been a long day for her. I'm tired too.'

'I'm not surprised. How many beers have you had?'

'I've lost count. I haven't had a drink in ages and it's my party!' he declared. 'I've had a great day. Thank you, sweetheart.'

'Don't thank me, Ingrid and Axel planned it. They love you… everyone loves you,' she told him, proudly and kissed him.

'I'm very lucky to have such a lovely family. It'll be your 30th in the summer.'

'Don't remind me, we're all getting old.'

'Martha, I'll love you at 90. You're beautiful, whatever your age. But what shall I give the girl who has everything?' he joked. 'I think I'll take you away, just you and me, to some exotic beach where it's nice and hot. What do you say?'

'That would be nice. So, tell me, when you blew out the candles on your cake, what did you wish for?' she whispered in his ear.

Kissing her, he declared, 'I've all that I could ever have wished for, right here in my arms. I love you.'

'I love you, too.'

They kissed again and rested their foreheads together.

'Surely you want something?' she asked. 'I mean, you don't think there's anything missing from our lives?'

Felix shook his head. 'I'm the luckiest man alive to have you and Peonie.'

'Maybe there's more to come,' said Martha, unable to keep her precious, six week old secret to herself one moment longer. 'Because, my darling, our holiday will have to wait until next year. Hopefully, I've saved the best birthday present until last… we're having another baby.'

21. Standards

Dr Jonas Roth arrived at Berlin's Brandenburg gate police station first thing on Monday morning carrying a briefcase. He signed in at reception and took the lift up to Kruger's office, marching in and slamming the door behind him. In the room was Kruger's deputy, Detective Inspector Stefan Glockner, a dark-haired man in his 30s of medium build and height, sporting a goatee beard. He was dressed in a favourite brown suede jacket, sitting in an armchair close to the window, mulling over a case file and drinking coffee.

Kruger and Glockner both sat upright at the abrupt intrusion.

Dr Roth was fuming. 'Kruger! What on earth's going on?'

Kruger was flummoxed. 'Sorry?'

'I thought I made it very clear that any of Lotte's details you released to the press were going to be censored, but yesterday the Lady in the Lake was the lead story on the television news!'

'Do you want me to leave?' Glockner asked his boss, rising from his chair.

'No, you stay. I need someone to witness his outburst.'

Glockner sat down.

'Herr Doktor. Don't come barging into my office! We agreed, the press would be drip fed to avoid a media circus - and it's Kommissar Kruger to you,' he added, churlishly.

Jonas slammed a newspaper down on Kruger's desk. Lotte Holler was front page news.

'And this? What have you got to say about this, Kommissar?'

The newspaper headline jumped out at Kruger and Glockner: LADY OF THE LAKE WAS PREGNANT.

Kruger was adamant. 'I didn't tell the media a bloody thing!'

Jonas felt indignant. 'Damn it! It's an invasion of privacy!' he shouted.

Glockner stepped in to calm things. 'If I recall, back in 1992 when the crime took place, the press somehow got hold of the victims' details about her pregnancy. It'd be worth considering if it was the staff in the hospital who told the press or if the journalists simply looked back in the archives.'

This idea momentarily stopped Jonas in his tracks.

Kruger could always count on Glockner's logic. 'Dr Roth, this is my deputy, Detective Glockner, who is assisting me on the case.'

The doctor shook Glockner's hand.

'Unfortunately when the media have a story to tell they have a habit of sensationalising, and Lotte Holler's private life is merely fodder for them,' continued Kruger. 'I'll investigate whether it was leaked by hospital staff, but it stops now!' Dr Roth insisted. 'It was an invasion of the family's private grief. Isn't it enough that someone spends years in a coma? Yesterday it was all over the television news and today it's in the morning papers so the whole country knows Lotte Holler was pregnant and lost her baby.'

'As I said, some clever journo probably looked back to the attack in 1992,' Kruger reassured the doctor. 'After all, this was common knowledge at the time.'

The tense atmosphere in the room began to ease.

'Julia - Frau Kessler, Lotte's sister - was quite upset by it all. She was in tears yesterday at the hospital. Lotte must be protected- she's very fragile.'

'Please pass on my apologies to Frau Kessler,' Kruger said sincerely. 'We don't want the patient or her family upset.'

The doctor nodded appreciatively. 'Thank you.'

'Can I get you a coffee?' Glockner asked.

'No, thanks, I'm due at the hospital. I believe I'm meeting your colleague Hanne Drais this afternoon. I've arranged for Frau Kessler to be present and then the process of interviewing Lotte can begin. Thank you for your time. Good day.'

Jonas left the room in a civilised manner, closing the door quietly behind him. He'd been incensed on Julia's behalf with the media coverage. As Lotte's doctor, he understood the ramifications of the media intruding on her fragile psyche but it was also Julia he wanted to protect. Jonas kept his growing but unspoken feelings for her private but even so, he didn't want Julia hounded by the press for photos, interviews and statements in her role as next of kin to the victim. On his way back to the hospital, he felt a bit embarrassed about how he'd handled himself in front of the police officers, but at least they were now under no illusions that this case had to be handled with sensitivity or they'd have him to deal with.

Oskar and Stefan simultaneously let out a huge release of air.

'Fuck that for a Monday morning briefing,' Oskar exclaimed. 'Who the hell did he think he was, storming into my office like that?'

'Doughnut, boss? I feel like something sweet.'

'Yeah, and while you're raiding the staff canteen, get Drais in here.'

Carrying a small tray with an assortment of biscuits and pastries, Stefan bumped into Hanne in the corridor.

'The Kommissar wants to see you in his office,' he told her. 'We've just had Lotte Holler's doctor in, shouting and stamping his feet at the press intrusion. Be warned, Kruger might be a little grumpy.'

'Nothing new there,' Hanne remarked, distracted by the

tray of goodies. 'I see you want to sweeten him up?'

'One of us has to. Here, Drais, have a doughnut,' he said, placing one gently into Hanne's open mouth.

Hanne wasn't in the best frame of mind. She had a hangover from her outing last night with her friends where she had met Brigitte, her blind date, and they'd got on well and agreed to meet up again. To steady her nerves Hanne had drunk too much beer and was now suffering the consequences of her over-indulgence. At breakfast, Audrey had enthusiastically asked her lots of questions which Hanne was not in the mood for. All she wanted to do was return to her bed and mother and daughter had parted company on grumpy terms.

Hanne went into Kruger's office in an apprehensive frame of mind.

'Drais, there you are. Grab a seat, a coffee and a cake.'

His pastries were mostly all gone and only a few biscuits were left over. Stefan had doughnut sugar all over his goatee beard. Hanne passed him a tissue and he wiped his face. They were like brother and sister, friends one minute, arguing the next, and as colleagues on good, collaborative terms. With their mutual, dry sense of humour there was rarely a dull moment.

'I've had one, thanks. Got to watch my figure.'

Hanne looked at Kruger with a 'best he said nothing' kind of look.

'Right.' Kruger began reading information from the open file on his desk. 'This is what we have... You've both read the files, haven't you?'

Hanne and Stefan nodded.

'Ok. In the winter of 1992, Lotte Holler was found unconscious after blows to the left side of her forehead. She was found the following morning by a dog walker, on the back of her car, an old, red VW Polo Estate on the banks of Muggelsee, near Kopenick.'

They all perused some gruesome photos of Lotte Holler

taken at the crime scene.

'Blows to the left side at the front would indicate the assailant was right handed,' Stefan said. 'Do we have any idea what object caused the injury?'

Kruger shook his head. 'A hard, blunt object, but not a rock, and possibly the handle of a gun. The victim's clothes had been cut and shredded. Her clothes and coat had been placed over her like a blanket, indicating someone else had dressed her. Her mobile phone was right beside her and her handbag hadn't been touched. There were no signs of sexual assault, nor after examination was there any evidence of sexual intercourse.'

'So we can rule out theft, rape and a sexual motive,' stated Stefan.

'I think so,' said Kruger. 'Even though her clothes were cut-off at some point.'

'Sounds like the assailant asked her to strip, possibly to make her feel the cold and be afraid for her life. Or to humiliate her, you get control by humiliation,' Hanne ventured. 'Maybe that's why he asked her to dance.'

Kruger quipped, 'Yeah, dancing on ice! Ok, we'll agree there was some sort of power struggle going on.'

'There's the old adage that most murders or attempted murders usually have a sexual or financial motive. So if it's not sexual, maybe it was about money, some sort of blackmail?'

'Unlikely, Glockner,' Kruger mused. 'Lotte was a security guard working at Karstadt and living in a high-rise building in Kreuzberg, and hardly the sort to be blackmailed.'

'Not far from where I live now,' Hanne remarked. 'Not much money in my area- and even less back then.'

'Well, you're not due a pay rise,' Kruger said, trying to read between the lines.

Hanne did not react to her boss's gibe.

Stefan perused a different avenue. 'A large percentage of women who are attacked know their assailant.'

'I'm certain they had met before, even if Lotte didn't

know who it was - he was probably wearing a mask,' Hanne explained. 'This crime has revenge written all over it, and the man simply wanted to punish her.'

'The bastard did a damn good job of punishing her. Putting her in a long term coma is a pretty severe kind of revenge.'

'Oskar, I believe he set out to kill her but for some reason couldn't go through with it,' ventured Hanne. 'He even left her mobile phone beside her in case she woke up to call for help. That's a big U-turn - but why? He went to a lot of trouble kidnapping her in Berlin and taking her to Muggelsee, planning it down to the smallest detail.'

Kruger frowned and scratched the stubble on his chin. 'But if he didn't plan to kill her, why be so violent?'

Hanne was quite animated. 'Violence equals control. I think he changed his mind and was torn. Of course he could have helped her if he didn't want her to die, and he could have called an ambulance instead of leaving her overnight to freeze in a car. But in case Lotte did survive, he left her with access to a phone and dressed her to give her half a chance. My guess is he didn't care about the outcome in the end and left Lotte's fate in the lap of the gods.'

'Fine, we agree that Lotte knew her attacker. What about an ex-lover?' Stefan asked. 'I believe the father of her child was a married man, so he'll be worth revisiting.'

Kruger stated. 'Sadly, in 1992, Lotte's married lover was ruled out at the time with a cast iron alibi.'

Rolling her eyes, Hanne said, 'That doesn't surprise me. Besides, I don't believe it was a crime of passion. There's every indication that Lotte Holler was afraid, which is why the music freaked her out. When a victim is afraid, the assailant is more likely to be a stranger to them but often a stranger who knew her and had something against her, if that makes sense.'

'Maybe a work colleague, then?' Stefan suggested. 'We'll try and get hold of all the old timesheets, records of Lotte's colleagues at Karstadt, see if anyone had a grudge against her and take a fresh look at it from that angle.'

'Ok. So, let's look at what clues were left at the scene of the crime,' Kruger stated. 'A Herbertz boat knife, with special attachments, was found under the wheel of the car, and some boat rope was left on the ground near the water.'

'That could have been there already. It's a lake, people fish at lakes.'

'Obviously, Stefan, your papa never took you fishing,' quipped Kruger. 'It was too cold for fishing! The boat knife and its leather sheath was the only piece of evidence that had unidentified fingerprints on it. We've kept it at our forensics storage unit along with Lotte's car. Back then, we didn't have a criminal DNA data base but now, thanks to some Oxford professor, we do.'

'Our chief forensic officer- Korfsmeier, would beg to differ, if he were here. Don't you remember he told us that it was Sir Alex Jeffreys, who discovered the variations in DNA in genetic fingerprinting back in the mid-1980s? Yes, he went to Oxford but he's actually a professor at the University of Leicester.'

Kruger scoffed, 'Well, Glockner, like Korfsmeier, you're a know-it-all, so take that smug look off your face.'

'Will you two stop throwing your dummies out of the pram?' Hanne told them.

'Drais, we're enjoying ourselves,' Kruger grimaced and quickly returned to his notes. 'The boat knife had a minuscule strand of anchor rope attached to a lanyard. It's possible the knife belonged to the assailant and he works with boats, angling, or aquatic sports, something of that nature.'

'So, we're looking for a Marine Boy,' Stefan declared.

'Hey, everyone, that's our new nickname for our assailant - Marine Boy,' confirmed Kruger. 'An opera-loving Marine Boy!'

Hanne ignored the two of them. 'Did forensics pick up any fibres in Lotte's car?'

'It'll all be gone over again. Korfsmeier will love that,'

Kruger said. 'Of course, there's the risk of cross contamination after all these years.'

Hanne reminded them, 'I'm meeting Dr Roth and Frau Kessler at the hospital in Tempelhof this afternoon.'

'Well, you'd better mind your manners with Lotte's doctor. He came marching into my office earlier this morning, shouting the odds. I think he's programmed like the bloody Terminator Two - a robot, protecting Lotte Holler at all costs.'

Stefan piped up, 'Yeah, you should've been here with Dr Caveman.'

'Whatever you do, Drais, don't talk to the fucking press!'

'There's a small number that camp daily outside the hospital entrance,' Stefan added.

'I've no intention of talking to anyone about the case outside of this office. I'll use a different entrance,' Hanne told them. 'You know what really intrigues me about this case? What incensed this man to attack Lotte Holler so violently?'

'Marine Boy might just be some kind of a nutcase.'

Drais was adamant. 'No, Stefan, he's not some random nutcase. And if I'm right about them knowing one another, maybe Lotte did something to provoke her assailant and whatever it was, precipitated the attack - not that I'm condoning it.'

'You mean, tit for tat?'

'Possibly, Oskar. Maybe they shared some bad, past experience. But something pricked this man's conscience which says he was capable of showing empathy to his victim.'

'Just because he didn't kill her doesn't mean he's a nice guy. Marine Boy took Lotte Holler there with the intention to harm her. It's attempted murder,' stated Stefan.

'I didn't say Marine Boy was a nice guy,' Hanne replied, realising she was joining in with her colleagues's penchant for nicknaming suspects. Oh what the hell, she thought, if it helps lighten the mood when working with dark and grisly cases.

'Marine Boy is, or was a troubled soul. Of course he's damaged, but he's also capable of being normal.'

Glockner was flabbergasted. 'Normal? Murder isn't normal?'

Drais continued. 'To show empathy, you have to be taught it. Marine Boy's complex for sure, but he has a conscience. Even if he planned it, he couldn't kill Lotte Holler, so someone loved him at some point and taught him about empathy.'

'What do you mean, that he was a troubled soul? Do you think he's dead?'

Marine Boy may be dead, who knows? What I mean is, it's 12 years ago and a lot can change in a person's mental health in that time.'

Kruger requested. 'Enlighten us, Drais.'

'Sure. Well, the definition of a psychotic is; what they are thinking is their reality. If Marine Boy thought about killing Lotte, then he had to act on his feelings.'

'So, we're looking for a pretty screwed-up individual,' Kruger surmised.

Hanne continued. 'Marine Boy's state of mind could be worse or better. Mental health often fluctuates throughout our lives, depending on our circumstances. There are low and highs and manic episodes or just a steady, ok kind of flow. It depends if Marine Boy is emotionally literate or in denial.'

'Oh, Marine Boy knows he's done it all right and he's got away with it up until now, but I'm going to nail the bastard,' Kruger pledged.

'I meant, Marine Boy probably thinks he's normal or at least pretends to be. Take us three as an example, we're hardly normal but we think we are.'

'Yeah, yeah, Drais, very droll. Don't overload on psychobabble,' said Kruger. 'So, what are you really saying about Marine Boy?'

'I'm saying, when he attacked Lotte, it could have been a

stage in Marine Boy's life. Maybe his mental health has improved and he's put his past behind him - and now he's just as normal as the three of us.' Hanne smiled when she said this, watching their astonished faces.

Hanne waited in Dr Roth's office. She noticed how pristine everything was; a tidy desk with in and out trays, flowers in a vase that gave a sweet fragrance to the room, but it was a place bereft of personal photos.

Jonas Roth opened the door allowing Julia Kessler to pass through before him. Hanne rose from her chair and held out a hand to Julia, which was grasped warmly.

'Thank you for coming, Frau Drais.'

'Please, call me Hanne.'

'Ok, Hanne. Pleased to meet you. Do call me Julia.'

'I'm so very sorry about the press release of your sister's private details,' Hanne said, sincerely, hoping to start on a good note.

'Jonas... Dr Roth explained everything,' Julia said, appreciating Hanne's gesture. 'From my point of view, it's a fresh start for all of us.'

'Thank you. We'll drip feed the media from now on and everything will first be approved by you and Dr Roth,' Hanne reassured her.

'That's good to hear,' said Julia, looking at the doctor in the hope that he would take over the conversation.

Dr Roth cleared his throat. 'Lotte's doing very well and making a slow but steady recovery. She's reluctant to talk to the police but she knows she has to. May I suggest we schedule weekly meetings with her lasting no more than an hour?'

Hanne nodded. 'Will either of you be present at these meetings?'

'I think Lotte will be more comfortable if I'm with her,' Julia declared.

That's fine,' Hanne replied. 'And shall we have a briefing meeting with you, Dr Roth, before and after our sessions?'

Jonas nodded. 'Yes, of course. We can schedule that in.'

'I'd also like to speak with the nurses on duty the night Lotte woke up, if possible?'

'That would be Lena and Martin,' Jonas informed her.

'I'd like them to come to the station to be interviewed so my colleagues can be present.'

'I'll let them know.'

'Thank you, Herr Doktor,' Hanne said.

Julia's smile was friendly. 'I'll think you'll find my sister is quite chatty and she'll tell you all you need to know in her own time. Just let her do the talking.'

Lotte Holler was dressed in a tracksuit that hung loosely on her thin frame. She was sitting in one of the armchairs by the window in her room when Julia and Hanne entered.

'Excuse me, if I don't stand up,' Lotte announced, eyeing the police intruder. 'I had a work-out in the gym this morning and my legs are a little achy.'

Hanne noticed Lotte was physically frail. There was a Zimmer frame and a walking stick close by. 'Please, don't get up on my account,' she said.

Julia did the introductions. 'Lotte, this is Hanne, Hanne, this is my sister, Lotte.'

'Julia, don't be so formal,'Lotte said gruffly. 'I can speak for myself.'

'Thank you for seeing me,' Hanne said, stretching out her hand to Lotte.

Considering the patient's condition, it was quite a strong handshake, thought Hanne, noting the determined, almost steely look in Lotte's eyes.

Lotte instructed, 'Have a seat. Julia, you can sit on the

bed.'

'Thank you,' said Hanne, sitting in the armchair.

Lotte got straight to the point. 'So, after all this time, what do you think the chances are of catching the bastard who put me in here?'

'I can't guarantee anything but we'll certainly try.'

'Ok, but it'll be like chasing a phantom in the night,' Lotte declared, with more than a hint of bitterness.

Hanne took out her notepad. 'What do remember about that night?'

'I remember everything!'

'Please, talk me through the events.'

'I was abducted outside my flat in Kreuzberg. He put a gun to my head and duct tape over my mouth to stop me from screaming, tied my hands behind my back and shoved me into the back of my car. I was at the mercy of a madman! Next thing I knew, I'd been taken to a lake.'

'That would be Muggelsee. Go on.'

'I tried to kick out at him but he was too strong - I'd freed my hands and pulled off the duct tape and I was screaming, but no one could hear me. It was pitch black except for the headlights on the car.' Lotte's voice faltered. 'He held a gun against my head and told me to strip.'

'Lotte, if it's too painful, you can stop any time,' Hanne assured her.

'No, it's ok, I won't cry. I won't give that bastard the satisfaction. I was afraid he was going to rape me but he told me that wasn't what it was about.'

Hanne noticed Julia had tears in her eyes as her sister retold her story.

'I was so cold in the water. He told me to dance, and perversely it did me a favour, because it warmed me up. But being made to dance to that bloody opera song… I'm not a fucking toreador! Just saying it makes me so angry. I've never felt so humiliated in all my life!'

'What do you think that was all about?' Hanne enquired.

Lotte bellowed. 'Revenge, that's what! He knew me, the

boy knew me.'

Hanne queried, 'The boy?'

'Well, I didn't think he sounded older than about 20,' Lotte ventured, looking at Julia and thinking, if I don't tell this psychologist, they'll find out some other way. So, she braced herself. 'You see, I used to work as a warden at a youth correction centre near Dresden, in East Germany. You may have heard of it… Torgau.'

Indeed she had. Hanne hid her surprise. Her ex, Claudia, knew of a girl who'd been sent there and the tales of cruelty and abuse inflicted on the children by the adults were horrific. After her release from Torgau, Claudia's friend had suffered many breakdowns and had been in and out of mental institutions for years.

'Yes, I've heard of Torgau,' Hanne replied carefully, beginning to wonder if Lotte Holler could be guilty of cruelty and abuse as a Torgau warden.

'I think my attacker knew me at Torgau- he had some sort of grudge against me, and I wasn't the only one! There were others.'

Hanne was intrigued. 'What sort of grudge?'

'Oh, I don't know, I probably told him off a few times. You know kids, they can't take much discipline.'

Julia couldn't agree with such a sweeping statement. 'Oh, I don't know. My boys don't give me much trouble.'

'Julia! Your boys are saints, just like you,' Lotte said, mockingly. 'Torgau kids were troublesome, to say the least.'

Hanne ignored the siblings' banter and continued with her line of questioning. 'Lotte, you said there were others?'

'That's right. He was deranged, he said he'd killed three of my old Torgau colleagues and they were lying dead at the bottom of the lake! And I'd be next.'

'But he didn't kill you,' Julia interjected. 'So, maybe he was lying about the three men and he only told you that to frighten you.'

Lotte confessed, 'I was frightened. Not just for myself, I was frightened for my baby. He killed my baby!'

173

'Yes, so I gather. I'm sorry,' Hanne told her.

'I don't want to be pitied. I want the Torgau boy caught and I want to meet him again when he's not hiding his face behind a balaclava and waving his gun. He'll be wetting himself like I did, the next time we meet,' Lotte insisted.

'We'll investigate to see if there's any truth in it, as it might help us find him,' said Hanne. 'Did he tell you the names of your colleagues?'

Lotte nodded. 'Horst Gwisdek; Gunther Schukrafft, and Harald Plaumann.'

Hanne thought Lotte's mind must be razor-sharp to reel off these names so quickly after all this time.

Julia asked, 'If it's true and this Torgau boy killed Lotte's ex colleagues, could you search the lake?'

'That's a good idea. We've a team of experienced scuba divers and I'll inform my colleagues straight away,' replied Hanne. 'Ladies, you've been a great help, thank you, but I think we'll leave it there for now.'

Lotte was adamant. 'I want to be kept informed. You've got to tell me what you find out, every step of the way, and don't skimp on the details.'

Julia frowned. 'Lotte, don't get yourself all worked up now.'

'Worked up? I'm glad to be feeling anything after all this time!' Lotte snapped.

Julia understood. 'Yes, sorry, of course you are.'

Hanne stood up to leave. 'Lotte, you'll be kept informed of any developments but please understand, it's going to take time to unravel this case.'

Lotte nodded. 'Time, is what I have.'

Jonas Roth was waiting for Hanne in his office.

'She's all there,' Hanne told him, wryly.

Jonas smiled. 'Isn't she just? Hopefully you've got some information to help with your psychological profiling of the case. Any clues to what sort of person would commit such a crime?'

'Yes, I have. Thank you,' Hanne replied, somewhat non-committal. 'Crimes often tend to be committed by the most likely candidate.'

Dr Roth didn't press Hanne further. He knew most of Lotte's story via Julia and she would inform him of the details of Lotte and Hanne's meeting later on.

23. Déjà vu

Hanne Drais left the hospital in Tempelhof and cycled back to Unter Den Linden, stopping off at a Starbucks café near the Brandenburg Gate. She bought a blueberry muffin to take home to her daughter as a peace offering. If she couldn't bake a cake she could buy Audrey one. As she drank her cafe latte at a window seat, trying to clear her thoughts before returning to the station to fill in Kruger on her meeting with Lotte Holler, she watched her fellow citizens pass by.

She couldn't quite believe what she'd heard or what she was thinking. She didn't want to be too judgmental this early in the negotiations yet she couldn't help thinking how tough Lotte was. She hadn't evoked as much sympathy in Hanne, as she would have expected in the circumstances. After witnessing Lotte's dismissive and bossy manner with her sister, Lotte had shown herself to be pretty authoritarian. Julia was a far softer character. When Lotte had mentioned the kids at Torgau, Hanne had felt her hackles rise and unusually, a growing sympathy for the boy: Lotte's assailant; Marine Boy.

In just one meeting with Lotte, Hanne had discovered some of her preliminary profiling was accurate. The motive was apparently established as revenge and there was a distinct possibility that Marine Boy was a serial killer. If it turned out to be true - and she had the feeling it could be - Hanne wondered how deep the Torgau boy's suffering must have been to make him turn to murder.

She wanted her colleagues to consider this newly discovered information and to look at the case from a different perspective, hoping Kruger and Stefan would find some compassion for Marine Boy, but she wasn't counting on it. Hanne was adamant that it wasn't just about finding Marine Boy to lock him away for the rest of his life. No, this was now about justice for him as well. Marine Boy might need psychological help after his suffering at Torgau.

Hanne cycled down Unter Den Linden towards her old university and her thoughts drifted to her happy but arduous time spent as a psychology student in the magnificent and prestigious neo-classical building, the Humboldt, situated across a large courtyard at the back of police headquarters. The Humboltd was Berlin's oldest and highly regarded university where 29 Nobel Prize winners were educated, including the scientist Albert Einstein. Hanne wasn't in such an esteemed league of alumni but allowed herself to feel a sense of pride and achievement having gained her degree in such hallowed halls. She hoped Audrey would follow in her footsteps and go onto greater things.

Kruger's face turned white.

'Oskar? Are you ok?'

'Drais, please tell me I'm not hearing things? Did you just say Horst Gwisdek; Gunther Schukrafft and Harald Plaumann?'

Hanne nodded and looked at Stefan, who seemed just as concerned.

Kruger undid his top button on his shirt collar. 'Fic! Remember the case I was on back in 1992, when we went after the paedophile ring? Out of roughly 60 names from an anonymous list there were around seven suspects who disappeared into thin air. We never found them, never got to question them, put them away or log them on a sex offenders' register, but I remember all the names by heart that got away.'

Hanne gasped. 'Mein gott!'

'You can say that again, Drais. Because Lotte Holler's ghost has just walked over my grave. Her three colleagues at Torgau - Horst Gwisdek, Gunther Schukrafft and Harald Plaumann - were on that paedophile list.'

Stefan was gobsmacked. 'No! That puts a new light on things.'

Hanne agreed. 'These missing men, they're likely to be at the bottom of Muggelsee lake and Marine Boy really did go after his Torgau abusers.'

'And he was fucking successful by the sounds of it!' Kruger quipped. 'We've got to search the lake. Stefan, get me the case notes of the paedo ring from 1992.'

'Sure. So, if the Torgau three are at the bottom of Muggelsee we're looking for a vigilante and a serial killer.'

'Oskar, do you think Marine Boy was the one who sent you the anonymous tip off and posted you the list in 1992?'

Kruger smiled at Hanne's insight. 'Could be, could be. It wasn't any of the Torgau kids that came forward to identify their abusers- they had no knowledge of any such list.'

Hanne concluded, 'Marine Boy is not to be underestimated.'

The team quickly gathered, including the junior police officers assigned to assist the case, and researchers for a meeting. Kruger had written the following on the incident board:

Lotte Holler: Marine Boy: Gunther Schukrafft: Horst Gwisdek: Harald Plaumann: and the year: 1992.

Kruger turned to address his colleagues. 'Anyone recognise these names?'

This drew a blank.

'Maybe you're all too young to remember and anyway, some of you weren't even here when Lotte Holler was first in the headlines. Schukkraft, Gwisdek and Plaumann were her ex-colleagues at Torgau and suspected paedophiles who went missing back in 1992, around the same time that Lotte Holler was attacked. Seems our Marine Boy outsmarted everyone, as Lotte Holler told Drais all three men are at the bottom of Muggelsee.'

Stefan added, 'Which is why they've never been found-they're most likely dead.'

Kruger confessed, 'It's the likeliest possibility as to why they've never been caught. I hope so, because I wouldn't like to think they escaped my clutches and they've been at large to do more damage.'

'And Muggelsee is where Marine Boy left Lotte Holler. That's a question in itself,' mused Hanne. 'I'm assuming Lotte Holler wasn't on the paedophile list?'

Kruger shook his head. 'No women were on the list. Glockner, what can we get from the cold-case notes?'

Stefan referred to the 1992 file. 'I haven't checked the others yet, but Plaumann was a security guard at Schonefeld Airport back in 1992 when he disappeared out of our clutches leaving a wife and two small children. He was never found, nor was his car.'

'We assumed he'd skipped the country,' added Kruger.

Stefan continued. 'It says here, a bicycle that was hidden in the bushes at his gym was linked to a theft in Kopenick. If Plaumann is in the lake, the bike that is kept at forensics storage can be checked for fingerprints. It's a long shot, but at least we might have a link to the fingerprints on the knife found the night Lotte Holler was attacked, and a direct link to the lake and Marine Boy.'

'We are looking at a possible serial killer,' Kruger interjected. 'So we're going to send a team of scuba divers to Muggelsee, tomorrow.'

Hanne was adamant. 'All four were wardens at Torgau. In my opinion, it puts a new slant on this case, especially if Lotte Holler is connected to these missing paedophiles.'

'The motive is revenge. Marine Boy is apparently a Torgau kid but on no account is this to be leaked to the press,' Kruger stated. 'Is that clear?'

Everyone in the room nodded.

'It would detract from sympathies towards Lotte Holler if she's found guilty of any crimes from her time at Torgau,' Hanne ventured.

'If Marine Boy hated her enough to attack her we will find out why,' Stefan said with assurance. 'Let's not forget, even if Marine Boy is crazy; he's guilty of a violent attack which resulted in Lotte Holler losing a baby and spending 12 years of her life in a coma. She is the victim of a terrible crime.'

Hanne commented, 'He's not necessarily crazy but possibly suffering from paranoia. Remember, deadly logic is a characteristic of acute mania. However, Marine Boy could be living a normal life now after violent episodes in the past. That's if he's still alive.'

Stefan didn't necessarily agree, 'Or he could still be out there, acting like a vigilante, with anyone associated to Torgau. So, keep an open mind.'

'Well, I'll be meeting with Lotte Holler next week to get more details but this is what we have to go on so far. She described Marine Boy as tall and athletic.'

'That could describe anyone! However, Drais, you've made a good start keeping on the good side of Dr Roth and his patient,' Kruger praised.

Hanne said nothing. It pleased her that Kruger respected her work and contributions.

Stefan concluded, 'It's important to establish a definite link between Lotte Holler and her missing Torgau colleagues because it'll help us find a trail to Marine Boy.'

'Right, we've all got a job to do,' Kruger barked. 'Let's get on with it.'

The team dispersed from the room and only Stefan and Hanne were left behind.

He patted Hanne on the back. 'Well done, you've truly opened up the case.'

'I've only repeated what Lotte Holler told me.'

'I wish I had your modesty,' Stefan confessed. 'Well,

Hanne, don't forget to dress up warmly tomorrow. It'll be a long, cold day at Muggelsee.'

24. Out of the depths

A team of experienced police scuba divers arrived at the crack of dawn to brave the cold of the Muggelsee water. With the exception of the ferry services from the centre of Kopenick to Berlin, the boating lanes around the rest of the lake were closed and the police divers had a few clear days to make safe and extensive underwater searches. They divided into four teams of four divers, with two divers in the water and two on the banks awaiting their turn. The most obvious place that a car could enter the water and stay hidden at depth was the area immediately beyond the jetty. The divers plotted an estimated triangle of the projected distance a car could travel at speed, and went a little further and wider just to be sure.

The east team divers waded into the murky water and kept in close proximity with their dive buddy, especially as the visibility was less than two metres. The torches attached to their heads beamed powerful lights to illuminate their paths as they descended to around 15 metres - the deepest part of the lake. It wasn't long before they found a car, partly hidden amongst the mud and weeds on the riverbed. Inside this watery grave, camouflaged by the roots of a tree, were the remains of a body with its feet tied together. The police and forensic officers arrived in droves soon after and quickly cordoned off the area around the jetty. A haulage firm duly arrived with a truck and mini crane to pull the car to the surface.

When Kruger, Glockner and Hanne Drais arrived at the east banks of Muggelsee, they were given the usual protective clothing of rubber gloves, plastic overalls and paper masks by Rutger Korfsmeier, the forensic team leader. A portly man of 50, he was a well-liked colleague whom they often worked with, and they followed him to the car.

Rutger showed them the body in the back of the car. 'We had to prise open the back doors as they'd been locked. The victim was entombed by branches of a tree blocking the exit in the front and his feet were tied so there was no chance of the corpse floating to the surface. This male, aged around 40, has nothing to identify him so we'll check dental records. I've already given the car registration details over to Vehicle Licensing.

Stefan noticed something shiny on the floor of the car and picked up a silver crucifix. 'Could this have been some kind of weapon?'

'Quite possibly,' Rutger replied, popping the evidence into a clear, plastic DNA bag.

'His feet are tied together but not his hands. There must have been a struggle but he didn't have time to free his legs and swim to the surface,' Stefan surmised.

Kruger quipped, 'That and a bloody great branch through the front window!'

'However, someone was swimming!' Rutger stated, showing the others an aqua shoe in a forensic bag. 'A size nine, whereas the victim looks more like a size 11.'

Kruger and Glockner looked at one another, reading one anothers' thoughts.

'Marine Boy!' Oskar and Stefan cried in unison.

Rutger looked bemused. 'Marine Boy?'

Kruger took a call on his mobile phone.

Stefan enlightened Rutger. 'The nickname for the assailant. He left a boat knife at the scene of the crime when he attacked Lotte Holler, told her he'd killed three of her ex-colleagues here at the lake, and it looks like he wasn't lying.'

Hanne had remained quiet throughout, studying the body

and the scene of the crime, lost in her thoughts. 'Rutger, have you checked in the boot?' she queried.

Rutger nodded. 'We had to force the car boot open because it had rusted and we found a few shredded clothes in a sports bag, nothing else.'

'Mein Gott!' Kruger bellowed. 'The divers at the north and south jetties have discovered two more cars in the lake with bodies in them!'

Stefan clapped his hands. 'Bingo!'

Kruger received another call and listened intently then suddenly punched the air.

'That was HQ, Vehicle Licensing checked the registration records of all three vehicles and the cars belonged to Gwisdek, Schukkraft and Plaumann!'

'Just like Lotte said. Marine Boy buried them in a watery grave,' stated Hanne.

The police released the minimum amount of detail to the prowling press but they quickly picked up on the story. The news spread throughout Kopenick and journalists and cameramen from local and Berlin television companies began turning up at the lake, hoping for an exclusive on the breaking story. The police team at Muggelsee were under strict instructions not to reveal the names of the three bodies pulled from the lake. Television networks were allowed to film briefly and Kruger was interviewed but that was it.

All three cars were retrieved from the depths and moved to a confined area at the south jetty - the one furthest away from the town and the most remote part of the lake. Here, the forensics squad would be less likely to be disturbed by the public stumbling across the cordoned off area where a forensics tent had now been erected. The cars with the Musketeers inside were parked in a row on the southern banks of Muggelsee, together again in death as they were in life.

Allowing forensics to get a head start, Kruger, Stefan and Hanne joined Rutger in the forensic tent later that morning and inspected all the evidence and bodies in their cars. Hanne kept a sang-froid attitude looking at corpses whilst looking for the mystery in the story in the tale of death.

'So, our Marine Boy is a confirmed serial killer,' Kruger announced. 'And three of Lotte Holler's Torgau colleagues, as predicted, were found dead in their cars in the lake.'

'Their dental records will confirm identifications,' Rutger reminded him. 'But we are assuming it's them- Gwisdek, Schukrafft and Plaumann.'

Who else would they be? Kruger thought. That would only leave four men that I failed to catch from the paedophile ring - four men too many who got away. Kruger carried misplaced guilt about the case and in an unusual paradox, found he was feeling grateful to Marine Boy.

Hanne was keen to tap into Rutger's meticulous mind, knowing he was blessed with an exceptional memory. 'I want to understand about homicidal drowning so don't spare me any details,' she said.

Rutger was happy to oblige. 'I'll have to wait for the autopsy report to distinguish between post and ante mortem bleeding but all three men suffered several blows to the head, although it could be the constant buffeting of the water which creates head banging, and this commonly produces post-mortem injuries that sometimes makes for diagnostic confusion. Horst, for instance, had bruising to the front and the back of the head, sharp incisions close to the scalp, possibly indicating some sort of hair scalping and his ear lobes were hacked with a knife. There were rope marks around the wrists and feet and we believe his eyes were gouged by a sharp object - there was damage to the socket bones.'

Hanne was curious. 'So, do you know if any of them were alive when they entered the water?'

'If a body is alive when entering the water, a white froth or foam is usually found in the airways. The lungs over-inflate and become heavy with fluid and the middle ears show haemorrhaging, plus foreign bodies are found in the airways and stomach.'

'Such as?'

'Sand, silt or weed, which would suggest rapid death by drowning. Do you know, there's not a universal diagnostic lab test for drowning?'

Hanne looked surprised. 'You're kidding!'

Rutger shook his head. 'Fortunately, the autopsy findings are usually consistent with the circumstances of the corroborative evidence, such as why the victim entered the water, why they were unable to survive, etc, etc, which usually gives us the answers.'

'They've been down there 12 years, if Lotte Holler is correct. Rutger, how decomposed are the bodies?' Hanne asked.

'Well, the normal changes of decomposition of a body in water are delayed in cold, deep water and here at the lake it's cold most of the year, and around 15 metres is deep and dark enough to keep the bodies from turning too skeletal. If the fish hadn't nibbled them they'd be quite well preserved. Bodies recovered in the water show signs of anserine cutis and adipocere which protects against decomposition,' Rutger explained.

'Korfsmeier! Layman's talk please, we're only mere mortals,' Kruger said.

Rutger nodded. 'Sorry... The bodies have goose skin, skin maceration and the fatty layer beneath the skin has transformed into a soap-like substance. Corpses normally tend to float upwards once the natural gases explode but as two of the bodies were tied to the door handle and the third was entombed by a tree, there wasn't any chance of that.'

Kruger grimaced and said wryly, 'Is that all?' His flippancy was an attempt to lighten the gruesome sights he had to deal with, but Kruger trusted Rutger and was eager to hear the minutiae about the corpse. Rutger was not only a good forensic officer, he also had imagination.

'Rutger, can I look at the DNA evidence you've collected?'

Rutger showed Hanne the evidence collected in labelled DNA bags. There were three watches: a sports watch; a gold Rolex and a practical watch with a brown leather strap; a size nine aqua shoe; some boat rope, and a silver crucifix on a chain.

'Well, Marine Boy's no thief!' Stefan jested. 'He didn't steal the Rolex, which would have been worth 1,000 marks back in 1992.'

Hanne spoke her thoughts aloud. 'We've not found any mobile phones. Didn't you tell me Harald Plaumann's wife received a text message on the night he disappeared?'

Kruger's eyes lit up. 'That's right Drais, she did. A convenient texted confession, so if the mobile wasn't lost in the depths someone must have it, and it's likely that that someone sent the text to Plaumann's wife.'

'Marine Boy!' cried Stefan.

Hanne remarked, 'I noticed the links of the silver chain are not open or broken.'

Rutger was intrigued. 'Meaning?'

'Maybe it didn't belong to the victim or the assailant and just happened to be in the car but neither man was wearing it.'

'You're right, Drais,' Kruger said. 'It would probably have broken in a struggle.'

'Doesn't matter if someone wore it or not, is it significant?' Stefan queried.

For a little while she was lost in her thoughts, digesting all the evidence. Eventually she announced: 'I've been thinking about the evidence in the cars. I think Gwisdek was the first to be murdered.'

'But does it matter who was killed first? It's the end result that counts and three men are dead,' said Stefan 'Anyway, how can you be sure?'

'I can't, but he was the only one with shreds of clothes on. I think Marine Boy got into his stride later on, repeating patterns with the others, tying them up, making them strip or playing music. At some point, Plaumann was the only one to break free, which would account for the struggle that followed and the gouging of his eyes.'

Rutger liked Hanne's logic. 'Marine Boy had to be in the front of the car and Plaumann had to be in the back from the angle the crucifix went in.'

Hanne agreed. 'I think Marine Boy drove Plaumann's car into the water to drown his dazed or semi-conscious victim as he'd done with the others but Plaumann mounted a surprise attack from behind. The crucifix must have been hanging in the car on the rear view mirror and Marine Boy somehow managed to grab it. So, Plaumann must have been blinded and in agony before he ran out of time, and he couldn't untie his legs and escape. Marine Boy swam to the surface leaving a clue behind: his aqua shoe.'

Kruger grimaced. 'The psychotic kid escaped to strike again - a bloody shame for Lotte Holler that he survived.'

'What I find strange is the hair: a few balding patches where there should be hair, with all three victims,' Hanne told them.

'Maybe Marine Boy wanted a trophy from his victims?' queried Stefan.

Hanne was adamant. 'No! An abused person does not want a trophy from their abuser. It would repulse them to have any keepsakes or reminders. Marine Boy would have cut his victims' hair for some other reason.'

'Or just for fun?'

Hanne found Stefan's remarks irritating but held back her opinions.

'Oh, yeah. It's a fucking funny crime scene,' quipped Kruger.

'There's something else, ' Hanne mused. 'Marine Boy is true to his nickname. The way he tied the rope in a figure of eight, isn't that the best way to moor a boat?'

Rutger smiled. 'Yes, Hanne, it's called a Flemish knot, you tie a boat in a figure of eight to secure it to the mooring. It seems Marine Boy is a keen boatman.'

Kruger scoffed and grimaced. 'Yeah, and we're looking

for Flemish knots and a Marine Boy in an area of 100 lakes! Ok, let's inform the relatives before the press get hold of the names. I gave an interview earlier and they'll be panting for more.'

'Glockner, take Drais with you to break the news to Plaumann's wife in Schonefeld and onto Leipzig afterwards, to Schukrafft's mother's old place. If I remember rightly she died not long after her son went missing but maybe there are neighbours that remember them. Try to see if there's anyone at Gwisdek's old home too, and let's hope someone will shed some light on the victims.'

Stefan nodded. 'Sure. I'll need to liaise with the Schonefeld and Leipzig police- don't want to step on anyone's toes.'

Kruger remarked, 'We're here at the lake with the co-operation of the Kopenick police, so why should the Schonefeld and Leipzig police be any different? Besides, it's good to step on someone's toes; it gets the wrong people out of the way!'

25. Confessions

Ingrid and Angele took turns to look after Peonie whilst Martha continued working in Berlin. She planned to give up her job before their second baby was due in the middle of September. This week it was Ingrid's turn. Peonie would be tired from her morning at the village kindergarten and hopefully fast asleep at some point in the afternoon, Klaus was up at the golf club and didn't plan to return for lunch and Axel was at school. Ingrid was hoping for an opportune moment to catch Felix alone and have a long, overdue talk with her nephew.

Felix tried to find time to see Peonie during his working day and often came for lunch at his tante's cottage. Before he went back to work at the boathouse he would put Peonie to bed in the spare bedroom for her afternoon nap. As he came back into the living room, a television news bulletin shattered his peace with some breaking news.

A male reporter was reporting live from Muggelsee where in the background a haulage truck was pulling a car out of the water. Felix turned white. Ingrid came in from the kitchen and saw not only Felix's ashen face but how he was frozen to the spot, as he had been when Susanne had died. She was suddenly afraid for him and time was suspended as they listened to the television report.

'Here on the banks of Muggelsee, three cars have been pulled out of the water. Each car contains a body. With me is the investigating officer, Kommissar Kruger.'

At the south jetty of Muggelsee, Kruger was dressed in forensic clothing, in stark contrast to the smart reporter in his suit.

Kruger was succinct and to the point. 'Three bodies in their cars have been recovered at various points around the lake. The names of the victims are known to us but we can't release this information until the relatives have been informed.'

The reporter asked. 'What led you to carry out a search of this lake?'

'We received information relating to another case that led us here. We had to close the boating lanes but they will reopen in due course after police scuba divers have concluded their underwater search,' Kruger explained.

'Does the evidence you've found so far indicate murder?'

Kruger looked annoyed at this question. 'Well, it's not suicide.'

Ingrid switched off the television with the remote control.

'Hey! I was watching that,' Felix said, raising his voice.

'Don't raise your voice to me!'

Felix grabbed his coat, ready to leave.

'No!' Ingrid barked. 'You are not leaving until we've talked.'

'Shush, you'll wake Peonie.'

Quickly, Ingrid softened her tone. 'Felix, it's me. You can tell me anything.'

Felix looked in her eyes, knowing she was telling the truth. How long could he carry this burden alone? But wouldn't telling her be a selfish act? Ingrid would then have to deal with the nightmares and her safety too would be compromised. Tante knows anyway, Felix told himself, and there's no hiding it from her. He would only be confirming her worst fears.

'Young man, it's time you told me what's going on.'

'What can I say?'

'The truth! Felix, please tell me the truth.'

'I've tried to carry this burden alone, and I'm going to be a father again. I really want another child but bloody hell, this is such bad timing.'

'Felix, I know you. You haven't been yourself these last few weeks and you've started obsessively washing your hands again. Don't fob me off with, 'It's just my eczema' and I'm sure Martha is getting suspicious, too.'

'Both you and my dear wife worry too much,' he told her, in a final attempt to stave off her questions.

'Felix! On your birthday I watched you go outside and throw up behind a tree.'

'You did?'

'Yes, I was worried. It was after the news report about 'The Lady of the Lake' waking up from her coma, wasn't it? And at your birthday party, you really didn't like onkel Bernd giving you a Herbertz knife. Why? And seeing how you've reacted to the news coming from Muggelsee today, I have the feeling they're all somehow connected.'

Felix was tired of lying and tired of keeping secrets. If he couldn't tell his beloved tante, who else could he tell? Ingrid was the woman who reminded him of his mother in many ways, the woman who had given him a home and loved him as if he was her own son. It was true; he had been washing his hands excessively of late because his nerves were getting the better of him. He'd been finding it hard to relax, worried every time he turned on the news and he was drinking, albeit surreptitiously, more than usual.

'If I tell you, then you'll be collaborating with me,' he said.

'I don't give a damn!'

'Tante, you promised. No questions.'

'Promises go out of the window when you're in trouble.'

Felix could not resist a moment longer. 'Ok, but I'll put your life in danger... as an accessory to murder.'

Ingrid's face dropped a million miles. 'I knew it. I just knew it.' Instinctively, she took Felix in her arms as they sobbed together. Once their tears had abated, they both found the courage to speak.

'With these hands of mine... I've loved my wife and daughter - and I've also killed three men and nearly killed a woman. I can't quite believe I am a murderer, that I was capable of it. At the time I thought I was going mad but it all seemed so clear to me, I just had to do it. I'm sorry I've let you down.'

'Why didn't you talk to me or Klaus?'

'It was part of being a man, something I had to do on my own.'

'So, let's get this straight. The coma lady and the three bodies discovered today at Muggelsee, they're all connected to you?'

He nodded. 'The three men were wardens at Torgau, and they all abused Susi and me.

The coma victim was their go-between and collaborator.'

'I see. Did you kill these men in the autumn of 1992?'

He lowered his head in shame.

'I remember exactly when it was. You came home with bruises and rope burns around your neck. I told you my secret then, about my shame regarding Sofie, and you half told me your secrets. Felix, I've waited a long time for you to confide in me and I won't judge you, just as you didn't judge me about Sofie,' she promised.

Felix looked Ingrid in the eye. 'Tante, I'm ready to tell you the whole truth. One of them, Horst, turned up at the golf club at the end of the summer. He recognised me, said he would come after Axel. I didn't plan to kill him, just to frighten him away, but then he told me he'd contact his paedophile friends. I couldn't have that so I attacked him, tied him to the car door and drove his car into the lake at Muggelsee.'

'Did you use Klaus's gun?'

'Only to gain control. I never wanted to shoot anyone, and I hit him over the head with the gun, stunning him. But I didn't shoot him.'

'Then you drove him into the water and swam to safety.'

'Yes. Tante, now you know, how can you keep this a secret?'

'The truth has versions. My version is that I've been your collaborator for a long time. I've known, deep down,' she confessed. 'Did anyone see you?'

'If they did, no one has turned me in so far. I wore a disguise - that old wig you bought for me, and a balaclava.'

'That's good. How did you know where to find the others?'

'Horst kept a diary, with all the names and addresses of his sick friends.'

'Where's this diary?'

'It's hidden in a safe place.'

'Felix! It's evidence, get rid of it!' she urged.

'No. You never know when I may have to use it again.'

Ingrid realised at that moment that if it was necessary, Felix would repeat his crimes. 'Surely you won't have to. Anyway, after Horst, who was next?'

'I stalked a second man using the same methods, and he ended up at the bottom of Muggelsee without much trouble. However, the third man wasn't so easy. That's when I got the rope burns around my neck. I nearly drowned in the car with him.'

Ingrid began to cry.

Felix felt ashamed. 'Look what I've done to you... I should go away.'

'No! That's what Sofie did and it broke my heart. I'm not crying because I'm ashamed of you,' she said, wiping away her tears. 'I'm crying because I nearly lost you at the bottom of some lake. We would never have known.'

'Just as you never knew when Sofie died.'

'Yes,' Ingrid said, softly.

'Shall I go on?'

She nodded, trying to compose herself.

'The last one, their go-between Lotte Holler, the one the press call the Lady of the Lake, well, she used to take Susi and me from our beds and lead us to the three men, Horst,

Gunther and Harald. They called themselves the three Musketeers. One for all and all for one, that was their sick motto.'

Ingrid was outraged. 'The bastards! You should have killed that woman too.'

'Tante, I couldn't go through with it.'

'Was it because she was a woman?'

'No. Lotte Holler would have ended up at the bottom of the lake just like the others, which is where they all deserved to be so I could keep my family safe from the paedophiles. But she told me she was pregnant and I couldn't go through with it. I know she lost her baby but at least I didn't knowingly kill her baby.'

'Funny sort of mother she'd be. Felix, you did the right thing.'

'Tante, surely you can't mean that? You can't condone murder. I took the law into my own hands. I killed the Musketeers after the fall of the Stasi regime, so what excuse do I have now, living in a democracy?'

'If you hadn't acted, they would have gone unpunished and continued torturing others with their sordid lives. Felix, you were traumatised! You'd been through a lot and you were only 17 when you committed these crimes - still a minor, in legal terms.'

'That's what I told myself,' he mused. 'And neither the Musketeers nor their go-between showed any remorse.'

'Well, you get what you deserve out of life and they got what was coming to them. Their downfall was self-inflicted.'

'Will you tell onkel Klaus?'

'Will you tell Martha?'

They both had their reasons and both shook their heads.

'Do you think the police will catch me?'

'I hope not. Let's go over it, to settle your mind, and mine. Did you leave any clues?'

'I tried not to but I left my Herbertz knife at the scene of the crime when I was with Lotte Holler. It had my fingerprints on it, although the police don't have my fingerprints on file. Tante, they'll be looking for someone who has a boat or a connection to a lake, I'm sure of it.'

'Don't worry, with all the lakes around here they'll be looking for a needle in a haystack. But no wonder you didn't want Onkel Bernd's knife!' she ventured. 'So, how many of them saw your face?'

'Two of the Musketeers saw my face.'

'They don't count any more, but what about the coma woman?'

'No. I kept my balaclava on.'

'Good. She's the only one who can help the police now but it's a long time ago and hopefully nothing will be fresh in her mind after 12 years in a coma.'

'I was a coward. I couldn't show her my face.'

'You're not a coward. It's good that she won't recognise you.'

Felix grew agitated and started rubbing his hands.

'For God's sake, leave your hands alone!' she pleaded.

Putting his hands on his head, he began to cry in frustration.

Ingrid was concerned. 'It's all right, everything will be all right,' she said softly.

'Do you know why I couldn't tell Lotte Holler who I was? Because Felix Waltz died a long time ago, and as Felix Baum, I'm alive again.'

'Felix, you have to calm down,' she begged him. 'Think of Peonie, Martha and the new baby. Please, focus on them.'

There are not many people in life that we show our weaknesses to, but it's usually with someone who offers the nearest thing to unconditional love. Ingrid had become that person for Felix. He could cry in her arms like a little boy and feel safe.

'You're right. I'm a husband and a father and my family needs me to stay strong. Tante, you've been a second mother to me,' he told her.

'Felix, your mother would have wanted me to look out for you. Whatever happens; we're your family, we love you

196

and we'll stick by you,' vowed Ingrid.

Ina Selge was an attractive woman approaching 50. Her husband Harald Plaumann went missing about the same time as the paedophile ring was broken and once the police searches for him had ground to an inconclusive halt, Harald became persona non grata in her family. He may not have been found guilty but there was guilt by association, and Ina quickly reverted to her maiden name, changed her children's surnames and applied for a divorce in his absence.

Ina had not remarried but enjoyed a relationship with an old flame called Dieter. They were happy together, yet both preferred living separately in the Schonefeld area, south of Berlin. When her children were younger, Ina felt they needed the stability of the same school and friends, especially after the press first got wind of the story and labelled her guilty just for being his wife. She moved to the other side of town where she'd lived ever since and her family and friends protected her and the children, closing ranks against outsiders.

It was a modern and immaculately kept home. Photos of her children adorned the walls. Her son, Peter, now 20, was away at university and her daughter Marie, just turned 16, was away on a school ski trip. Ina ran an online shopping service and worked from home. At 9.30 a.m. her doorbell rang. When she opened her door, Stefan Glockner and Hanne Drais were standing on her porch, sheltering from the gusty winds.

'Ina Selge?' Stefan presumed, showing his police identification.

Ina looked at his ID. 'Yes?'

'I'm Detective Glockner and this is my colleague, Hanne Drais. May we come in?'

Ina opened the door and beckoned them in. 'It's not my children, is it? She was worried now. 'There's not been any bad news about my children?'

'No. Not at all,' Hanne said, reassuringly.

'Have you by any chance seen the recent news from Muggelsee?' Stefan asked.

Ina nodded. 'They've pulled three bodies out of the lake.'

Stefan was careful in his delivery. 'It's about your ex-husband. Dental records have just confirmed that one of the bodies is that of Harald Plaumann.'

Ina slumped into a chair. 'I see.'

'I'm sorry. Is there anyone you'd like to be here with you?' Hanne asked.

'No, I'm fine. Will I have to make a formal identification?'

'That won't be necessary. We're treating his death as a homicide. In fact, all three men pulled out of Muggelsee a few days ago, were murdered,' Stefan told her.

'I didn't think Harald would kill himself. He was far too vain. I believe he left me and the children because he'd been found out and fled the country.'

Hanne thought Ina's bitterness towards her husband was justified. 'We've some of your late husband's personal belongings - a sports watch and a silver crucifix.'

'The crucifix was a present from his mother and he hung it on the driver's mirror so she'd notice it from time to time. Then he wouldn't have to wear it,' Ina explained. 'But I don't want any of Harald's keepsakes.'

Hanne sighed, 'I understand.'

'How was he murdered?' Ina asked.

Stefan gave her the facts. 'He was taken to Muggelsee by force, and after a struggle his car was driven into the water where he drowned.'

Ina showed no emotion. 'He was my husband and the father of my children and we had 10 happy years together, or so I thought. But Harald was living a lie.'

'Is it ok if we go over the evidence that you gave in 1992?'

'Of course, Detective Glockner. I've only kept one thing - the message Harald sent to me on an old mobile phone the night he disappeared, because it had vital information that helped the police. I'll go and get it. Can I get you both a drink?'

'A pot of coffee would be nice, thank you,'

In due course, Ina returned with refreshments and her old mobile, a Nokia 101, the lightest and innovative mobile phone of its time and massively produced in 1992.

'I'll have to charge the battery so you can read the text, but it won't take long,' she said. Over coffee, they made some small talk, talking about their children. Eventually, Ina passed the mobile so Hanne could read the text message.

'Darling Ina,

I have to get away as news is about to break and the police will come after me for what I did as a warden at Torgau. I sexually abused the kids. Tell no one. I've got to lie low. I'm sorry. Kiss my children for me.

Your loving husband,
Harald

Hanne was full of empathy for Ina. 'I'm sorry. Receiving that must have ripped your world apart.'

Ina nodded, tears in her eyes. 'I didn't want to believe it at first but when he didn't return and the police turned up looking for him, the only thing that mattered to me was finding out if Harald had touched our children. Can you imagine? I had to ask them and put them through something like that! I'm angry at myself for not seeing past his façade, and for not protecting my children. So, you see, we had a very lucky escape. Harald never touched his own children.'

Delighted to hear this, Hanne passed the mobile to Stefan, who while reading the text, stayed uncharacteristically quiet.

Ina conclude, 'And now, after hating him for living a lie and turning our whole family life into a lie, and doing that to other people's children, all I feel nothing for him.'

Stefan suddenly spoke up. 'Harald sent you this text at 9.15 p.m. on the night of 16th November 1992. We didn't find his mobile at the scene of the crime which leads us to question whether Harald actually sent the text himself. It's possible it was sent by the man who killed him.'

'It doesn't matter who sent it. Harald was found guilty in his absence when some abused kids from Torgau gave evidence against him as part of a trial of another paedophile warden from Torgau,' said Ina. 'The truth is clear for all to see, my ex-husband was a paedophile. This young man who killed Harald was most likely abused at Torgau too.'

'We think so,' Hanne admitted. 'And if the man who killed your husband and the others sent you the text, he was telling us about his motives and why he murdered them.'

Ina furrowed her brow. 'Then you have a very clever killer, because he helped you catch a paedophile ring.'

Hanne agreed. 'Yes. He can be viewed either as a vigilante hero or a psychotic villain.'

'I imagine the other men found at Muggelsee were just as sick as Harald.'

'Yes, they were his ex-colleagues at Torgau. They suffered the same fate, death by homicidal drowning,' Stefan told her.

Ina nodded. 'So, he's a serial killer. I can't say I blame him, getting his revenge. He did me a big favour too.'

Stefan grimaced. 'He's not a hero in my book, he's a killer and he needs to be caught.'

Hanne didn't offer an opinion about Marine Boy. She asked, 'Now, if it's ok, we need a profile of Harald - who he was and who he mixed with - clues to help us catch the Muggelsee killer.'

Ina thought for a moment then reluctantly recalled some details. 'Harald's life with the children and me was obviously a cover for his other life. I imagine he got up to all sorts when he went on trips with his Torgau pals but I never suspected a thing. It all made sense once he'd disappeared.'

Hanne was intrigued. 'Trips? What sort of trips and with whom?'

Ina spoke with frankness. 'With his best friends- Horst and Gunther. Horst had a motor home and they travelled all over in it. Supposedly, they were fishing and hunting trips. That's what I was told, but now I'm sure they hunted kids to abuse. I've never heard from those two again and I'm wondering if they are linked to Harald's disappearance?'

Hanne and Stefan looked at one another and wondered what Kruger would say and if it were prudent to tell Ina that Horst and Gunther were the other two bodies recovered from Muggelsee. They decided she merited hearing the truth.

Stefan broke the news. 'We'd like you to hear it from us, before the media gets hold of any information. The other two bodies pulled from Muggelsee were Harald's friends, Horst Gwisdek and Gunther Schukkraft.

Lotte Holler had been unwell. She had caught a bad dose of flu and Julia worried it would turn into pneumonia. Dr Roth quarantined his patient and the hospital staff, including Julia, wore protective masks when attending to her.

Julia's sons had yet to meet their tante Lotte, so their inaugural meeting was tentatively on hold. The interviews with criminal psychologist Hanne Drais were also postponed until Lotte recovered.

After a few weeks of lying in bed, reading and watching television, Lotte gradually recovered her strength, and was eager to get back into the gym to exercise and swim in the hydrotherapy pool. She enjoyed her daily regime of physiotherapy but not the long, psychological rehabilitation. She didn't need the psychobabble talks', as she called them, with the hospital's team of psychologists. She found the sessions laborious but endured them because she knew it was expected of her and worried that if she didn't comply she wouldn't be allowed to begin her life outside the hospital walls.

The days grew longer and the scent of spring was just around the corner. Lotte began to walk without a Zimmer frame or walking stick, albeit slowly, and those who visited her were no longer required to wear protective masks.

Much to Lotte's chagrin, Julia and Dr Roth decided the television from Lotte's room should be removed until she had fully recovered from the flu that had devastated her vulnerable immune system. Protecting her from journalists eager for news of her progress, and thus avoiding any disturbing information such as the three bodies discovered at Muggelsee, was paramount. They also decided to keep the daily newspapers out of sight, so she didn't have access to them.

One morning before Dr Roth's rounds, Martin- Lotte's favourite nurse, came in to check her blood pressure pushing a refreshments trolley.

'Sleep well?' Martin asked.

Lotte nodded. 'Yes, thank you. I'm a bit bored without television and newspapers, but it's Dr Roth's orders.'

Martin's hospital beeper sent a message and he stopped to read it. 'Got to pop out but I'll be back shortly,' he said, leaving his trolley. He'd forgotten he'd left a newspaper on the bottom shelf, and Lotte noticing his error, took a sneaky look. Though the Musketeers had been discovered over a month ago, the Muggelsee killings were still being written about and she was furious to read that her former colleagues, the Three Musketeers, had been murdered and nobody had told her. Lotte's temper rose quickly. She threw her shoes across the room and screamed. 'Scheisse!'

Later that morning, Julia arrived with a fresh bouquet of flowers. She kissed and hugged her sister warmly and asked. 'Good morning. Sleep well?'

Lotte was livid. 'Don't you good morning me! I've heard about the Muggelsee murders! I told you that sick bastard had done it. Why didn't you tell me? Get that policewoman, what's her name? Hanne, Hanne, Drais. I want to talk to her.'

Julia tried to placate her sister. 'Jonas and I felt it best that we didn't tell you straight away because you've been so ill. And we were right, look how it's upset you.'

'Oh, now it's Jonas and I, is it? Lotte said cynically. 'How dare you? I'll decide for myself. I don't want to live in a cocoon and lose touch with the outside world.'

Julia didn't enjoy seeing her sister in a state. 'Lotte, please try and calm down.'

'Julia, I've got to get out of this place before he finds out I'm in here! That Torgau boy will come after me.'

Julia thought her sister was showing signs of paranoia. 'Don't be silly. The wards are policed and we'll ask for police protection once you leave hospital.

Lotte cried. 'I'm afraid!'

Julia held her sister's hand. 'I know - but it will be all right and with your help the police have found your ex-colleagues, just as you said they would.'

'At the bottom of Muggelsee, just like he said. You see what he's capable of?'

'He won't get near you, I promise. Lotte, Jonas has just told me some good news about the compensation you're entitled to as a victim of crime. You remember I said after ten years of you being in a coma, I put in a claim - there's a government rehabilitation scheme for victims of crimes or serious traffic accidents that helps their families too.'

Nodding, Lotte mumbled, 'I vaguely recall you mentioning it.'

'Well, your claim is being finalised, as we speak. It's calculated from the projected earnings of the victim's lifetime and the victim's quality of life, post-accident or trauma. Our solicitor has managed to get it inflation-linked. The rehabilitation scheme has advanced us some money and is ready to release the rest in due course.'

Lotte sat upright. 'How much?'

'Enough to rent and eventually live in a house overlooking the lake at Wannsee,' Julia told her, excitedly. 'You always wanted to live in Wannsee.'

The news appeased Lotte's grumpy mood. 'That's the kind of news I like to wake up to,' she said in a cheerful tone.

'Hopefully you can leave hospital before the end of March,' Julia informed her.

'Is that what you're saying, or Dr Roth?'

Julia felt Lotte was envious of her relationship with Jonas.

'I just happen to agree with him because he knows what's best for you.'

Lotte was adamant. 'I decide what's best for me! If I don't get out of here I'll go mad. I'll discharge myself.'

Julia wasn't going to argue with her sister. 'Try and relax. Why don't we go for a walk in the hospital gardens?'

'Maybe later. You and the boys, you will come and live with me, won't you?'

'Lotte, I can't just change their schools, they're happy there. I know it'd be better for them to live in a nice suburb like Wannsee rather than in a rough area like Wedding, but that's where their school is and where all their friends are.'

Lotte's voice faltered. 'I can't be alone in a big house. We'll make it nice for them and they can have a boat to go out on the lake - anything they want.'

'We'll see,' Julia replied firmly, not wanting to be manipulated by her sister.

Lotte could see the reticence in Julia's face. 'Please Julia… for me?'

'Lotte, we'll come at weekends at first, you haven't even met the boys yet. And you need to get better, so you need peace and quiet, besides, you're not used to a pair of rowdy boys, and they have to get used to you.'

Julia was adamant that it would be her decision and the needs of her boys would come first and foremost.

Calming down a little, Lotte realised what her sister was saying made sense. 'You know what happened to you in the last 12 years? You grew up and became a mother.'

Julia smiled at the compliment. 'Aren't parents supposed to be grown up? Besides, you'll see me most days and have professional carers with you for the foreseeable future.'

'Will I? Who's going to pay for all this?' Lotte inquired, raising her brow.

'The lawyer says it will come out of the compensation fund.'

Lotte shook her head in disbelief. 'So, are you telling me, I'm really going to be rich?'

Julia nodded. 'All you've been through and all the publicity has, perversely, pushed up your price. The lawyers are confident that you'll be a millionaire.'

28. Leipzig

Hanne Drais and Stefan Glockner arrived in Leipzig at noon to meet Monica Hirsch, who had worked with Gunther Schukkraft at the library after German reunification. Recently retired, she was happy to be of help.

'We're hoping you'll help us with our investigation by giving us a picture of Gunther's life, his daily habits, who he mixed with, that kind of thing.'

'Yes, of course, Detective Glockner. Well, Gunther was my boss from 1990 to the time he went missing in the autumn of 1992,' replied Monica. 'I never thought he'd killed himself because he wouldn't have left his Mutti. Nobody at the library suspected a thing.

Believe me, I'm not the only who found it shocking to read that he was involved in a paedophile ring and ended up at the bottom of Muggelsee.'

Stefan resisted the temptation to be flippant and say, 'It's the quiet ones you have to watch'. Instead he said, 'Did he get on with his colleagues?'

Monica was defensive. 'Nobody had a bad word to say about him until… Yes, Gunther was a good boss and got on with everyone in his own quiet way. Some people mistook his shyness for being aloof, but he was always polite.'

Hanne phrased her question carefully. 'Do you know if Gunther was in a relationship at the time of his disappearance?'

Shaking her head, Monica began to waffle, 'Not to my

knowledge. Marlene - his mother - used to say that Gunther took after his father and was just shy, that he'd never found the right girl. When the police came looking Gunther, I'm sure that's why Marlene died from the shock. It was such a tragedy. She was a nice old lady.'

Trying to get Monica back on track, Hanne asked: 'Do you remember if Gunther had any friends outside of work?'

'It's a long time ago. Let's see, there were two friends Gunther went on trips with.'

'Trips? What sort of trips?' asked Stefan, knowing full well.

'Fishing, hunting, that sort of thing, but for the life of me I can't remember their names. I can picture the three of them, passing me in the motor home. Don't you two get old, the mind and body decays, it's very frustrating- old age is not for whimps! Now, what were they called?'

Stefan thought he'd give Monica a gentle reminder. 'Horst and Harald?'

'Yes, that's right, Horst and Harald. Gunther spoke of them from time to time.'

Then it dawned on her. 'Genau! Weren't these the names of the other men discovered in the lake alongside Gunther?' exclaimed Monica, visibly shocked.

'Yes. All three men died due to homicidal drowning.'

'Someone had a vendetta against Gunther, Horst and Harald because of what they did to the kids when they worked as wardens at Torgau,' Hanne told her. 'Did Gunther ever mention his job at Torgau?'

Monica shook her head. 'Only that he ran the library there. He had to tell us that because it was on his CV.'

'Any other friends you remember Gunther hanging out with?' Stefan asked.

Her eyes lit up. 'Yes! Gunther had a male friend who used to visit.'

Stefan sat upright.'Can you recall his name?'

'Yes, Gunther called him Witzig. I never knew his real name.'

Hanne was intrigued. 'Did this friend, Witzig, also work at Torgau?'

Monica was growing tired. 'Sorry, I don't remember.'

When they were alone, Stefan and Hanne mulled over their meeting with Monica Hirsch.

'Glad we won't need to interview her again.'

'Stefan, we can't dismiss her as some dotty old girl; she remembered Horst and Harald, and that matches Ina Selge's evidence. I'm wondering about the Witzig connection?'

'We can check if he was on the 1992 list.'

'Good idea. You know, it's a pity Marine Boy didn't go through the legal system and take Horst, Gunther and Harald to court and get them locked away to rot in a prison. That would be sweet revenge too, but he preferred the more complex option.'

Stefan was adamant. 'Hanne, I'm a man and if I'd been buggered by a bunch of sodomites, there's no way I'd stand in front of a jury and give evidence in court.'

'Marine Boy probably came to the same conclusion,' Hanne surmised. 'Let's get over to Gwisdek's old residence.'

On the other side of Leipzig they visited Horst's last home. They found, not to their surprise, that many tenants had lived in this apartment over the past 12 years. Luckily, the landlord; a retired businessman called Detlef Biegel, remained the same.

A tenant in the building gave Glockner his mobile phone number. Biegel was out of town but he answered his phone. He told them that after a few months without any news of Horst and with the rent overdue and no relatives or friends to contact, he'd moved Horst's belongings and his motor home to a timber yard near Zossen owned by Biegel's family.

Telling Biegel that the police would liaise with forensics and in the very near future would need to inspect the motor home, Stefan hung up.

The case was beginning to get to Stefan on a deeper level than usual. 'Don't know about you, but delving into the minds of paedophiles makes me worried for my own kids.'

Hanne sighed, 'I know exactly what you mean. How are your kids?' she asked.

'Fine. I have them on alternate weekends and see them most days after school. Daniel's into football, plays in the school team and on Saturdays I freeze my nuts off watching a bunch of nine-year-olds kick a ball around.'

'What about Steffi?'

'She watches her brother play - I think she's got a crush on the football coach's son. He's 12 and suddenly my 11-year-old daughter's into make-up. Luckily, my girlfriend's around to help. I can't believe how fast they grow up.'

'In the blink of an eye,' Hanne said, thinking of her beloved Audrey.

29. Axel.

Axel Felker was a strong, active young man of 15. He was a popular boy with many friends in the village, both male and female. His long fair hair and good looks meant he could have his pick of female admirers and he often dated one girl or another but never for very long. He had an independent, self-reliant streak and getting a good education was important to him because he hoped to go to university to study languages and travel the world. The annual foreign trips he made with Klaus, Bernd and Felix following the best golf tournaments gave him a love of languages, especially English, and served to whet his appetite for more travel.

Throughout the tourist season, Axel was forever practising his language skills with visitors from England, France and Spain. Whenever Felix's father-in-law, Jens, came to Motzen, the two of them would go off to a corner together to converse in English. Most foreign visitors to the lake and golf club didn't speak German but understood some English and this was the universal language adopted by the family when dealing with the foreign tourists.

Axel enjoyed working at the boatyard and the golf club outside of school hours and it earned him some pocket money to spend on his hobby: buying materials for building and fixing up motorbikes. Felix allowed him to ride his old Schwalbe on quiet roads and this opened his eyes to the joys of biking. Although finances were available to him from the coffers of the family business, he'd inherited the same work ethic as the rest of the family and he had learned that hard graft brings its own rewards.

Klaus and Ingrid told Axel from a young age that he was adopted as a baby and that Susanne; Felix's twin sister, was his mother. He was nonchalant about his origins and saw Klaus and Ingrid as his papa and mutti, even though they were in fact his great onkel and tante. However, Axel's closest natural bond was with onkel Felix, who had always been special to him. When the family thought Axel was old enough to understand about the death of his mother, they told him it was a tragic accident. Axel was 12. He asked some questions at the time but was trusting and accepted what he was told, apparently untroubled by the information. Until the spring of 2005.

In early March, Felix was sanding down a boat in the boatyard when Axel suddenly appeared at the door, his long hair blowing about in the gusty wind. Felix was surprised to see his nephew and could see immediately that Axel's mood was dark and potentially explosive.

'Onkel, is it true?'

'Is what true?' Felix enquired, putting his tools down.

'That my real mother didn't fall in Das Kino. She jumped and killed herself!'

Felix had been dreading this day. 'Who told you that?

'Some new kid at school has picked up on some gossip. Is it true?' Axel persisted.

'Right, we're going back to school to have a word with this boy. What's his name?'

'Alexander Blisse.'

Feeling indignant, Felix said, 'I'm going to talk to this lad, and the principal.'

Axel was adamant. 'I'm not going back to school today.'

'They'll be on the phone to Ingrid. Try saying no to her!'

'I'll tell her the truth. Onkel, am I the joke of the village? Am I the only one who doesn't know the truth about my mother?'

'I want Klaus and Ingrid to hear this. Wait here!'

'Onkel!' Axel cried. 'I'm asking you!'

Felix faced Axel. This was a defining moment where secrets and lies held no place. 'Yes, it's true.'

Axel felt let down. 'Why didn't you tell me? Why didn't anyone tell me?'

Fudging the issue, Felix said, 'We told you Susanne died, falling in Das Kino.'

'That's not the same thing. My mother didn't want me, that's the truth, isn't it?'

'No! She wanted you - ask Jens if you don't believe me. We think Susanne was suffering from postnatal depression, but nobody realised it at the time.'

'Why the big secret? I knew from a young age that Klaus and Ingrid adopted me, so why didn't you tell me the truth about my mother?'

Felix sighed, 'We thought you were too young and the truth would be too painful. It seems we were right.'

'Secrets just cause more pain,' Axel muttered.

'We didn't want you to grow up stigmatized. We were only trying to protect you.'

Axel was adamant. 'Onkel, you're the person I trust most in the world. Please, I want some answers.'

'You can talk to Klaus and Ingrid, they're your parents.'

'Yes, but you're closer to me in age.'

'I can talk to them about anything, and so can you. Axel, don't shut them out.'

'I'm conscious of having older parents. I don't want them having heart attacks because of my troubles,' Axel said, with insight. 'Onkel, please, you were with my mother at that place in East Germany. I've heard stories about the abuse that went on there; I've even Googled it on my laptop.'

'So, now the whole fucking Internet knows about our Torgau abuse!' Felix yelled, instantly incandescent.

'It's true then, you and Susanne... you were sexually abused?'

Felix nodded, his throat catching with the painful,

suppressed memories.

Axel's anger subsided. 'And this led to my mother's depression?'

'Naturlich. And having a baby at 14.'

Axel reached out and touched Felix on his arm. 'Onkel, I can't imagine how you must have suffered. It must have depressed you too.'

'Yeah, I was a little crazy for a while.'

'But, you're ok now?' Axel asked, eager to hear a positive answer.

'Well, we're all a bit crazy in this family, so I don't tend to stand out.'

'Onkel, you're trying to laugh it off, as usual. These people who did this…'

Felix interrupted his nephew. 'Paedophiles, that's the word you're looking for.'

'Those paedophiles, we can take them to court; to make them pay for their crimes.'

'Too late for that, because it's hard even talking about it with the family.'

Feeling outraged on his onkel's behalf, Axel spat, 'I'd like to kill them for what they did to you and my mother.'

'That's what I thought you'd say.'

'Onkel, you can't let them get away with it and go unpunished.'

'We all pay for our crimes, sooner or later. Trust me, they've been punished.'

In his frustration, Axel pleaded, 'I feel as if I should do something, in my mother's memory. Please, let me help you bring these men to justice.'

'Axel, please don't try to rekindle a flame that has already been extinguished.'

'Onkel, I don't understand, you're talking in riddles.'

Felix felt his pulse race and his frustration rose. 'You don't need to understand. All you need to know is your mother Susanne loved you, your parents love you, your family loves you - and I love you.'

'I know. I'm a lucky kid.'

'Axel, you've got a lot going for you and I imagine that that boy in school, Alexander, wants to compete with you in some way and found out some information about you to try and weaken you. No one else in the village would do that because you're well-liked and popular. Remember, criticism usually stems from jealousy.'

'I gave him a black eye for his troubles,' Axel said proudly.

'Good for you! Just don't show him you're sensitive. It's your Achilles heel.'

'Onkel, what's your Achilles heel?'

'I think you already know the answer: Torgau.'

'I'm sorry.'

'Don't be. I'm a survivor. My dear Axel, I know you need answers but let me tell you something, it's the here and now that counts, that's all we've got. We can never go back and change anything. It is as it is.'

Axel nodded, seeming to understand. 'Onkel, one last question,' he began and took a deep breath. 'Who is my real father?'

Felix had been dreading this question for years. 'I can't answer that,' he said, softly.

Axel frowned. 'Can't - or won't?'

Felix had sent off the Musketeer's hair samples to various DNA experts many years ago to determine Axel's parentage but could not and would not reveal the identity of Axel's father to anyone. If he did, he'd have to explain how he got the hair clippings in the first place and that would mean confessing to three murders - and only Ingrid knew the truth in that regard. But he had to give an answer, so he chose to tell his nephew a version of the hard and tragic truth.

'Axel, I'm sorry. With all the abuse that went on at Torgau; no one can be sure who your real father actually is,' he said, gently.

This upset Axel so much he covered his ears. 'Scheisse!' he screamed, running out.

Felix ran out, calling after him. 'Axel!'

Axel ran into Das Kino, where Felix caught up with him.

'Did she jump from up there?' Axel cried, pointing to the balcony in the rafters.

'Axel, please; let's not go there.'

'Tell me!'

Felix saw the pain in the young man's eyes. They reflected his own pain, which he now was reliving. Finally, he nodded, 'Yes. She jumped from up there.'

'And you? Couldn't you have stopped her?'

'Are you blaming me?' Felix asked, incredulously. 'It all happened so quickly, I was half-way out of the door. Ask Ingrid if you doubt me!'

'Onkel, I've never doubted you. But please, what did my mother say? What were her last words?' Axel asked, needing to know.

'I don't remember.'

Axel was livid. 'You must know!'

Suddenly, Felix snapped, 'I don't want to remember! It's too painful. It wasn't my fault. And nothing I say or do will bring her back.'

'Onkel, please, I know it's not your fault but I need to know.'

'Ok. We'll do this now but we'll never talk about it again. Agreed?'

Axel nodded in tacit agreement. Felix was shaking, visualising Susi standing up in the rafters, on the brink of jumping. The image had never left him; it was indelibly printed in his mind. They had exchanged harsh words and regrets and he'd ended the argument by walking outside.

'Before she jumped she said, 'I can't live like this, I can't do this anymore' and I got really worried for her state of mind. I asked her to come down.'

Axel looked puzzled. 'What couldn't she do anymore?'

'Torgau haunted her; it was all she ever thought of. She said she couldn't live with it going around in her head anymore.'

'Is that all she said?'

Felix could see Axel desperately needed a few comforting words and even though he knew he was omitting specific details, he tried to oblige and say something his nephew could always take great consolation from.

'She wouldn't come down and Susi's last words were, 'Look after Axel, tell him I love him.' Then she jumped.'

'You're just saying that, to make me feel better.'

'It's true, I swear! Your mother told me to look after you,' Felix insisted. 'She loved you… and when she lay crushed on the floor, I cradled her in my arms.'

Axel and Felix threw their arms around one another and wept. It was difficult to tell which one of them was more in need of comfort.

30. Evidence and concepts

Kruger called an impromptu meeting with the team to review the case.

Rutger opened the discussion. 'The cause of death of all three men at Muggelsee was drowning. They were all alive before they entered the water - dazed, but alive.'

Kruger quipped, 'Well, I didn't think they were going skinny dipping in their cars.'

As usual, Rutger ignored Kruger's flippancy and smiling, didn't take offence. 'A blunt object was used on each of the victims' heads and they were each hit several times.'

'What sort of object?' Stefan asked.

'An unknown, blunt object,' said Rutger, wryly.

Hanne stifled a laugh. She wanted to express some ideas of her own. 'The Muggelsee victims worked at Torgau in the 1980s and this would mean when they met their demise in 1992, Marine Boy was probably no older than about 20. Gwisdek and Plaumann were big, strong men, but not Gunther and to overpower someone you need a lot of force... or a gun?'

Rutger concurred. 'Yes, the blunt object could have been a gun, the back of a gun.'

'But he didn't fire it. It's much easier to shoot someone than to go to all the trouble of kidnapping them and driving a car into a cold lake,' Hanne mused.

'Why do you think that is?' Rutger asked.

'Well, it's almost biblical: revenge, an eye for an eye.

Marine Boy wanted to punish them, to make them to feel the same way he'd felt - controlled and humiliated. He tied them up, cut their hair and their ears, and stripped away all their defenses, as if he wanted his victims to atone for their sins,' Hanne told them.

'Then he killed them anyway.'

Hanne nodded. 'That's right, Stefan. Marine Boy couldn't let them get away. Would you, in his place? Shooting his abusers would be too quick a death and I think he wanted them to suffer before they died.'

Kruger offered his insight. 'He'd have to kill them anyway if they saw his face and knew his identity... Any updates on the fingerprints?'

'Yes and no. The stolen bike from Kopenick found in the bushes at Plaumanns' gym had none, but fingerprints belonging to an unknown male were found on the Herbertz knife by Lotte Holler's car. However, there's no record of these fingerprints on our national criminal data register.'

'Marine Boy seems to be a first time offender,' Kruger ventured.

Nodding in agreement, Rutger mused, 'Maybe he's just too clever to be caught.'

Kruger was adamant. 'Oh, we'll catch him, Rutger, I usually get my man - not as quickly as I'd like, but Marine Boy will turn up sooner, rather than later.'

'Indeed! Now, I've taken fingerprints and DNA samples from all three corpses, but we weren't able to retrieve any information from the saturated fibres in the cars pulled from Muggelsee. Unfortunately we couldn't get any DNA from going over Lotte Holler's car again either.'

Stefan chipped in. 'Drais and I got lucky on our trip to Leipzig. Horst's motor home ended up in Zossen. Also, there's another name that's been brought into the frame. Gunther's ex-colleague at the Leipzig library said he used to hang out with some guy called Witzig. I've crossed-checked the 1992 list, but he's not on it. But somewhere, there's another warden from Torgau out there. Dead, or alive.'

'Indeed. But we're concentrating on the men found at Muggelsee for now,' stated Kruger. 'The three Torgau wardens used to go away on trips together in the motor home so we'll need forensics there asap. Delving into their backgrounds will help us find not only their killer but Lotte Holler's assailant, too: the elusive Marine Boy.'

Hanne piped up. 'I've an idea. Why not release details and photos of the Torgau wardens found at the lake? Say the police are looking for witnesses from Muggelsee back in 1992 and would welcome anyone coming forward with previously held information. Some of the abused Torgau kids might recognise them and be brave enough to come forward again, like they did when you broke the paedophile ring. Knowing the police are on his trail, Marine Boy may just crack under the strain and give himself away.'

'I like your idea, Drais,' Kruger said, perkily. 'But I'll have to handle the fall-out for Plaumann's wife and family. Let me think about it and I'll let you know.'

Winding up the meeting, Stefan ventured, 'So, Marine Boy's around 30 to 35 years old, and if he's still alive, someone must know him and suspect him.'

Stefan's words were prophetic. Although she didn't realise it, Hanne had already met Felix, the boy who went on to kill three of his Torgau tormentors and attempted to murder Lotte Holler. His photo, taken at the time of the collapse of the Berlin Wall in 1989, was still on her wall at home. They had shared a brief encounter on an historic night; and they were destined to meet again.

Kruger clapped his hands. 'Ok, listen up, team. In the next five days I'm expecting the following: Gwisdek's motor home brushed for fingerprints: Drais, Lotte Holler is well enough to be interviewed again so get onto Dr Roth and arrange it: I want the old files starting from 1992 relating to sexual abuse, especially the Torgau cases, looked over again. Maybe one of the victims will be prepared to repeat their evidence, or maybe they'll have an idea about our phantom killer. Let's get to it!'

'Yes, sir, echoed the team.

'Oh, one more thing… Make sure you're free on the 15th next week to celebrate our colleague's birthday.' Kruger said, looking directly at Hanne. 'Drais, you'll be the birthday girl and the drinks will be on you.'

31. Hospital revelations

Hanne's second meeting with Lotte's nurses Lena and Martin took place in Dr Roth's office. Their first had been at police headquarters where Lena and Martin had given statements explaining the events of New Year's Eve and how an innocuous playing of the Toreador song precipitated Lotte Holler's miraculous awakening.

Lena and Martin were still in their white hospital uniforms. Lena had let down her long dark hair that she kept back when working on the wards. She had dark rings around her eyes and Martin's shaved, bald head was shiny and a bit grubby. Both looked in need of a good night's sleep.

'Thank you for staying after your night shift, I'll try not to keep you long. I guess you're wondering what further information you can offer me? Well, I want to know your views on the patient, what she's like as a person, how she's coping, etcetera. Please speak freely and what you tell me will be strictly confidential.'

'Well, I made a gaff last week,' Martin confessed. 'I left a newspaper on a trolley, against Dr Roth's orders, and Lotte, somewhat sneakily read it. So, it's my fault she knows about the Muggelsee killings.'

'Jonas has forgiven you,' said Lena. 'Don't worry, Martin, you can't shelter her from these things. Lotte would've found out sooner or later, she's a determined lady!'

'That's precisely the sort of information I need to help me build up Lotte's profile,' confessed Hanne.

'I thought you only profiled those who committed crimes?'

Hanne nodded. 'Well, Martin, that's true, but in profiling the victim as well you discover much more. When you find out who the victim is and what sort of person they are you find out the reasons why they were attacked - and how.'

Lena commented, 'I think Lotte's a realist. She's getting on with things and is determined to get fit and restart her life. It can't be easy after missing all those years.'

'And she's making plans for the future,' added Martin.

'What sort of plans?'

Martin loved a bit of gossip. 'A move into a big house in Wannsee, you know, with an advance of her compensation money.'

Hanne was intrigued. 'I see. When will this take place?'

'When Dr Roth discharges her - not that I'd want a million euros in exchange for losing 12 years of my life,' he replied.

Lena smiled. 'Martin wants to go and work for her. He's Lotte favourite.'

'Lotte likes all the staff but she's a man's woman, more at ease with men. Even camp men like me! Lotte knows I'm gay but it seems to make no difference.'

Lena scoffed, 'So it shouldn't. Anyway, I think Lotte's competitive with women, except for her sister.'

'Lotte can be a cow to her sister!' Martin exclaimed.

'Agreed. Lotte dominates her sister, manipulates her and tries to be in control,' Lena stated. 'I find myself feeling sorry for Julia! Does that sound terrible? And I don't mind patients asking for anything they need, but Lotte's a prickly and demanding character. If she doesn't get it, she gets impatient and moody, and easily cross.'

'You're saying she's quick-tempered?'

Trying to rephrase her words, Lena said, 'Maybe it's being judgmental, but let's just say Lotte's intolerant and a bit spoilt. She gets frustrated easily and then huffs and puffs.'

Martin winked. 'Don't we all? Nothing wrong with some

huffing and puffing!'

'And most of us don't like to hear the word 'no', eh?' Hanne stated, with her thoughts drifting to Marine Boy, wondering how Lotte Holler behaved with him. If Lotte was manipulative with people to get her own way, including her sister, and used her temper as a means of control; that's the behaviour of a bully.

'We don't seem to be very tolerant or sympathetic to the patient, do we?' Lena asked, jolting Hanne out of her thoughts.

'You're only expressing an opinion. Thank you both for your time.'

It was a crisp spring morning and there wasn't a single cloud in the bright, azure sky. Julia and Lotte were waiting for Hanne in the gazebo in the hospital gardens. Lotte was in a wheelchair, wrapped in a blanket.

'You are late, Frau Drais,' Lotte commented. 'Good job it's not too cold.'

Julia was embarrassed. 'Good morning, Hanne. Lotte, don't fuss, it's warm in here and the gazebo windows are double-glazed. Look at the garden- daisies are flowering.'

Hanne ignored Lotte's comment. 'I'm sorry I'm late,' she said, sincerely. 'I had to speak with Martin and Lena.'

Lotte frowned. 'What did they have to say?'

'They told me how well you're doing with your exercises and your rehab. Are you feeling better?'

'I'm fine. If you're wondering why I'm being pushed in a wheelchair, well, I can walk but Julia needs the exercise!' Lotte replied, laughing.

Julia chuckled. 'Hanne, Dr Roth is hoping to discharge Lotte before the end of the month. You'll have to come and see her in Wannsee.'

'Yes, come and see us in Wannsee,' Lotte echoed, looking at her sister, then giving Hanne a discerning look. 'I'm going to be rich. Compensation for my 12 missing years, lost in a bed. Do you think it's a fair exchange?'

Hanne's tone was serious. 'I don't think the loss of time has a price.'

Lotte liked this answer but she didn't trust the police psychologist and the way she was probing into the past. For perceived sins against the Torgau kids, Lotte believed her coma was punishment enough. 'No. It doesn't,' she said flatly.

Julia tried to lighten the conversation. 'Hanne, where do you live?'

'I live with my daughter, in Neu Kolln.'

Julia was pleasantly surprised. 'You have a daughter? You never said.'

'Audrey will be 16 at the end of the month.'

'Must be nice to have a daughter- but I'd not be without my boys.'

'My daughter's into role reversal and sometimes behaves like my mother!

Interrupting them, Lotte brought the spotlight back to herself. 'I'm only 41, it's not too late for me to have kids,' she announced.

'No, course not,' Julia said. 'You've still time to meet someone nice.'

'Failing that, I could find a sperm donor,' Lotte stated, hoping to shock them.

Again, Julia felt a little embarrassed and anxious that Lotte's outspoken nature might cause offence to those who didn't know her well. Julia knew Lotte said outrageous things, sometimes for a laugh and sometimes to shock people. Also, her comments could be quite barbed. She was different to her sibling: Julia usually wanted approval from others whilst Lotte didn't give a damn what people thought of her. Julia often found herself wondering what the pleasant police psychologist thought of her sister and herself.

Hanne also noticed how Lotte liked to provoke. She'd had enough of small talk by now and asked Lotte about the father of her child she'd lost.

'He was married. It was a bit of fun for both of us and I

hadn't told him I was pregnant and was keeping the baby. Why? Is he a suspect?'

'Not at all,' Hanne replied.

'You know, Dr Roth advised me against reading or watching the news but I found out about the three bodies pulled from the lake anyway - my former colleagues Horst Gwisdek, Harald Plaumann and Gunther Schukrafft.'

Hanne nodded. 'It's looking like we have three similar murders on our hands.'

Lotte looked worried. 'This Torgau boy who you suspect, he'll be a man now. What if he's been watching the news and has seen that I've come out of my coma? Do you think he'll come after me again?'

'Try not to get too anxious. You have police protection for as long as necessary. I believe if the Torgau boy wanted you dead, he would've done it while he had the chance.'

Julia took umbrage on Lotte's behalf. 'He left my sister for dead!'

Lotte intervened. 'He would have killed me by driving me into the lake like the others but my car wouldn't start! Psycho boy left me unconscious in the car to freeze to death in the middle of winter, hoping I'd be dead by morning.'

Hanne explained, 'We're looking into the backgrounds of the three dead men to try and find a link and a trail back to their killer - possibly the same man as the one who attacked you. Lotte, you said he was masked and wore a balaclava. Were there any parts of his face you could see; his skin colouring, his height, weight, the colour of his hair?'

Lotte closed her eyes and her thoughts returned to that fateful night. Her face contorted and suddenly she opened her eyes.

'He was about two metres tall. Oh my God, I remember! I saw his face in the headlights,' cried Lotte, suddenly animated. 'He had a wisp of fair hair, peaking out of the balaclava, and blue eyes… Yes! Piercing blue eyes.'

Hanne jotted this down. 'Was there anything he did or said that reminds you of who it could be?'

Lotte remembered quite a lot from 12 years ago but knew she had to be selective with any information she gave to the police. She wasn't about to tell Hanne her attacker had said she was a cruel bully and a Nazi, nor that he'd accused her of assisting the Musketeers in their sordid, debauched activities. As for being pregnant, he'd quoted something in Latin - in loco parentis, whatever that meant. No, Lotte could never tell Julia or anyone else about the part she played at Torgau, because she worried she might never be forgiven.

'I asked him why was he doing this to me? He said he wanted revenge. I think I told him he was in Torgau as a punishment and that he had to be disciplined. He replied that he was an orphan, not some delinquent. He felt the punishments at Torgau were too severe and the wardens deserved to be punished. I can't remember any more.'

'Well done, Lotte, Julia cried, hugging her sister.

Hanne repeated this new information. 'He told you he was an orphan?'

Lotte nodded. 'He was probably lying.'

Suddenly, Hanne asked Lotte a loaded question: 'What kind of punishment do you think he was talking about?'

Lotte and Hanne looked at one another. They both had incisive minds and neither was easily put off their stride or outsmarted.

'Well, some of the wardens were quite rough with them, to control them. They used their fists, the back of their hands, that sort of thing.'

Careful not to be accusatory in her questioning or tone of voice, Hanne probed deeper, 'Did you witness any of this?'

'I know some of the wardens used to find it funny to take some of the unruly kids, strip them and hose them down with ice cold water.'

Julia held her hands over her face. 'If anyone did that to my boys, I wouldn't find it funny at all. It's unforgiveable.'

Continuing with her story, Lotte began to lie to protect herself. 'As for me, most of the kids were taller and stronger than me and I used to shout at them, I don't deny it. I kept control by threatening to tell the male wardens, and the kids knew if they didn't behave with me, the men on duty would punish them.'

Julia was hearing this for the first time. 'No! What sort of punishments?'

'The kids would spend the night in a dark cellar, knee deep in water.'

Hanne informed her, 'Lotte, you need to know that some Torgau kids made accusations of abuse against some of the wardens. These cases came to court over the past decade and a number of ex-employees at Torgau were found guilty of abuse, and punished.'

Lotte held her nerve, keeping her temper in check. 'But that boy, whoever he was, he was a sick psycho! I didn't do anything to justify what he did to me.'

Julia hugged her sister. 'Course not, sweetie, it's not your fault.'

'Absolutely, you're the victim,' Hanne stated, without conveying her doubts.

Lotte stared at Hanne, steely-eyed. 'That's right, it's not my fault. I am the victim in all of this.'

Julia ventured, 'I've faith that the police will catch this madman and put him on trial.'

Challenging her to answer one final question, Hanne asked, 'Lotte, was there, to your knowledge, any form of sexual abuse taking place at Torgau?'

Contorting her mouth, and biting back barbed words, Lotte shook her head. 'Not to my knowledge. If anyone was abusing the kids, they were doing it secretly and certainly not broadcasting it. Anything like that must have all gone on behind closed doors.'

'I think we'll leave it there. Thank you. Sorry if it's been upsetting for you- you've given me quite an insight.'

'Yes, Lotte, you've been very brave,' Julia praised her sister. 'And I'm sure Hanne will remember everything you've said and put it to good use.'

'I will. Oh, one more thing. Lotte, your private papers,

diaries, photos, have they been kept somewhere?'

'Julia emptied my rented flat several years ago.'

'I've kept them in my cellar but there are only a few boxes,' Julia declared.

'Did you have any photos of the staff or the kids at Torgau?'

'I think so. Why?' Lotte asked.

'May I have a look through them?'

Lotte thought she could read Hanne's mind. 'Oh, you'll be looking for an orphaned boy with blond hair and blue eyes? There were plenty like that at Torgau. But he's an adult now and he might have a family. His hair might not be blond any more - but his eyes will still be blue.'

Hanne smiled and gave a false compliment. 'You have a detective's mind.'

Smiling wryly, Lotte agreed. 'Yes, I do. And yes, you can look through my old papers and things. Julia, I'm getting tired now, take me back to my room. Frau Drais, I'd like you to keep me updated with the case.'

'Of course. Julia, I'll send a police officer to collect Lotte's boxes.'

Julia nodded and wheeled her sister away. Hanne looked at the empty cups on the table, and a cheeky thought crossed her mind. She didn't have Kruger's official permission but nevertheless she wrapped the cup Lotte had been drinking from in tissues and placed it carefully in her bag. If Lotte's fingerprints and DNA were found in Horst's motor home, it would prove that she knew the Musketeers after Torgau's closure.

32. The Motor Home

Kruger came into Hanne's office and slammed a newspaper on her desk.

'Our case is on page 17, but look what's made the front cover!'

Hanne read the headline news:

'The film Downfall, about Hitler's last days in his Berlin bunker, has been nominated for best foreign film at the Hollywood Oscars later this month.'

Kruger was livid. 'So much for the important things in life! It'll be this Oskar's downfall if I don't catch the Muggelsee killer!'

Hanne quipped, 'And that's an Oscar performance.'

Kruger managed a rare smile. 'Very droll, Hanne,' he said.

Hanne flicked over the pages and found photos of Horst, Gunther and Harald. 'Funny, I can't relate to these photos after seeing them in their cars at Muggelsee,' she said.

'Well, the images of death stay more powerfully in our vision. Your idea of printing these old photos was approved, and will hopefully jog a memory or two.'

'Fingers crossed. Now I went through Lotte Holler's private papers last night. Sadly, she didn't have any incriminating numbers in a diary, just a few family photos, letters and some unpaid bills.'

Kruger scoffed, 'Lotte won't need to worry about unpaid bills when she's in her new home in Wannsee.'

Hanne nodded. 'It's severance pay, for all her years in a

coma.'

'That's one way of looking at it.'

'Oskar, do you know what really gets to me? Everyone knew abuse went on at Torgau but did nothing about it,' cried Hanne, sounding bitter. 'Lotte has denied all knowledge of any abuse that went on there. Unfortunately, we've no proof to nail Lotte, only the fact that Marine Boy hated her as much as the other Torgau wardens and wanted her dead.'

Kruger was a father and sympathised to some degree. 'You know, back when I was working on breaking the paedophile ring, not one Torgau victim in court who gave evidence about the male wardens, mentioned abuse from female wardens.'

'Did you ask any of the abused victims if they knew Lotte Holler at Torgau?'

'How could I? Lotte wasn't on the list that helped break the Torgau ring. Nobody knew she was even connected to that appalling place!'

'With respect, it doesn't mean she's innocent.'

'Listen Hanne, you often feel for the underdog, and I can see your sympathies are with Marine Boy. However, we can't let bias affect our decisions in a police investigation.'

'I know and I have sympathy for Lotte as a victim but as a parent, I can't help feeling Marine Boy was a victim too.'

'Well, until Lotte's well enough no one will accuse her of anything. She's owed that much because she was a victim of a terrible crime,' Kruger stated. 'You want justice for Marine Boy but what about justice for Lotte? When we catch Marine Boy he'll get sentenced for his crimes and we'll take into consideration what he went through at Torgau. That'd be fair, but we can't, as law enforcing officers, excuse murder, not even

for those who've been abused. Hanne, I promise we'll find out about Lotte's role at Torgau, but give it time.'

On the journey out of Berlin, Glockner and Kruger bantered away about politics whilst Hanne remained quiet in the back, lost in her thoughts. The German Chancellor, Gerhard Schroeder, was on the verge of stepping down or being usurped within his own party and an election announcement was imminent.

'There'll be an election soon, a new Chancellor and coalition party,' mused Stefan.

'Who'll be Chancellor then?' Kruger asked.

'There are women rising in the ranks. I reckon a woman is due to take control.'

Kruger laughed. 'Not in my lifetime!'

'Twenty euros says I'm right.'

'Easy money. You're on. Do you hear that Drais? Glockner reckons we'll have the first female Chancellor. What do you say?'

'Our country needs a Hausfrau in charge!' Hanne remarked, trying not to smile.

Kruger grimaced. 'Speak for yourself, Drais.'

Hanne returned to her thoughts. She liked getting out of Berlin although she didn't take Audrey to the countryside now as often as she'd like. When Audrey was little, Hanne and Claudia would go on cycling trips to the vast areas of countryside and lakes surrounding Berlin, with Audrey secure in a harnessed basket at the front of the bike. She sighed inwardly and told herself not to get melancholy or stuck in thoughts about the past. Audrey was older and they still did mother and daughter outings together but in the natural evolving state of any parent and child, they now led more independent lives. Claudia was long gone and Hanne had a new girlfriend, Brigitte. They'd been dating for six weeks and were getting on nicely, so things were looking up.

Passing Schonefeld Airport on the motorway they turned off onto quieter rural roads, meandering through winding lanes of open countryside and alleys of trees towards the small town of Zossen. Hanne, quietly happy in the back, was enjoying the view.

Detlef Biegel, an active and friendly 70-year-old, met the

police and forensic team at a modern timber yard where business had ceased for the duration of the police visit. He was eager to help. Introductions were made and any small talk ended.

'Thanks for seeing us,' said Kruger. 'What can you tell us?'

'Well, Kommissar. In the winter of 1992, after three months of watching the post piling up and waiting for Horst to return to the flat in Leipzig where there was rent owing, my brother and I packed up his things. We put them in the motor home and brought it here, to my brother's field at the back of the timber yard,' Detlef explained.

'We'll need fingerprints from you and your brother today.'

Detlef looked worried. 'You want our fingerprints? I'd better fetch Ulrich.'

Stefan put his hand on Detlef's shoulder. 'Don't worry, it's just routine. You and your brother have been inside the motor home so both your prints need to be ruled out.'

'Ok. Yes, I understand. Well, we just let the moss grow over it and after a while it was a blot on the landscape, but we didn't dare get rid of it in case Horst came back.'

Hanne was intrigued by the old man's choice of words. 'You didn't dare?'

Detlef shook his head. 'Herr Gwisdek was quite a tricky character. He didn't mix with the neighbours. He was a loner, not polite but not particularly friendly either.'

'Did you ever see any of his friends or family?'

'Not really. Horst never spoke about a family or even what he did for a job, and I didn't ask. He paid the rent, so I couldn't complain. Nobody messed with him because he was a tough, ex-army type.'

Kruger's ears pricked up. 'Ex-army? How'd you know that?'

'When Ulrich and I packed all his things, we found a photograph of Horst in a Russian Army uniform,' Detlef told them.

'Could be fancy dress costume,' Kruger surmised. 'Time we saw this motor home.'

Horst Gwisdek's motor caravan was in a field behind the timber yard, obscured by trees and partly covered in moss. Inside it was cold and damp. Rutger- who'd travelled down separately, had set up a forensic tent outside and the area was cordoned off. Everyone who entered the motor home wore protective latex gloves and plastic overshoes.

After a brief perusal, Kruger wandered off to Rutger in the tent, leaving Hanne and Stefan in the caravan, looking through a few discoloured white envelopes, pulling out old photos, mostly in colour but some in black and white. There was a photo of Horst as a younger man in the distinctive uniform of the Russian Army with red lapels and epaulettes emblazoned with the hammer and the sickle, and other army photos where Horst was dressed in desert combat gear.

Hanne turned over a photo: the words 'Afghanistan 1982' written on the back.

'Stefan, take a look at this. Horst served in Afghanistan.'

Looking at the photo, Stefan ventured, 'No one wins over there except the Afghans.'

Finding a photo of a large group of men and women in a cobbled courtyard, Hanne looked closely, hoping to recognise someone in the myriad of faces. On the back of the photo was written: Dresden 1988.

'This has to be Torgau. So, after his Army days it's looking likely that Horst went to work at Torgau as a warden and the dates would fit. But what did he do after the Wall came down?' she mused. 'Let's hope these files will give us some answers.'

There were several files in boxes including old records of Horst's rental contract for the Biegel's flat in Leipzig, Horst's car and motor home insurances, his landline and mobile phone bills alongside utility bills like electric and gas, old receipts for food and petrol and invoices to and from various places of work.

Stefan read an invoice. 'Bingo! Horst was a self-employed

security guard.'

'Prima!' Hanne exclaimed.

'Ok, let's see what else we can find.'

'Stefan, I've had an idea,' Hanne said, and left in a hurry.

Biegel had provided the police and forensic teams with sustenance from the small kitchen in the timber yard. Copious amounts of hot, freshly brewed coffee were available plus sandwiches and pastries and most important of all, a warm room to sit in.

'This looks nice, thank you. Detlef. May I ask you a question?'

Biegel nodded. 'I don't know if I can help, but go on, young lady, ask away.'

'Did you know Horst was a self-employed security guard?'

'I always thought he was self-employed but I never knew exactly what Horst did.'

'Well, we've got some of his old invoices and I imagine he sorted his taxes out himself because there's no sign of an accountant. So let's assume Horst was working up and until the time of his disappearance and was invoiced for a job at his last place of work.'

Detlef had a bright spark in his eyes. 'You mean, did Horst receive any letters or invoices after his disappearance?'

He'd read her mind and Hanne smiled. 'Exactly!'

'Let me see. If I remember correctly, I put the last few months of his post in a manila envelope and dated it: Autumn 92.'

Hanne could have kissed Biegel. 'Thank you. I'll be back for coffee and cake.'

Returning to the motor home, Hanne found the manila envelope. Inside, were details of Horst's last places of work. Two invoices and cheques were sent to him in the autumn of 1992, one from the organisers of the Berlin Marathon dated September 1992. The other was from Motzen Mayor golf club for his security services at their tournament, dated October 1992.

Stefan commented, 'These two sporting events never had to pay him. Horst never cashed their cheques. His death saved them more than 300 Deutchmarks each!'

'That was a good day's pay in 1992. We'll mention these cheques to the Berlin Marathon organisers and the Motzen golf club. I wonder who Horst banked with?'

Pulling out a piece of paper from a file, Stefan told her, 'It's with Deutsche Post and here are his account details. I'll contact the bank.'

Hanne was curious. 'If it's a hibernating account, I wonder who gets the money?'

'Not Lotte Holler, that's for sure. She'll be rich enough.'

Kruger came inside the motor home.

Hanne had a wry smile, 'Good timing, Oskar.'

'Take a look at this,' Glockner said, handing Kruger the letter from the manila envelope.

Kruger read the letter and asked. 'How many bloody security people do you need at the Berlin Marathon?'

'Quite a few. You don't think they'll remember Gwisdek?'

Kruger shook his head. 'No, Stefan, I don't. But there's less staff at a golf tournament. Where's this Motzen Mayor Golf club?'

'Not far from here. Don't think we'll have time to check it out today, though.'

Kruger, Glockner and Hanne took a break in the warmth of the staff room at the timber yard just as Detlef's brother Ulrich arrived, bringing with him a local and distinguished guest: the Mayor of Zossen, Bernd Felker.

Bernd didn't want to make a fuss; he just wanted to know what was going on in his jurisdiction. Zossen was his home and whether the news was good or bad, he liked to be informed. He knew the Biegel brothers and many of the townsfolk by name and when Ulrich bumped into him in town and told him what was going on at the timber yard, Bernd immediately dropped all of his plans and followed the old man back.

Detlef greeted the Mayor and his lookalike brother Ulrich, who was in fact five years younger, shaking hands warmly with both men. Bernd perused the room and instinctively noticed Kruger's air of authority with his colleagues, which told him that this man was in charge of proceedings.

Detlef cleared his throat, to address the team. 'This is the Burgermeister of Zossen.'

Kruger shook the Mayor's hand. 'Kommissar Oskar Kruger, and these are my colleagues; Stefan Glockner and Hanne Drais. News travels fast in these parts.'

'You could say that. May I?' Bernd asked, gesturing to join them at the table.

'Of course, sit yourself down.'

Bernd shook hands with Stefan and Hanne.

'Bernd, help yourself to a cake. What can I get you to drink?'

'No cake, Detlef, just a cup of tea, danke,' Bernd said, and turning to the police team he told them, 'My wife worries about my expanding waistline and coffee consumption.'

'So does mine, but she's not here,' Kruger said, laughing and taking a second pastry. 'How can we help you, Herr Burgermeister.'

'Please, call me Bernd. Well, if anyone in town starts asking questions and wants to turn up here out of curiosity, can you advise me what I should say?'

Kruger thought Bernd was experienced at diplomacy and lowered his gruff exterior for the friendly Mayor. 'Firstly, the motor home is not to be tampered with and other than that, I'm sure you'll know what to say to the townsfolk. Now I'd like you to accompany me to the police station in town and help me liaise with them once we've finished here.'

'No problem, be glad to help.'

'So, Bernd, let me fill you in on some details. You've heard about the three bodies pulled out of Muggelsee last month?'

'Yes, I hear it's the talk of the town over there.'

'Well, the motor home belongs to one of the deceased men, Horst Gwisdek. Have you heard of him?' Kruger asked.

Bernd shook his head. 'Is he… was he from around these parts?'

'From Leipzig. He went missing back in 1992.'

Detlef brought Bernd a cup of tea, and chipping in, said, 'Horst Gwisdek was one of my old tenants.'

'I see. Thanks, Detlef. Don't forget to tell Ute, I haven't cheated with the cakes,' Bernd said, grinning.

'We'll be in the kitchen if you need us,' Detlef told them and with Ulrich, left the room.

'Where were we?' Kruger asked.

Glockner reminded him. '1992, Leipzig and Gwisdek.'

'Oh, yes, Horst Gwisdek. The motor home belonged to him and we're hoping anything we find inside amongst his personal possessions will help us track his killer.'

'I see. Well, I don't suppose it's easy to find killers, let alone killers from 1992, but I wish you luck with your investigation,' Bernd said, enthusiastically. 'I have to tell you, Kommissar, the excitement of your presence here in Zossen has spread all over town.'

Kruger seemed unperturbed. 'Can't be helped.'

Hanne ventured, 'It's like a traffic accident. Passing cars slow down to take a look.'

'Lots of folk like a bit of blood and gore.'

'Speak for yourself, Glockner,' quipped Hanne.

Bernd could see the police team enjoyed their own brand of humour. 'You said there were three men pulled from Muggelsee. Are they connected to one other?'

'Yes,' Kruger replied flatly, lighting a cigar.

Bernd didn't probe. He took Kruger's tacit response as 'Don't ask' and took a swig of his tea, gulping it down in one go thinking maybe he should leave. 'Well, here's my card. If there's anything I can help you with or you need, just get in touch with me.'

Kruger liked the Mayor's diplomacy. 'Don't go just yet. I'll finish my coffee and we'll go to the police station in Zossen, if that doesn't interfere with your plans for the day?'

'Not at all,' Bernd said, thinking his round of golf with Klaus could wait. Police work was much more important than keeping up his golf handicap. Bernd liked to feel his work was worthwhile, serving the community of Zossen. He preferred presiding over meetings with the town council to discuss environmental and fiscal developments rather than being simply a figurehead, holding banquets and opening fetes, and Ute enjoyed playing the perfect host as the wife of the Mayor. Today was real work, helping the police with a murder investigation.

'Bernd, I presume you take an oath of secrecy to serve the community and country?'

'Yes, Kommissar. Every time I'm re-elected as Burgermeister.'

'How long have you been Mayor of Zossen?' Stefan asked.

'About 15 years.'

'The news will be breaking any day now, therefore I'm not being indiscreet. To answer your earlier question, yes, all three men found in the lake worked together in East Germany, as wardens at a notorious institution near Dresden.'

Bernd had a gut feeling Kruger was talking about Torgau. He didn't think it was a good idea to mention his family links to such a place.

'Have you heard of a place called Torgau?' Kruger asked the Mayor.

Bernd sighed, thinking of Felix. 'Who hasn't?'

Kruger confessed, 'The killer seems to be an ex-inmate with a grudge who took his revenge on the wardens on the banks of Muggelsee. As far as we are aware, he was successful at least three times.'

Bernd was intrigued. 'You mean, he tried to kill others, but was unsuccessful?'

'In 1992 there was a fourth crime at Muggelsee, where he left a woman, the 'Lady of the Lake' for dead.'

'Kommissar; wasn't she the coma victim?'

Kruger nodded. 'We'll put photos up of the Muggelsee three in all the towns in this area and maybe someone will come forward with new information.'

'Sure. Maybe the murderer is from around here or lives near a lake, being that he likes water crimes. Maybe he's under your very noses,' Bernd said, prophetically.

Hanne celebrated her 37th birthday on 15th March. It was going to be a busy day. Brigitte left earlier that morning after breakfast, taking Audrey and dropping her off at school. Hanne worked at home till lunchtime, and allowed herself the rest of the day off; a rare treat.

Lotte Holler's case had troubled her more than usual. As a mother, she knew that sexual abuse of a child was one of the worst things that could happen to her daughter and she found it hard to stay neutral. She had formed a certain bias in favour of Marine Boy, even though she didn't have all the facts. Hanne couldn't hide this from Kruger, yet behind his gruff exterior, he had insight and empathy, which was edifying.

The same questions kept repeating in her head. What had happened to Marine Boy that had compelled him to kill these three Torgau colleagues and include Lotte Holler in his murderous plans? Unless he was insane, which Hanne didn't believe, what was his motive? Marine Boy seemed to find all four of them equally culpable for crimes against him. Surely it wasn't a case of mistaken identity where Lotte was concerned?

Hanne didn't think so. On her last visit to the hospital when Lotte revealed details of the abuse that went on at Torgau, Hanne had the feeling she was hiding much more than she was letting on and skirting around the details. When she'd asked Lotte outright if she knew of any sexual abuse that took place, she scrutinized Lotte's facial movements for any signs of discomfort. Hanne felt Lotte was being selective with the truth and lacked empathy - and without empathy, she thought, there's usually little compassion for others because it has been replaced by a narcissistic projection of the self.

Hanne often found herself wondering what had happened to Marine Boy. He'd let his mask slip, albeit briefly, when he told Lotte he was an orphan. Surely there was one family relative that could have looked after the boy, protecting him from ending up in Torgau? The system in East Germany had failed him but what had become of him after Torgau's closure? Without the love of a family, had he drifted in and out of mental institutions or managed to find a job? Did Marine Boy continue the cycle of abuse with children once he himself became an adult, as is sometimes the case, or was he connected and involved in the Torgau Three's activities before he murdered them? It was even questionable whether Marine Boy was still alive and quite possibly he had died at some point after he'd completed his mission at Muggelsee.

There were so many imponderables. Hanne had a gut feeling Marine Boy was still alive and was sure he'd never told anyone about his long-forgotten crimes. She hoped he'd found some happiness and security with a new family of his own. Was it coincidence that Marine Boy encountered one of the Torgau Three, and this changed his destiny?

Going by the evidence, Hanne, thought, Horst's murder was likely to be the first and the primary motive was revenge. There was no other explanation for such horrific crimes. If Marine Boy found his stability threatened he would feel the need to act, especially if there was someone he wanted to protect in the process? A child, possibly?

Unfortunately, Marine Boy's mental health could be troubled again, hearing news reports about Lotte Holler and the Torgau Three and knowing the police were on his trail. In her job, working alongside the police, there was the belief in the rule of the law: Marine Boy should be caught and punished. Hanne had been politically correct most of her life but with this case she felt she was losing her bearings. As a parent, Hanne sympathised with the rule of revenge: paedophiles are rapists and rapists get what they deserve.

Of late, Hanne was juggling her time more than usual and often went to bed exhausted but she tried to make sure she made enough time for Audrey, and now Brigitte. Today she decided she would try to switch off from the case and enjoy her birthday. It was a bright, breezy, sunny spring day when Hanne cycled into town and met up with Brigitte for lunch at her workplace – Kadewe; one of the most prestigious department stores in Berlin, where she worked as a pharmacist. The food was expensive yet exquisite and staff had a 10 per cent discount. Regarding quality, Hanne thought, you get what you pay for, but expensive food often tasted better at a reduced price.

Lunch was a compromise for Hanne and Brigitte. They'd decided they wouldn't spend the evening together as Hanne's mother Traudl was coming for an evening meal, which Audrey was cooking. As yet, Traudl hadn't met her daughter's new girlfriend, and Hanne and Brigitte agreed it was better left as a family affair. The most important thing was that Brigitte was adjusting to Audrey and so far, enjoying the process. There was no need just yet for her to have the extra pressure of meeting her prospective mother-in-law.

Hanne met her girlfriend on the restaurant floor. Brigitte had kept on her white, clinical work coat with her name badge but removed her protective cap revealing her short, chestnut hair. Brigitte was a few years older than Hanne and shorter in stature- like Audrey, so Hanne towered over her. Brigitte never felt the urge to become a mother but enjoyed being around kids of all ages, and liked Audrey and hoped it was reciprocal.

It was too early for Hanne and Brigitte to be talking of future plans, but after six weeks they were getting on rather well and just trying to go with the flow.

Brigitte could see that Hanne's job as a criminal psychologist was highly pressurised, on top of bringing up a teenager. Hanne didn't talk about her work with Brigitte, partly because it was highly confidential but also because she discussed it enough during her working day and tried not to bring her work home with her. If anyone asked her what case she was working on she painted an overall picture but was careful not to divulge sensitive facts.

In Kadewe, Hanne and Brigitte enjoyed a pleasant hour together in the busy food hall, toasting one another with a glass of champagne filled with strawberries. Brigitte had bought tickets for them to see the German singer Nena in concert in a few weeks and presented Hanne with the tickets.

Hanne smiled. 'Danke. That's so lovely. I'll look forward to it.'

'You're welcome. I asked Audrey to join us at the concert, but she said no.'

'I feel bad you're not coming tonight. Are you sure you won't come?'

Brigitte shook her head. 'You haven't seen your mother since she came back from her trip to South Africa.'

Rolling her eyes, Hanne commented, 'She's annoyed I didn't pick her up at the airport last week but Audrey wanted me to go to the opening of her art exhibition at school. Mutti thought I could see Audrey's artwork any time but it was a chance to talk to some of her teachers. As it transpired, though, only her art teacher was there.'

'My mother's the same. She doesn't think my time is limited,' Brigitte remarked.

Hanne was adamant. 'I'm not apologising. No; Traudl clicks her fingers and expects me to jump.'

'I've only known you a short while and you don't jump to anyone's tune.'

Hanne laughed at Brigitte's insight to her character. 'Well, maybe Audrey's tune. No, I simply couldn't disappoint my daughter and not go to her exhibition on opening night.'

'Kids come first; I'm sure your mother knows that.'

Hanne laughed. 'You don't know her! Traudl likes to come first, and that's only one of the reasons why we clash!'

Brigitte observed wryly. 'Families, eh? Is your brother Rolf coming?'

'Rolf called earlier; he flies to the States tomorrow for a month. He'll also miss Audrey's 16th birthday later in the month, but never mind.'

'Is Audrey's father coming to her party?'

'Yes, but I'm not sure if his wife's coming.'

Brigitte seemed somewhat tentative. 'Audrey invited me to her party. Is that ok?'

'Naturlich. Audrey wants you there, and I want you there.'

'Then I'll be there,' Brigitte told her, smiling.

'Good. Then you'll have the pleasure of meeting Traudl.'

'It's a bit ominous, but I think it's time I met your mother. I guess you'll have to meet mine, too.'

'Ok, I'd like that. Now, be warned, when you meet my mother; don't forget to bring a thick skin with you.'

Brigitte winked. 'Sounds like you! We all have to take after someone.'

Hanne reached out to squeeze Brigitte's hand under the table. Berlin was a gay friendly city, but public displays of affection, especially in middle class areas and establishments such as Kadewe, could be seen as inappropriate. Before parting, Hanne and Brigitte enjoyed a few private kisses and hugs on the fire exit stairwell.

A little tipsy, Hanne cycled slowly along the cycle paths to the office for the pre-arranged celebration with her colleagues. Kruger and the team were in the staff canteen. Rutger made an appearance, bringing with him a few bottles of champagne to drink with the spread of sandwiches and cakes. Hanne was still full from lunch but appreciated the gesture and forced herself to eat a little and have another glass of champagne, although she worried that later, she'd be caught drink-driving on her bicycle.

Kruger raised his glass. 'To Drais, our psycho cop!'

'Cheers!' echoed around the room followed by everyone singing 'Happy Birthday'.

'Thank you all,' Hanne told them, warmly.

Rutger rose to speak. 'Of course, 15th March is an auspicious day. Not only is it our dear Hanne's birthday, but many centuries ago the Emperor Julius Caesar on this day - known as the Ides of March - was murdered.'

'What are you trying to say, Rutger?' Kruger queried. 'Is there a Brutus among us?'

Rutger smiled, wryly. 'No, only Brut champagne.'

Cringing, Stefan declared, 'Drais, I do believe Rutger was attempting a joke.'

'Danke,' Hanne told Rutger, giving him a hug.

Before long, Kruger took Hanne aside. 'We got a breakthrough with the case today. Rutger found other fingerprints in Horst's caravan, and Harald and Gunther's were among them.'

'Prima!' Hanne exclaimed. 'That verifies the witness statements about the Torgau Three and their trips away.'

'I know. But listen to the best news of all. A man called Wolfgang has turned up at a police station in Minden, near Hannover; he was a Torgau inmate in the 1980s.'

Hanne was excited to hear more. 'Did he recognise the Torgau Three from the photos we put in the newspapers?'

'Yes, and Wolfgang's saying all three of them sexually abused him.'

'Bingo!' Hanne said, clapping her hands.

'As far as I know, Wolfgang, didn't give evidence back in 1992 but that's probably a good thing because he can shed new light on the case and only add more credence to the evidence against the wardens,' Kruger said, waving Stefan over.

Joining them, Stefan asked, 'What's up?'

Kruger instructed, 'You two, whatever your plans were for tomorrow, they've just been changed. I've booked us all on the first flight to Hannover.'

34. Klaus and Ingrid

Ingrid hadn't been sleeping well. Her boys were troubled and when she went to bed at night she couldn't switch off because she was worrying incessantly about Felix and Axel. Since Felix confessed to the Muggelsee killings and his attempted murder of the coma victim, Ingrid felt she'd helped him by letting him get it off his chest. By listening to him, though, she had taken on the mantle of an accomplice and she felt responsible for letting him down in some way.

She didn't feel any differently about her beloved nephew, refusing to judge him because he was only 17 at the time, and probably not in his right mind. On the contrary, Felix had taken these extreme measures to rid himself of the threat from his abusers, avenging Susanne's death in the process. Ingrid felt a certain admiration for his bravery. An eye for an eye, Ingrid believed, and loved Felix nevertheless, knowing he'd also acted to protect Axel, Susi's son and now her own.

However, Ingrid was finding it hard to block Felix's actions from her mind, especially with the constant reminders in the media. The case was updated regularly on the news and the victims' photos were often in the newspapers and on the television. She did her best to make sure it was switched off- especially when Felix visited and reports of the case in the newspapers were hidden away. They had a tacit understanding to talk about it, but only if Felix first brought up the subject.

As yet, he hadn't spoken about it again. Felix was trying

to put it out of his mind and concentrate on his life and the arrival of his second baby. He knew it was a ridiculous fantasy, as if by not talking about it made it unreal and it had never happened. It was foolhardy for Ingrid and Felix to live in denial but after all the secrets they had to keep in the former East Germany, they were both well practised at hiding information.

Then there was Axel. Felix told her that Axel now knew the truth about his mother's demise. Ingrid and Klaus wondered why their son hadn't come to them first but understood why Felix was the one Axel wished to talk to. They spoke with Axel and resolved to put it behind them. When Axel's school contacted them about their son's behavior - he had hit another pupil - this too, was dealt without fuss, swept under the carpet and forgotten.

Feeling the pressure, Ingrid began to suffer from insomnia. She considered taking sleeping pills instead of admitting to herself that she was emotionally tired from the recent revelations and the stress of keeping such terrible secrets.

Klaus noticed a change in his Ingrid over the last month and challenged her for an explanation for her mood swings and low energy. She told him it was because she was worried about Axel fighting at school in the aftermath of him finding out the truth about his mother. Klaus reassured her that any anxiety and violent reaction that Axel felt, would soon pass.

One night, Klaus awoke in the middle of the night to find Ingrid fast asleep in the living room, with the television on low. Something serious was troubling her. At first, Klaus wondered if it was the menopause because Ingrid had been suffering from hot sweats and insomnia, but instinct made him wonder if it went deeper than that.

The following day, Klaus insisted Ingrid join him on a walk, away from the cottage and saying he needed to talk to her alone. Ingrid conceded Klaus was worried about her and a conversation between them was long overdue. It had been a while since they'd walked the circumference of the lake so they went at a steady pace, with the spring sunshine peeping through the tall pine trees shading the wooded pathways.

'Are you going to tell me what's troubling you?' Klaus asked, taking her hand.

Although she felt guilty about not confessing secrets to her beloved husband, Ingrid had promised Felix it would be their secret. 'How'd you mean?'

Klaus wasn't put off. 'My dear, we've been together since we were teenagers. You're not sleeping, you're tired during the day and your rosy cheeks have lost their glow.'

Ingrid was flippant. 'It's called menopause.'

'No!' Klaus insisted. 'You're worried about Axel and Felix. Axel I understand, but you and Felix? When you think I'm not looking, the pair of you exchange odd looks. What's the big secret?'

She blurted out, 'I promised I wouldn't tell! I must keep his secrets.'

'Ingrid! If you don't tell me, I'll ask him! There'll not be any secrets between us.'

'No! Don't ask him, he'll never forgive me,' Ingrid pleaded.

Klaus realised the importance of her words. 'What's happened? Ingrid, please.'

She sighed. 'You and me, we kept Felix a secret from the Stasi, and we both know the importance of keeping secrets. Klaus, I've hated lying to you.'

Klaus stopped in his tracks, faced Ingrid and put his hands on her shoulders. 'Then tell me the truth, let me help you.'

'Ok. But you must keep it a secret… Felix's life depends on it.'

Klaus felt his pulse race and could see the fear in his wife's eyes. 'What's he done? Has Felix done something… something bad?'

'You mustn't judge him, because he was only 17 at the time.'

Klaus cast his mind back. 'Has this got something to do

with the time he came home with rope burns around his neck?'

She nodded. 'In 1992... You know the Muggelsee killings?'

'Nein!' Klaus snapped, shaking his head. 'Don't tell me... No! Not our Felix.'

'Those three men abused him and Susanne in Torgau,' Ingrid confessed. 'Felix felt he didn't have a choice. One of them turned up at the golf club- working for us as a freelance security guard at our September tournament.'

Klaus put his hand over his mouth. 'Scheisse! The police rang the club the other day. They were asking if we remembered someone called Gwisdek. Apparently we sent him a cheque for his services, only he never cashed the cheque.'

Ingrid gasped, 'No! What did you tell them?'

'I said I'd look through our old files and get back to them.'

'You've got to protect Felix. Klaus, promise me you'll protect him.'

'Of course. I love Felix just as much as Axel. Oh, the stupid boy! Ingrid, I want all of it, all the details. How many has he killed?'

'The three men found at Muggelsee. He drove their cars into the lake and also left a woman for dead, you know, the one that's been in the news, the woman who woke up from a coma. She was at Torgau; she was their accomplice, a cruel go-between.'

Klaus was adamant. 'Then she deserved all she got, just like those sick bastards. An eye for an eye, that's my belief.'

'I'm so sorry I didn't tell you.'

'Now you have, maybe you'll sleep better. I've been so worried about you.'

Ingrid began to cry. 'I'm sorry. Sofie will be turning in her grave if I don't protect Felix. Klaus, I can't lose him, he's all I have left of my sister.'

Klaus held Ingrid in his arms. 'She'd be proud of you

because you're a good mother. We couldn't have stopped him, you know. Felix had to do it or he wouldn't have found any peace knowing those people went on abusing and living. Don't worry my love; no one will take our Felix from us.'

35. The Magic Flute

A few days after Hanne's birthday, Stefan Glockner picked her up at 6 a.m. and drove to Berlin's Tegel Airport. Their journey across the city was spent in happy mutual silence. Both were bleary eyed and in need of large doses of caffeine at breakfast in the departure lounge while they waited for Kruger, who, as usual, was running late.

'Sorry, I forgot to ask. How did your birthday meal go with your mother?'

Hanne quipped, 'Audrey was the referee! There were a few fouls but no red cards.

'Was your new girlfriend there?'

'No, Traudl and Brigitte will meet for the first time at Audrey's birthday party.'

'Am I invited?'

Scoffing, Hanne commented, 'Stefan, if you want to give Audrey a present, feel free, but don't use it as an excuse to meet Brigitte and take the piss out of me.'

'Drais, would I?'

Kruger arrived, a little out of breath. 'Don't anyone say if I stopped smoking cigars, I'd be as fit as you two and get here on time. It's my wife's fault; she insisted on driving!'

It was a short flight to Hannover and all three of them had a quick doze. Kruger, Stefan and Hanne were collected by two officers from the Minden police who briefed them as they drove for an hour out of Hannover into the countryside towards Minden, a small town on the river Weser.

Wolfgang Feuer was waiting in the police interview room. In his early 30s, tall and slender with wavy, brown hair that covered his ears, and smartly dressed. His fingernails were bitten to the core- the only visible signs that under his relaxed, outward appearance he was an anxious man.

The team introduced themselves to Wolfgang.

'Thank you for coming all the way from Berlin to see me,' he said, warmly.

'It's our case; the Minden Police were obliged to contact us,' Kruger told him.

Wolfgang was adamant. 'Kommissar, I want to make something clear. I'm not doing this to get compensation. Besides, who'd pay for all the crimes committed at Torgau?'

'Let me assure you, the police have investigated a lot of accusations of paedophilia linked to Torgau; many suspects were caught and tried,' Kruger announced, proudly. 'They've paid all right and if your evidence helps us catch others, we'll ensure the legal system won't let you down. Any compensation due to you will be forthcoming.'

Wolfgang appreciated this. 'Thank you. Kommissar, I remember the trials in the early 90s when you put away some of the Torgau paedophiles, but back then, I didn't have the strength or the courage to give evidence. When I recognized the wardens' faces in the papers recently, I was ecstatic. They'd got what they deserved and I thought it was time I spoke up; time their families knew the ugly truth about them.'

'The men found at Muggelseee were suspects in the paedophile ring of 1992-3. Rest assured, their families know the truth about them now,' stated Stefan. 'They didn't get away with it and they paid for their crimes with their lives.'

'Good! I can't libel the dead, but I'll happily stick another nail in their coffins,' Wolfgang said, clapping his hands.

Speaking softly, Hanne asked, 'How old were you when you were at Torgau?'

Wolfgang had been waiting a long time to tell his story. 'I

was 13. I was imprisoned for three years. Gunther, Horst and Harald were known by their nicknames at Torgau - they called themselves the Musketeers. I was one of their 'boys' they sexually abused.'

Hanne was concerned. 'Is this the first time you've spoken about this?'

Wolfgang confessed, 'I've had therapy. Erich, my husband, encouraged me to come forward and tell my story to the police.'

Kruger and Stefan looked at one another, which didn't go unnoticed by Wolfgang.

'And just in case you're thinking, oh, he's gay, and must have enjoyed being passed around by the Musketeers- three at a time! That is NOT the case!' snapped Wolfgang, banging his fist on the table.

Kruger whispered in Stefan's ear and then Hanne's. To Wolfgang's surprise, Kruger and Glockner then left the room.

'They're not homophobic. I'm gay and I wouldn't allow it,' Hanne told him, gently.

Wolfgang composed himself. He felt Hanne was sincere - after all, she didn't have to divulge her sexuality to him, a stranger, but she had. He decided to trust her. 'I'm a bit touchy, sorry.'

'That's understandable,' Hanne said. 'Please, go on.'

'Ok. Well, the Musketeers did the night shift at weekends; for them it was party time, and we were taken from our beds. Once they'd had enough of us, we were discarded and left alone for our wounds to heal for a week or two; until the next time.'

'Was there anyone you could tell?'

Wolfgang's bitter tone was full of irony. 'The Stasi.'

Hanne understood. 'Well, this is a murder inquiry and maybe you can help us, give us some clues as to who might have killed the Musketeers?'

Scoffing, Wolfgang cried, 'All the kids at Torgau will be suspects!'

'I can imagine you kids must have hated the Musketeers.'

'Do you know what their motto was? 'One for all and all for one'. Yeah, I hated them all right; the Torgau kids hated the Musketeers with a vengeance.'

Hanne needed to know. 'Did you hate them enough to want to kill them?'

Wolfgang shook his head. 'Given half the chance, but I'm not brave enough. Am I a suspect? I'm happy to take a lie detector test and voluntarily give my DNA.'

'No, you're not a suspect. Wolfgang, explain how did you ended up in Torgau?'

'You won't believe me, but I told a joke in school. Someone told the authorities I was making anti-Russian jokes, and that I wasn't a good Communist. I was 13! They took me from my family and put me in that terrible place. My parents had no right of appeal or allowed to visit me. As if I was forgotten - weggesperrt.'

Hanne was shocked. 'I'm sorry. Dare I ask what the joke was about?'

'I was disrespectful to Stalin's memory. Stalin had been dead for years when I told a joke I'd made up; it went like this: Stalin was visiting the people in Berlin and went up the TV tower in Alexander Platz with the East German cabinet. Stalin asked them, "What can I do for the people of this Russian enclave of mine" The cabinet replied "You could jump". I don't tell jokes anymore.'

Hanne gasped, putting her hands up to her face as tears welled in her eyes. What could she possibly say?

Wolfgang appreciated her empathy. 'It's ok, I went back to my family and made something of myself; I wasn't going to let those bastards define my life. Maybe the person who killed the Musketeers felt the same?' he ventured.

'I think so too,' she admitted, taking a tissue and blowing her nose.

'Do you need a break?' he asked.

'No, I'm fine. This case is getting to me, I have a daughter, she's 16 next week and I couldn't bear the thought of her… Sorry.'

'There isn't a day goes by when I don't think about Torgau,' he confessed.

'Have you kept any photos of your time at Torgau?'

Wolfgang nodded. 'A few. The Minden police have them, but I don't think they'll be of much use. I kept a diary - now that's an interesting read. I kept it hidden under the floorboards and recorded all my abuse in it. Don't read it on a full stomach.'

'The Musketeers, did they have favourites?'

'They could pick and choose. I believe they had about fifty, including myself that they regularly raped, mostly boys. Oh, yes, I remember the orphans - a brother and sister at Torgau. The Musketeers liked to get them to dance for them.'

Hanne heard alarm bells ringing in her head. Hadn't Marine Boy told Lotte Holler he was an orphan and asked her to dance for him? 'Dance for them?' she probed.

'Yeah, they had a sick sense of humour. They called them the dancing twins, because their surname was Waltz,' Wolfgang told her.

'Twins?'

He nodded. 'Susanne and Felix Waltz.'

'How old were they?'

'About my age, or maybe a few years younger. You see, the Musketeers had nicknames for all of us.'

'What did they call you?'

'The Magic Flute - after Wolfgang Mozart's famous opera; only I couldn't sing or play the flute. It's as if calling people by something other than their real name dehumanised them, so abusing subordinates doesn't feel like a crime.'

Hanne thought about how her colleagues used nicknames and even though it wasn't the same as the Musketeers at Torgau; she felt a little guilty and understood exactly what Wolfgang was trying to convey.

'Can you describe the Waltz twins?' she asked, eager to

hear more about them.

'It's a long time ago, but I'll try. We all kept to ourselves as much as possible. Let's see… They were both fair haired like me.'

'Blue eyed?'

'Couldn't say.'

Wolfgang was curious. 'You've got me wondering; do you think Susanne Waltz killed the Three Musketeers?'

Hanne was confused. 'A woman couldn't physically commit these crimes.'

'That's what I think. But neither could her brother.'

'I don't understand,' she said.

Wolfgang explained, 'In the spring of 1989, Felix Waltz tried to escape. It was a shame he couldn't stick it out a bit longer, not that anyone knew Torgau would be closed by the end of the year. Felix jumped into the River Elbe and drowned.'

Hanne gasped, 'No! What happened to his sister?'

'She was pregnant. Dr Jens somehow got her out of there, before the Wall came down.'

'Dr Jens?'

'Some of the doctors were kind, especially when the Musketeers left us, you know… sore. Dr Jens was the kindest; he used to let us stay overnight in the hospital wing.'

'And you say he helped the Waltz girl leave Torgau?'

'I think so. Rumour had it, that Susanne gave birth to a little boy in late September or early October 1989 at some nursing home in Dresden.'

Hanne was quite moved by this story. 'Poor girl. I wonder what happened to Susanne Waltz and her baby?'

Shrugging his shoulders, he declared, 'It's not as if us Torgau kids keep in touch. It'd be a constant reminder of what we all went through.'

Suddenly, the interview with Gunther's ex-colleague filtered through Hanne's mind. 'Did you know or hear about someone called Witzig?'

'He might have been at Torgau but it was a massive

place. I was in one wing of the building, the Musketeers' wing.'

Hanne had an idea. She pulled the photo of a young Lotte Holler that she had borrowed from Julia from her briefcase, placing it on the table in front of Wolfgang.

'Do you recognise this woman?'

Wolfgang was not expecting to see Lotte Holler's face stare back at him. Tears welled in his eyes, which gave Hanne her answer. Resting her hand briefly on his arm, she said, 'I'm so sorry.'

Wolfgang wiped his eyes but the tears started to roll down his cheeks and drop onto the table, muttering, 'Why have you shown me her photo?'

'She's alive,' Hanne told him.

'Where is she; Torgau's infamous, Fraulein Holler?'

'Have you heard about the Lady of the Lake case?'

Wolfgang gasped. 'That's her? I thought it could be her but I dismissed it, thinking there's more than one Lotte Holler in the country, especially as the press never printed her photo. I read she was pregnant when she was attacked.'

'They weren't supposed to print that private information. Lotte's recovering well in a Berlin hospital.'

Swiftly, Wolfgang's tears abated and he began to laugh. 'Now, that's poetic justice for the go-between.'

'The go-between? Is that was you called Lotte at Torgau?'

'Yeah, that's what she was. Fraulein Holler would disturb us from our sleep, collect us from our beds and take us to the Musketeers. Afterwards, she'd escort us back to our beds and order us not to cry out loud in case we disturbed the other kids. She said we'd feel better in the morning, after a good sleep... Sleep? After a session with the Musketeers? We wanted to sleep and never wake up. Ha, that is fucking ironic! The go-between slept for a very long time.'

Wolfgang had confirmed Hanne's suspicions about Lotte Holler. The go-between had paid a price - a long-term coma - for her complicity, she thought. Hanne began to feel sickened by the idea that Lotte was going to be compensated financially for being a victim of crime. She hoped once Lotte had been charged as an accomplice to the Musketeers, that some of the money could go to her victims; the abused children of Torgau. But of course this was an area that Hanne wouldn't have jurisdiction over: unfolding events would decide the outcome.

'The Torgau boy who killed the Musketeer more than likely attacked Lotte Holler. He didn't go through with it, but he caused her injuries that put her in a coma.'

Wolfgang was incensed. 'Idioten! He should have finished her off when he had the chance! Have you met her? Fraulein Holler?'

'Yes, I've met her. She's helping us with our enquiries.'

Wolfgang started to shout. 'She's the bitch who committed the crimes! What's she told you? Don't believe her, it'll be a pack of lies. She never cared!'

Hanne tried to calm him down. 'It doesn't matter what she says because we'll read between the lines. Wolfgang, trust me and my team, we'll uncover the truth.'

He snapped, 'I want to talk to that bitch!'

'Well, that's your right, of course, but she's not fully recovered and I don't believe Lotte's doctor would allow you anywhere near her, just yet.'

'How fucking convenient!' Wolfgang yelled. 'It's amazing, how did a Torgau boy outsmart them all?'

Hanne nodded. 'That's what we'd all like to know.'

Wolfgang was animated. 'Wow! That's one hell of an adrenaline rush, coming face to face with his abusers, and knowing for the first time that he had the upper hand.'

'He's a serial killer and however warranted he felt it was he has to face justice and pay for his crimes,' Hanne stated, trying not to show her bias towards Marine Boy.

'Justice! The system fails us all the time. Why don't we get rid of expensive judges and all the victims of crimes can decide about justice? Real punishments can only be dished out by the victims of crime. How's that for a vision of democracy?' insisted Wolfgang, his eyes wild and furious.

Hanne couldn't disagree. 'A judge and jury is supposedly the fairest system. But I like your idea.'

Wolfgang made a statement of intent. 'I'll talk to Fraulein Holler at some point. But like you said- when she's better. She has to look me in the eye and finally face the truth about herself, what she did and how her choices affected me. She owes me!'

Nodding, Hanne understood. 'Are you going to bring any charges against her?'

'She'll lie; say it's her word against mine.'

'Wolfgang, I would help you with the evidence,' she told him.

This surprised him. 'You would?'

Sighing, she declared, 'I think you've been very brave to come forward.'

'I don't feel brave, I'm shivering in my bones,' he said, tears welling again.

'Don't you start me off,' she said, and passed him a tissue.

Wolfgang blew his nose. 'I've run away from this too long. Not anymore.'

'That's why you're brave. I think Marine Boy was just as brave, in his own way.'

'Marine Boy?'

Hanne was a little defensive in tone. 'We give suspects a nickname before we find out their true identities; but not to dehumanise them.'

Wolfgang understood and wasn't offended. 'And you call him Marine Boy because he drowned all his victims?'

Hanne was embarrassed. 'Something like that. Silly, isn't it?'

'Marine Boy, I like it, it suits him. After what happened at Torgau, facing his abusers, it doesn't get any braver than that,' Wolfgang said, smiling. 'He knew, just like I do, that paedophiles never change and if no one stops them they carry on abusing children most of their lives. Marine Boy's actions, though unlawful, have saved other children the pain of all that. He deserves a medal!'

'Well, as a mother, this case has me quite torn,' she confessed.

Wolfgang was curious. 'If you find Marine Boy, would you let him go?'

'I'm afraid that's unrealistic.'

'But morally, you'd want to let him go, isn't that right?' he insisted.

Hanne dodged the issue. 'Most parents would.'

Wolfgang smiled. 'For his sake, I hope you don't catch Marine Boy. Though it would help my case if he was caught because he'd be another witness against that bloody bitch; Fraulein Holler.'

'We'll do our best to catch him,' Hanne promised. 'Here's my card, you can call me if you remember anything else of significance.'

'Sure. I hope it was worth the flight from Berlin.'

'You've helped, more than you know.'

They took a little break whilst Wolfgang went to speak with his partner; Erich, who was waiting for him in another room. Hanne found Kruger and Stefan going through some paperwork in the police canteen, and filled them in on all the details.

Kruger spoke with pride. 'I know. We watched you through a one-way mirror. You did great, Drais.'

Hanne was pleasantly surprised.'Danke. What now? Lotte's not well enough yet to be confronted about her past. Besides, we'll have to wait and see what Wolfgang decides.'

'Maybe we should let the judges decide, not Wolfgang, or anyone else from Torgau who comes forward,' Stefan replied.

Hanne thought about a different vision of democracy. 'The victims are usually the best judges,' she said, echoing Wolfgang's sentiments.

Kruger agreed with Hanne. 'Glockner, without witnesses it's not so easy to build a case and get a guaranteed conviction. Drais is right, let the dust settle.'

Stefan was a little indignant. 'So, we wait for Wolfgang to make a choice? Is that what you're saying?'

Hanne was adamant. 'We all have choices. In my opinion, Lotte should be made accountable for what she did at Torgau. According to Wolfgang, she never cared and wasn't sorry for what she did. Lotte's in denial and doesn't want to admit she made the wrong choices. I think even when she's well enough she won't admit the truth, but she'll have no choice in avoiding police charges.'

'That may be true, Drais, but don't forget Marine Boy made the wrong choices too and he has to be caught and punished for his crimes,' Stefan stressed.

'Shut up the pair of you! You're both right, so let's celebrate our breakthrough today that the truth's out about Lotte Holler. She was a go-between who committed unforgiveable crimes,' Kruger barked. 'She collected the kids, held the doors open and led the kids to their doom with the Musketeers, as we'll now refer to them. One way or another, justice will be done.'

Feeling overwhelmed, Hanne couldn't listen to Kruger's brutal summing up. She thought of Audrey and all those Torgau kids - Marine Boy and his sister, and now Wolfgang amongst many others. There had been no one to hear their cries for help; they'd had no voice and many of them still didn't. Hanne had heard enough tales of cruelty for one day, and she broke down and cried.

36. Audrey's Birthday

Audrey's 16th birthday fell on Easter Saturday, a sunny, windy spring morning. Hanne got up early to take a short walk to the bakers to get some fresh rolls and pastries for breakfast for her daughter, still sleeping. Returning home, she brought up Audrey's birthday present from the cellar, a new mountain bike in deep purple. The previous night she'd tied a red and blue ribbon to each of the handlebars and a two large, helium pink balloons with 'Happy Birthday' and '16' written on them.

It was going to be a busy day. The visitors would be arriving at lunchtime, each bringing something to eat and drink, and she needed to clean the flat before they turned up. As Hanne waited for Audrey to stir, she went over her agenda for Monday. There was a list of things she had to do regarding the case and details to follow up.

After the devastatingly sad but insightful meeting with Wolfgang, Hanne had instructed the police clerks to look into all the births registered in Dresden between September and October 1989. She was hoping to find a young girl called Susanne Waltz and the present whereabouts of this Torgau girl and her child, believed to be a boy, born roughly six months after Audrey. Hanne felt a statement from Susanne Waltz could only add to the case against Lotte Holler. She would also be fascinated by her story: a girl from Torgau who lost her twin brother, and became an under-age mother before she was 16. How on earth had she coped?

Audrey crept up on her mother. 'Mutti! Not today. We promised each other, you won't work at the weekends and I'll get all my school work done during the week.'

'Happy Birthday, sweetheart,' Hanne said, bursting with pride, and kissing her daughter. 'I was just keeping busy, waiting for you to wake up.'

Audrey looked at the pile of unopened birthday cards and breakfast treats on the table. 'Danke. Mutti, I can't see any presents?' she said, cheekily.

Hanne smiled. 'Your father, oma and the guests will bring you lots of presents. Your present from me is in my room. I lied, we can afford it.'

Audrey was an excitable child-woman and ran into her mother's room. It was the bicycle she'd shown Hanne when they were out shopping a while back, and had been told it was too expensive.

'Thank you. I love it!' Audrey declared, wildly, hugging her mother.

Bicycles seemed to be the theme of the day. Hanne's mother, Traudl was the first guest to arrive bringing an enormous 16th birthday cake in the shape of a bicycle. Traudl Drais was very proud of her descendants from Heidelberg, despite the fact they were from her late husband Kurt's side of the family. In 1817, Karl Jasper Von Drais had invented the first known bicycle and called it the Draisine, or hobbyhorse. It had a front wheel that could be turned for steering but had to be pushed along with the feet. For many years, people in Germany, France and England, especially, were enthusiastic about this new activity of hobbyhorsing. The bicycle industry really began later in the century when other entrepreneurs added cranks and pedals onto the wheels of the hobbyhorse. However, nine generations or so later, Traudl Drais unfortunately had never seen any financial profits from the bicycle industry.

'Happy Birthday, mein schatz,' Traudl said, kissing her granddaughter.

Audrey feigned surprise. 'Oma, what a lovely cake! Thank you.'

Hanne embraced her mother. 'Mutti, lovely to see you.'

Hanne looked nothing like her mother; Traudl dressed for the male admirers in her life and at 62 was a tall and very attractive woman. Hanne rarely wore a skirt or dress or make-up, yet was attractive in a different way. However, in character they were similar: stubborn, impatient and wanting to be right.

Kurt had died several years ago and after an acceptable period of mourning, Traudl tended to divide her time flitting between the men at her social club, not wishing to be tied down to marriage again.

'It just had to be a bicycle cake, given that our family invented the bicycle. Such a pity the nobility of Von in the title was dropped somewhere along the line. Traudl Von Drais has a nice ring to it. Nobility opens doors. Maybe Kurt should have made a claim on the Heidelberg fortune. I asked him many times but he wouldn't. He always said there's no shame in being a proletariat.'

Hanne bit her lip. Traudl bought a bicycle cake every year for family occasions and always said the same thing.

'You and Papa did ok without a fortune, or title. You were happy- you can't buy that.'

Traudl sighed. 'Yes, we were happy… Audrey, I see you've a brand new bike.'

'Mutti's present, Audrey told her.

'I've got your presents in the car, I couldn't carry them all in. One of them is a GPS watch for your bike trips, which means you can plot your routes more easily.'

Audrey put her arm around Traudl. 'Oma, danke. That's a fantastic present, though the cake would have been more than enough. But there's something you can do for me.'

Traudl raised her eyes. Her granddaughter never asked for much. 'Yes, anything?'

Audrey looked at Hanne and Traudl. 'It's my birthday so, you two, promise me you won't have any silly tiffs today.'

Hanne nodded in agreement and Traudl followed suit. Hanne thought her 16-year-old daughter had the measure of both of them.

The guests arrived in dribs and drabs. Half a dozen of Audrey's friends, who would later be going out together once the family celebrations were over, mingled with themselves. Alongside a few of Hanne's friends, was Brigitte, waiting patiently in the wings. Before long, Kruger and Stefan turned up.

'Oskar, lovely to see you. And you, Stefan,' she said, offering her hand.

Happy to humour her, Kruger kissed Traudl's outstretched hand. Stefan followed suit.

'How many criminals did you catch last week?' Traudl asked them.

'Not as many as we'd like,' Kruger replied.

'We stay on a case until it's solved,' added Stefan.

'What are you working on now?'

'The Lady of the Lake case.'

This was news to Traudl. 'Wirklich? My daughter never tells me anything.'

'And I never tell my wife, it keeps home and work life separate.'

Traudl ventured, 'Well, I suppose it does. I'm sure Hanne is a great help to you, with all her psychobabble.'

Kruger smiled politely. 'We wouldn't solve cases as easily without her.'

'Thank you, Oskar. That's what a mother likes to hear,' Traudl said, and moved off to greet her daughter's new girlfriend.

'Good thing that Drais is nothing like her mother,' Stefan whispered to Kruger, once Traudl was out of earshot.

Hanne introduced Brigitte to her mother and quickly left them alone to work out their own relationship. Audrey's father Rafael was the last to arrive with a grand bouquet of flowers for his daughter. He always spoke in Spanish to Audrey because he wanted her to know and practise his language. Hanne watched their South American way of talking, with gesticulating arms all over the place: father and daughter were physically very alike.

Hanne understood what they were saying but usually replied in German, to be polite and in deference to the others, especially her mother, who got quite annoyed when she wasn't at the fulcrum of conversations.

Traudl nudged her daughter. 'What's he saying?'

'Mutti! Audrey is half-Chilean and speaking Spanish is important.'

Audrey suddenly flung her arms around her father. 'Oh, Papa, please tell them.'

Audrey tapped on a table and the conversations around the room came to a halt.

Rafael cleared his throat to speak in German with a heavy Spanish accent. 'My beautiful daughter wants you all to know… Audrey's going to have a brother or sister.'

Polite echoes of congratulations filled the room.

Hanne quickly crossed the room to join Audrey and her ex-husband. 'Rafa, that's great. Where's Clara?'

'Morning sickness, only it lasts all day.'

'When's the baby due?' Hanne asked.

'Early October.'

'Papa, why make me wait until I'm 16 to get a brother or a sister?'

Rafael smiled and winked. 'I've been trying for ages!'

'And I wasn't going to give you a sibling,' Hanne exclaimed with a grin.

'Mutti, just because you're gay it doesn't mean you couldn't have another. You had me.'

Hanne smiled. 'One child is more than enough for me!'

Brigitte joined them and Hanne introduced her ex-husband to her new flame.

'Hi. Congratulations.'

'Gracias, danke. Pleased to meet you,' Rafael said.

Traudl waved from the other side of the room.

'Papa, I think Oma wants a word,' Audrey said, nudging

him.

'Brigitte, my advice to you about Traudl - when she says jump, you jump, but she doesn't get to say how high,' Rafael said, with a smile, before Audrey dragged him away.

'You never told me you could be the heiress to a bicycle fortune,' said Brigitte.

Hanne shook her head. 'Liebe Mutti. Have you seen the cake?'

Kruger and Stefan sauntered over to Hanne and Brigitte.

'So, you're the lady who has put a smile on Drais's face of late,' Stefan blurted out.

'Ignore him,' Kruger said, deadpan. ‚I'm Oskar Kruger, Hanne's boss.'

'Pleased to meet you, Kommissar. Or may I call you Oskar?'

'I'm only the Kommissar at work.'

'And I'm Stefan, the sous-chef. Oskar, Hanne and myself are the three…'

Kruger interrupted. 'Glockner, it's Kommissar, to you.'

'And I'm not having a nickname that's associated with you two!' Hanne cried.

'Quite right, Von Drais,' Kruger said, winking. 'Brigitte, you see what Hanne has to put up with… Please excuse us, but we've got to go soon, and there's police business that simply won't wait.'

'Sorry,' Hanne told Brigitte.

'No problem. I'll mingle.'

'Don't breathe a word to Audrey, I'm forbidden to work at weekends.'

Brigitte winked. 'What's it worth?'

Hanne blew Brigitte a kiss and went outside with her police colleagues onto the balcony overlooking the river where Kruger felt sufficiently at ease to light a cigar.

'What couldn't wait till Monday?' Hanne asked.

'That's just it. I'm telling you now so you and Glockner know where you're going first thing Monday morning.'

'Dresden,' Stefan told her. 'Don't worry, I'll drive.'

Kruger announced, 'Our researchers have come up trumps. And Wolfgang was right. A baby boy called Axel was born to Susanne Waltz, on 30th September 1989 at a nursing home in Dresden. She would've been 14 at the time.'

'That's a good team effort.'

'But that's not all,' said Stefan.

Kruger spoke softly. 'Brace yourself, Drais. Our clerks at police HQ checked for records of births, marriages and deaths. Sadly, Susanne Waltz died in December 1989. Her death was registered in Kopenick.'

Hanne sighed. 'Nein! That's very sad.'

'We'll go to the nursing home to speak with the staff. Apparently there's someone still working there who remembers her,' Stefan informed her.

Hanne looked out onto the water and for a few minutes was deep in thought.

Kruger looked puzzled. 'However, there's no record of an Axel Waltz. He seems to have disappeared along with his mother, but we'll keep looking.'

Hanne had a brainwave. 'Susanne Waltz left Dresden with her son and two months later her death was registered in the Kopenick area. So, let's assume the baby was alive and was taken into care or even adopted,' she pondered.

'Good idea, Drais. I'll get the team onto that.'

'I want to check Susanne's birth certificate; it'll state the names of her parents and her mother's maiden name. Then we can check for any living relatives,' Hanne ventured. 'But even if we find Axel Waltz's birth certificate, I'm sure the name of the father will be recorded as unknown.'

'She was fucking 14! No one will admit to fathering a kid with a minor,' Kruger cried.

'There has to be someone alive in the Waltz family,' Hanne suggested. 'Or what about the doctor who got her out of Torgau; he might still be around? Maybe he even signed the death certificate.'

Kruger was annoyed with himself. 'Damn! I've left the copies of the certificates in files, back at H.Q.'

Stefan volunteered, 'I'll pick them up before we go to Dresden.'

'What did Susanne Waltz die of?' Hanne asked.

'Multiple head injuries; I guess from some kind of fall. The coroner recorded a verdict of death by misadventure,' Stefan informed her.

Hanne sighed. 'Poor kid, sent to Torgau after losing her parents and her brother, she gives birth and dies so young. How unlucky can you get?'

'I wonder if Lotte Holler remembers the Waltz girl or Wolfgang?'

'I could ask her, next time I see her.'

'You do that, Drais. Now, Rutger said Wolfgang's prints don't match those on the Herbertz knife, plus he's a size 11 shoe, so he's in the clear. Oh, I forgot. Rutger sends his apologies to you and Audrey, his wife had a fall and he's with her at the hospital.'

Hanne was concerned. 'Nothing too serious, I hope.'

'Twisted her ankle,' Kruger explained. 'But Rutger asked me to pass on some news for you regarding Lotte Holler's fingerprints.'

Hanne was a little embarrassed. 'Oh, sorry. It was a spur of the moment thing. I was waiting for the right moment to tell you.'

Kruger raised an eyebrow. 'That moment is now. So, you illegally collected fingerprints. Drais, you're as underhand as me! Unfortunately, Lotte Holler won't lose any sleep on it because her fingerprints weren't found in Gwisdek's motor home, so her activities and connection to the Musketeers seems to have ended at Torgau's closure.'

Traudl came out onto the balcony.

'There you all are! Come inside, I'm about to make my speech, Traudl announced.

'Did I ever tell you, Drais, you're nothing like your mother.'

Hanne kissed Stefan on the cheek. 'That's the nicest thing you've ever said to me!'

Inside, the guests quietened their conversations and Audrey and Hanne linked arms to give each other moral support, as Traudl's unscripted speech began.

Traudl cleared her voice. 'Today is Easter Saturday and my granddaughter is 16. Audrey was born on Easter Sunday, on 26th March 1989, and that's not the only reason she's a special child. She was my first grandchild and she's a direct descendant of Karl Jasper Von Drais; the inventor of the first known bicycle in 1817, the Draisine.'

Klaus slept uneasily after Ingrid's revelations. He observed Felix at close quarters and noticed how jumpy he was when the news came on and quickly decided the promise he'd made to Ingrid would have to be broken. Klaus knew it would cause trouble within the family, but it would eventually blow over and they would be a stronger unit for facing their problems and fears together. There was no time for procrastination, he needed to confront Felix. A man that dealt with problems through action, Klaus cleared his diary to arrange a round of golf with Felix early on a Sunday morning.

They arrived at the golf club in separate cars and met on the first tee at their allotted time. Even as owners they had to book a tee off time, careful not to disturb the club's etiquette rules and upset any members on their regular days of golf.

Felix was a bit bleary eyed. 'I thought onkel Bernd and Axel were playing with us?'

'No, it's just us today. We've a nice morning for it.'

They enjoyed some competitive banter as they played. Half-way around the course, Klaus sliced his tee shot into the woods on purpose.

'Damn!' Klaus cried. 'That's my favourite ball.'

'We've got time to look for it- we're ahead of play. We'll find it, I saw exactly where it went in,' Felix said, with confidence.

They left their golf trolleys at the edge of the woodland,

both taking a golf wedge to help them search the undergrowth for the missing ball. Once out of sight and earshot of any passing golfer, Klaus put his arm on Felix's shoulder and looked him directly in the eye.

'Felix… I know. I made Ingrid tell me.'

Felix understood. He swung his golf club hard at the ground. 'Fic!' He turned to storm off but Klaus held his arms with as much force as he could muster.

'Stop! Felix, we've got to talk about it.'

'Who else knows?' Felix demanded.

'Just the three of us.'

'I had the feeling you hit that ball in here on purpose.'

Klaus nodded. 'Now my lad; I want the truth. Did you really do it?'

'What can I say? Yes, I did it. I killed three men and left that woman for dead.'

'You killed three Torgau men; that's the difference, and that woman helped them. They all got what they deserved,' Klaus stated.

'I'm a murderer. It isn't right, but I had no choice.'

Klaus shook his head. 'No, Felix, you had a choice. Why the hell didn't you talk to me? I could have helped you.'

'One of them turned up at the golf club and threatened to set the paedophiles on Axel. I panicked. I didn't plan to kill him.'

'But you took my gun?'

'Yes, onkel. Simply to protect myself. I knew Horst would threaten me, and when he wanted things back the way they used to be and said he'd go after Axel, I knew I couldn't let him live. So I drove his car into the lake at Muggelsee. The others had to follow.'

'You nearly lost your own life in the process.

'Axel's life is worth more than mine. Onkel, sometimes in life we have to run towards the things that make us want to run away.'

Klaus put his arms around Felix. 'Thank you for protecting Axel.'

'So, how do I tell my wife and child who I am?' Felix cried.

'You certainly don't tell Martha while she's pregnant,' Klaus advised. 'When the baby's born you could tell her, though. Martha loves you, she'll understand.'

'It might repulse her to be touched by me, a murderer.'

'Never! Martha knows what they did to you at Torgau; she's always known and loves you, no matter what.'

'I'm not the person Martha thinks I am,' Felix said, with tears in his eyes. 'I've let her down. I've let you all down. Onkel, I feel so ashamed.'

Klaus was outraged. 'What about the Torgau rapists and their shame? My poor lad, doesn't anyone ever learn? Isn't it enough that Germans have always felt a ceaseless sense of shame? And yes, we were a disgrace, and to atone for Hitler's war it might always be this way, this perpetual mantle of feeling ashamed. Felix, for different reasons, you'll just be another generation of Germans that learns to live with your shame.'

'I think we all hide as human beings and we only show the parts of ourselves we want others to see. Onkel, I've hidden so much that I've become an expert at hiding.'

'Good. Felix, if you'd committed unforgiveable crimes without any provocation, I'd turn you in myself. Just don't tell me you feel shame for getting your own back on those bastards. Rapists and paedophiles get what they deserve.'

'And Ingrid?'

'It's always been us as a family against the world. Felix, promise me you won't be too hard on Ingrid for telling me?'

'I promise.'

'Good lad. But be on your guard, the police are on your trail. They rang the golf club a few weeks ago, asking if we remembered employing a security man in September 1992.'

Felix was concerned. 'Fic! That'd be Horst Gwisdek. What did you say?'

'I told them I can't remember last week, let alone over 10 years ago. They mentioned a cheque we sent him for his work because he never banked it. To think he was there, on our doorstep and we would have paid him for his contributions. It makes me feel sick just thinking about it,' Klaus confessed.

'Did they believe you?'

'I think so. They know there are lots of people that come and go over the years at a golf club. But I remember him and I'd bet Bernd would too. This Gwisdek was cocksure and sycophantic around the celebrity golfers.'

'What if the police question Bernd?'

'After all his years in the Politburo, Bernd can smell a rat and would speak with me before he spoke to the police, so try not to worry.'

Onkel, I left clues at the scenes of my crimes.'

'You did? You can't obsess about that now, it's done and you can't change anything.'

'Shall I give myself up?'

Klaus was unsure how to reply. 'That's your decision.'

'It would bring shame upon the family,' Felix surmised.

'I'm not ashamed of you. Whatever you decide, we'll cope and stick together and it doesn't matter what others think. Stuff the law! We understand your motives.'

'Onkel, in the eyes of the law, there are no excuses for murder.'

'I might be wrong but I think you'd be tried as a minor. Felix, you were 17 when you committed these crimes. You'd be tried with older laws and subject to the legislation that was in force at the time.'

'How many years would I get?'

'Who knows? But they haven't caught you yet,' Klaus replied.

Stefan Glockner collected Hanne on Monday morning and they set off for Dresden. As he drove, Hanne looked through the case file and studied the birth and death certificates relating to Susanne Waltz and her son Axel, and was full of imponderable questions.

Sighing, Hanne said, 'We have to find the missing gaps.'

'Such as?'

'Well, such as, who kept Axel after his mother's death.'

Stefan reminded her. 'I thought you said we were going to check adoption records.'

Hanne grimaced. 'There's not been time and getting evidence from old, East German records, is like asking Kruger to stop being grumpy - bloody difficult!'

Smiling, Stefan agreed. 'You're not wrong there! You don't think Axel died too in the same accident as his mother, and it was all covered up?'

'I've a gut feeling Axel's alive. So, we have to ask ourselves who would be likely to adopt him. Someone must have helped Susanne Waltz after she left Torgau.'

'Drais… You can't present evidence in court on gut feeling alone.'

Hanne read aloud. 'Her Father was Jakob Waltz, age 21, and her mother; Sofie, nee Baum, age 20. If we get their marriage certificate it'll show where they married.'

Stefan understood the direction in which Hanne's mind was travelling. 'Normally, you marry in your local church or town hall.'

'Genau! My bet's a town hall because Communism and Christianity were an unlikely alliance. Faith wasn't predominant in a Russian, Stasi-run state.'

'And maybe Jakob and Sofie had brothers and sisters?' suggested Stefan.

'Once we know where Susanne's parents lived at the time of their marriage, we'll check the census records - it might give us a list of possible siblings.'

'Drais, do you talk about the case in your sleep?'

With a cheeky grin, she replied, 'Ask Brigitte!'

'I liked her. Hanne, I'm pleased for you.'

'Thanks, Stefan. I don't want to tempt providence and say I'm happy. but I am. Besides, if my girlfriend can handle my mother, she's doing well.'

'Your mother is quite a cabaret act.'

Hanne laughed. 'Yes, she is!'

'Are you really related to the inventor of the first known bicycle?'

'Stefan! Don't start!'

Arriving at the Dresden nursing home a few hours later, they were greeted by a wizened and feisty Uwe Muller. He was the manager working there when Susanne Waltz gave birth, but had long since retired. His daughter was now manager of the home, currently catering for elderly, retired folk. Uwe visited daily to take part in yoga sessions, play cards, darts or bingo with his fellow pensioners.

The interview would take place in a conservatory overlooking a garden where the signs of spring were evident, with daisies and daffodils pushing through the earth. Hot and cold refreshments were provided and Stefan and Hanne were invited to help themselves.

Stefan and Hanne echoed their sentiments. 'Thank you for the refreshments.'

'You're welcome,' Uwe replied. 'When I heard the police were interested in a girl from Torgau, I was a bit surprised. I hope I'll be able to help in some way.'

'When did this place stop being a nursing home?' Stefan asked.

'Oh, not long after the Wall came down. It was rather sad taking in all those young girls with their teenage pregnancies, so we modernised the place and turned it into a retirement home, and a more respectable establishment.'

Hanne tried not to be judgmental of this old man. 'Were there many under-age teenage pregnancies from Torgau?'

Uwe nodded. 'And you're interested in Susanne Waltz?'

'You remember her?'

'Yes, she was a sweet girl. Never said much, she seemed lost in her own little world. She was the last Torgau girl to give birth here,' Uwe told them.

Stefan read from his notes. 'Susanne Waltz gave birth to a boy, Axel, on 30th September 1989. Who delivered the baby?'

'That'd be Dr Jens. He brought Susanne here, said he wanted to help deliver the baby and we were to call him when she went into labour.'

Hanne recalled Wolfgang mentioned Dr Jens. 'The doctor brought her here?'

'Yes. Dr Jens worked at Torgau.'

'What was his full name?'

Uwe confessed, 'My memory's not what it was. We all just knew him as Dr Jens. He bought a lot of girls here to have their babies, before they returned to Torgau, sadly without their babies.'

Hanne was intrigued. 'Who kept the babies?'

Uwe felt uncomfortable but knew he had to answer the questions truthfully. 'The state authorities decided; the children were put up for adoption.'

'Including Susanne Waltz's son?'

'No, Sir, that was down to Dr Jens. He felt there was imminent change in the air, what with all the demonstrations and the fall of Communism in the Eastern Bloc. He told us Susanne was keeping the baby and was to stay here under his jurisdiction until she'd recovered from the birth. And he'd pay all her costs.'

'And when the Berlin Wall fell and Torgau closed? Susanne Waltz was free to leave with her baby son?'

'Yes, Sir. That is correct.'

'Could your old records tell us when she left and where she went to?' Hanne asked.

Uwe shook his head. 'I don't have any records. Who wants to be reminded of that era?'

Hanne sighed. 'That's a shame, but I understand.'

'It's funny isn't it? Us old people talk about the past because we don't have much of a future, and want to be selective. Most of us don't care to talk about the past in East Germany, as if we're ashamed about our lives,' Uwe told them, wistfully.

Hanne grimaced, 'We'll have to find another way of tracing the boy, Axel.'

Uwe was confused. 'I thought you wanted to trace Susanne?'

'Sadly, no. Susanne's death was recorded in Kopenick in December 1989. She died as a result of a fall.'

Uwe was genuinely dismayed. 'Nein!'

'I'm sorry to be the bearer of sad tidings,' Hanne said, apologetically.

Stefan thought without records, they were wasting time. 'Herr Muller, thank you for seeing us.'

Suddenly, the old man's eyes lit up. 'Wait a minute… It's all coming back to me! When Dr Jens quit his job at Torgau, he came to goodbye to Susanne. I remember the poor girl saying, Dr Jens told her he'd got a job at a surgery in Kopenick. He paid her bills in advance but never came back to see her, and I think Susanne felt abandoned all over again, until…'

Looking at the death certificate, Hanne interrupted, 'Do you think Dr Jens registered the death?' I didn't spot it before; the doctor's name is illegible! Here, take a look.'

Uwe shook his head. 'Even with my glasses I can't read

that signature. I was about to tell you, to everyone's surprise, Susanne's relatives turned-up here, and took her away.'

Suddenly, Stefan perked up. 'Susanne's relatives?'

Uwe nodded. 'We all thought she was an orphan. Apparently, they knew nothing about her being in Torgau, and when the Wall fell, they came looking for her.'

Hanne was very pleased to hear this. 'Do you remember anything about them?'

'The relatives were brothers. Susanne was their niece.'

'Do you recall their names?'

'No, Sir. It was a long time ago... Wait! One of them was a politician.'

'A politician?' Stefan repeated.

'In East Berlin,' Uwe recalled. 'He came to assist his brother in an official capacity and waited in the reception area. Yes, I remember. It was his brother who was Susanne's onkel... Onkel Klaus! That's right, his name was Klaus.'

'That's great that you remembered,' Hanne enthused.

'I asked Klaus for proof of who he was, even though Susanne knew him, and he told me he was her onkel. I insisted on seeing some sort of proof before I let any girl leave the home with two men.'

Stefan queried, 'What proof did onkel Klaus offer?'

'It was a will that stated Susanne would inherit her grandmother's house. Klaus showed his marriage certificate to prove he was married to the grandmother's daughter.'

It was a long shot. 'Do you remember where Klaus lived?' Hanne asked, thinking her question would be in vain.

Uwe nodded his head. 'They lived by a lake, around the Spreewald.'

'If you do remember any names or any other details, please, give us a call,' Stefan said, handing Uwe his card.

'Thank you, Herr Muller; you've been a great help,' Hanne said, appreciatively.

When Stefan and Hanne were alone in the car, Hanne began to cry.

'This case has got to you, eh?'

'More than usual, and more than I thought possible.'

'Because there are kids involved?' he surmised.

Hanne nodded and blew her nose. 'It's silly, I know, but I was really happy to hear Susanne had a family and they didn't forget her; they found her. But she didn't get a happy ending, did she?'

'Does anyone? Onkel Klaus arrived a few years too late for her. You're a big softy inside your tough shell, eh Drais?'

Hanne rested her head briefly on Stefan's shoulder. 'I don't believe Axel was given away; because he's all they had left of Susanne. My bet is that onkel Klaus and his wife adopted him.'

39. Wannsee

In the middle of March, Lotte Holler decided she'd had enough of hospital life. No one could get her to change her mind and wait any longer. Lotte presented her sister and Dr Roth with a fait accompli. She would continue her rehabilitation in a home of her own and much to Julia's annoyance, she discharged herself from hospital and moved into her beautiful, modern rented home on a hill scattered with pine trees overlooking the River Wannsee, in this verdant, south-western suburb of Berlin.

Lotte had insisted on four bedrooms because she wanted her nephews to have their own rooms, complete with ensuite bathrooms, when they came to stay. There were two reception rooms and a conservatory overlooking a south-facing garden containing a pond and rockery. In secluded areas of the expansive grounds were seating areas and a summerhouse amid the topiary. A large hut for Frank and Tomas to play in was filled with games, a computer console and large screen plus a billiards table.

Julia and the boys spent the Easter holidays and every weekend at the Wannsee house, and their routine was soon established. They would go there on Friday evenings through to Monday mornings and quickly adjusted to their new life on the lake and surrounding countryside. They enjoyed living between two places - Berlin city life during the week and the wealth and luxuries at Wannsee - courtesy of their kind and generous benefactor, Tante Lotte - at weekends.

After two years of negotiation, which started way before she came out of her coma, the courts compensated Lotte for being a victim of crime. The Berlin solicitors representing her secured Lotte a settlement of just over one million euros, which meant she was financially comfortable for life.

Lotte was at last feeling well again and enjoying her new-found wealth. She bought a new car for Julia and one for herself, which she drove tentatively. She tended not to drive anywhere far and kept to local roads for the time being. There was a lot more traffic now and drivers seemed far more aggressive and prone to outbursts of road rage. She began attending events at her new social club in the area, keeping herself busy during the week while she looked forward to Julia and the boys arriving on a Friday evening. She didn't get the chance to feel lonely because she had company most of the time, and could afford to employ nurses on a rota and a housekeeper. The local police checked on her daily. Plain-clothed police officers were stopping by to check on her every couple of hours and were only a phone call away should she need them.

Julia could see her sister felt she was part of a family again and the signs were there that Lotte was looking forward to returning to a full and prosperous life. For Julia, helping Lotte achieve a positive outcome was worth making a temporary sacrifice for the next six months or so. As yet unbeknown to her sister, though, Julia had other plans for her own future: she had fallen in love with Dr Roth and he felt the same about her.

On a Sunday afternoon in the middle of April, Frank and Tomas were playing football in the garden. Julia asked Lotte to keep an eye on them whilst she popped into town on the pretext of arranging a surprise for Tomas's birthday the following weekend. In truth she was eager to see Jonas.

Their rendezvous was at a coffee shop in town where they kissed warmly and held hands.

'I miss you, but it won't be for long,' Julia reassured him. 'I'd like to have a weekend with you, but at the moment it's not possible.'

'I know. Besides, we're together most weekdays.'

'Yes. But not the quality weekend time together, when you're not so tired.'

'I'll be patient.'

Julia quipped, 'Instead of being my sister's doctor?'

Grinning, Jonas declared, 'And that's why I love you.'

'And I love you. Why did we wait so long to get together?'

'Both of us, all that time, we only saw Lotte, and not each other.'

They kissed and stared lovingly into one another's eyes.'

'Have the boys said anything about me to Lotte?' Jonas asked.

'That we're together? Not yet, but I'm not going to ask them to keep it a secret. If they let it slip, Lotte will ask me straight away, you can be sure of that!' Julia declared.

At the house in Wannsee, Frank and Tomas stopped playing their game of football when a tall stranger with a pale face came into the garden. It was Wolfgang Feuer.

Smiling, Wolfgang spoke in a relaxed manner. 'Hi, I rang the bell, but no one answered. I'm here to see Lotte.'

Frank was a streetwise kid in his usual city neighbourhood. He looked at the smartly dressed man and didn't feel too worried he was about to commit a crime. 'Ok, I'll go and get my tante Lotte for you,' he told the stranger.

'Danke,' Wolfgang replied.

Tomas didn't take any interest in the man and accidently kicked his ball into the pond.

'Damn it!' Tomas cried.

So these boys were Lotte's nephews, thought Wolfgang. It was a shame he was about to change their lives, too. 'I'll help you get the ball out.'

'Danke,' Tomas said, pleased for the help.

It started to rain. Lotte came out into the garden looking a bit perturbed, Frank following her. One of her nurses had gone off duty and her housekeeper was running late. Who was this strange man, in her garden? Wolfgang turned to face her. The last time he'd seen her was when he was a 15-year-old boy at Torgau. She was exactly as he remembered.

'Go inside boys, you'll get wet,' Lotte instructed her nephews and waited until the boys had gone inside to speak to the stranger. 'And you, sir, are trespassing.'

He scoffed, 'Indeed! Let me introduce myself. I'm Wolfgang. You used to call me the "Magic Flute" at Torgau.'

Immediately recognising him, she spat, 'Get out of my garden!' through gritted teeth.

'So, Fraulein Holler, you do remember me.'

'I'm calling the police. They'll be here in a shot. Get out!' she barked.

Wolfgang was fearless. 'Yes, call them. Let's talk in front of the police.'

Lotte froze. 'Are you the man… Did you attack me?' she uttered, her voice trembling.

Wolfgang shook his head. 'That's not my style. The Torgau boy that attacked you, he left fingerprints on a knife found at the scene of the crime. The police know the fingerprints are not mine and I'm in the clear.'

Lotte felt suspicious. 'Do you know who attacked me?'

'If I did, I'd buy him a drink.'

Wolfgang was deadly serious and Lotte knew he meant business. It was clear he had no sympathy for the years she had spent in a coma. She didn't react to his acerbic remark, just asking, 'What do you want?'

'The truth.'

'How did you find me?'

'I'm a property developer with many contacts. Nice house. I believe you've come into a lot of money.'

'So, you're after my money,' she guessed.

'Blackmail is not my style,' he told her.

The clouds grew very dark and soon, rain started to fall

heavily.

It was at this moment that Julia arrived home with shopping, entering the house from the front. She called out for her boys. 'Frank, Tomas, please help me unpack the shopping. Where's Lotte?'

Tomas appeared, somewhat bemused. 'Tante Lotte's in the garden, talking to a man in the rain. Why don't they come inside?'

Julia dropped the shopping bag and ran outside. Lotte and Wolfgang were soaked and appeared frozen to the spot, and staring at one another.

Julia felt afraid. 'Lotte!' she cried. 'And who are you?' she asked the intruder. 'Lotte, come inside.

Looking menacing, he announced, 'We're staying here.'

Lotte's hair and clothes were drenched. 'It's all right, Julia. I can handle this. Go inside and call the police.'

'Your sister might be interested in what I have to say,' Wolfgang ventured.

'Will one of you tell me what's going on?' Julia bellowed.

Lotte tried to take control of the situation. 'Julia! Just do as I say!'

Suddenly, Wolfgang moved to stand in front of Julia, blocking her path. 'Your sister had a nickname at Torgau. Aren't you curious to know why all the kids at Torgau named Fraulein Holler the go-between?'

Glancing at Lotte, Julia saw fear in her eyes.

'The go-between?' repeated Julia. 'Lotte, what's he talking about?'

Ltte cried, 'Don't listen to him. He's trying to blackmail me!'

Wolfgang was outraged. 'I wouldn't touch your blood money, Holler. Go on; tell the truth for once in your life. Tell your sister what you did to us kids at Torgau!'

All three of them were quite drenched by this time, that it was impossible to see that Lotte was crying.

'What did my sister do to you at Torgau?'

Wolfgang could see Lotte was dumbstruck and wasn't

going to admit the truth. He spoke on her behalf. 'She collected us kids from our beds and took us to the Musketeers.'

Julia was confused. 'The Musketeers? I don't understand.'

'The three men found dead at the bottom of Muggelsee; they were paedophiles,' he explained. 'Your sister helped them at Torgau; she was their go-between. She led us to our abuse and when it was all over, when the Musketeers had finished raping us, your sister escorted us back to our beds and told us not to cry!'

'No!' Julia screamed. 'It's not true… Lotte?'

Lotte lowered her head in shame.

Suddenly the sound of police sirens could be heard and Frank came running outside.

'I called the police, they're here,' Frank cried, trying to catch his breath.

Wolfgang confessed, 'That's what I wanted from you, Fraulein Holler, a confession and your shame. I hope your sister shows you some mercy - mercy that was so lacking in you towards us Torgau kids.'

Two armed police officers entered the garden and Wolfgang readily handed himself over to them for his crime of trespassing, It didn't worry him. His mission had been successful and was now complete.

Julia looked at her sister. 'Lotte! Why did you do it?'

Lotte had no valid answer. 'The wardens stuck together.'

'Nein!' Julia shouted. 'Mein Gott! What have you done?'

Witnessing the disgust and disappointment in Julia's eyes, Lotte pleaded, 'Forgive me, please forgive me.'

Julia shook her head and turned to go. 'I thought I knew you.'

Lotte tried to stop her sister leaving. 'Julia! Bitte! Don't go!'

Finding it hard to look her sister in the eye, Julia announced, 'I'm taking the boys home.'

'But this is your home. Julia, please,' Lotte cried.

Julia was outraged. 'If my sons had had the misfortune to

be sent to Torgau, they'd have suffered the same fate. You would have taken my Frank and Tomas from their beds to those men, wouldn't you? Lotte, how could you?'

Lotte fell to her knees in the pouring rain. 'Julia, you're all I have. Don't leave me!'

Julia sobbed as she walked away but she didn't turn around or answer her sister's pleas. She had to get away from Lotte, and the boys were hurried out of the house.

'Mutti! What's wrong?' Frank asked.

'Don't ask! Play with your Nintendo with your earphones in, and please don't talk. I need time to think,' Julia instructed.

The boys obeyed their distraught mother without question. They'd never seen her quite like this before.

Outside in the street, a handcuffed Wolfgang was in the back of a police van. He watched Julia and her sons leaving the house. On his face was a satisfied smile.

Safely in her car, Julia phoned Jonas on her mobile to tell him she was on her way, and she'd explain why when she saw him. She drove out of Wannsee and back to the city with her sons, to the safety of Jonas's arms and his home in Pankow.

Lotte stood in her garden, unable to move as the rain poured down around her. She was utterly alone.

It was getting dark. It took a few frantic calls from Kruger to round up his team on a Sunday. Kruger was attending his wife's parents' 50th wedding anniversary party and couldn't possibly leave. It was down to Glockner and Drais.

Stefan drove Hanne to Wannsee police station at breakneck speed. When they arrived he was brought into the interview room. Wolfgang had been more than happy to spend the rest of the day in the police cells awaiting their questions, and even be charged with mere trespassing. Although his clothes were semi-dry, his hair was still wet from the rainstorm and pushed back behind his ears, revealing small, faded scars on the lobes. Hanne noticed

Wolfgang's ears and immediately, had a feeling of déjà vu that she couldn't quite place. She'd seen scarred ears like that before but couldn't quite recall when or where.

'What the hell do you think you're playing at?' Stefan yelled at him.

'It was my right,' Wolfgang replied, calmly.

'How the hell did you find her?'

Wolfgang smiled. 'Well, Sir, I have contacts. I don't want to prosecute her or sue her for damages - she can choke on her money for all I care. I just wanted to confront her.'

'What did you say to her?' Hanne asked, trying to stay calm.

Wolfgang was callous in his reply. 'I told the truth, and in front of her sister. I wanted that bitch to own up and feel the shame I've felt all these years.'

Stefan's mobile rang and he wondered off along the corridor to take the call.

Hanne shook her head in disbelief. 'Are you satisfied now?'

'Don't tell me you feel sorry for her? Fraulein Holler helped scar me for life! Look at my ears. The Musketeers liked to brand their "boys" with cigar butts, like fucking cattle! It's a permanent reminder every time I look in the mirror!' he shouted, pulling his hair over his ears to hide the scars.

'I'll have to go and see Lotte Holler. Am I to tell her that you won't be bringing a case against her?' Hanne asked.

Wolfgang nodded. 'I've had my revenge. When other Torgau kids find out about her new found wealth, they'll go after her and her money and good luck to them.'

Slowly, Stefan came into the room. His face was looking pale and stunned.

Hanne was concerned. 'Stefan, are you all right? What's happened?'

'That was the police, over at Lotte's house. Lotte Holler's been found dead. She walked into the River Wannsee and drowned.'

291

40. The Letter

Lotte Holler's funeral was a sombre and quiet affair. To avoid any media circus, Julia and Jonas kept the arrangements quiet and had a private family cremation. The members of the press who'd reported her death and mentioned it for several consecutive days on national television news, were outwitted by the police telling them it would be at a certain place and time, before spiriting Julia and her boys and Jonas to a crematorium far away. A small number of disgruntled journalists camped outside the house in Wannsee hoping for an exclusive interview with Julia, but she'd abandoned the house and returned with her sons to her Berlin flat, hoping for obscurity.

A few days later, Julia welcomed a visit from Hanne.

'I'm so sorry for your loss,' Hanne sighed, giving Julia some flowers.

'Thank you. I'll put these in water. Coffee?'

Hanne nodded in appreciation and looked around the small living room. There were photos of Julia's sons at various stages in their young lives, one of Lotte as a younger woman and a recent photo of Julia, Lotte and the boys at Wannsee. Hanne was staring at this photo when Julia returned with a tray of biscuits and freshly brewed coffee.'

'She loved that house,' Julia remarked. 'But it wasn't meant to be.'

'It must have been a shock, Wolfgang turning up.'

Sighing, Julia mused, 'The truth always comes out in the

end. I would have tried to forgive my sister eventually but she didn't give me the chance. I don't know if I could have forgotten, though.'

'The wardens hid the abuse at Torgau and stuck together to hide the truth.'

'Just like the Nazis, they stuck together - no one questioned or challenged them and like the Torgau wardens, they admitted nothing,' Julia said, bitterly.

Hanne nodded in agreement. 'Be prepared, more Torgau victims may come forward.'

'Let them. It's their right. I'll not touch Lotte's money, her victims can have it.'

Contradicting Julia, Hanne declared, 'I think you're wrong. You were at your sister's bedside all those years until she woke up. Your sister made some terrible mistakes at Torgau; but she was also a victim of a crime and you suffered greatly as a consequence.'

Julia's eyes welled with tears. 'But when I think of all those children... Instead of helping them, Lotte betrayed them.'

'Agreed. But even if you don't want to touch the money, I think some of it should go to your sons. A bit of money in the bank might give them a few more options; if they have to deal with Lotte's ghost in the future.'

Julia could see the sense of it. She got up, went over to a dresser and searched for a letter, then passed a small, white envelope to Hanne. 'My sister walked into the river on Sunday night. She couldn't swim. Here's her last testament; it doesn't absolve her but in the end at least she was honest.'

Hanne read the letter.

My dearest Julia,

I've been ringing your mobile all day and have left several messages. When you left and didn't come back I realised you were ashamed of me. When we faced each other in the pouring rain, I saw the pain and disappointment in your eyes and how much I'd hurt you and let you down. I didn't dare come and see you in Berlin because I knew you needed time away from me. Then dark clouds descended on me and I finally admitted my guilt to myself, realising what I had done to all those poor children. Was that really me? Why did I do it? I have no excuse; I did it because I could. No one questioned or challenged us.

At Torgau, we did what we liked to the children. We repeatedly physically, mentally and sexually abused them. Julia, you'll probably doubt all I tell you now, but please believe me when I tell you I did not touch the children in a sexual way.

My crimes were plenty. I was a persistent, cruel bully who belittled the kids, I didn't care how I made them feel, and it was all about me.

I was in control, I felt superior and I was always barking orders and unleashing my moods on them without mercy. It didn't even occur to me to disobey orders from the male wardens, so I took the kids from their beds and led them to the paedophiles.

I read somewhere that when a person is unable to show empathy, it's an extreme form of narcissism. My inflated ego played a large part in the choices I made and the actions I took. Most normal people would wrap a crying child in their arms to protect them from such misery - but not me, I didn't want to be an outsider and I enjoyed being part of a gang. Because I co-operated, it was as bad as joining in the abuse. 'Do what you like, just don't get caught', that was our motto. At Torgau it was similar to how mankind commits atrocities in wartime: it was about the total failure of the human spirit.

It was the opposite when I came home from Torgau in the evenings and looked after you. I felt the maternal love that was so lacking in me there. How can anyone easily explain the dark side of themselves? I am doing my best to be honest with you now. When that young man attacked me on the banks of Muggesee, did I tell you how I begged for my life and told him I was pregnant? He said I was unfit to be a mother. He quoted Latin to me - in loco parentis. I had to look it up in a dictionary to understand the meaning. He was right. I was unfit to be a mother.

Julia, you're so different to me. You're a sweet and loving mother and your boys are a credit to you. They don't deserve the stigma of being associated with me; their tante. I've brought trouble into your life ever since I awoke from my coma. I feel I've been a ball and chain around your neck for too many years.

I'm sorry I wasn't brave enough to tell you the truth and it's because I got caught that the truth came out. Tell Wolfgang I'm sorry, though I know they are futile words after all he went through. If I came face to face with my attacker I'd ask why the hell he changed his mind and showed empathy, and didn't finish me off when he had the chance.

I'm sorry to leave you such a mess and so much shame to deal with. I know you'll forgive me in time, we're sisters and we love each other. Do you realise, Julia, I've never known any other love but yours. I leave all I have to you.

You know I can't swim so I've weighted down my coat pockets with stones. Hopefully drowning won't be too painful a death and it'll be over quickly. I'm not afraid. Death will be a release from the torments that now haunt my mind. What I am afraid of is never feeling at peace with myself - even with my new-found wealth it would be more painful to stay alive. I think a part of me died that night on the Muggelsee. I wish I had died then but at least I got to have your love again and hold you in my arms. I hope Dr Roth will look after you, he loves you and I can see you love him.

Please don't define me by my shame at Torgau. Think of me kindly, once in a while. Remember the days when it was just you and me against the world. Forgive me. I love you, my sweet, darling sister. I've been lucky to have your love.

Your devoted sister,
Lotte.

Folding the letter carefully, Hanne placed it on the coffee table.

Pretty strong stuff,' Julia said, stonily.

Hanne sighed. 'Indeed. I guess we never really know anyone.'

'What are you going to do with this letter? Do you need it for evidence, to help Wolfgang or any other Torgau victim that comes forward to get justice and compensation?'

'Possibly. You keep it safe, for now. The truth is, we've known for a while Lotte was involved with the paedophiles at Torgau as a go-between.'

Julia looked surprised. 'I see. So, you'd questioned Lotte

at some point and charge her?'

'Yes. We decided we'd question Lotte when she was well enough to give evidence and face trial.'

'Please tell me the truth and don't spare me any details,' Julia demanded.

Feeling uncomfortable, Hanne braced herself. 'Ok. Lotte was involved with the three men found in the lake at Muggelsee. Evidence suggests that these men - who called themselves Musketeers - were involved in paedophilia at Torgau. They were named in a paedophile ring that the police broke back in 1992, only we thought they'd disappeared and escaped justice. Little did we know; they were murdered, drowned in their cars and hidden in the depths of the lake!'

'So, the motive of Lotte's attacker was revenge?'

'Yes, the Musketeers were copycat murders of each other, but he didn't go through with killing Lotte. When we catch him, we'll find out why.'

Julia ventured, 'Maybe, this abused Torgau boy, did you all a favour, getting rid of the Musketeers.'

'In a way he did, but we can't excuse him even if he does turn out to be a paranoid schizophrenic. You can't take the law into your own hands, so if he's alive and we catch him he'll be assessed and sentenced accordingly.'

'Do you think he's still alive?'

Hanne nodded. 'I have a feeling that he is.'

'Thank you for telling me. Now I understand his motives, I can't blame him any more for what he did to Lotte,' said Julia, calmly. 'If I were in his shoes I'd take the law into my own hands. I think most people would, especially if it were their child that was abused.'

Hanne concurred but couldn't admit that she sympathised with Marine Boy. She felt great compassion for Julia. Every time she reads her sister's confessional letter it will be a reminder of everyone's pain, she thought, and had an overriding desire to tell Julia to burn the letter.

'By the way, I was pleased to hear that you and Dr Roth

are together now.'

'Yes, danke. Lotte was observant enough to know Jonas and I had fallen in love,' she said, smiling. 'Funny isn't it? All that time she was in a coma, Jonas and I had separate lives. I guess if we hadn't admitted our feelings before Lotte was discharged as his patient, we'd have missed our chance.'

Hanne thought about how she had prolonged letting go of her past regarding Claudia but when she'd finally summoned up the courage, she had met Brigitte.

'I guess love happens when you're least expecting it. Isn't that the old adage?' Hanne surmised. 'Julia, I'm glad for you.'

'Thank you. You know, it's weird how long it took Jonas and me to get together. I guess it was all down to timing. I've lost Lotte but gained Jonas. I feel so unbalanced.'

'Buddhists believe that to feel unbalanced is to have a balanced life,' Hanne ventured.

Julia smiled. 'It would be nice to keep in touch with you- if it's not too painful.'

'I'd like to think it's possible,' Hanne replied. 'One last question, did Lotte ever mention anyone called Witzig? He was possibly an ex-colleague from Torgau.'

'No, sorry. I've never heard that name before.'

41. Martha

At the end of April, Martha Baum was nearly five months pregnant and knowing she could afford a longer maternity leave than most, didn't intend to work past six months of the pregnancy. With only another 25 working days to go at her Berlin law firm, she marked each day off on the calendar. She was looking forward to putting her feet up and relaxing for the rest of her pregnancy at the lake. She'd been thinking that Peonie would benefit from some exclusive nurturing time, just mother and daughter, before the new baby came along in September.

During her last scan Martha and Felix had discovered the baby would be a boy. The happy, expectant parents told the family and there was much enthusiasm although Martha noticed that after the initial excitement her husband quickly returned to seeming ill at ease and troubled. They usually spoke honestly with each other but they hadn't found the time for a heart-to-heart for a while now. Martha felt Felix, who was usually quite open and frank, had recently become emotionally secretive and closed-off to her.

When her parents took Peonie to Kopenick that weekend, Martha thought it would be the perfect opportunity to have a discussion and a snuggle-up time with her husband. Felix came out of the shower and grabbed a beer. He was looking forward to spending the weekend alone with his wife. They had something to celebrate, not that Martha knew it. Lotte Holler was dead. He'd seen it reported on the news and it meant she could no longer help the police with their enquiries. Maybe he could relax a little and pamper his wife as she deserved. He had been so preoccupied since Lotte Holler had awoken from her coma; it was time he put it to the back of his mind.

After long discussions with Klaus and Ingrid, Felix had decided in the near future, to tell Martha the truth. For moral support he would have his onkel and tante present when he did. If they still loved him after all they'd discovered, Felix felt confident his wife would also come round and take his side. However, because Martha was pregnant it was decided with Klaus and Ingrid that his secrets should remain hidden until after the baby was born.

Martha came out of the bathroom to be greeted with a kiss from her husband and served with a simple meal of spaghetti bolognaise.

'Delicious,' she said, tasting a mouthful.

'I can't remember when I last cooked for you. Tante Ingrid always sends me home with a meal for the three of us,' Felix confessed.

'She knows you! After a long day at the boathouse you don't want to come home and cook, and after a day in Berlin, neither do I.'

'Martha, this time next month you can put your feet up. I've been a bit lazy of late and I haven't looked after you as well as I could, but I'll try and make it up to you.'

Martha was curious. 'Why haven't you been extra attentive when your wife is carrying your son?' she asked, a little mischief in her eyes and voice.

'I guess I got complacent. I hit 30 and realised I had everything I'd ever wanted - a beautiful wife, kids, money, a loving family. Maybe, I'm afraid of losing everything.'

'You won't lose us, sweetheart,' she assured him, with a kiss.

Swiftly, Felix switched the subject. 'So, what shall we call our son?'

'Well, didn't we say we'll call him Oskar or Guido, and let

Peonie decide which one of the two she likes best? And you, my dear husband, are changing the subject. Is that what you've been feeling since I told you I was pregnant: fear?'

'No man wants to admit to his wife he's afraid.'

'Do you feel under pressure? Has my pregnancy added to your worries?'

'I want this baby, my son.' Felix said, softly. Suddenly, there were tears in his eyes.

Martha was shocked. The last time Felix had cried in front of her was when Peonie was born. She knew suddenly that there was something serious wrong, something more than he was admitting to. Martha suspected Felix confided in Klaus and Ingrid, especially tante Ingrid. In the last few months the two of them often stopped their sotto voce conversations in mid-sentence when anyone else walked into the room.'

'Sweetheart, what's wrong? I'm worried, please tell me.'

Felix threw his arms around her and broke down. 'Look at me, a grown man crying,' he cried. 'I'm so selfish, and there's you, carrying our son. You're the brave one out of the two of us.'

Martha was deeply concerned. Without discussion, she picked up the phone and called Klaus and Ingrid and told them to come over straight away. Felix tried to compose himself but he couldn't stop shaking or crying.

Klaus and Ingrid arrived within five minutes. Along with Martha, they too, thought Felix was on the verge of a nervous breakdown.

'I think I should call a doctor, or maybe papa,' Martha declared.

'I don't need a doctor!' Felix shouted, suddenly furious.

'Come on, lad,' Klaus encouraged Felix. 'Think of Martha, she's having a baby. You don't want to go upsetting her.'

Ingrid added, 'But we can all see you're not well. You need to rest.'

Felix screamed. 'I'm not cracking up. I just can't lie to my wife anymore!'

Martha looked at Klaus and Ingrid. It seemed they knew what Felix was talking about. 'Felix, what do you mean, you've been lying to me?' Martha demanded to know.

Ingrid pulled Felix into an upright position. 'Pull yourself together. We'll help you tell her. Go on; tell your wife the truth. All of it.'

'Ingrid!' Klaus cried. 'Not now!'

'Tell me what?' Martha screamed.

'If he doesn't, he'll go mad!' Ingrid yelled back.

Martha pleaded, 'Felix! Please, you're scaring me and I can feel my heartbeat racing.'

This jolted Felix into the present and he led Martha to a comfortable armchair and sat her down. 'Ok. Tante Ingrid and onkel Klaus know because they found out.'

Martha covered her mouth with her hands and shook her head. 'You're not having an affair are you?'

Felix shook his head, gasping, 'Never. I love you. But I've kept something from you, to protect you and protect your opinion of me. Now, I'm afraid to lose your love.'

'Whatever it is; tell me. I'm your wife, and you know I love you.'

'But you're pregnant! And my news isn't good news.'

'I'm tougher than you think,' Martha insisted.

'Ok.' Felix took a deep breath. 'You remember the three bodies pulled out of Muggelsee in February?'

Martha nodded.

Blurting it out, Felix confessed, 'They were the men that abused me at Torgau. I put them there. I killed them! I drowned them in their cars and left them at the bottom of the lake!'

She was shaking her head in disbelief, 'No! You couldn't have,' Martha cried.

Klaus intervened. 'Felix was 17. One of them turned up at the golf club and threatened to go after Axel. Martha, please understand.'

'Don't reject him,' Ingrid implored.

Felix and Martha stared at one another, both with tears running down their cheeks. Felix reached out his hand to touch his wife; she recoiled. Martha felt strange sensations in her womb but ignored them, thinking her baby was merely as uncomfortable as herself.

'Martha, please forgive me,' Felix begged her.

Martha was outraged. 'Forgive you... for murder? And for lying to me, all these years? Scheisse!' she screamed at him.

Ingrid was frantic with worry. 'Martha, we've lied to you, too. I'm sorry.'

Martha scoffed, 'That explains the secretive behaviour. Thick as thieves; you two!'

Klaus intervened. 'We've always protected Felix.'

'Martha, what are you going to do?' Ingrid asked.

'I don't know! But don't worry; a wife can't testify against her husband,' she cried, sarcastically.

Klaus insisted, 'We can keep it secret, Felix hasn't been caught in all this time. I'm so sorry, Martha, we've all lied to you.'

Martha shouted, 'It's a hell of a secret to keep! Felix, what else have you lied about?'

'Only this, I swear,' Felix promised, solemnly.

'It's not every day I hear my husband has killed three men.'

'If I'd had an affair, would that be worse?' Felix asked, pathetically.

Martha did something out of character, something she'd never done before. She slapped her husband's face hard on the cheek. 'Don't you dare joke about it!' she snapped.

Felix was shocked. He rubbed his sore cheek and stayed silent.

'Martha, Felix has been under a lot of pressure,' Ingrid began. 'Last month the police were asking questions at the golf club about one of the men who worked for us during a golf tournament in 1992. Felix didn't want to tell anyone- I dragged it out of him!'

'So now we all share his burden,' Martha mocked.

'Felix! Say something,' Klaus urged him.

Felix was flummoxed. 'Martha, do you want me to leave?'

'NO! You stay here and explain yourself!' she ordered.

Haltingly, Felix told her all the details of how he had disposed of the three Musketeers. His wife listened intently as Klaus and Ingrid looked on. When his story was finished, Martha realised she couldn't hate him; she loved him. She would never think of her husband as a murderer and knew she would eventually forgive him in time. He was a damaged Torgau boy, she'd always known that. He'd taken his revenge on his abusers and his reasons were apparently valid. But for now she was in shock, and Felix would have to wait until she calmed down for this unexpected and horrific news to sink in - and for her considered reaction.

Swiftly and instinctively, Martha's legal brain kicked in. 'Did you leave any clues at the crime scenes?'

Felix nodded. 'A size nine aqua shoe in Plaumann's car, and my Herbertz knife. There's one more crime I need to confess to. I left my knife at the lake when I attempted to murder a woman; the one that fell into a long coma. She drowned herself last month in the Wannsee.'

Martha's face crumpled. 'No! Not Lotte Holler.'

Felix nodded. 'She was a warden at Torgau and helped the Musketeers.'

Suddenly, Martha clasped her lower abdomen. The pain was instant and agonising. Then she felt fluid leaking out of her.

'What's wrong?' Felix asked, suddenly anxious and concerned.

'I don't know... I don't feel well,' Martha cried, as the room began to spin around her.

Felix rushed his wife to the hospital in Zossen. Her blood pressure was high and she'd had a slight womb bleed. The baby was fine, which was a great relief to both of them, but as a precaution and on the doctor's advice she stayed in hospital overnight. Felix phoned Klaus and Ingrid to tell them the good news and returned to his wife's private room. Martha was on her mobile phone to her parents, reassuring them.

'Yes… I'll not go to work on Monday. I promise. Is she asleep? Ok, Mutti, I'll ring tomorrow at breakfast time to speak to Peonie. Tschuss.'

'The nurses said they'll bring me a camp bed to sleep in here with you,' Felix told her.

'I'm fine. Go home and sleep in a proper bed,' Martha said, curtly.

'I don't want to leave you.'

'Felix, I need some space to get my head around all this.'

He held his head down in shame. 'If you lose the baby, it will be my fault.'

'Stop! The baby's fine. Just go. I'll see you in the morning.'

Felix felt pushed away but he understood. 'Ok.'

Relenting suddenly, Martha held out her arms and Felix hugged her gently.

'I'm sorry, I'm so, so sorry,' he cried.

'I know you are, but it doesn't change the facts. Felix, you realise I'm now compromised by you: I'm committing a crime by keeping your secrets.'

'Do you want me to give myself up?'

Martha shook her head. 'I know you'll do what you think is right, no matter what I say.'

Raising a half-smile, Felix said, 'You know me all too well.'

She whispered, 'Well, now you've unburdened yourself, maybe I'll have my husband back. I felt I was losing you. I didn't think your troubled mood of late was because you'd committed 3 murders, and were worried your crimes were catching up with you!'

'It's not been easy to tell my wife who I am and what I've done.'

Martha sighed. 'I guess not. I believe it was Freud who

said there are no coincidences. I'm going to break client confidentiality for the first time in my life. Felix, it was my legal firm that won Lotte Holler her compensation settlement.'

What an incredible coincidence, thought Felix. 'Did you ever meet her?'

'No, but my colleagues said she was a tough and uncompromising character. Do you know why she walked into the Wannsee?'

'The papers said she was depressed.'

'Obviously! But as her legal team, we got to hear the truth from the police.'

Felix was intrigued. 'Go on.'

'A man turned up at her home- one of the kids she'd abused at Torgau Apparently, she couldn't live with the shame of her sister knowing the truth, and she couldn't swim.'

'So, she drowned herself, 'Felix mused. 'That's what I wanted to do to her, drown her in the depths of Muggelsee.'

'Why didn't you drive her car into the lake like the others?'

'The car wouldn't start. Had I known she couldn't swim, I could've thrown her into the lake from the end of the jetty.'

'But you didn't kill her.'

'No. Lotte told me she was pregnant; I couldn't knowingly harm an unborn child,' Felix confessed. 'Martha, I was 17 and I don't think I was in my right mind after everything that had happened. Maybe I was paranoid or schizophrenic at the time but I felt I was entitled to choose revenge after everything I'd suffered at the hands of those monsters. It's been hard living with the torment of having killed them and I don't get much peace, but it would have been worse if I hadn't done it. If they were still alive, the Musketeers would have haunted my dreams all my life, and they might have come after Axel, who was only a little boy then. The one good thing to come of it all, the one thing that justifies my actions; they will never rape another child again.

'Putting them behind bars meant they wouldn't be able to hurt kids either,' Martha said, in a matter-of-fact way.

'I'm not trying to defend myself or condone what I did, but I'm glad I did it. Does that shock you?'

She nodded. 'I didn't think you were capable of such violence.'

'Everyone is capable of violence when pushed to their limits,' he stated.

Martha thought for a moment. 'I suppose that's true. If anyone touched my daughter...' She stopped in mid-sentence, traumatised at the thought.

Felix took her hand. 'When you've been violated as a child, it takes away all your happy childhood memories and robs you of a future. I wanted to move on but I couldn't. Once I'd got rid of the Musketeers, only then did I really feel free.'

'I'm trying to understand,' Martha told him. 'Only because I love you; but it's hard.'

'I love you too, and I never meant to hurt you. I'm glad you know.'

'That's what I have to get my head around. I understand your motives, but I can see clearly, you're not sorry. In fact you're rather proud you've killed your abusers.'

'I'm not proud, how could I be? Martha, I can't lie and say I'm sorry, because I'm not; Axel is safer because of what I did, and I'm no longer stuck in limbo.'

'No!' cried Martha. 'You are stuck in limbo again; we all are. We're all waiting for the day when the police figure out it was you... So, what do we do now?'

'I don't know,' Felix replied, candidly. 'Pray for a miracle.'

42. Brothers in Arms

Kruger was in a foul mood early on Monday morning with Stefan and Hanne 'I've got the Leitender breathing down my neck, demanding progress with this case,' he snapped.

Stefan was defensive. 'It's not an easy case to solve…'

Kruger interrupted him. 'Quatch! Glockner, get your arse in gear and help me solve this Musketeers case by the end of the month. Is that clear?'

Hanne took umbrage at Kruger's outburst. 'With due respect, Kommissar; Stefan's been working hard to solve this case but can only go on the leads given. Events from 12 years ago aren't fresh in anyone's memory, not even yours. It doesn't help that certain records in East Germany have disappeared, denying us vital information.'

Kruger admired Hanne for standing up to him, but he wasn't about to relent. 'Haven't either of you got any bloody leads to go on?'

'Yes, as a matter of fact,' Stefan replied, calmly. 'I got a call from Uwe Muller, the old man at the nursing home in Dresden late last night. He remembered the politician who came to collect Susanne Waltz - he saw him recently on television, said he looked older but was sure it was him.'

'Well, who the hell is it?

Looking pleased, Stefan announced, 'It's the Burgermeister of Zossen.'

This surprised Kruger. 'What? The Mayor at Gwisdek's motor home?'

Hanne declared, 'Yes, Bernd Felker. But he's not Marine Boy. He can't be; he doesn't fit the age group, the height or the profile of the Torgau boy.'

Stefan added, 'But he's connected to Torgau and the Waltz girl who died; so he must know what happened to the child, Axel.'

Kruger's mood lightened. 'Lotte Holler couldn't be sure of the age of her attacker - he might have told her a pack of lies. It could be the Mayor or his brother as revenge for their niece's death. Get him in.'

Stefan nodded. 'Will do.'

'Tell Korfsmeier, I want his fingerprints to see if they match those on the knife. And find out his shoe size. Tell the Mayor to bring his brother, too… And thanks,' Kruger said, smiling. 'Good work, both of you.'

Much to his surprise, Bernd received a call from the police asking him to come into Berlin for questioning; and to bring his brother.

On hearing the disconcerting news, Klaus cried out. 'Mein gott!'

Bernd nodded. 'Sorry, I wish it wasn't true. I don't know what's going on, but they want to speak to you as well.'

Klaus's heart sank. 'Are we suspects?'

'How the hell should I know?'

'Bernd, I think I know what's it's about and you've got to trust me. They're on a trail, and it leads to Felix,' Klaus confessed.

Bernd was concerned. 'What's he done?'

'I'll tell you on our journey to Berlin, but whatever you do, don't tell the police about Felix. As far as they know, Felix Waltz died in Torgau in 1989. They have no record of his new name. I'll tell Felix to stay away from the golf club for the time being and I'm also hoping, the police don't know about our family links to the lake.'

'I have a bad feeling about all this,' Bernd said.

Klaus put on his coat. 'I'm not telling Ingrid or Felix where we're going.'

'Best not. I haven't told Ute, or the girls.'

'Good. Let's hope by going there and answering their questions, it'll keep them from paying us a visit here,' Klaus said, crossing his fingers.

'You've got some explaining to do,' Bernd told his brother.

When the Felker brothers arrived at the Berlin police station they voluntarily offered to have their fingerprints taken. Bernd now knew the whole shocking truth about Felix and was taken first to the interview room. Glockner and Kruger sat opposite Bernd, who tried to look and stay calm even though he was nervous. In an adjoining room, Hanne watched the interview through a one-way mirror.

Stefan turned on a tape recorder. '11.42 a.m., 3rd May 2005. The interviewing officers are Kommissar Kruger and Detective Glockner. Bernd Felker is willing to be interviewed without a lawyer present.'

'What's this all about?' Bernd asked.

Stefan stated, 'In December 1989, you and your brother Klaus Felker, visited a nursing home in Dresden. You took your niece, Susanne Waltz home with you. Is that correct?'

Bernd was surprised. 'Yes.'

'The owner of the nursing home remembered you. He said you told him you were a politician in East Berlin.'

'Yes, I was a functionaire in the DDR Politburo.'

'And after German reunification?'

'I stayed in politics. I became the Mayor of Zossen in 1990.'

'What happened to your brother's niece?'

Bernd recalled sadly. 'Susanne died, not long after leaving the nursing home.'

'How did she die?'

'In an accident. She fell from a height, hit her head and broke her neck.'

Kruger probed without sensitivity. 'What was she doing?

Climbing trees?'

Bernd knew he had to be careful with his answers, so as not to compromise himself or his brother and in particular, Felix. 'I don't know; I wasn't there. It's a long time ago and we've never spoken about it again. It's still too painful,' he confessed.

'Susanne was at Torgau youth prison in East Germany. Is that correct?'

'Yes, Kommissar. Susanne was sent to Torgau. She didn't do anything wrong- it was simply because she was an orphan.'

Kruger snapped, trying to provoke Bernd into reacting. She had a family!'

Ignoring any provocation, yet Bernd was adamant. 'We didn't know!'

'I see. And when you collected your niece, she had a child, a boy called Axel. Did that make you feel angry? Your brother's niece; a mother at 14?'

'Yes, Kommissar. Angry and sad. Klaus's wife, Ingrid, fell out with her sister- Susanne's mother, who subsequently died. We didn't know that either, or as I've said, that Susi and Felix had ended up in Torgau.'

'Where's Axel?'

'Axel? Klaus and Ingrid adopted him,' stated Bernd, plainly.

Kruger nodded and changed the direction of his questions. 'What's your shoe size?'

Bernd looked puzzled. 'Eleven. Why?'

Kruger held out his hand. 'Herr Burgermeister. May I see your shoe?'

Bernd handed over one of his shoes.

'Size 11,' Kruger repeated, aloud. 'For the benefit of the tape, it's confirmed that Bernd Felker's shoe is size 11.'

Stefan's mobile phone on the table vibrated.

It was Hanne, texting a question. Reading her text, Stefan turned to address the Mayor. 'You've been careful not to mention Susanne's twin; her brother, Felix. Why's that?'

Bernd felt under pressure and sweat began to trickle down the back of his neck. 'Felix… We don't like being reminded that as a family we failed those kids,' he said, hoping he'd given a satisfactory answer.

'No more questions for the moment,' Kruger informed Bernd.

Stefan switched off the tape and left the room with Kruger. Bernd was escorted out by a police officer.

Kruger was interested to hear Hanne's take on the Mayor's interview.

'You wouldn't wear an aqua shoe two sizes too small: one size smaller maybe, to but not two, the shoe wouldn't fit,' Hanne ventured.

Stefan suggested, 'Maybe the aqua shoe is a red herring and just happened to be in Plaumann's car. Has anyone ever considered this?'

Kruger agreed with both of his colleagues' observations. 'Whatever the truth is about the aqua shoe, the Mayor's a smooth operator. Let's get onkel Klaus in.'

Klaus was not a smooth operator but was adept at hiding the truth to protect his family, even though he was nervous and less composed than his brother and rather overwhelmed by his surroundings.

In the interview room, Stefan switched on the tape. Kruger stared at Klaus; it was his usual gruff look, which strangers often interpreted as intimidating, but Kruger was just being himself.

Stefan spoke into the microphone. 'Time, 1.23 p.m., 3rd May 2005. Interviewing officers; Kommissar Kruger and Detective Glockner. Klaus Felker has agreed to be questioned without a lawyer present.'

Hanne watched from the other side of the mirror. She felt some empathy for Klaus, and had been happy to hear that Susanne Waltz's son had been adopted. Axel was not a weggesperrt child, she thought, he wasn't forgotten like the kids in Torgau. Ingrid had become his mother.

Kruger began with a different approach. 'Herr Felker, are you close to your brother?'

'Yes, we're a close family.'

'And families protect one another,' ventured Kruger.

Klaus replied, emphatically, 'Naturlich!'

'Did you take your brother in his official capacity as functionaire, to help get your niece Susanne Waltz out of a Torgau in the winter of 1989?'

Klaus nodded. 'I did, but it was in the process of closing down. Susanne had been sent to a nursing home in Dresden and given birth to Axel, her son.'

Kruger was challenging in tone. 'And you and your wife adopted Axel. Was that before or after your niece's early demise?'

Klaus felt his blood boil at the insensitive question, but bit his lip. 'Susanne was allowed to keep Axel, if that's what you mean, unlike other pregnant girls that gave birth at that nursing home. Axel was a direct result of the systemised abuse that went on at Torgau.'

Hanne listened intently. Klaus was standing his ground with Kruger.

'But when she died, you adopted Axel?'

'Yes, Kommissar. My wife and I never had children. We were approaching 40- a bit late for first-time parenting some might say, but there was no way Axel was going to be given away. He was all we had left of Susanne.'

Klaus had taken the exact sentiments out of Hanne's mind and mouth.

Stefan asked, 'How did Susanne die?'

Klaus felt the police already knew the answer to this question and were trying to catch him lying. Also, he didn't have a clue how Bernd had answered this question, but knew if his brother didn't know what to say, he'd usually be evasive or say he didn't know.

'She was suffering from post-natal depression, only no one knew at the time,' Klaus cried. 'It was snowing; Susanne climbed a tree and lost her footing, slipped and fell, and broke her neck.'

Hanne texted.

Klaus heard Glockner's phone vibrate and saw the policeman glance towards the blackened mirror behind him. He guessed there was someone watching in another room.

Stefan read the text and asked Klaus, 'Was Dr Jens the doctor who helped you?'

Klaus was surprised by this. The police had done their research. 'Yes, Dr Jens was Susanne's doctor in Torgau, and he helped get her into the nursing home. Ingrid, my wife, rang Dr Jens when Susanne fell and he came straight away.'

'How did you know his telephone number?'

Klaus bluffed his way along. 'Susanne told us about how kind he'd been. Dr Jens had given her his number if ever she should need him.'

'I see,' Kruger said. 'What's the doctor's surname?'

'No idea,' Klaus lied.

'Convenient,' Kruger mused. 'And the doctor's signature on Susanne's death certificate is, illegible. Your niece's death was recorded in Kopenick.'

'Dr Jens said he'd take care of it and yes, he lived in this area. I believe he posted us a copy of her death certificate,' Klaus replied.

'Are you still in contact with Dr Jens?'

'No. It would only remind us of that tragic event,' Klaus declared, lying again.

Probing, Kruger asked, 'Axel must be around 15 now. Does he know the truth about his real mother?'

'Axel's known he was adopted since he was old enough to understand.'

Kruger could see Klaus was guarded. The silence in the room was broken by Glockner's mobile vibrating again. He tried to hide a smile reading Hanne's text. This question would probe even deeper.

Stefan queried, 'And the house Susanne was to inherit from your wife's mother. Do you live in this house, with your wife and son?'

Klaus was taken aback but tried not to show it, wondering if they knew there was a link to the lake and the boatyard.' 'Yes, we've kept it. It will belong to Axel someday.'

'Where is this house?'

'At Motzen, near our golf club,' Klaus answered, trying not to sound perturbed.

Stefan continued probing. 'And what do you do for a living?'

'I'm a carpenter by trade. After the Wall came down, Bernd and I invested our savings and bought the Motzen Mayor Golf club. It's a family business - even Axel works for us at weekends on the driving range, collecting golf balls.'

This rang a bell in Stefan's head. 'Do you remember a security guard working for you in September 1992, a man called Horst Gwidek?'

Klaus could have kicked himself. He'd told them about the golf club to divert attention away from the Felix, the boathouse and the lake. 'I've already told the police clerk who rang me at the club. Do you know how many security guards we've employed over the years? No, I don't recall him,' he said, hoping his answer was convincing enough.

Hanne texted another question.

'Herr Felker, like your brother, you've said nothing about your nephew, Felix Waltz. I find this a bit strange,' Stefan declared.

Klaus was prepared for this question. 'My wife has lived all her life with the guilt of falling out with her sister Sofie. She died before they were reconciled. To discover our twins ended up abused at Torgau was heartbreaking. Felix jumped into the River Elbe trying to escape, and those bastards at Torgau, didn't even bother recording it. To them, our Felix was just a forgotten kid. No, as a family, we don't talk about Felix; it's too painful; it reminds us how we failed him.'

Kruger butted in. 'Like you said, you protect your family. How do you feel about the people that abused your niece and your nephew?'

'I hate them. Wouldn't you?' Klaus replied, honestly.

'I guess I would,' Kruger replied. 'What if I told you Horst Gwisdek was a paedophile and one of the Torgau wardens who abused Susanne and Felix?'

This was the optimum opportunity for Klaus to release the tension he was feeling.

'Nein! Scheisse! And I had him within my grasp.'

'More importantly, Gwisdek was murdered. And if you don't already know; last month, he was one of the three men found dead in his car, at the bottom of Muggelsee.'

'Good fucking job that bastard ended up dead in the lake, or I'd have given him a taste of his own medicine!' Klaus bellowed.

Kruger observed, 'You've a temper on you, Herr Felker!'

Stefan added, 'Giving you and your brother a motive.'

'What shoe size are you?' Kruger asked, going off at a tangent.'

Klaus thought this was an odd question. 'Size 11.'

'Same size as your brother,' Kruger muttered under his breath. 'A size 11 shoe was found at the scene of the crime,' he lied, to see how Klaus responded.

Klaus banged his fists on the table. 'And you think Bernd and I have something to do with it? Don't waste my time! Find the real culprits,' he barked.

Rutger came into the room where Hanne was watching Klaus being interviewed.

'Hanne, I've done the fingerprint checks on the Herbertz knife. The Mayor and his brother are in the clear as far as the knife is concerned,' Rutger told her.

Hanne seemed pleased. 'Thanks. Kruger will be disappointed. Look at this, Klaus Felker is giving Kruger a run for his money.'

Rutger smiled. 'That's a first. Who's going to tell him, you or me?'

'You can put them all out of their misery. Wolfgang told us about the Waltz twins and that is Klaus Felker's only and unfortunate connection to Torgau,' Hanne surmised.

Rutger agreed and left Hanne, quietly entering the interview room, handing over his findings, and creeping back out.

Kruger scanned Rutger's notes. 'Interview terminated,' he barked, storming out.

Klaus wondered what evidence Kruger had received but breathed a sigh of relief, feeling he'd performed well and matched the abrasive Kruger. Hanne continued watching through the mirror and saw Klaus visibly relax. She smiled, thinking that thanks to onkel Klaus, Susanne Waltz's little boy had the chance of a happy childhood.

43. Serendipity

Audrey went off early on her new purple bicycle on Saturday morning for a lesson with her maths tutor and afterwards, planned to spend the rest of the day on a cycle trip with friends. As Brigitte was working at Kadewe, Hanne found she had the day to herself. They were planning a long weekend away together at the end of May, around the lakes beyond the Spreewald. It was a sunny spring morning and on impulse she decided to take a reconnaissance drive and peruse the area around Zossen.

After listening to Klaus Felker's interview at the police station earlier in the week, Hanne was still curious to catch a glimpse of Axel. She remembered Klaus saying Axel worked at their golf club at weekends and it was in the area where she was planning the mini- break with Brigitte. Hanne wouldn't be recognised by the Felker brothers because they hadn't met her- she'd stayed hidden behind the scenes at the police station. What harm could it do, simply to satisfy her curiosity and take a peep at the boy whose story had touched her heart?

Hanne took her top-of-the-range GPS tracking data pusher with her, an essential piece of modern technology designed to help the police with covert operations. She programmed the route and her journey was mapped out within seconds.

About an hour out of Berlin she passed Zossen; a little

further beyond was the verdant area surrounding Mellensee Lake. On its northern edges, the vast lake filtered into a lock and the Notte Kanal. Boating enthusiasts could sail all the way up to Kopenick via this canal where the river widened, eventually joining the River Spree which led to the heart of the capital; Berlin. Now she was deep into the countryside, with picturesque windmills and castles, and Mellensee offered lakeside aquatic activities and a designated trail for walkers or cyclists along the canal. It was an ideal oasis for city dwellers to take a holiday so Hanne booked three nights in a local guest house feeling sure Brigitte would approve of her choice. She had a quick bite to eat in a café overlooking the lake at Mellensee before heading to the Motzen Mayor golf club, a short drive away.

The large car park was busy with golfers arriving and departing. Hanne parked and wandered into the reception area of the clubhouse and was greeted by a friendly face. It was Carsten Berger, Felix's old school friend, and now one of the managers of the club who had worked his way up from barman.

Carsten watched Hanne enter and browse through the brochures in the foyer.

'Entschuldigen? Can I help?' he asked.

Hanne feigned interest. 'Yes, I'll be holidaying near here at the end of the month and we thought we'd play a round of golf. Do you have to be a member to play here?'

Carsten shook his head. 'Not at all. But you'll need to book a tee off time in advance,' he told her, pointing to a brochure. 'All the details are our brochures.'

'Danke. Mind if I look around?'

'Kein problem.'

Axel Felker was out on the driving range with his mini-tractor; collecting golf balls. He had an iPod attached to his waist and was listening to music, humming some tune or other as he drove the tractor around. Intermittently, he hopped out to gather the balls in a scooper, loaded them into the container at the back of the tractor and once full, drove to the machine at the entrance of the range to refill it with golf balls. Then he had a wait of about half an hour before the golfers on the driving range had hit enough balls for him to collect again. Often, Axel took this opportunity to practice his own golfing game or chat with the members.

Near the driving range, someone called out his name; Axel turned in response and Hanne knew she'd found him; the son of Susanne Waltz. Surreptitiously watching him, Hanne noticed how at ease Axel was, not only with himself but with everyone he came into contact with. He was very pleasing to the eye with his athletic build and fair hair tied in a ponytail, and exuding an air of friendliness. She noted that he was always ready with a smile that was mirrored infectiously by those who came into contact with him. There was something familiar about him, too. Hanne felt she'd met Axel or seen him before. Of course it wasn't true but nevertheless, she had a strong feeling of déjà vu. Now that she'd seen him, she thought she'd better stop loitering and head back to Berlin.

Walter, one of the experienced golf instructors at the club, was warming up on the range and struck up a conversation with Axel which Hanne couldn't help overhearing.

'Hey, Axel. Who do you think will win the German Masters next month?'

Axel smiled mischievously. 'Fancy losing another bet?'

Walter smiled, enjoying the banter with the boss's son. 'You won our bet last year, when you said Padraig Harrington would win, so this year I get to choose first.'

'Ok.'

'Ten euros says K.J Choi wins.'

Axel thought about it for a moment and shook his head. 'No. He won it two years ago. The only person to win the German Masters golf tournament more than once is Bernhard Langer because it means so much to him. So, I'll say someone that hasn't won it before, someone in form…

Retief Goosen.'

The two of them shook hands on the deal.

'Haven't seen your Onkel Felix up here in weeks,' commented Walter.

'Onkel Felix is working on the boats over at the lake, getting them ready for the summer season. He'll be back-you can't keep him off a golf course for too long,' Axel replied, and went off in his tractor.

Hanne heard the name Felix and it registered immediately. Onkel Felix, that's what Axel had said; but didn't the Felker brothers say their nephew Felix Waltz had drowned in the river Elbe? She thought back to the recent interviews. No, she recalled, they hadn't said that exactly. Both brothers had been slightly evasive, as if they'd made a secret pact not to mention their nephew. What Klaus Felker actually said was that Felix jumped into the River Elbe and Kruger, and everyone assumed he died from drowning. Klaus never actually uttered the words 'Felix died'. Klaus also said Felix's death wasn't recorded at Torgau and she and the team concluded that the police team must have failed to establish whether this information was true or false, although records in those days were sketchy to say the least.

Were the Felker brothers lying with their carefully worded script? Surely there couldn't be two onkels in the family called Felix? That would be too much of a coincidence. Had Klaus and Bernd Felker outsmarted them? Axel's onkel Felix was working at a lake. If so, which lake? This was an area full of lakes.

At a lake, Hanne repeated to herself... Marine Boy probably came from a background where boats and water sports were predominant. And if Felix Waltz was alive he would fit the profile and motives of the young man who killed the Musketeers and the attempted murder of Lotte Holler. In 1989 he would have been the right age, strong enough and angry enough to take revenge on his Torgau abusers. He could be Marine Boy.

Logically, it slotted into place. If Felix Waltz escaped

from Torgau, his first port of call would be the safe haven of his onkel Klaus's home. Was Felix hidden and protected by his loved ones until after the Wall came down, when it was prudent to re-emerge back into society? Obviously the family would have been extra cautious after Susanne's tragic demise; anyone incarcerated in Torgau would need gentle handling and copious amounts of time to recover and heal.

Hanne questioned if it was possible that a few years later, with business booming in the former East Germany, Horst Gwisdek had turned up unexpectedly at the family's golf club and backed Felix into a corner, triggering him into turning vigilante and committing unpremeditated murder. She simply had to find Axel's onkel Felix. With simultaneous anxiousness and excitement, her heart was pounding. And then a memory hit her. Axel looked exactly like the boy in her photo; the boy she and Claudia had met the night the Berlin Wall came down. The photo that had adorned her kitchen wall for the past 15 years… This boy had called himself Jens. His hair was fair under his dark wig and the cigar scars on his ears were similar to the scars on Wolfgang's ears. So that was why Hanne had had that feeling of déjà vu when she'd seen Wolfgang's ears. Branded by the Musketeers and remembering how Jens had the same scars.

Were Jens and Marine Boy the same person? Hanne's mind was racing. Marine Boy slashed his victim's ears. Was he branding the Musketeers to make them feel like the Torgau boys felt? It was an incredible coincidence that could be true. Could this Jens possibly have been - and still be - Felix Waltz? Hanne could see the image of Jens that night clearly in her mind. The similarity between Axel and Jens was uncanny. But this was perfectly natural, and given that Felix and Susanne were twins it was likely that Axel would resemble the male version of his mother.

She simply had to speak to Axel, so she returned to the club shop and bought a seven iron and a glove on the advice of the sales assistant, who informed her that this was the first club a golfer used when starting out. She kept the receipt to get the money reimbursed as a work expense before making her way back to the driving range.

For two euros, the machine dispensed a basket full of golf balls and Hanne was lucky to find an empty golf bay on the driving range close to Axel's parked tractor where he was sitting listening to music and playing with his mobile phone.

It was now or never.

'Bitte,' Hanne cried loudly.

Axel took his earphones out and looked at her, half smiling.

The feeling grew stronger: Hanne could see the boy Jens in Axel's face.

'Sorry to disturb you. But I'm a bit new to this. You work here, and I was wondering, are you any good at golf?'

'I've a handicap of 14,' Axel replied.

'Is that good?' Hanne asked, embarrassed by her golfing ignorance.

'It's ok. It could be better.'

'You wouldn't mind giving me a few tips, would you?'

Axel hopped off the tractor. 'Sure... But I could go and ask one of the golf pros to help you if you like? Where's Walter?' he said, looking around for him.

'No, sorry. I'm trying to keep costs down,' Hanne told him.

Axel smiled. 'I understand. How can I help?'

'My partner wants me to take up golf, so I'm doing this on the quiet as a surprise. I just don't know how to hold the club or how to stand.'

'Have you warmed up yet?'

Hanne shook her head. 'I don't know how to.'

Axel showed Hanne a few warm-up exercises. He was patient with her awkwardness, helping her to understand the basics of holding a golf club. After some practice swings and shots, eventually, Hanne made contact with the ball and to her surprise, it travelled quite straight for about 50 or so yards.

Axel praised her encouragingly. 'You're a natural.'

'And you are very polite. Thank you.'

'Just keep at it and keep your head down. Don't be tempted to look where the ball goes before you've finished the follow-through with the swing,' he advised.

'Ok. Sounds bit too technical, but I'll give it a try.'

Hanne repeated the success of the previous swing and Axel clapped politely.

'Beginner's luck,' she grinned. 'How long have you been playing?'

'Since I was old enough to hold a golf club, when I was about five,' he told her.

'And you love golf so much you work here on Saturdays?'

Axel was a little embarrassed. 'Kind of. My family owns the club.'

Hanne knew time was running out and she had to be more audacious if she was to find out what she wanted to know. 'Oh, yes, I remember now, it's a very prestigious golf club you have here, run by your father Klaus, your onkel Bernd and… Onkel Felix. Must be nice; working for the family business.'

Axel smiled. 'If I want pocket money, I have to work.'

'Your father and his brother, the Mayor, were entertaining everyone in the club house the last time I was here, but I didn't get to meet your onkel Felix.'

'Onkel Felix is working at our boatyard over at Motzen Lake. My mother runs the café on the waterfront - you must try the food there; it's great,' Axel said, with enthusiasm.

'Oh, I will. What a busy family you have.' Hanne told him. 'I mustn't keep you. You've been very kind, thank you.'

'You're welcome. Good luck with the swing,' he said.

Axel started up the tractor and drove off. Hanne left the basket half-full of golf balls and hurried back to her car. She threw the golf club and glove into the boot and quickly reprogrammed the GPS tracker to direct her to Motzen Lake. Briefly, she thought about calling the team for back up, just in case things got tricky, but the ambiguous feelings she'd developed over the past five months spent working on this case made her hesitate. She still felt a surprising amount of empathy for Marine Boy. Possibly she'd soon face him in his home environment. Would he be violent? Hanne didn't think so, although she carried a Taser stun gun in the car. Strangely unafraid and with resolve, she decided to go alone. Was this foolhardy? It was a calculated risk that she was willing to take.

What if her imagination had gone into freefall and was playing tricks on her? Then it wouldn't be Marine Boy after all. It would simply be Felix Waltz; a boy whose family wanted to protect his identity and veil his past associations with Torgau. Either way, Hanne was about to find out.

44. The Banana Lady

Martha came out of hospital and returned home to Motzen having been ordered to rest by the hospital doctor and her father. Jens and Angele offered to keep Peonie for an extended stay but Martha wanted her daughter at home with her. Her parents stayed for a few days and this helped Felix and Martha ease gently back into a united front. In pretending all was well, they fooled not only the others but themselves, too. Once Jens and Angele returned to Kopenick, Felix and Martha were left alone to pick up the pieces after the recent traumatic revelations and try to rebuild trust within their relationship.

Martha needed time to come to terms with the fact that her husband was a serial killer and find a way to learn to live with such a terrible secret. Her focus was her unborn child and she was worried about the effect her negative thoughts would have on her baby. Felix was careful not to mention the subject of his crimes, unless Martha wanted to discuss the matter. He didn't want to upset her again and risk losing the baby.

Usually so happy together, their laughter was replaced by a subdued atmosphere that Peonie was fortunately oblivious to. Topics of conversation were limited to perfunctory exchanges and their usual tactile behaviour was cast aside. But they continued sleeping in the same bed and when either of them turned during the night they would instinctively reach for each other's hand to hold before falling back to sleep.

However, Martha could not reject Felix for long. After a few days of uncharacteristic distance between them, and her forlorn face mirroring his, she burst into tears. He held her in his arms and kissed her and only then did she begin to feel all would be well again. Ingrid was taking Peonie off their hands during the afternoons whilst Martha had a siesta or rested in bed watching television. Felix had taped a lot of comedy programmes for her, and despite the recent traumatic events, Martha laughed easily as she tucked into her favourite chocolates. Felix meanwhile occupied his thoughts and days with plenty of work, fixing up the pleasure boats and crafts for the tourist season, which would soon be in full swing.

Hanne arrived at the lake, parking her car at the old aircraft hangar. She took her Taser stun gun from its case, primed it and hid it inside her jacket. Although nervous, she felt very strongly that the events over the past five months had led her here for a reason.

There weren't many people around this early in the season. Hanne could see the beauty and tranquillity of the place and imagined the tourists would flock here when it became warmer. The lake was an expanse of calm, which was juxtaposed to her feelings of angst. Passing the waterside café she made her way to the boathouse. One of the stable-style doors was open and the sounds of a drill inside punctuated the air. This is it, Hanne told herself, there's no going back. She took a deep breath and went inside.

He was just as she'd remembered. Axel's onkel Felix; the boy who called himself Jens on that cold, crisp November night in 1989, were one and the same. She looked at the young man who stood directly in front of her and noticed the scars on his ears had faded.

Felix stopped in his tracks. He didn't recognise the tall woman who stood by the door but immediately had a weird feeling about her.

'Hello. Can I help you?'

Hanne showed him her police identification badge. 'Hanne Drais, I'm with the Berlin police as a criminal psychologist. I'd like to ask you some questions.'

Felix's heart sank. Had the moment finally arrived where he was to be brought to account for his crimes?

'Not here, my little daughter might come in,' he said. 'Please, follow me.'

Hanne followed Felix to Das Kino; the doors were left ajar. A large screen hung from the rafters and a light blue Schwalbe was parked in a corner of the auditorium, alongside rows of collapsible chairs and tables. In another corner was an old boxing punch bag.

'Nice bike. Do you still use it?' she asked.

'Yes, in summer.'

'What's this hangar used as, a cinema?'

'Just at weekends.'

'And what's up there? Hanne asked, pointing to the balcony.

'A store room.'

Hanne was curious. 'I'd like to see it. What's in there?'

Felix answered candidly. 'Not much. A bed and a sink.'

'Is that where you stayed hidden, after Dr Jens helped you escaped from Torgau?'

He sighed, 'That's right. I got lucky.'

'We interviewed Klaus and Bernd last week at police headquarters in Berlin and they told us some little white lies. Felix Waltz didn't die in the river Elbe, did he? He ended up here. You're Felix Waltz, aren't you?'

Felix knew nothing about his onkels's trip to Berlin but felt sure Klaus with his measured and astute mind wouldn't have given anything away. However, it would be wise not to underestimate this woman, he thought. He'd dreaded this moment, the moment of his capture, and speculated why the police hadn't arrived with all guns blazing, as he'd often imagined they would. Instead, the atmosphere was eerily calm and this lone policewoman had come to interrogate him. His feeling of finally being able to let go and confess came as a great release and he decided there was no point in lying or trying to run away.

'Yes, I'm Felix. You seem to know a lot about me.'

'All our enquiries have led me here,' declared Hanne, her face giving nothing away.

'Onkel Klaus has always been protective because he didn't want me ending up like my sister. Susi fell from up there,' he told her, pointing to the balcony, high in the rafters.

Hanne looked up. A wave of sympathy swept over her. 'I'm sorry.'

'Thank you.'

'I must confess; I met Susanne's son, Axel, at the golf club,' Hanne told him.

Felix raised his eyes. 'Axel knows the truth about his mother, and Klaus and Ingrid have done a great job bringing him up.'

'He seems like a good kid.'

'He is. Have you come to arrest me?' Felix asked.

Hanne replied carefully, 'Escaping from a hell hole like Torgau isn't a crime.'

'No, but I'm done with living a lie. If you took my fingerprints you'd find they match those on a Herbertz knife found in 1992; by Lotte Holler's car, at the scene of the crime. And I'm a size nine shoe - Plaumann grabbed hold of me during the struggle in the car as it sank,' Felix confessed.

Hanne was strangely subdued hearing this candid confession. Felix, as she suspected, really was Marine Boy.

'What you say may be taken down and given in evidence against you,' Hanne began. 'You have the right to remain silent...'

Felix interrupted her. 'That won't be necessary. I have no rights and I'm ready to take the consequences for my actions. I may have been a crazy 17 year old, but drowning those three paedo's was the best decision I ever made. I took the law into my own hands and it was sweet revenge for the sexual abuse they inflicted on me and my sister.'

'I understand your motives but I can't condone them,' Hanne told him, although her heart was telling her otherwise.

'I didn't plan the first murder- Gwisdek turned up at the golf club.'

'I see. You must've felt threatened.'

'Yes. Gwisdek told me he would send his friends after Axel. Becoming a vigilante was my only option. I took his diary and went after the others.'

'Gwisdek kept a diary of names?'

'A diary full of sodomites.'

Hanne suddenly had a vision. 'Was it you who sent the anonymous letter to the police which precipitated the cracking of the paedophile ring in 1992?'

'Yes, that was me,' Felix announced, with a hint of pride.

Hanne was flabbergasted. 'Mein gott! How clever. We thought the Musketeers had escaped until we discovered them at Muggelsee; they didn't escape your justice.'

Felix looked surprised. 'How did you know their nicknames at Torgau?'

'Do you remember a boy in Torgau called Wolfgang Feuer?'

'There was only one Wolfgang. They called him The Magic Flute.'

Hanne nodded. 'That's him. He came forward when Lotte Holler got into the news.'

'Wolfgang told you about me?'

'Yes. Wolfgang gave us vital information: that you drowned in the Elbe and that your sister got pregnant. But you didn't drown. I believe Dr Jens helped you escape, just as he helped get your sister into a nursing home.'

Felix was curious. 'How did you find out I hadn't drowned?'

'It was what your onkel Klaus didn't say that got my attention. I'm a psychologist, I read between the lines,' she told him.

'I see. And Lotte Holler? You know she was the go-between for the Musketeers.'

'Yes. We know the truth about Lotte, our suspicions grew each time we talked to her. Between the lies and the rumours, there's always some version of the truth.'

Although he should have been petrified of the punishment that was to come, what Felix actually felt at this moment was great relief that everything was finally out in the open.

'The go-between- I heard she drowned herself in the Wannsee last month.'

Hanne explained, 'Wolfgang went to see Lotte and told her sister what she really did at Torgau. Lotte couldn't face the shame of her sister knowing.'

Felix was unforgiving. 'Hmmm. Being found out is not the same as owning up. You'd think when you are faced with possibly the last moments of your life you'd confess the truth. Not her, nor the Musketeers!'

Hanne interrupted. 'Lotte left a letter to her sister. She confessed everything, in the end... just so you know.'

This didn't appease him. 'Lotte left it too late. The Musketeers said sorry but only to try and plead for mercy and their lives; none of them showed any guilt or remorse. They were all in denial, lying up to the very end. Well, I won't do that. I killed the Musketeers by driving their cars into Muggelsee and attempted to kill their go-between, and I'd risk my life and my sanity again if my family were threatened.'

Hanne felt another twinge of compassion for Marine Boy. 'Are you saying you were insane back then, but now you're normal now?'

Felix wanted to laugh. 'What's normal? Moral constraints of society define normality. All I know is that I had all this anger inside me and I took my anger out on the right people. I'd like to think in their dying moments the Musketeers, and Lotte Holler for that matter, thought how the hell did a Torgau boy get the better of us?'

Hanne found his confession brutally honest. 'Lotte awoke from her coma to the aria Toreador. What was that all about?'

'They all used to make me dance so I thought I'd humiliate them, let them see how it feels, jigging about naked in the cold water. The music I chose for all of them was Toreador because it's about a Matador, and that's how I felt when I faced them all. It was like being in a bullring facing possible death,' he admitted.

'I see. Tell me, why didn't you drown Lotte, just like the others?'

'She told me she was pregnant and that would have meant I'd be killing an innocent baby too. I know she lost the baby, but I didn't set out to kill it.'

'Lotte said you told her she wasn't fit to be a mother and you said something in Latin... in loco parentis,' Hanne recalled.

Felix was shocked. 'Lotte Holler remembered that after 12 years in a coma?'

'When she woke up it was if the past 12 years had been a dream. It was incredible; she was as sharp as an eagle. She remembered everything but of course, was selective with the part she played and with all that went on at Torgau. In my opinion, she played the victim right up to the very end.'

Instinctively, he felt the psychologist understood his motives and didn't condemn him. 'Lotte wasn't fit to be a mother. I'm glad you could see through her lies.'

Hanne agreed. 'I had the feeling right from the start. Don't get me wrong, Lotte was a victim, but so was Marine Boy: you.'

Felix smiled. 'Marine Boy! Is that what you call me?'

A little embarrassed, she said, 'On account of the boat knife, the rope and the aqua shoe.'

Felix gave a little laugh, to ease the tension. 'Marine Boy,' he repeated aloud.

'We'd better be going now. Hopefully handcuffs won't be necessary. Please, gather your things and come with me to police headquarters in Berlin.'

Felix was indignant. 'No handcuffs, please, allow me some dignity. My wife's pregnant with our second child and my daughter is two. I don't want them seeing me being led away in handcuffs.'

Hanne agreed to his request. 'Ok, Herr Waltz. No handcuffs.'

'I'm not Felix Waltz, I'm Felix Baum. I changed my name when I was 21,' he told her.

She gave a wry smile 'I see. Your oma's family name. Do you live in her house?'

Felix replied rhetorically, 'Is there anything you don't know about me? Yes, it's here in the village.'

'That explains why it was hard to trace you. We were looking for a Felix Waltz. You and me, is it fate or just coincidence?'

Felix looked confused. 'Bitte?'

'You don't remember me, do you?'

He shook his head. 'Should I?'

'When the Berlin Wall fell, I bought a crate of bananas to give to the East Germans as they came through to the Western side. You and I had a photo taken together with my baby daughter- she pulled your wig off. I saw your scarred ears as you scurried away.'

Felix was astonished. His thoughts drifted back 15 or so years to that eventful night in Berlin. 'That was you? The Banana Lady?'

Hanne smiled. 'Is that what you called me? We all seem to have nicknames. You told me your name was Jens.'

'It was the first name that came to mind, I'd just seen Dr Jens in the crowd.'

Hanne gasped, 'Dr Jens! What's his surname? Do you know if he's still alive?'

'Jens Wissemann is alive and well. He's my father-in-law.'

Smiling, Hanne said, 'How ironic. Freud said there are no coincidences.'

'That's what my wife says and I'm beginning to believe it.

You know, that was the best banana I've ever eaten,' he declared.

'I kept your photo on my wall at home and it's still there. I've often wondered what happened to you,' Hanne confessed. 'Life's strange, eh?'

'Indeed! Please, have something to eat in the café whilst I gather my things. And I'll settle the bill,' Felix insisted. 'You know I won't run away this time.'

Hanne's mobile sounded out a tune.

'Ok. Excuse me, while I answer this. Hello... Herr Lankwitz...Yes, this is Frau Drais, Audrey's mother.'

Felix headed to the doors of Das Kino; upon hearing this name, his ears pricked-up. Alarm bells rang in his head. He'd heard this name before, just once, in a dark and dismal place, but he'd never forgotten it. Felix stayed in Das Kino listening, riveted to Hanne's phone call.

Hanne looked a little worried. She repeated what she was being told. 'What do you mean; Audrey didn't turn up for her maths lesson this morning? Really? She left at nine o'clock; it's midday now. Have you tried her mobile? Where could she be? Ok, Herr Lankwitz, I understand, you can't wait any longer for her. I'm sure she'll turn up somewhere. Thanks for letting me know. Tchuss.'

Felix was very concerned. 'Is everything ok?'

Furrowing her brow, she repeated, 'My daughter didn't go to her maths tutor. Where the hell is she? I'll phone her friend Kati, they were going biking today.'

Something didn't feel right. Hanne phoned Audrey's friend whilst Felix climbed up to the balcony to his former hideaway. Rummaging in a box he found Horst Gwisdek's diary, next to the Musketeers' mobile phones. It was a long time since he'd opened this infamous book and copied all the names to send off to the police - the list that had helped break the paedophile ring. He turned the dusty, yellowing pages to the letter L.

There was nothing entered regarding Lankwitz. Suddenly Felix's brain shifted back in time to his school lessons in

Torgau. The wardens had called Lankwitz by another name - Witzig - so he turned to the back pages of the diary. There he was, Bruno Witzig, but the address next to it was illegible, smudged by a coffee stain. Felix could just make out the name of the town: Potsdam.

'Fic!' he gasped.

He hurried back down to Hanne who was pacing up and down, somewhat distraught.

'I've phoned her friend, Kati, who said Audrey's mobile's been off all morning. It's not like her. I've just spoken with her father but she's not with him. He said not to worry, she'll turn up, and I'm just overreacting. Hell! My 16-year-old daughter's missing and her laid-back father says I'm overreacting!'

'Maybe he's right and there's nothing to worry about. But just suppose, Audrey's mobile has been turned off for her, so she can't be traced? I don't want to alarm you but this teacher, Lankwitz; do the kids call him Witzig?'

Hanne felt suddenly chilled. She remembered the name Witzig but not because of Audrey. No, wasn't he a friend of Gunther Schukrafft?

'I don't know what they call him. Herr Lankwitz is the one who's just told me Audrey's missing!' Hanne cried.

Deeply concerned, Felix stated, 'Paedophiles are very clever at subterfuge. This is the diary that belonged to Gwisdek. There was a young guy at Torgau, he came the last year I was there. I wasn't one of his 'boys' but he used to teach us maths. The wardens called him Witzig because he was always joking around, but I remember the kids had to call him Herr Lankwitz. What's Lankwitz's first name?'

She was shaking, 'Bruno, I think.'

Felix's faced dropped as he showed Hanne the diary.

'No! Witzig's got my daughter!' she screamed.

'It's a long time ago, but when I sent the police, I just copied the names from the diary and wrote Bruno Witzig,' Felix cried, berating himself. 'I'm sorry, I could kick myself.'

Hanne burst into tears. 'We've got to find them!'

'If we could make out the Potsdam address they might be there.'

Hanne had a brainwave. 'Wait! My mother recently bought Audrey a new mobile phone and a watch with GPS tracker modem devices. It maps out cycle routes even if there's not a good signal in the area. Witzig might have turned off her phone, but if her watch isn't broken, please God I'll find her.'

Hanne and Felix raced outside to Hanne's car. She turned on her GPS.

'How's this going to work?' Felix asked.

'As long as the satellite signal is strong enough, both Audrey's mobile number and watch registration number is programmed into my tracker. It's a bit like a suspect out on bail, wearing an ankle monitor. We can locate Audrey's position within five to ten metres.'

As suspected, Audreys' mobile was switched off but her GPS watch and the details of her whereabouts soon popped up on the screen. She was at a place called Caputh - or the watch was.

'That's near Potsdam,' Hanne exclaimed and looked skywards to the heavens in gratitude. 'Mutti! Thank you! I'll never argue with you again.'

Felix made an unusual suggestion. 'Ring Witzig; to trace his whereabouts.'

She agreed this was a good idea. Hanne checked her mobile for the number of her last caller and programmed Witzig's mobile into the GPS. She rang his phone and waited anxiously: his phone was on but he didn't answer. However, the GPS information on the screen read... Caputh.

'Got you!' cried Hanne, punching the air.'

'The bastard! I'll get my gun,' Felix insisted. 'Now, call the police.'

'That paedophile has got my daughter,' she cried.

Felix put his arm around Hanne's trembling shoulders. 'It'll be ok, I know how to deal with these Torgau bastards. I'll drive you and we'll be there in less than an hour. Now, programme in the address on the GPS and wait here for me.'

'If he's touched her....' Hanne stopped mid-sentence. It was unbearable to think about.

Felix took the words right out of her mouth. 'You'll kill him.'

He'd read her mind correctly. 'Yes. I'll fucking kill him!'

'If Witzig kidnapped Audrey and left Berlin this morning, they can't have been at Caputh long,' Felix ventured, trying to reassure her.

Looking at her mobile, Hanne gasped, 'Fic! My mobile battery's almost dead and it takes half an hour to recharge it!' she cried.

Felix took out his mobile. 'Damn, mine too. Wait! I've got a multi-mobile portable charger at the boathouse. We'll take it with us. There's a landline phone in the boathouse; you can call the police for back up before we go. Los gehts!'

At the boathouse, with her hands shaking uncontrollably, Hanne called the police. Meanwhile, Felix swiftly packed a bag with some essentials: his gun, a knife, torch and binoculars, some boat rope and the mobile charger. He had a feeling of déjà vu and was afraid of what was about to happen but he couldn't back out. His hands were moist with sweat, so he threw a pair of work gloves in his bag thinking that he if had to use his gun or knife, gloves would stop a weapon from slipping in his hands.

'Bitte! Hilfe! Is that the police? Danke... I'm Hanne Drais. I'm with the Mitte Police in Berlin. My daughter's been abducted by a suspected paedophile; I need back up. I'm heading over to Caputh, near Potsdam. My GPS tracked my daughter to a house on the lake - 25 Kleine Havel Weg, Caputh. Please contact me on my mobile in about half an hour- I've got to charge it, my number is 01606 659942. Please, please, hurry.'

Hanne was still shaking when she put down the phone but Felix took her by the arm and they hurried off to her car.

Ingrid had just returned home with Peonie, who was asleep in the back seat of her car. Seeing Felix coming towards her, hurrying from the boathouse with a strange woman, she was instantly alert and anxious.

'Felix, what's going on? Who's this?' Ingrid asked.

'Tante, this is Hanne, she's with the police. They know the truth about me. Don't tell Martha yet, please, just look after Peonie for me,' he requested, and ushered Hanne into the passenger seat of her car.

Ingrid's face turned ashen. 'No! Where are you going?'

He cried, 'Tante, I've no choice, I've got to go. One of those bastards from Torgau has abducted Hanne's daughter.'

Audrey awoke in a windowless room in a basement bereft of natural light. She was feeling drowsy from the effects of a sleeping pill. Herr Lankwitz had surreptitiously emptied a sleeping pill capsule into her drink during the tutorial at his Berlin flat. Where the hell was she? She stood up slowly and walked around.

The room had all the requirements of a bedsit: a double bed, an armchair, a fold-up wooden chair against a desk, a shower, a sink with a tap and mirror above the basin, and a toilet. A mini-fridge was stocked with food. On a shelf was one cup, one glass, one plate, one plastic spoon and one fork, but no knife. It was quiet except for the gentle humming of the air conditioning unit on the wall. Hidden in the overhead light, unknown to her, was a security camera.

Audrey tried the pulling the door open; it was locked and bolted from the other side. She saw her rucksack on the armchair and searched frantically for her mobile phone. It was missing. Her watch was there, the one Traudl had given her for her birthday in March: the time was 3pm. The last thing Audrey remembered was arriving at Herr Lankwitz's flat in Berlin that morning. Where had the time gone in between?

She opened the chest of drawers and found female clothes and lingerie. She rummaged through the skirts, jumpers and negligees. Everything was a size 10 - her own size. Surely that must be a coincidence? A chill shivered up her spine. Hoping that her mobile had fallen under her bed, she saw an old, dusty shoe box and pulled it out. Inside was a stuffed, human foot. Audrey screamed, dropping the box, and the foot tumbled out. Grimacing, she kicked the foot and the box back under her bed. Why was she here? She felt a sudden terror. Had she been abducted?

At that moment there was a knock. Audrey sat upright, anxiously waiting for the door to be unbolted and unlocked from the other side. Herr Lankwitz came in and flashed his captive prey a cheery, yet sinister smile.

A handsome man of almost 40, with dark, wavy hair and long eyelashes, he was of average height but had a strong, athletic build. Audrey, on the other hand, was a petite teenager just 5ft 4ins tall.

'Ah! You're awake.'

Audrey was confused. 'Herr Lankwitz?'

'Please, call me Bruno.'

'Where am I? What's going on?'

'Well, Audrey. Thank you for accepting my invitation to come and stay.'

What could he mean? She hadn't said she'd stay with him. And where on earth was she? Did her mother know he'd taken her away? These thoughts raced through Audrey's brain and were quickly replaced by fear. Herr Lankwitz only meant her harm.

'Invitation?' she queried.

He smiled. 'It's a euphemism.'

'I want to go home,' she pleaded.

'Well, you can't.'

Audrey began to cry.

'Now, now, don't go spoiling that pretty face of yours with tears. Give me a smile. That smile of yours is so gorgeous, and the moment I saw it, I just knew I had to take the risk. You had to be mine.'

On impulse, Audrey made a dash for the door, trying to push her kidnapper out of the way, but he blocked her exit and pushed her hard, back onto the bed.

'Let me go!' she screamed. 'You know my mother works with the police.'

Bruno was taken aback. He had no idea Audrey's mother worked with the police. 'You're kidding! You told me your mother worked in Kadewe.'

'I always say that, to protect her identity.'

Shaking his head, he insisted, 'Well, it's too late now. No turning back. Besides, I have got away with it before. You're 16, it's legal now. Are you a virgin?'

'You're sick!' cried Audrey, refusing to answer his question.

His tone was sinister. 'Audrey, you're going to be here a long time. No one will find you. So, when you feel like being nice to me, I'll take you outside for some fresh air. Think about it. It'll be nicer this way... then I won't have to force you.'

Audrey's heart was beating so loudly she was surprised it wasn't audible. She needed time to think and work out a strategy to escape. Don't cry, she told herself- don't let him see you're afraid. Then she remembered something her mother told her: when there's nothing else you can do, show your strength. She took a deep breath.

'They'll all be looking for me,' Audrey announced.

'Let them. I'll not go down without a fight. There's only been one person who managed to find me here- a boy from Torgau. Have you heard of a place called Torgau?'

Audrey nodded. 'My mother's involved in a case about a boy from Torgau.'

He raised an eyebrow. 'Really? Well, I worked there, though it was a long time ago. He was a real crazy, blue-eyed, orphaned kid from Torgau, on a mission to kill paedophiles. There were many who fucked with him, literally, including me. By the time he found me a few years after reunification, he'd already killed and disposed of roughly half a dozen of my ex colleagues.'

Audrey needed to know, and muttered, 'What happened to this boy?'

With pleasure, he told her. And bending down to pull out the foot and the shoe box from under the bed, announced, 'Let me introduce you to David. Size nine feet.'

Audrey recoiled. She could see Bruno's eyes were glittering and animated and realised how extremely dangerous he was.

Bruno continued, 'David came at me with a fancy knife. There was a struggle. He stepped on my toes, and as you can see, I kept his foot as a souvenir. David is in the lake here; hidden in the depths.

46. Caputh

Hanne and Felix were feeling ill at ease, but for different reasons. What could they say to one another? Their situation would have been ludicrous, even funny, if it hadn't been so serious… Felix was a murderer, helping Hanne, a criminal psychologist, in an attempt to rescue her abducted daughter from a suspected paedophile. These two strangers, who once shared a brief moment together at the fall of the Berlin Wall in 1989, had been brought together again by a series of bizarre coincidences. They were now involved in a race against time.

Instinct told them both that Bruno 'Witzig' Lankwitz meant to harm the missing Audrey. He'd blatantly lied to Hanne about her daughter's whereabouts, clearly not expecting them to harness modern technology to trace them to the same place; the village of Caputh. For any parent this was a truly frightening scenario but for Hanne, with her encyclopedic knowledge of paedophiles; it really was her worst nightmare.

Felix knew the country lanes like the back of his hand and it wasn't too long before they were on the main motorway towards Potsdam. He drove as fast as safety would allow whilst Hanne kept looking impatiently at the mobile phone attached to the portable charger. After about 20 minutes, it was semi-charged.

'I've got enough battery now to ring Stefan,' she cried.

'Who's Stefan? Your partner?'

'No; I'm gay. Stefan Glockner is a detective; my police colleague in Berlin.'

Felix liked her forthright approach. 'Have you rung Audrey's father?' he asked.

'I tried; because he needs to know. But he's cooking for some wedding party somewhere in Rostock and his mobile's turned off. I'll try again later.'

'Then ring Stefan.'

Calling Stefan's number, Hanne tapped her hand on the dashboard, waiting and praying for him to answer.

Stefan was at the barbers getting a haircut. He answered, 'Hello, Drais. Can't get enough of me, even on a Saturday, eh?' he joked, bantering with her as usual.

Hanne had never been so relieved to hear his voice. 'Stefan! Audrey's been abducted. I'm on my way to Caputh-near Potsdam. Help me!'

'Fuck!' Stefan yelled. 'Hanne, it'll be ok. Text the address-I'll be there as quickly as I can. Are you going alone?'

Hanne looked across at Felix but couldn't bring herself to tell Stefan the truth. 'I've got help. Stefan, please hurry,' she urged.

'Hanne, don't do anything stupid,' Stefan told her and hung up.

Hanne texted the Caputh address to Stefan. She couldn't tell him she was in a car with a confessed murderer. How stupid was that? It was the most imprudent thing she had ever done, but the most ridiculous thing of all was that Hanne felt she could trust Marine Boy. In this nightmare situation she was now facing to get to her daughter in time, Felix was the one person she felt who might make all the difference.

Thinking out loud, she confessed, 'I couldn't tell Stefan I was with Marine Boy.'

Felix understood. 'I'll give myself up later, you have my word. Right now it's not about me. We need to focus on your daughter.'

'Thank you,' Hanne said, sincerely.

Felix nodded and concentrated on the road ahead. Hanne, full of angst, stared out of the window at the countryside, whizzing by. She had the need for just a little small talk, as a diversion to their predicament.

'You know, I saw your little daughter in the back of your tante's car, so innocent and lovely. What's her name?'

'Peonie. She's two-and-a-half. And yes, I'm biased; she's lovely- when she's not screaming! She's looking forward to having a brother. My wife is five months pregnant and they've told us it's a boy.'

'One of each, that's nice. Audrey is my only child but she was - is - the best thing that ever happened to me,' she declared, feeling tears welling in her eyes. 'I don't know what I'd do without her.'

'Now, don't go upsetting yourself. We've got to stay focused. I've been racking my brains trying to remember what Witzig was like at Torgau.'

'Anything would be helpful.'

Felix's memories of Torgau were still vivid. 'I seem to recall Witzig liked older boys and girls but was more interested in girls,' he told her.

Hanne's head spun as she tried to tap into her scientifically trained mind. 'Let's think about his profile.'

'Ok. I think when people have secrets to hide they pretend to be something they're not - I know I did. Because it's not who you are, it's who people think you are,' he ventured.

Hanne agreed. 'Witzig could be a groomer. He waited till Audrey was of age, just so he wouldn't be accused of paedophilia before he made his move.'

'The cunning bastard! Yeah, and I remember at Torgau, Witzig only chose the most beautiful girls, as if he was collecting them like trophies.'

'Audrey is beautiful,' Hanne stated, in a matter-of-fact way. 'But if her teacher made a pass at her, I know she'd reject him.'

'That would hurt his ego,' observed Felix.

344

'Have you read a book called 'The Collector' by John Fowles?'

Felix shook his head. 'What does he collect?'

'Girls,' Hanne replied. 'The Collector keeps them prisoner in some remote place and hopes eventually the girl he's obsessed with, will fall in love with him.'

'You mean Stockholm Syndrome, where the victim falls for her abusive captor?'

Hanne nodded. 'Something like that.'

'And when she doesn't fall in love with him?' he queried.

'He can't let the girl go free because she knows too much... so he kills her and moves onto another girl,' Hanne cried, bursting into tears.

'Then he's in it for the long term. Witzig won't touch or hurt her straight away,' Felix said, trying to reassure her. 'Not long now, we're nearly there.'

The small, picturesque village of Caputh, just south of Potsdam in the Brandenburg area, is surrounded by numerous lakes. Its most famous resident was Albert Einstein, who kept a summerhouse in the village at number 7 Waldstrasse; now a long established museum and open to the public.

Felix and Hanne arrived in Caputh within the hour. The GPS tracker eventually led them to Kleine Havel Weg; a gravelly road with fields on one side and houses on the other backing onto dark, leafy woods where a sandy pathway to the lake. Felix drove past number 25, parking beyond the house, which was set back 50 metres off the road.

'That's it, number 25. We don't want to raise the alarm by being in view of the house,' Felix said. 'No sign of the police yet, but there's no time to lose. Hanne, stay here, I'm going in.'

Hanne was adamant. 'I'm coming with you!'

They both got out of the car. Felix collected his bag and put on his gloves. 'No!' he insisted. 'You are far too emotional. Please, let me handle this. Witzig's got Torgau in his bones, just like me.'

Hanne thought this situation had a twist of irony: she was the law enforcer and Felix was the law breaker, but somehow she knew he was right.

'Ok, but please; get my daughter out of there alive.'

'I will; I promise. You stay here, just in case Witzig tries to escape from the front of the house and wait for the police to arrive. I'll go round the back.'

Hanne took her Taser stun gun out of her pocket. 'Felix... here, take this.'

Realising the Taser had originally been intended for him if he'd acted up, he replied, 'I have my own gun in my bag, and I've got my knife as back up.'

'Then I'll use it if Witzig comes out,' she said.

Felix took his binoculars and moved behind a tree to get a good look at the house. There was a car parked at the side.

'Someone's in,' Felix told her, asking, 'What type of car does Witzig drive?'

Hanne shook her head. 'No idea, I've never met him. I just assumed all of Audrey's teachers were police checked, so I didn't worry about it.'

'There's a purple mountain bike attached to an Audi.

Hanne gasped, 'Audrey's bike!'

Felix surmised, 'I guess he couldn't leave her bike outside his flat in Berlin; it would have been too suspicious. Hanne, I need to know his precise whereabouts. Check the tracker on Audrey's watch and call Witzig. If he answers, hang up.'

Hanne followed his instructions. Witzig didn't answer his phone but Audrey's watch indicated they were both in the house, just 50 metres away.

'They're in!' she cried.

'Good, and within touching distance. Don't worry, I'll get that bastard.'

Squeezing his hand, Hanne said, 'Felix, be careful.'

Felix made his way carefully through the woods towards the house, running from tree to tree, hiding briefly and checking in all directions before moving forward. Eventually he ran out of the trees and into a sandy clearing. The glimmer of the sunshine on the lake behind the house was visible.

Leaving his rucksack by a tree, Felix put his knife and some boat rope in one pocket and his gun in the other. He ducked to the ground and crawled, shuffling his body to the rear of the house. The house was eerily silent. Carefully, he checked the windows for signs of life inside. Nothing. The back door leading to a kitchen was unlocked. He reached for his gun in his pocket but it wasn't there. It just have fallen out somewhere between the Copse and the house. Luckily, he felt the reassuring sharpness of his Herbertz knife in another pocket and crept inside.

Soon, Witzig emerged from the cellar into the kitchen with a tray containing an empty plate, a glass and some plastic cutlery, and catching sight of the intruder, he grabbed a knife from a sideboard. The tray crashed to the floor, shattering the glass in the floor.

Felix and Witzig faced each other with knives.

'Who the hell are you?'

'Where's Audrey?'

Witzig hid his surprise. 'What are you talking about? You're an intruder in my home.'

'Kein witz; Witzig. I'm with the police, my back up team will be here any minute,' lied Felix. 'Give yourself up, Lankwitz.'

Witzig thought for a second. Was this man with the police, was it game over? He took a quick check out the window. No sign of a police team. No, he decided; this man was acting alone to rescue Audrey, who was hidden in a soundproofed room in his cellar.

'You know me?'

'We were at Torgau together.'

'I see. So, you've come to get revenge.'

'No. Luckily I wasn't one of your boys. I've come to rescue Audrey. If you've touched her, I'll kill you.'

It all happened so quickly, that neither man had time to

think- Witzig launched himself at his intruder. Felix, raised his arm to protect his chest, as the knife slashed into his upper arm, forcing him to drop his knife. Wildly, Witzig stabbed again, and Felix, adrenaline pumping, did his best to dodge the onslaught. Feinting sideways, Felix managed to land a punch on Witzig's face, stunning him and causing him to drop his knife. Now both men were without their weapons. Moving quickly, Felix grabbed Witzig's arm and there was a brief struggle before he managed to twist it and snap it hard. Witzig dropped like a stone, falling onto the broken glass on the floor, with a bone protruded from his forearm, but this didn't stop Felix binding his opponent's arms together with some boat rope in his pocket as Witzig writhed, screaming in agony.

As Felix grabbed a towel to stem the blood pumping from his own arm he heard the sound of police sirens. Frantically, he searched the house, eventually heading downstairs to the cellar, and unbolted the door, turning the key in the lock. Inside, a frightened, ashen-faced but feisty Audrey was hiding behind the door, with a chair raised above her head, ready to strike.

Felix felt the full weight of the chair crack against his back and stumbled. Audrey was confused, realising she'd hit the wrong man, but relieved to hear the police sirens.

'Who are you?' she cried.

'Audrey, Hanne's outside. It's all over. Lankwitz has been dealt with,' Felix told her, getting up from the floor. He ushered her upstairs to the kitchen where two armed police officers and Stefan rushed in, followed swiftly by Hanne.

'Mutti!' Audrey cried, running into her mother's arms.

The police saw Witzig screaming on the floor and Felix with a bloody arm, holding a young girl. Not knowing who was who; they pointed guns at both men.

'No! Not him,' Hanne cried, pointing at Felix. 'He saved my daughter.'

Hanne looked at Audrey. 'Did he touch you?' she asked, afraid of the answer.

Trembling, Audrey shook her head. 'No. But he told me if I was nice to him, he wouldn't have to force me.'

Hanne was livid. She'd never felt such anger and suddenly acted on it. She jumped on Witzig and hit him repeatedly with her fists. 'I'll fucking kill you!' she yelled.

'Mutti!' Audrey screamed, shocked by her mother's actions.

Witzig groaned pathetically, cowering, 'I never touched her!'

'You sick bastard!' Hanne spat.

Stefan pulled Hanne off Witzig. 'Hanne! It's over. It's over.'

Sealing off the house, the police waited for a forensic squad to arrive. Bruno 'Witzig' Lankwitz was swiftly taken away. Stefan told Felix to get his arm bandaged by the paramedics who'd recently arrived on the scene. Audrey had just been checked over in the ambulance, and Hanne led her daughter out as Felix arrived with Stefan.

'It's only a shallow wound. I'll be fine,' Felix ventured, bravely.

'You were very brave. What's your name?' Stefan asked him.

Hanne looked at Felix and quickly addressed him. 'Jens, thank you so much.'

Leaving Felix in the ambulance, Stefan accompanied Hanne and a shaken Audrey to their car parked out in the street. His mobile rang. It was Kruger.

'Kommissar. Yes, she's here,' Stefan said. 'Hanne, Kruger wants to talk to you.'

Stefan could hear Kruger shouting at the other end of the phone. 'Is Audrey ok?'

Hanne gasped, 'She is now. Her teacher worked at Torgau,' she told Oskar.

'What the hell? Drais, you're the psycho officer, not the bloody cop!' bellowed Kruger.

'She's my daughter!' retorted Hanne.

'Ok, Hanne, try to calm down. Audrey's safe. Now, don't be rushing to question that bastard. Promise me you'll let the Potsdam police deal with him, because if you see him again, you may do something you'll regret. Ok?'

'Hanne sighed, 'Yes Oskar. I promise.'

'I'm on my way to Caputh, but I'm stuck in traffic in Potsdam due to some sodding concert, so, if you're both really ok, I think I'll turn back to Berlin. We'll need to arrange a de-brief meeting, but I guess you don't want Audrey out of your sight right now. I'll come to your flat on Monday, ok?'

'Thank you, Oskar,' Hanne said, hanging up and passing Stefan his phone.

'We'll look into how Audrey's teacher fooled the school authorities. I'm sure this isn't the first time he's brought some unsuspecting kid here.'

'Thanks Stefan. Audrey had a lucky escape,' Hanne responded, looking at her daughter sitting quietly in the back of the car. 'I won't be long, sweetheart. There's something I have to do.'

'Drais, who's this Jens; Audrey's hero?' asked Stefan.

Hanne fudged the question. 'He was passing by and offered to help. I must thank him. Stefan, stay with Audrey and don't let her out of your sight.'

Felix was in a state of shock. Knowing he was capable of such violence sent his head spinning back to the nightmares of his crimes against the Musketeers. This time, he told himself, he'd not committed a crime but had put his strength to good use. Yet, he was feeling vulnerable at a crime scene. He trusted Hanne to some degree after confessing to her, but paranoia had set in and compounded with the shock of the day's events, all he wanted to do was escape. He found his gun on the ground at the edge of the copse of trees, and retrieved his rucksack, secreting the gun and knife in an inner pocket and shoving the bloodstained towel and gloves into his bag.

Hanne approached Felix as he sat propped up against a

tree with his arm in a sling.

'How's your arm?'

'I'm ok, really. The sling's just a precaution to keep the weight off it. Is Audrey ok?'

'She's fine, thanks to you. We got here just in time. Felix, I really do understand how you felt when the Musketeers threatened your family,' Hanne told him. 'Until it happens to you, it's just words. You're right; parents would kill to protect their kids. I really wanted to hurt Witzig- even kill him.'

He confessed, 'I've not killed anyone else in more than 15 years. Today brought it all back and I know in the same circumstances, I'd do it all over again if I had to.'

'Thank you, Felix,' Hanne reiterated.

Felix was curious. 'Why did you tell Detective Glockner my name was Jens?'

How could Hanne explain to Marine Boy that she was torn? Felix's bravery had helped save her daughter's life and certainly, rescued Audrey from sexual abuse. How could she ever thank him - or turn him in? On the spur of the moment, to protect Felix's identity she'd lied to Stefan.

'I wanted to buy us both a little time- to think,' she told him.

He had no right to make any demands, however, Felix was desperate. One last favour, he thought. It was worth asking.

'You wanted to help me… Then please can you give me a few days to be with my family, before I'm locked away?'

Hanne was unsure. 'I don't know.'

Apologising, he said, 'Sorry, I've no right to compromise you.'

Hanne took a deep breath. 'Ok. Felix, you need to be with your family and I need to look after Audrey after her ordeal. I'll see you in one week, in Berlin. I'll do my best to get you a reduced sentence on account of your age at the time and mitigating factors from your time at Torgau. Also, for the heroism you showed in rescuing Audrey.'

'Thank you, Hanne,' he said, quietly.

'There's a new memorial for the holocaust victims, it's just opened near the Brandenburg Gate. I'll collect you there at midday, a week on Monday. I'm trusting you, so make sure you come.'

Felix nodded. 'You have my word.'

Stefan was waving. Hanne hurried to the car, anxious about Audrey.

'You all right, my sweetheart?'

'Take me home, Mutti,' Audrey pleaded.

'Ok; sweetheart.'

Stefan looked around. Felix had quietly slipped away. 'Where's he gone, Jens the hero? He needs to make a statement.'

Hanne was secretly pleased. 'I don't think he likes the limelight. Don't worry, Stefan, I know where to find him.'

47. Das Kino

Felix caught a local bus in Caputh that took him to the centre of Potsdam where he rang Klaus and waited to be collected. He passed time wandering around the park at the palatial chateau of Sans Souci that once belonged to the Prussian King, Frederik the Great, in the 1700s. He found a quiet place in the Orangerie, where he had a view over the former vineyards and extensive landscaped gardens. Feeling numb and lost, he sat staring ahead until Klaus turned up and took him in his arms. Klaus didn't ask too many questions- he could see how exhausted Felix was, and let his nephew fall asleep in the back of the car on the journey home.

Within a few days of returning to the lake and to his loving family, Felix grew calmer, yet troubled about how he'd cope in prison. He was going to pay the ultimate forfeit for his terrible crimes, losing his liberty and his loved ones. His actions when he was an angry, damaged 17-year-old had caught up with him and the repercussions would impact on all those he loved most in the world. Not only would they lose him for years, they were at risk of being unduly maligned and forever stigmatised for their association with him. For this, but not for his actions – he'd never be sorry for ridding the world of those paedophiles; he felt ashamed.

Felix hoped he would be locked up for no more than 20 years, given his age at the time of the crime and time taken off for good behaviour in prison. He would miss out on all those precious years with his children as they grew up and his new baby would be raised entirely without a father. The risk of Peonie and the baby becoming strangers to him was high, as well as the probability of losing his wife. After all, why should she wait for him for two decades or more? She was still a young and beautiful woman, and she deserved more than being the wife of a convicted murderer.

For her part, Martha was devastated knowing that her beloved husband would soon be incarcerated and wouldn't be around to support her or help bring up their children.

'I'd understand if you wanted to divorce me,' Felix told her.

Martha shook her head. 'No! I just don't want all this to be true. When I've had the baby, I'll appeal to the courts for leniency, given your age and the mitigating circumstances at the time. We've got to fight this.'

Felix felt the luckiest man alive. 'I love you.'

Martha kissed him. 'I love you too. We'll get through this together.'

Klaus and Ingrid cried together in private but showed a united and brave face in front of Felix.

'I promise, everything will be here waiting for you when you come out,' Klaus told Felix.

'How's Martha taken it?' Ingrid asked.

Felix broke down in tears and Ingrid held him, just like she always had done.

The hardest part for Felix was admitting the truth to Axel. He took him aside, into Das Kino to tell him the devastating news in private.

'Onkel! What are you saying?' Axel cried. 'That you're a serial killer? Is this some sort of joke?'

'It's true, Axel. I did it, to protect my family.'

Axel began to cry. 'I can't believe it. What am I supposed to say?'

Felix was close to tears. 'Tell me you don't hate me?'

Axel threw his arms around Felix. 'No! Never. But Onkel, you are a bloody fool,' he shouted, and ran out.

'Axel!' called Felix, but he had run into the woods and Felix felt it best not to chase after his nephew.

If he was to face his 17-year-old self now, Felix wondered what he would say to him. Could he make his younger self see sense? He knew his actions as a teenager were not rational or reasonable but neither was he in those days. He'd been troubled, deeply damaged by his experiences and was angry and grieving for his sister. But this thought ran parallel with a feeling of deep satisfaction that he'd protected himself, his family and particularly Axel from further damage at the hands of the Musketeers. If they hadn't disappeared his life could have continued to be compromised by his abusers. If he hadn't killed them and taught Lotte Holler a lesson, would he have become the man he was today? Felix began to believe it was part of a process, a journey he had to take to reach his destination.

His thoughts flashed back to the day Susanne died. The memory still haunted his dreams. He was in Das Kino, just as he had been that tragic day, making a baby crib for Axel when his sister walked in.

'Susi! It was meant to be a surprise,' Felix said, a little grumpily.

'Felix, you know I don't like surprises… What a lovely crib, I didn't know you were so clever at making things. Thank you,' she said, adding, 'We need to talk. You left me alone in that terrible place. How could you?'

He felt ashamed all over again. 'Susi, I'm sorry but I couldn't stay another day. It was killing me. When Dr Jens offered to help me escape, I just had to go.'

With tensions bubbling, they surfaced and Susanne snapped, 'It was killing me too!'

'I'm sorry,' Felix repeated, feebly.

'Why didn't you take me with you?'

Feeling looked at his sister, imploringly, 'In your condition?'

'I felt betrayed… you didn't even say goodbye. Maybe you wanted to get away from me too,' she ventured.

'Torgau changed us and not for the better,' he replied, flatly.

'I cried for weeks without you,' she admitted.

'Me too.'

'I thought you were angry at me for keeping the baby.'

Shaking his head, he insisted, 'No. How could I be angry with you? Keeping the baby, well, that was your decision. I just ran away from the truth.'

Then out of the blue she made an announcement that shook Felix to the core.'

'Axel's your son,' she declared.

Felix gasped, 'You can't be sure Axel's mine?'

Susanne was adamant. 'Well, I'm almost 100 per cent sure. You remember when I fractured my ankle and Dr Jens kept me in the hospital for a few weeks? It was just after my first period and we... anyway, three weeks later I was throwing up. He's yours, I'm certain of it.'

'Have you told anyone?' he asked, concerned.

Scornfully, she replied, 'You mean have I kept our secret?'

'Susi, if you have discussed it, no one will understand or forgive us.'

'No, I'll take our secret to the grave. Let them all think Axel's father is unknown, a product of my abuse at Torgau,' she said, bitterly. 'No, Felix, I'll never tell a soul; no one knows we were lovers.'

'Don't say that word,' he told her.

'What... lovers? Or incest? We comforted each other sometimes in the hospital ward. With all that sex going on around us... it just happened.'

He snapped, 'It was wrong! We can't ever touch each other again.'

'Do you still want to?'

'You're my sister!'

'And you're my brother.'

Felix breathed out heavily, 'What the hell are we going to do now?'

'I don't know… Axel's the image of you.'

Grimacing, he ventured, 'We're twins. No one will suspect.'

She scoffed at his suggestion, 'But we know! It'll always be, nagging away at us and staring us in the face. When we grow up and get married we'll have to lie to our spouses, and lie to everyone for the rest of our lives… and lie to our son.'

He was adamant, 'We can't admit to incest! It would destroy Axel.'

'It has destroyed me,' she confessed.

'Don't let it. We'll get through this and the nightmares of Torgau together.'

Unsure, Susanne shook her head. 'I don't know. Can we?'

'Please, Susi. We've got to try. What other choice do we have?'

They smiled at one another and there was a brief moment of uncomfortable silence. A change of subject was necessary.

'So, tell me; how did you escape?' she asked.

'Well, Dr Jens and me, we fooled that bitch Lotte Holler. She thought I'd tied bedsheets together and jumped into the River Elbe. Dr Jens told her I'd drowned.'

Sighing, she said, 'You fooled me, too. I thought you'd drowned and that I'd lost you.'

'That must have been hard for you. I'm so sorry. I was hidden under a blanket in Dr Jens car all night. He got me out of Torgau and brought me here, where I could hide.'

'I see. Once you'd gone, Dr Jens was kind to me and looked after me. He never told me you'd escaped, though. I guess it was safer for everyone if he kept it a secret.'

'Susi, we don't have to hide anymore.'

She was curious. 'Where did onkel Klaus hide you?'

Felix pointed to his hideaway in the rafters. 'Up there. Want to see my room?'

Susanne followed Felix up the stairs to the top of Das Kino. She looked at the sparsely-furnished room and imagined herself living in it, and felt glad her brother had survived in this safe haven.

'Come and look out of the window. At night, when the moon is bright; it's lovely. I used to run in the dark or go out in one of our boats,' Felix told her.

'Weren't you afraid of the dark? I know I am.'

'After Torgau, there was nothing left to be afraid of,' he replied.

Susanne stood close to Felix, their cheeks almost touching as they looked out of the window onto the lake's snowbound edges. Their close proximity reminded them of the forbidden warmth they once shared.

'It's a lovely view in daylight too,' she observed.

Brother and sister looked at one another and smiled. They turned to one another in a clumsy embrace and felt their bodies trembling as familiar feelings stirred inside them. Losing all self-control they began to kiss as lovers do. Suddenly, Felix pulled away. He could see the hurt and confusion in her eyes, mirroring his own feelings and sadness.

'No! Susi, we can't!' he cried and ran out.

'Felix,' she shouted. 'Stop! Please.'

Felix had quickly descended the stairs. He shouted up at her. 'Susi, it's not right.'

Susanne screamed. 'I don't know how to be with you!'

Once he was outside in the snow, Felix hesitated about leaving. He didn't want to run away again, and thought maybe they should sort things out, once and for all. So, he went back in, intending to talk to Susi again.

Looking up, he called, 'Susi, I'm sorry. Please, let's sort this out, once and for all.'

She wasn't listening; she was in a trance state.

'Are you ok?' he asked, concerned at her blank expression.

Suddenly, Felix saw his sister climb over the balcony railings. Her mind was made up.

She mumbled, 'I know a way out. It's the best solution for you, and Axel.'

Felix was freaking out, unable to get to her quick enough.

'What are doing? Susi! Don't be silly!'

Looking at Felix, she managed a brief smile. 'Look after Axel. Tell him I love him.'

'Susi! No!' Felix bellowed.

Blowing Felix a kiss, Susanne cried, 'I love you,' before jumping to her death.

In Das Kino, in December 1989, Felix had cradled his sister's lifeless and bloody head. He carried her back to the cottage, and drops of blood from her head splattered a path on the pristine white snow. It was the last time he would touch her, and he held her until the warmth of her flesh ebbed away. To him, his beloved Susi's broken body; was a tragic symbolism of the sexual abuse and forbidden love at Torgau. Felix didn't want to end up the same way as his sister. He had a duty to survive, especially now that he was quite possibly Axel's father.

This possibility haunted his waking hours and his dreams. Felix had to find out the truth. Susanne told him the three Musketeers were the only ones who'd sexually abused her in Torgau, so; there was a one in four chance that he had fathered Axel. When he killed the Musketeers he'd decided to find out the truth once and for all, taking their hair for DNA samples. Felix sent the samples off under a pseudonym with strands of his and Axel's hair to a specialist laboratory in Berlin.

The wait for the results had been nerve wracking. Felix had always suspected Susanne's gut feeling was correct and the DNA results conclusively proved their suspicions. Axel was indeed Felix's son.

It was a strange paradox that Felix was not repulsed by these findings. He felt glad that none of the evil Musketeers had fathered Axel as a result of rape. Instead, he accepted that his nephew was his son as a result of incest and learned to live with the torment this caused him. Most importantly, though, there was a little boy who needed to be loved and protected. Axel belonged to him and although he alone would carry the burden of this knowledge, Felix was prepared to lay down his life to protect his son.

In May 2005, Felix walked out of Das Kino, with the memory of Susanne's death still clear in his mind and their incestuous secret still intact.

48. Debriefing

Kruger and Stefan arrived at Hanne's on Monday morning for their debriefing meeting. They brought flowers and cakes.

'Are you both all right?' Kruger asked.

Hanne nodded. 'We're fine.'

'Thank you for the flowers, I'll put them in water,' Audrey said.

'Audrey, we've brought your bike back. Forensics has finished with it, you know they have to fingerprint everything,' Stefan told her.

Audrey smiled. 'Great! I can't wait to get out for a ride.'

Kruger raised an eyebrow. 'Really?'

Hanne explained, 'You see, Oskar. After 24 hours holed up with me, Audrey is desperate to get out. But I said, give it a few days. I've arranged for a psychologist to come round and start some counselling, for the trauma.'

Audrey scoffed, 'I'm fine, Mutti. You're the best psychologist for me. I'll put the kettle on,' she said, and left the room.

Kruger made sure Audrey was out of earshot before speaking. 'That bastard Witzig has confessed to kidnapping Audrey, however, nothing else. Stefan and I interviewed him all day yesterday and he's not being co-operative. He said he knew nothing of the abuse that went on at Torgau, and couldn't understand why he'd be on the paedophile ring list. He insisted he wasn't friends with Gunther or any of the others at Torgau.'

Stefan added, 'And if you can believe this? Witzig said kidnapping Audrey was an aberration, as if it was his first offence! So, he won't admit to anything unless we provide the evidence to convict him.'

Hanne was incensed. 'What! Arschloch! And I suppose, he's not given any explanation for the hacked off foot he showed Audrey?'

'No, he said he got it from a science lab,' replied Kruger, with irony.

Stefan relayed better news. 'But we had some good news first thing this morning. Rutger called; said he'd found traces of blood in Witzig's cellar. He must have taken other girls there, so we're checking the house and the garden for buried bones.'

'So, how did Witzig escape being caught in the paedo ring of 1992?' she asked.

Kruger sounded bitter and resentful, admitting, 'There was a Bruno Witzig on the list, in the centre of Potsdam. When we did a dawn raid, the flat had been abandoned. Witzig was never caught because it was Bruno Lankwitz we should have been looking for.'

Hanne was sympathetic. 'Oskar, it's not your fault that some on the list got away. Sadly, the police were chasing a nickname.'

The irony of this statement was not lost on the three of them.

'Thankfully, Audrey had a lucky escape.'

'Oskar; you can say that again! Actually, Audrey wants to tell you something herself.'

Audrey had told her mother everything about her brief but traumatic ordeal. The details of her kidnapping would provide vital information that would help the team convict Bruno 'Witzig' Lankwitz.

'The severed foot that I found under the bed in the cellar,' Audrey began. 'Herr Lankwitz told me he was proud of it. I think he kept it as some sort of trophy and to remind others not to mess with him.'

'Did he tell you how he got this foot in his possession?' Kruger asked.

Audrey nodded. 'He said, a crazy, blue-eyed, orphaned kid from Torgau, turned up in Caputh, a few years after reunification, bragging about having killed and disposed of some wardens from Torgau.'

Stefan mused, 'Then this Torgau kid ran out of luck at Caputh.'

Audrey concluded, 'The Torgau boy was called David, with size 9 feet. Lankwitz said he'd 'stepped on his toes' so, he cut off his David's feet, and disposed of his body in the lake, behind the house at Caputh.'

Kruger smiled broadly. 'If this David's in the lake, police scuba divers will find him.

Thank you, Audrey. Your evidence will help us put Lankwitz away; permanently.'

'Good! I know I had a lucky escape- thanks to all those who rescued me and especially, because of the GPS tracker on my watch. I've never been so glad Mutti was able to spy on me!' Audrey said, grinning, kissing her mother and leaving the room.

'Are you thinking what I'm thinking?' Kruger asked Hanne and Stefan.

Hanne thought she steer the conversation in a certain direction. 'I'm thinking that this David could be our Marine Boy.'

'Me too,' said Stefan.

Kruger nodded. 'Maybe we can match the DNA from the foot with the fingerprints on the Hebertz knife found at Lotte's Holler's crime scene.'

'With respect, Oskar, the knife found at Lotte's crime scene could be a red herring,' said Hanne. 'Maybe someone dropped it or left it there after being out on the lake.'

'It's possible,' mused Kruger. 'The shoe fits. David's size 9 foot is the same size as the aqua shoe found in Plaumann's car.'

Hanne agreed. 'David planned to run Witzig into the lake at Caputh. That widens our search area beyond the Spreewald if David is, or was, Marine Boy.'

Kruger's eyes held a satisfied glint. 'I'd like to believe this Torgau David got rid of even more paedos than the three Musketeers, to make up for those I didn't catch, back in 1992. Even one extra sick bastard- dead or alive, would make this scheisse more palatable.'

Stefan and Hanne nodded in agreement.

'Hanne, I'd hate to profit from Audrey's misfortune, but if we solve the Lotte Holler case this way it'll be fucking amazing! You need to get a written statement from Audrey and that Jens fellow from Caputh.'

Hanne nodded. 'Yes, Oskar. Just give me a few days.'

'Sure. By the way, who is this Jens? All I've heard is that he came out of nowhere and was the hero of the day.'

Hanne would be economical in her reply. 'You see, Oskar, luck was with me, when he volunteered to help me. When I arrived at Caputh Lake, Jens was just passing by. He saw what a state I was in and when I told him why I was outside Witzig's home, he said he practised boxing and could take care of himself. There wasn't any time to waste, so, Jens insisted on helping me out until the police arrived.'

'I know I was stuck in traffic, but waiting for the police to arrive would've been the more prudent thing to do.'

Hanne was adamant. 'I couldn't leave Audrey alone with Witzig another minute!

'I understand,' said Kruger, softly.

'Jens is a hero; he saved my daughter's life. And the irony of heroism is; it's at its noblest when it's anonymous.'

Surmising, Stefan tried summing up, 'I guess, this means we've been looking for a phantom, if Marine Boy is already dead.'

'I guess so,' agreed Hanne.

Kruger was curious to know Hanne's opinion. 'So, do you really think this David is Marine Boy?'

Hanne fudged the truth with her answer. 'David does fit

the profile of Marine Boy… and the truth is often stranger than fiction,' she replied.

Hanne and Audrey spent the week following the abduction together at home. They received free counselling and a female psychologist came daily to help them come to terms with the trauma. They agreed not to constantly discuss what had occurred at Caputh outside of their therapy session, in an attempt to return to normality sooner rather than later.

Their family rallied around them, visiting and bringing them food. It was a week of international eating - Rafael brought South American cuisine and treats from the Spanish restaurant where he was working, whilst Traudl cooked traditional German food. Hanne told her mother, Traudl, how grateful she was that her present of a GPS watch had helped save Audrey's life. A truce was declared between Hanne and Traudl, which made a nice change. For, Audrey, this was the best outcome of her trauma.

Brigitte visited Hanne and Audrey intermittently, understanding that mother and daughter needed precious time to recover from their ordeal. She was sensitive enough not to interfere in this process. Hanne began to feel a renewed sense of happiness. She had her family, her girlfriend, a job that she loved and her daughter, healthy, safe and on the road to recovery.

On the following Sunday after a week of visitors, mother and daughter nestled together on the sofa watching television.

'When I go back to school tomorrow, I want to go on my

own,' Audrey announced, insistent in her tone.

Hanne looked concerned. 'Are you sure?'

'Mutti, it's been great; I've had a week off school. The best bit is you and oma getting on, but I can't take any more family lovey-dovey time or it'll get claustrophobic.'

Hanne laughed. 'Ok, little Miss Grown-Up, I know you're right.'

'And I can text you, but if you don't hear from me, don't worry. You can always track me on my GPS watch,' she quipped.

'Audrey! Don't joke about it.'

'Mutti, there's something that's been puzzling me. Who was that man, Jens, who helped rescue me? You haven't said much about him- and I don't think you even wanted to tell Stefan and Oskar. It's not like you to be evasive. You can trust me. Who is he?'

Audrey didn't normally ask too much about Hanne's police work, but this time it was different. Her daughter had been abducted and was the victim of a crime and had given evidence against the perpetrator. So, Hanne felt it was important to help Audrey heal, and besides, she knew her daughter wouldn't stop until she had unearthed some truth. Hanne weighed up her options: lying to her daughter, breaking police protocols or unburdening her own thoughts. Finally, deciding she couldn't share the burden of truth with anyone, especially not her daughter, she would offer some version of it.

Hanne smiled. 'You're observant- you'd make a good detective! Audrey, if I tell you, it must be kept a secret?'

'Cross my heart and hope to die,' she promised.

'Don't say that!' Hanne reminded her daughter.

'Ok, you remember I told you, I'd gone to the Spreewald, to look at possible sites for a holiday. Well, incredible as it sounds, Jens was working there. And he overheard me talking to your teacher. Upon hearing his name, he grew alarmed. He asked me if Bruno Lankwitz had a nickname- Witzig, and if so, he just might be one of the wardens, and one of his abusers, from Torgau.'

'Oh. I see. Mutti, why does it have to be a secret?'

'Because, I lied to the Kommissar. I told him, by some miracle; Jens was just passing by at the lake, at Caputh. Lying doesn't go down well with Oskar.'

Audrey was confused. 'So, why did you lie?'

'Well, Jens carries his shame as Torgau boy. He doesn't want to be questioned, or give evidence in court. He helped me because he knew how to handle himself, having gone after a few paedophiles who abused him. And he gave them a bloody good kicking.'

'Oh, I see. Mutti, you wanted to kill Witzig, so, now you really know how that feels. So, Jens is a hero; he saved my life.'

'I know. And there's my predicament,' Hanne confessed. 'So, do I let Jens keep his anonymity, or tell the Kommissar?'

Audrey understood her mother's predicament. 'You've lied to Oskar and Stefan, and you can't change that. You did it to help Jens. Instinctively, you made your choice, so why are you regretting your decision?'

'It doesn't sit well with me. Maybe, by going against my team, I'm not fit to work with the police anymore.'

Audrey scoffed, 'Quatch! Mutti, you're good at what you do. Of course I'm biased, but in fact, you're brilliant!'

'Danke, liebling,' said Hanne, smiling.

'For what it's worth, I'd want to help Jens too. Just keep his involvement a secret. After all, he was our guardian angel.'

During the night, remembering a previous occasion and a decision she'd deeply regretted, Hanne tossed and turned. A few years ago, investigating a case, she'd made the wrong decision and chosen the wrong path wherein, the suspect then committed suicide. She promised herself to never make the same mistake again; lives were at stake.

Going over the moral dilemma about Felix, as she now privately thought of him, Hanne finally fell asleep in the early hours of Monday morning after making a decision she knew would bring her lasting peace.

50. The Berlin Memorial

Audrey cycled to school without a care in the world. Hanne felt glad her daughter was so resilient and could recover quickly from such a trauma. It could have turned out so very differently if Audrey had been violated, or if Felix hadn't been there. How would the kids from Torgau have turned out if abuse and violence had not been so prevalent in their lives? Hanne thought about this all morning as she prepared herself for her meeting with Felix. Some Torgau survivors simply never came out of the darkness physically or mentally whilst others, probably in the minority, managed to find something resembling a normal life.

The Mahnmal-Das Denkmal is the German National Memorial to the six million murdered Jews of Europe murdered by the Nazis, and the Holocaust victims in the concentration camps. In May 2005, 60 years after the end of World War II, it had just been completed in Berlin. At a cost of 25 million euros, it consisted of a 4.7 acre site covered with concrete slabs or, as the locals called them, 'Stelae'. It was located on the former 'death strip' where once the Wall stood, a short walk from the Brandenburg Gate. The 2,711 dark grey, rectangular stelae were arranged in a grid pattern on a sloping field varying in height and size, like tombstones.

As promised, Felix arrived before mid-day at Potsdamer Platz, stopping in an Irish bar for a glass of Guinness, his last drink as a free man, before walking the short distance to the Denkmal. He strolled through the field of Stelae alongside the mass of tourists and had time to sit in the sunshine and contemplate his life in this symbolic place.

A few hours earlier in Motzen, warm embraces but few words had been exchanged as he said goodbye to his family at the train station. The image of Martha, his tearful, pregnant wife holding Peonie in her arms on the platform, lingered in his mind as the train pulled away. Klaus, Ingrid and Axel were also there, bravely waving him off. The next time he would see them all would be from a prison cell.

Within the hour, the scenery from the train window had changed from rolling countryside to the urban sprawl of Berlin. Felix was a wealthy man, but now all he carried with him in his rucksack. Inside the bag, was a change of clothes, some toiletries, photos of his family, sandwiches, fruit and a bottle of water.

Hanne arrived on her bicycle and found Felix sitting at the edge of the field of Stelae nearest to the Brandenburg Gate. 'You came,' she said, surprised.

'I always try to keep a promise. Besides, I wouldn't want you turning up again at the lake. How's Audrey?'

Hanne smiled warmly. 'She's recovering well, thankfully - she's so resilient. Felix, it's thanks to you, you rescued her before any further damage was done.'

Felix brushed away the compliment. 'Anyone would've done the same.'

'Not anyone. I really owe you big time and I mean that. How's your arm?'

'Fine. I had the sling off the following day. This is an amazing place,' he said, trying to be enthusiastic but failing.

She agreed. 'Yes. There's an underground information museum here with all the known names of the Jewish Holocaust victims. Did you see it?'

'Another time, maybe. I read in the papers this memorial has caused controversy within the German Jewish community, that it was unnecessary. How can anyone think a place like this is unnecessary? We must never forget the victims.'

Hanne sighed, 'Especially the children. You were a victim at Torgau. It shaped your life and your destiny.'

'It's hardly the same. I turned my abusers into victims,' he admitted.

'You took revenge, yes. When I was faced with Audrey's teacher, Witzig, I wanted to take revenge too,' she confessed.

'The difference was, you didn't go through with it; I did. That stopped me being a victim and turned me into something else,' Felix said, with brutal honesty.

'And if you spend the next 15, 20 years in jail, justice would be served, but you'd miss out on seeing your daughter and your new baby growing up. Wouldn't that be a crime? I'm sure your time at Torgau was enough of a life sentence,' she surmised.

Felix was confused. 'What are you saying?'

Hanne was animated, 'I'm saying, by the craziest twists of fate, there was a Torgau boy - a bit like you, out for revenge. He was called David, and he turned up at Caputh around the same time you were disposing of the Musketeers. Felix, do you remember a kid called David at Torgau?'

'Not really. There were so many kids coming and going.'

'Well, this David said he'd killed a few Torgau wardens, and he wanted to add Witzig to his list, only Witzig got the better of him.'

Felix found this unbelievable. 'No! You mean, I wasn't the only Torgau vigilante,' he exclaimed, gleefully.

'You've a doppelganger,' Hanne said, grinning. 'David's profile matches yours- and even size 9 feet. Sadly, Witzig kept one of his foot's as a trophy when he killed poor David. His remains are supposedly in the lake at Caputh.'

Felix read her thoughts. 'Is your police team thinking this David could be Marine Boy?'

'Yes. I want them to believe it. It seems by rescuing Audrey, Witzig has provided you with a window of opportunity, and the distinct hope of a possible way out.'

Felix was not entirely encouraged by this news. 'But if the police discovered I survived Torgau and my family hid me to protect me, I know that's not a crime. But how would I explain the fingerprints on my knife at Lotte Holler's crime scene?'

Sighing, she said, 'Then all the lies will tumble down, and let's hope it never comes to it,

because your fingerprints aren't on record anywhere. Felix, I can't promise the police won't ever turn up on your doorstep, but I promise, as for the Jens that saved Audrey's life; he will forever remain anonymous.'

'Thank you. I'll take that little ray of hope, and I'm used to living with uncertainty. Are you sure you want to do this?' he asked.

'I'm sure. I'll lie and say I believed David was Marine Boy. If someday my deception ever comes to light, please deny all knowledge of my ever having found you at Motzen. We'd have to convince others it was just some freaky coincidence that it was you, just a passer-by at the lake, who rescued Audrey. This would possibly give some credence to why the hero of Caputh disappeared as quickly as he appeared.'

Felix was concerned. 'Hanne, you're compromising your integrity for me. Why?'

She replied frankly and bluntly, 'Well, it may be politically incorrect, but I think I agree with the majority of people who don't really care what happens to paedophiles. Well, maybe their mothers find it hard to stop caring about them. I think the Musketeers got what they deserved.'

'And Lotte Holler?'

'At Nuremburg, complicity was a crime,' Hanne stated.

Nodding, he sighed, 'Indeed!'

'Besides, the Musketeers and Lotte Holler are dead, and I say let sleeping dogs lie. Felix, I'm not excusing your actions, although after Caputh, I understand them on a much deeper level. But your anonymous list helped catch paedophiles; that's invaluable.'

'Hanne, you'd better be good at keeping secrets.'

'Everyone has secrets, everyone lies,' she said, with a wry

smile.

'I've been keeping secrets all my life and they've a habit of coming back to haunt me,' Felix said, on tenterhooks, praying she really meant it.

Hanne promised, 'Some things should be left unsaid. This will be our secret.'

Excited, he told her, 'Agreed. Hanne, I can never thank you enough.'

'We are both in one another's debt. I got my daughter back and you get your freedom. The slate is wiped clean. Felix, go back to your family and your life.'

'They know the truth about me,' he confessed. 'They've known for a while. To outsiders I'm a murderer, but to them, I'm just Felix.'

Hanne smiled. 'Unconditional love, that's rare.'

At the edge of the field of Stelae, Hanne and Felix faced one another. The warmth between them was a mixture of compassion, gratitude and forgiveness that would forever connect them.

Felix took a banana out of his rucksack. 'Hanne. We'll never forget each other, but here's something extra to remember me by.'

Touched by his gesture, Hanne took the banana and put it in her bag. At first, they shook hands as they had done when they met in the crowd at the Brandenburg Gate more than 15 years ago. This time Felix did not run off into the crowds, instead he hugged Hanne warmly and strolled away.

Hanne knew she would have some explaining to do at work and more than a few white lies to invent for Oskar and Stefan. A future of secrets and lies... Life was made up of these things, but she knew she could do it and not regret her promise to Felix. Others would not necessarily understand or agree about why she wanted to give a murderer a second chance. Marine Boy was real; he'd taken human form as Felix and risked his life for Audrey. Ad infinitum; unlawful subterfuge at work was a price Hanne was more than willing to pay.

An ecstatic Felix rang his wife on his mobile. He could barely get his words out, and told her what had happened with Hanne at the Berlin Memorial. Martha was soon in tears. 'Sweetheart, I'm coming home,' he promised.

Felix hurried to the train station, feeling as if he was walking on air after years of walking through treacle, waiting for his crimes to be found out. He returned home to Motzen, to the family who loved and accepted him, intending to make the most of his luck and second chance.

Hanne never doubted her integrity regarding Felix. She remained happy with the choice she'd made. Fate had reached out and extended its hand, and she kept Felix's photo up on her wall as a reminder of life's fateful coincidences and its strange twists and turns.

THE END

Hanne Drais will return very soon in

FINDING COLOSSUS

Also published by Fahrenheit Press.

31861460R00223

Printed in Great Britain
by Amazon